SCORNED BY VENOM

ARGENTIUM VAMPIRE HUNTERS
BOOK TWO
P.S. NAIL

SCORNED BY VENOM

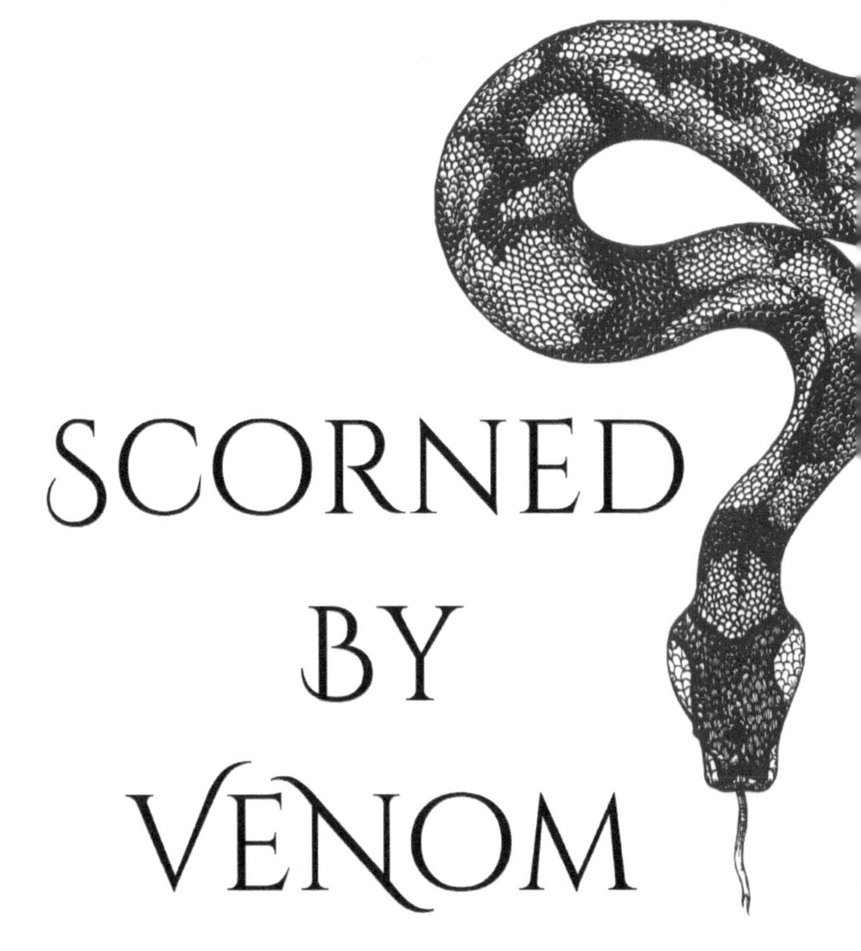

ARGENTIUM VAMPIRE HUNTERS
BOOK 2

To my team of Bloodsuckers
I appreciate and love every single one of you, even when
y'all annoyed the shit out of me for months!
With all the love in my heart, here's your damn book.

And to the readers
Never stop fighting for what you want.
My team didn't!

I HOPE YOU
LAVENDER
&
VANILLA
THIS BOOK

Author PS Nail

To purchase officially licensed merchandise, please vis-it: primordialtree.com

All social media: https://linktr.ee/authorpsnail

Free Book with Newsletter Sign-Up:
https://dl.bookfunnel.com/x395y7zcm9

QUOTE

"You only live once, but if you do it right, once
is enough." - Mae West

INFORMATION

Warning: This book contains scenes of explicit language, alcohol consumption, smoking, witchcraft, bloodletting, fighting, choking, blood, gore, death, murder, graphic violence, on page torture, and imprisonment. There is also on page, past recollection, sexual assault of a male.

There are topics discussed, including anxiety, depression, periods, infertility, endometriosis, pregnancy, newborn babies, and death of parents. There are no unexpected pregnancies.

It also contains explicit sexual content which includes unprotected sex, and swapping of bodily fluids, e.g., semen and blood.

If you find a warning I missed, please email me at peggysue@primordialtree.com

For information on this book, please visit the author's website: psnail.org

To purchase officially licensed merchandise, please visit: primordialtree.com

PLAYLIST

To help me get into the mood of each book, I make playlists to match the theme and feelings. Here is the one I listened to while writing Scorned by Venom.

Listen on Spotify

Listen on iTunes

Paperback readers, visit psnail.org for playlists links.

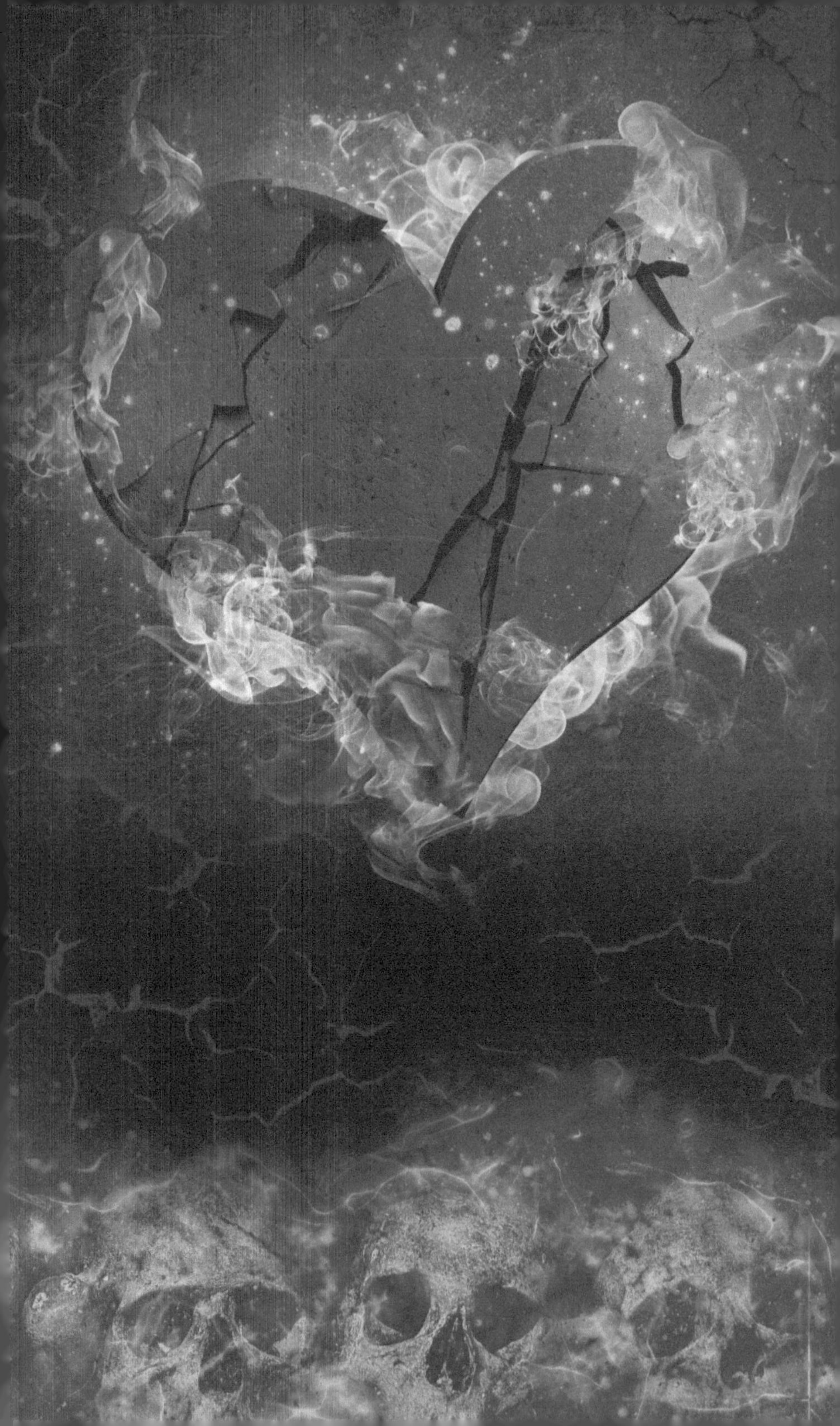

WINNIE

It's easy to shut down emotionally when you witness your sister's struggle to cope with the loss of her mate. But unfortunately, love is an epigenetic phenomenon even a vampire can't control.

It's an internal program of my brain that I don't have the software to hack.

My name is Winston Rodriguez and the story I'm going to tell you is about courage, loyalty, friendship, family, and falling in love while saving your friends and the vampire race.

SAGE

L ove is a tricky word. It's only four letters, yet the power it holds is immeasurable. People will go to great lengths to protect those they love and that's what he did. Luka sacrificed himself for me and I had to do whatever I could to get him back.

I'd give up anything and everything to save him . . . including my soul.

My name is Sagelynn Argent and the story I have to tell isn't one for those who don't understand boundless love. There's determination, family betrayal, heartache, magic, and death. Consider yourself warned.

LUKA

Sacrificing oneself for another is the highest form of devotion. I sacrificed myself for revenge, first for my mother and then for the woman I love. And without hesitation, I'd do it again.

I'd give up anything and everything to save Sage . . . including my life.

My name is Lukas Draven and my story isn't for those who are unwilling to sacrifice everything for the ones they love. It's a story of how the *torture* I endured was worth knowing Sage was safe.

Grab us some whiskey, we're gonna need it.

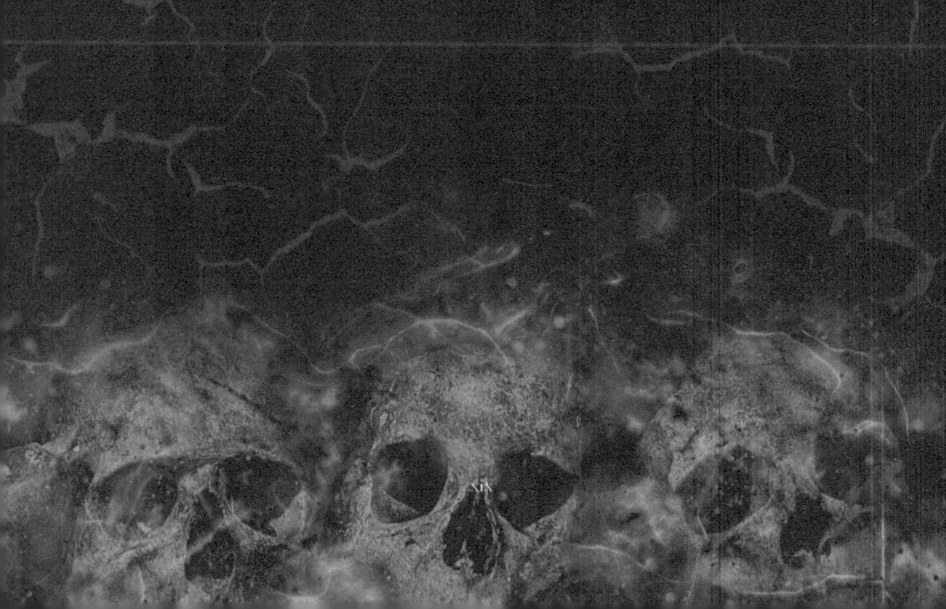

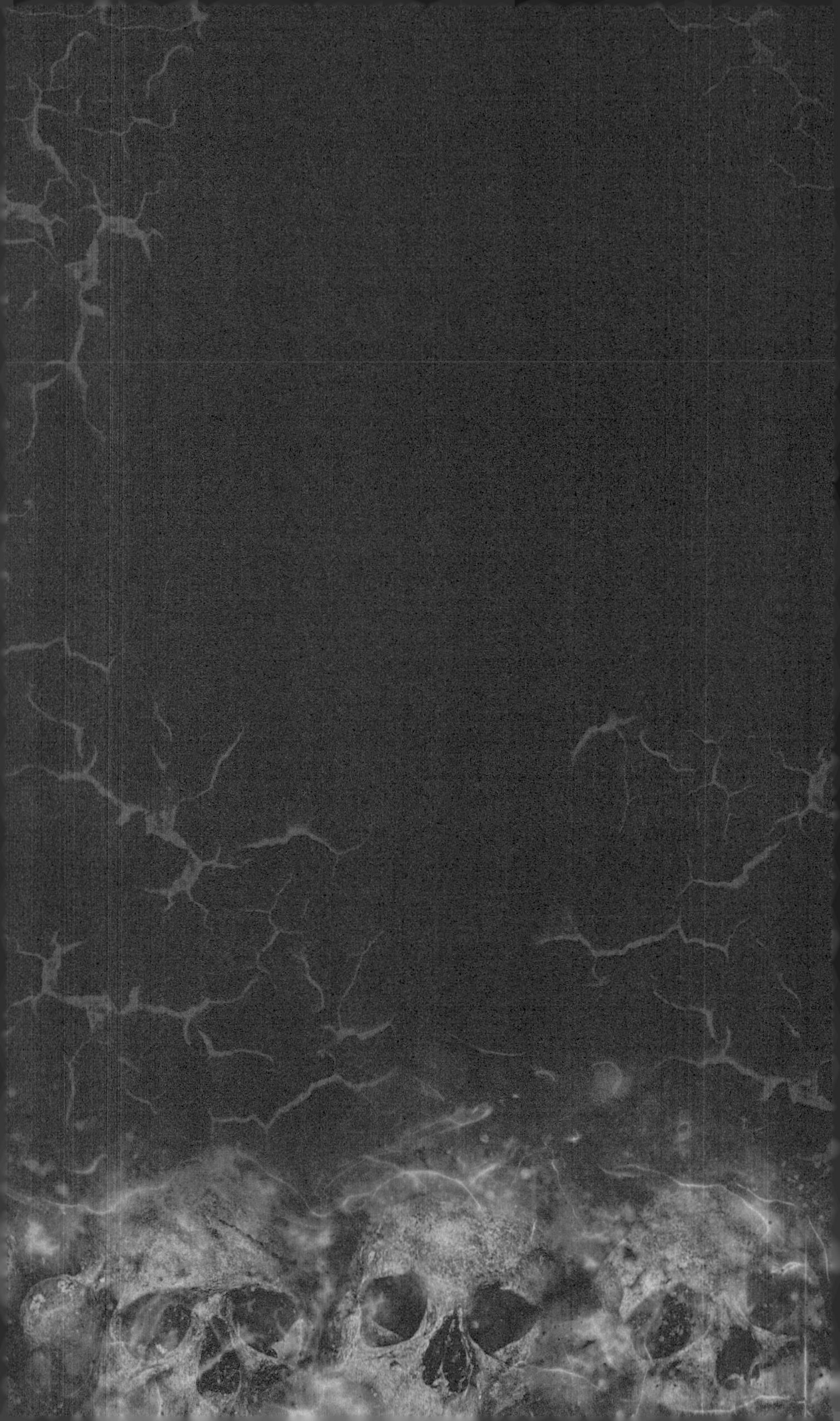

PROLOGUE

After swallowing hard, I lifted the gun to Sorin's head. "This is for Deren."

I pulled the trigger.

Cold blood.

I had killed someone in *cold blood*.

The sounds, the lights, the people all faded away into the darkness as my body went into shock.

The more I stared at Sorin's mutilated skull, the faster the waves of agony flooded through me, smacking against my heart and crashing against my soul. The pain eating me alive wasn't from the murder I'd committed. Not that I had a choice.

Kill or be killed, that's the old saying, right? It might seem like that's what I did, but it's far from being accurate. Vengeance had brought Sorin's death since he was the reason Deren died. I had a deep-seated fury that needed to be released. A punishment that needed to be served.

A life for a life.

But did it make a difference since they had taken Luka?

Not being able to save him caused me to be deeply disappointed in myself and truly *hate* myself.

I failed him . . .

Panic controlled me, causing each limb that used to be mine to tremble in defiance. Heartache and despair forced their way into me, propelling me to run and hide from the entire world.

"Give me the gun, Sage." My friend Erik's voice seemed distant, like a faraway echo from a place where I once lived.

Raw, unrelenting emotions took over my body, lacing it in invisible twine. A sinister force manipulated my every thought and every move as my eyes unfocused on the world.

The puppet master of darkness now owned my soul.

A hand landed on my shoulder and I lost the last bit of control I had. I whipped around and pointed the gun at Erik. "Get the fuck away from me!"

"Everyone back off!" Ravage commanded before putting his hands up in a placating manner and lowering his voice. "She's in shock. Give her some space."

"They took him! They just took him!" My heart thundered in my chest, true fear running through me. Dropping the gun to my side, I paced back and forth as a thousand thoughts bustled around my head. "They're going to kill him! I know they will."

The more I paced, the more the darkness consumed me. My chest tightened, my heartbeat thrashed in my ears as the walls closed in, stealing my air and suffocating my entire existence.

I halted my unsuccessful pacing, laid my hand on my chest, and gasped for air. "I can't . . . I can't breathe."

During my panicked state, someone grabbed me from behind, locking my arms against my body.

My instincts kicked in and I slung my head back, slamming them in the face, but it didn't stop them from keeping me restrained.

It only gave Ravage the opportunity to grab the gun from me, and I freaked out.

The terror in my voice scared even me when I let out another loud scream as I wiggled and thrashed, fighting for my life—for Luka's life.

"I need that! I can't protect him without it!"

Whoever held onto me nestled their nose into my neck. "It's okay, Sage Stick. You're safe."

"Let me go!"

I vaguely remember the smell of Winnie's cologne mixed with sweat when he yanked me from my feet and carried me toward an abandoned Venom van. He threw me inside, then climbed in behind me.

When he shut the van door, my screams swiftly turned into begging. "Please let me go. I need to save him. I have to save him. Please, Winnie."

He said nothing when he kneeled down and pulled me into him, causing me to start thrashing again.

"Stop! I need to . . . I have to—"

"We'll come up with a plan to get him back, I promise. But there's nothing you can do right now. Nothing any of us can do, so please stop fighting me."

In my mind, planning a rescue wasn't an option. If we didn't do something now, my father would have Luka killed and his death would solely fall on my shoulders.

Regretfulness filled my body, slowing it.

Time seemed to stand still as a shivering cold washed over me.

My emotions were now numb, paralyzed by the darkness.

With a deep breath, I squeezed my eyes shut and locked out the world.

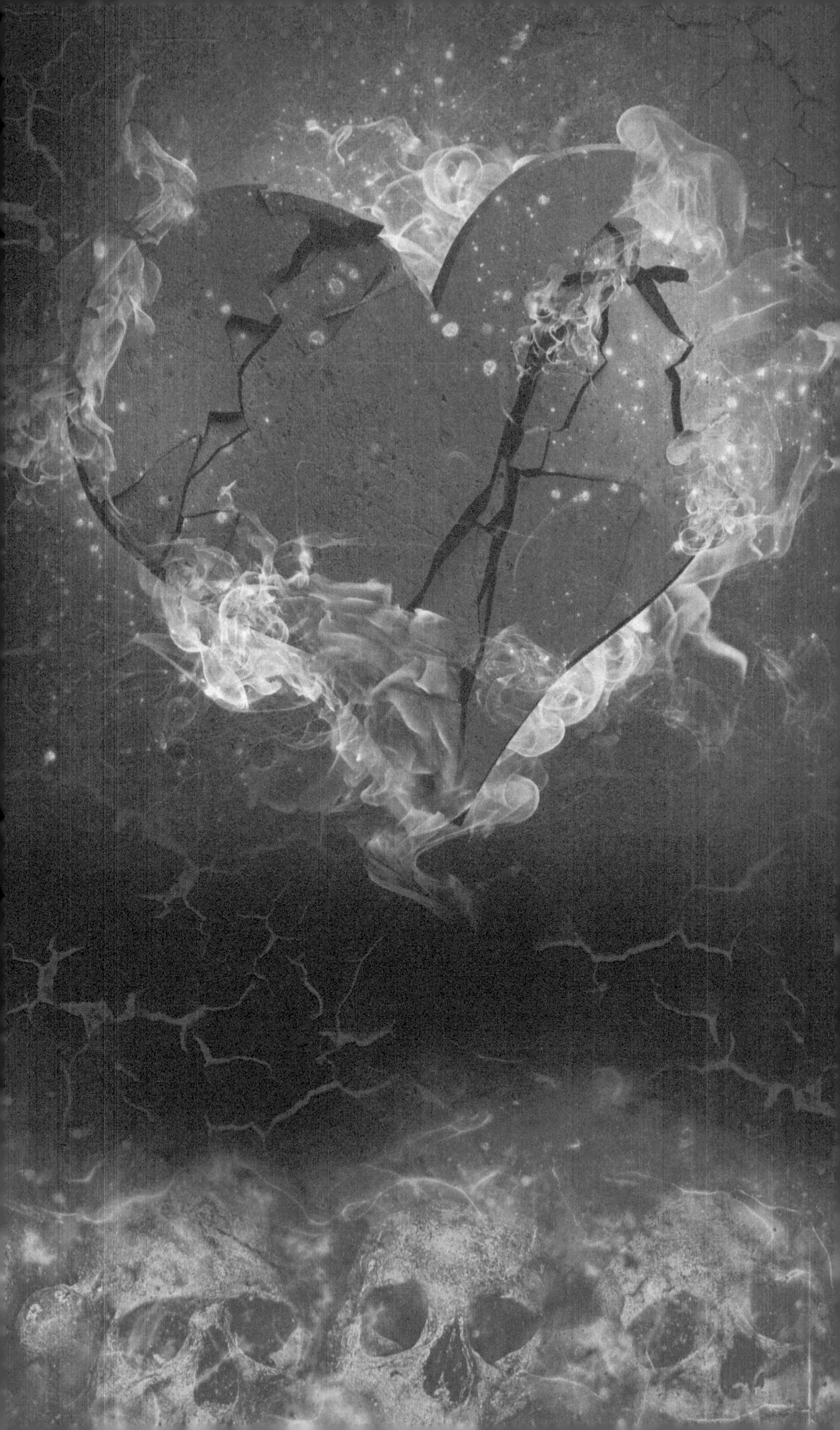

CHAPTER 1
SAGE

Five months after Luka was taken . . .

The night air was chilly, making the crisp wind that smacked against my skin almost unbearable. Not wearing my leather jacket and boots was my first mistake on this personal mission, but I would be lost without the prize.

Headlights appeared behind me on the once deserted back road, and when I looked in the mirror, barely seeing a black Venom van through the blinding lights, I knew someone found me.

The driver approached rapidly, blaring the horn, commanding me to stop.

Instead, I loosened my grip on the throttle, pulled the clutch in, and lifted the shift lever with the toe of my tennis shoe, popping the Harley into fourth gear.

I eased out the clutch and twisted the throttle, praying to whatever god listened that I didn't die from my stupidity.

The pavement beneath my tires was wet from thunderstorms that had passed through earlier in the day.

Because of that, and the fact it was my first time ever driving a motorcycle, when I swiftly approached the bend in the road, the bike began to wobble.

Shit! I should've watched more instructional videos on how to ride this damn thing.

With no idea what I was doing, I attempted to realign the bike I'd stolen by yanking the handlebars, but it refused to cooperate and I spun out of control.

The bike tipped, the ground approached rapidly, and I knew death stood over my shoulder like it had for months, ready to claim my foolish soul.

Winnie's beautiful dark-blue Harley hit the pavement first, then I slammed into it. The impact propelled my body across the asphalt, the surface eating away at my skin until I skidded into an embankment on the side of the road.

My heart thundered in my chest and my head spun as I sank into the cold mud wearing Luka's T-shirt and sweatpants. They were one of the few things I had left that still smelled like him, and my stomach knotted knowing I'd just ruined two of them.

That's just fucking great.

The van squealed to a halt, and I kind of wished I hadn't worn a helmet. I preferred dying from the road rather than being killed by any Venom member. Or worse, them taking me to my father.

The door flung open, and my breath caught in my throat as I instantly recognized the person on the other side.

Shit.

"What the fuck is wrong with you?" Winnie yelled, running to my side. He kneeled next to me and flipped open the shield on my helmet, his eyes boring into mine ready to scold me. "You could have fucking died, Sage!"

Marcus pointed a flashlight at my face, blinding me for a second. "Are you okay?"

"I'm fine."

Even though my captors weren't Venom, getting caught still angered me. I let out an exasperated sigh, feeling the weight of frustration settle in my chest. I attempted to push myself into a sitting position, but my body refused to cooperate.

My right arm hung motionless, completely paralyzed. The thought of it being torn off in the accident sent shivers down my spine. Reluctantly, I glanced downward and saw it was still with me but covered in road-rash and probably dislocated.

Seeing the damage I had caused, my body finally decided to announce all of my injuries. Every muscle and bone in my body throbbed with excruciating pain, starting from the crown of my head and cascading down my entire back, shooting sharp sensations through my legs.

I let out a wail, and Winnie shoved on my chest, pushing me back into the mud. "Stay down. You need blood."

Even with the severe pain, a weird tingle of shame ran through me, and I bit my lip, attempting to hide my feelings.

I'd never taken blood from anyone other than Luka, and despite it not having the same orgasmic intensity as vampire bites, it made me feel like I was being unfaithful to him.

As I thought about the last time I ingested some—when Mannie almost killed me—I knew I'd feel better once my wounds healed. But when I vaguely remembered the intense state of euphoria it provided me, I pushed aside my feelings.

Aware of that side effect, I had to make sure I got to keep what I went on this mission for. I hurriedly focused my attention on Marcus. He had a look of concern for my safety mixed with disappointment that made me feel horrible for my actions.

"I need my backpack," I groaned. "I had it strapped to the back of the bike."

He nodded and turned his flashlight away.

"I have to pick these rocks out before I feed you," Winnie said, bringing my gaze to him.

Though I knew it would hurt, I looked down at my arm and steadied my breathing, ready to get it over with. He pulled the first one from my wound, and I winced from the sting. "Fuck, fuck, fuck."

"This wouldn't have happened if you didn't go to Luka's house."

"How did you know where . . ." A realization dawned on me. "You have a tracker on my phone!"

"I do. But when I woke up and my bike was gone, I already knew it was you and where you went. I told you last night we couldn't go back there because we don't know if it's being watched or not, and you still didn't listen."

After Winnie denied my request, I snuck into his cabin while he was sparring and found the keys in a cup on his desk. I actually thought they were for Luka's Harley and that's why I swiped them.

Not knowing shit about motorcycles, I watched some YouTube videos on how to ride and shift gears until the sun came up, then mapped out a route. I set my alarm so I'd wake up before everyone to execute my flawless plan. When I attempted to steal Luka's bike, the keys didn't work. I'd almost given up, but decided to check Winnie's next and hit the jackpot.

It was quite a challenge to silently push Winnie's bike a mile away just to start it. Once I mounted the Harley and took off on my slow journey under the setting sun, I realized how much time I had wasted, which proved to be my second mistake.

"You guys went and got Annie. What's the difference?" I asked before gritting my teeth as he picked out another rock.

"We used a team of people and were careful when we went to get the dog. Obviously, you weren't since we easily found you without even using the tracker. You're lucky it was us." He shook his head, picking out another rock as I held my breath. "Had Venom found you first, they might have used you to breach the wards, and people could have died."

I thought I'd planned everything perfectly, mapping out my entire ride only using back roads and making sure to get in and out of Luka's house quickly. My safety wasn't important to me anymore, so if I'd gotten killed, I was okay with it. My suffering would have finally ended.

But what I never considered was the many lives of others. Because I didn't understand how wards functioned, I was unaware that someone could manipulate me to bypass the barriers protecting the camp.

More people would be dead because of me . . .

"So tell me, Sage, what was so damn important?"

It might appear foolish to Winnie and others, but I didn't have a choice but to go to Luka's house. Having his scent still on his clothes allowed me to be near him when I wore them. It was the only thing that brought me comfort. And although my stupid mission had scored me one of his T-shirts, two pairs of sweatpants, I'd ruined the ones I was wearing.

My chest tightened, and it wasn't from the impact of my crash. "This was the last set of clothes I had that smelled like Luka, so I went to get more."

Winnie let his head fall back, looking toward the dark night sky. He let out a long sigh that let me know he was done with my shit. "You're an idiot."

I ignored his candid remarks. "Whatever."

"Found your backpack," Marcus shouted from a distance.

When I turned my head to look at him, pain shot through me and I screamed.

Winnie's whiskey-colored eyes and unruly black hair came into my field of vision. "All the rocks are gone. Are you ready now?"

Unless I wanted to go to the ER and risk more lives, this was my only option. I nodded.

Winnie lifted a wrist to his mouth and bit into it, then held it in front of my face. I took a deep, painful breath before latching on to it.

With every sip, my weary body found relief, and I silently wished for my broken heart to be mended as well.

Winnie unlatched my helmet as the euphoria spread through me. Once his blood took over, my eyelids drifted shut, my mind falling into a state of ecstasy, landing softly into a fantasy world.

The mud below my body turned into a soft bed, and Luka was now wrapped in my arms, his blue eyes sparkling brighter than a star in the night sky.

And when he smiled at me, his fangs slightly showing between his lips, it was the happiest I'd been in a long time.

CHAPTER 2
WINSTON

It's weird how, in a blink of an eye, life can evolve into something you never saw coming. Only five months ago, I was just a vampire who had no plans for the future. A chill dude only seeking sex, blood, and a security system to hack . . . until my enemies killed some of my friends and imprisoned my best friend.

Not only did the internet suck out here in the middle of the woods, but Sage's stupidity ruined my night. The last thing I expected when I woke up was having to pursue her on a motorcycle, hoping she didn't die, while also wanting to kill her.

After seeing my wrecked Harley, I contemplated leaving her ass in the ditch on the side of the road. Good thing Marcus drove her back in the van or I might have.

Despite the horrible state my bike was in, to my surprise, it started right up. I trailed behind them on the way home, thankful for the opportunity to unwind in solitude.

When we returned, Marcus carried Sage to bed so she could sleep off the euphoria my blood gave her. An hour had passed before I heard her shifting around in her cabin. Although I knew she'd emerge soon, taking her normal spot in the woods, staring into the darkness, I wasn't ready to deal with her yet.

The fire in my chest was still blazing, leaving me feeling like a snake ready to strike at any moment.

Luckily, Marcus had been teaching me how to channel my anger into something positive, and I was determined to do just that.

Man, have things changed.

"Harder, Winston!" Lyric yelled, bringing me out of my murderous thoughts.

I arched my brow, fighting to catch my breath. "If I go any harder, I'm gonna hurt you."

She huffed out a sigh. "You're being a pussy."

Observing the dark-haired beauty in front of me, with one braid down each side of her head, I couldn't help but grin. "You're fucking gorgeous, you know that? Even when you're being serious."

"Stop messing around!" she screamed through fast breaths.

"I can't help it, babe. You're so damn sexy it makes my dick—" A fist slammed into my face, and to my surprise, it hurt. "Fuck!"

"Oh, my god. I'm so sorry. Let me see." Lyric dropped her defensive stance and stepped in close. Her elegant fingers grazed across my cheek in a smooth stroke.

"You socked my ass while I admired your beauty."

She giggled, dropping her hand from my face and placing it on her hip. "I'm polishing my moves and you keep messing around."

"You don't need to practice, mama. You're already packing a mean punch." Sliding my arms around her waist, I yanked her toward me and pressed my lips against hers.

"Are you two done flirting?" Erik shouted, causing Lyric to pull away with a blush.

My focus went to Erik and the scowl he had anytime my hands were on his sister. Even though I liked the guy, I loved torturing him, so I made sure to be extra handsy around him.

"Some of us would like to spar!"

"You and Kimber have been doing a shit ton of practicing," I retorted, sarcasm lining my voice. "You should already be pretty damn skilled."

Kimber's lightly tanned cheeks turned pink when she giggled, but otherwise she stayed silent. A sweet girl and the sister of my best friend Drag, she was cute, humble, and a magnificent fighter. A few days after we arrived here, she and Erik started "secretly" seeing each other. At least in Erik's eyes, it was hush-hush.

But the *lure* doesn't keep secrets.

When humans are horny, they release an aroma which is specific to them. A biological scent that sends out a sexual beacon to anyone in the vicinity. The more attracted to a person they are, the stronger the emotional response. Since only vampires and wolven could smell the lustful scents, I swore everyone to secrecy just to mess with Erik.

His now confused glare told me he didn't get the joke. "What are you talking about, Winnie? I spar with Marcus or Peach most of the time."

"It's Winston, " I reminded him before turning back toward Lyric with raised fists. "Come on, babe. Give me all you got."

Lyric threw out a punch and this time, I dodged it.

Despite my worry she'd get hurt during the rescue mission, she insisted on going. At least it helped to know how fast and efficient she had become.

Lifting my leg, I kicked out but in a gentle way—being my girlfriend, I couldn't help but go easy on her.

Apparently, she had no qualms about kicking my ass. In a flash, she crouched to the ground, swung out her leg, and swiped me off my feet.

I landed on my back, and she straddled me with a quickness most humans didn't have. Her fist came down as she attempted to stake me with an invisible weapon.

Reaching up, I caught her wrist and halted her attempt before grabbing the other one. I rolled her off me, throwing her hands above her head, and pinning her beneath me.

Her breaths were fast, her body warm as her chest rose and fell below me. A look of defeat settled on her beautiful bronze face, and I grinned.

"Don't *ever* let a vampire get on top of you. Unless it's me."

Her disappointed look turned sensual, her eyes darkened as the smell of sweet lilacs lit my senses on fire, the lustful aroma sending pulses of blood straight to my cock. If our friends weren't surrounding us, I would have fucked her right there in the dirt.

"Knee him in the dick!" Erik yelled, and I jerked my knees close—just in case.

Kimber giggled. "Don't do that. You're gonna need it."

"You most definitely will," I assured Lyric before leaning in and pressing my lips against her soft, full ones.

"For fuck's sake!" Erik yelled, making me want to punch him in his junk. "Can you violate my sister somewhere else?"

Lyric giggled in my mouth, so I pulled back with a fanged grin. "If a vampire gets on top of you, and it's *not* me, knee him in the dick."

I hopped up and pulled Lyric from the ground.

"What if it's a lady vampire?" she asked, dusting her butt off.

"You know what, I don't know." I clenched my brows, contemplating my answer when Kimber interjected.

"Punch her in the tit!"

Lyric laughed, strolling out of the ring. She took a seat on a log surrounding the fire pit, but facing away from it so we could still see the fighting ring, before peering up at me with her beautiful golden-brown eyes. "I may need to spar with someone else, Winston. You're too distracting."

I pointed at my chest. "*I'm* too distracting? You're the one in a tank top and yoga pants. You look hella sexy, by the way."

"They're leggings."

After I ran my fingers through my dark hair, making sure it wasn't messy, I took the spot next to her and slid my hand between her thighs. Her sweet smelling lure once again filled my senses. Taking a deep breath, I savored it, barely able to contain myself, knowing I'd get her naked later.

"I'm sick of the scents." Heston's spontaneous confession brought me out of the dirty visions of what I would be doing to Lyric.

Fuck.

If he didn't shut his mouth, he would ruin my secret.

"Her lilacs," the ebony-skinned wolven pointed to Lyric, "her gardenias," then to April, "and his pine trees!" then Erik before he threw his hands out in exasperation. "That's all we ever smell anymore!"

Drag grinned, running fingers through his long, dark beard. "You're just jealous *you* don't have anyone to smell."

"What are you talking about?" Erik asked, yanking his water bottle off the ground and twisting the cap off. "I don't smell like pine. That's the damn woods."

Drag barked out with a laugh. "Definitely *not* the woods. Maybe morning wood."

Kimber giggled, tying up her dark hair but still not saying anything. It surprised me when she agreed to keep the secret from her man, but I had a feeling she was also getting amusement from it.

Awaiting the perfect moment to tell Erik we knew when he was horny, I needed to change this conversation fast.

He bent over to set his water bottle back down and I whistled loudly, attempting to distract everyone from the scent topic. "Erik, your ass looks good in those jeans!"

Everyone laughed, and his head whipped toward me before scrubbing his hand across his forehead. "Someone kill me."

Vivi jumped to her feet, shoving her arm in the air like an honor-roll student. Her dimples were prominent as a cheeky grin engulfed her face. "I volunteer!"

Erik glanced over his shoulder with slanted eyes. "Why do I believe you?"

"Because my sister will," I chimed in with a grin.

Erik's face paled before he turned away.

To tell the truth, Viviana didn't despise Erik, she merely wanted to give the impression that she did. Not that she wasn't fierce. She'd killed people with far less motivation than most of us, but I'm assuming she had her reasons . . . most of the time. Although she wanted to appear tough and mean, I knew how kind and sweet she had been before the trauma.

Unfortunately, she had a lenxus—a supernatural bond between a vampire and another person—and had spent over twenty years with him.

When Venom took Strike from her, she changed, building an emotional wall to block herself off from people, much like Sage. But instead of hiding in a cabin, not speaking to people, and stealing motorcycles like Sage, Vivi kept her emotions veiled under a standing smirk, a snappy mouth, and a need to kill.

Once, Vivi informed me she knew Strike was still alive because she felt the pull of the bond. Despite receiving that constant validation, she experienced intense anxiety due to her inability to be with her bond-mate.

And that's why she's the person everyone else knew.

Since she was my sister, Vivi had always been a pain in my ass, but her heart was usually in the right place for the right people. She was just another anti-hero . . . like the rest of our camp.

Except for Lyric. In my eyes, she was perfect and nothing less than an angel.

"I know you don't like my brother," Lyric whispered, bringing me back to reality, "but you don't have to be mean to him."

"Why would you think I don't like him? I think he's cool."

She glared like she didn't believe me before shaking her head. Movement caught my eye, bringing my gaze back to Erik as he sauntered to the other side of the circle so his back wasn't to Vivi.

I chuckled, and Lyric swatted my knee. "That's why. Stop laughing."

My grin stayed put as I watched Peach enter the dirt circle we used for a makeshift fighting ring.

"I'm the next trainer. Who's my student?" Being an extremely old vampire, Peach was fast. She wouldn't tell me her age, but I had a feeling she was at least five hundred, maybe even a thousand years old.

Marcus had a severe attraction to Peach from the day they met, but she had remained closed off to his handsomeness.

Initially, I assumed playing hard to get had been a game of hers, but it eventually became clear something else was going on. I had my money on a possible past relationship trauma.

He stepped into the ring with a huge grin. "Me!"

Being a petite woman, around five foot three, when Peach stared up at the six-foot-four, mahogany-skinned human, it appeared she was admiring the moon.

"Marcus, you possess unparalleled skills and dare I say, you're the most impressive person I've ever encountered who is *not* supernatural. You clearly know you don't need training from me, yet every night, you persist."

Marcus's face gleamed, gazing down at her with pure adoration. "All I heard is you think I'm a god."

Peach's big blue eyes fluttered, unfazed. "Definitely *not* what I said."

Since the Venom society took Luka, Marcus and I had become close. He wasn't a stand in for the best friend I missed, but had become a person I looked up to. He was intelligent and a phenomenal fighter, and either of those attributes would've made me respect the shit out of him.

"Hey, Marcus!" I yelled, and his head whipped toward me. "I think you're a god."

He winked a brown eye at me. "Thanks, Winnie."

Peach ran a hand across her short hair. "I hate you both."

Marcus smirked. "Hate sex is hot, Peaches and Cream."

Because Peach had cream-colored skin with matching hair, Peaches and Cream became Marcus's new nickname for her. From my perspective, her hair appeared to be more sandy-blonde, but I'm just a hacker, not a hair specialist.

Peach ignored him and turned toward the half a dozen other people who were standing around watching, excitingly rubbing her hands together. "Who's sparring with me?"

No one moved or spoke, each of them avoiding her eyes.

Drag's gaze bounced from person to person before he finally cut in. "Nobody wants to fight you because you're *too* old and *too* fast."

"So, me again." Marcus grinned in triumph, and a large sigh left Peach before she finally relented.

"Whatever. Come on."

Since I'd watched these two lethal beings spar many nights, I turned my attention toward Lyric. She had been silent for the last few minutes and I wondered why until I noticed she had fixed her gaze on Sage's cabin.

Like Lyric and some other humans staying here, Sage was born into the Vampire Eradicating National Organization of Malice—also known as Venom. She worked for them, capturing vampires to send to the Vampire Research Center for testing.

We didn't know what they did with the specimens at VRC, we only knew the stories we were told from the two vampires who escaped from there—Viktor and Finneas.

Those two brothers also lead a group called Save—Supernaturals Against Venom Elitists.

Sage ended up here because she betrayed Venom—at least in her father's eyes since he was the president of the society. After a large battle between Venom and Save, all of us ended up moving to Drag's land.

Well, *almost* all of us.

My best friend Luka had sacrificed himself to save Sage and ended up being taken by Venom. If he had a chance to change the outcome, I knew he wouldn't have done it differently because love changes people.

Unfortunately, his capture sent Sage on a downward spiral. She shut herself off to everyone in the world, including Lyric.

Other than the stunt she pulled earlier tonight, she only came out of the house to stand in the woods and stare into the darkness. She also wouldn't speak to anyone for more than a minute.

Even though we knew how sad she had become, she wasn't realizing the hurt she caused her best friends.

Deep down, I knew Luka would want me to get Sage out of her current state of depression, then we could move on with the plans of saving him and his brother Strike. Maybe that would get shit back to *at least* a semi-normal state.

But perhaps such a useless word like "maybe" can't realign the world.

Turning her attention toward the firepit, Lyric inhaled deeply before letting out a long sigh. The light from the fire danced across her face, causing the sadness in her eyes to sparkle.

"Sage is fine. I gave her blood, and I'm sure her euphoria has worn off by now because I heard her moving around."

She crossed her arms, running her hands up and down them, then plastered on a fake smile before turning her head toward me. "I'm just tired and a little cold."

"I got you." Jogging up to the steps of our shared cabin, I retrieved the hoodie she had taken off before we started sparring and brought it back to her. "Here, babe."

"Thanks." She slid it on with another sigh before glancing back at Sage's cabin.

My eyes unfocused, my thoughts wandering off on a trip of their own as I thought about the plan again.

The details we laid out were as close to perfect as they could be. Absolutely solid. We had everything we needed: vehicles, blood, weapons, and a group of people who were willing to fight. We were only missing the most important thing . . . the location. Unfortunately, none of us, not even the ex-Venom members staying here, knew where the Vampire Research Center was located.

We had been prepared for weeks, doing everything in our power to find information. The Winter Solstice party came and Drag didn't want to go. He felt it wouldn't be right to look for a mate while other people were missing theirs. Christmas and New Year's had also come and gone, and now it was already April with no leads.

Dead. End.

As the night went on, Marcus grilled some food, and everyone joined us around the firepit. We had a blend of people in our group now. Vampires, wolven, and humans had banded together with one common goal: fighting for what's right.

We had another common component I realized as I watched everyone take their seats. Hope. The group possessed a formidable strength because of it.

Even though I could see the pain in Vivi's eyes, she still had hope that one day we would find her bondmate. She laughed at something Kimber said, showing her dimples before passing a bottle of whiskey to her.

A natural pink eyeliner lined the light skin around April's eyes, and even though she'd been crying all night, hope to one day have a family filled her. She wiped away a runaway tear, and her husband Zeke wrapped a blanket around her shoulders, comforting her.

Lyric's hope wasn't a secret. She told me every day how much she missed Sage and hoped she would get better soon.

Though it may sound sentimental, our collective hope was for peace. We just wanted to be happy with the ones we loved.

The wood planks on Sage's porch creaked when she finally stepped out of her cabin.

Her hope vanished several weeks ago. The strong, snarky, kind, yet stubborn as hell woman I once knew had been slowly fading away. She strolled past wearing the T-shirt and sweatpants she'd almost killed herself to steal from Luka's house and headed to the edge of the woods without making eye contact.

Lyric shifted, looking down at the ground, and I squeezed her hand, letting her know I would always be there for her.

Gazing past my girlfriend, I locked eyes on Sage as she took her normal standing spot, once again closing herself off from the world.

The way she had given up hope pissed me off. She had become family to me, and that was the only reason I held my tongue for the longest time. But not anymore. Even though she had given up on life, and on Luka coming back, I'd be damned if I gave up on her.

I needed to make her understand that we'd find where they were being held, and she needed to get her head out of her ass and get ready for this mission. Even if it meant hurting her feelings and jeopardizing our friendship.

Marcus and Drag appeared with handfuls of wood, laying them close to the fire pit. Nighttime in New Mexico brought in an icy chill, even colder deep in the woods.

Being the alpha of a wolven pack, Drag owned the small camp we stayed at, but few people outside of his pack knew about his leadership status. Most of his pack members stayed four miles away at the main camp, filled with mated couples and children. Drag went back and forth constantly between the two, but slept here since he was unmated. That's also why Kimber and a few other wolven stayed here. Camp Singleton, I liked to call it, though most of us were fucking somebody.

"We need to get a group together and head into town," Drag said, getting my attention. "We have more people than ever and we're running low on supplies."

"I need to go into town too," Peach added, strolling up with Marcus. "I still haven't paid Eddie."

"How much is he charging?" Marcus asked, perching himself on a wood log across from me.

Peach took the seat next to him, and my brows rose. She seemed to be growing to like him. "He said to throw him twenty, but it doesn't seem like enough. I have fifty to go toward it."

"It's definitely not enough," Ravage said. He was an older vampire, and Luka's origin, which means he turned him. "I'll add fifty to that, Peach."

He held his cup out and Lynx filled it with whiskey. She was his tattoo apprentice, a vampire, and cool as shit.

"I think I've got a couple of twenties in my wallet," Jimmy added, an ex-Venom member we obtained. Of course, I took a huge liking to him since he was a genius with computers. I'd been teaching him my knowledge on hacking. "I may be able to get money out of my bank, but I'm uncertain if Venom has frozen our accounts."

Ravage chuckled, appearing amused. "We appreciate the gesture, but I think adding fifty thousand to the fifty Peach has will be enough."

Jimmy's brown eyes enlarged under the thick lenses of his glasses. "Fif . . . fifty *thousand*?"

"He deserves it. Do you know how long it took to burn thirty-six bodies?" Peach asked, causing Sage to suck in a gasp.

Fuck.

Sage asked me one time how many people died and I told her I didn't know because I knew she would dwell on it.

Jimmy shook his head, then pushed his glasses back up his nose. "Wow. That's too many people to go randomly missing. Are the police looking for anyone?"

Heston busted out a laugh and squatted at the edge of the circle. "Of course not," the young wolven said. He plucked a stick from the ground before drawing in the dirt with it. "Venom has the police on payroll."

"More like the government," Ravage corrected. "They pay for Venom, the research, and the cover-ups."

Jimmy furrowed his brow. "It's weird knowing everything I've been taught is a lie."

Erik handed him a beer before twisting the top off of one for himself. "Welcome to the club."

Even though I knew they were better off without Venom, it didn't stop them from hurting. Everyone involved lost things they loved when they left the society. Houses, cars, family, friends, pets. The hard reality hit when it ripped away the life they once knew.

After numerous conversations with the now exiled members, I realized they truly believed in the validity of their actions. Their society had convinced them they were doing the right thing, and they regretted not seeing the truth sooner. If the ex-Venom members were willing to change and fight against the system, I welcomed them.

Knowing Lyric was one of the people screwed over by Venom, I trailed my fingers up and down her back, comforting her.

She turned toward me, her hazel eyes glazed over. "If you keep treating me so well, I might accidentally fall in love with you."

I took one of her dark brown braids between my fingers, slightly tugging her face closer to mine. "Maybe that's my plan."

"My grandson is such a romantic," Ravage interrupted, bringing chuckles from some and gasps from others.

"Grandson?" April's brows shot up before confusion settled on her face. Being Marcus's sister-in-law and a human, she ended up here after the war by proxy. She pushed some blonde locks off her shoulder. "How is that possible?"

"Don't get him started." I shook my head, and Ravage laughed.

Of course, he wasn't my real grandfather, but since he turned Luka into a vampire and Luka turned me, the jokes had been going for years.

My phone rang, interrupting our conversation. Ollie's name flashed on the screen, causing me to shift my gaze to Drag. "Dude, it's your dad."

He shot to his feet with a concerned expression, and I did the same, immediately heading away from the circle of people before answering the phone.

"What's up, Ollie?"

"Is my son around? I called him but no one answered."

I tipped the phone so it wasn't next to my mouth. "Where's your cell, bro?"

"At my cabin at the other camp. I didn't want to run the four miles to get it."

"Lazy ass." I laughed and turned my attention back to Ollie. "He's right here. Do you want to talk to him?"

"Put me on speaker, since it concerns you all."

I clicked the button and held the phone between us.

"Everything okay?" Drag asked, and Ollie sighed.

"Not really. There was a woman here. Venom."

Drag's panicked face told me he was ready to drive into town and take his father for a prisoner, but I knew Ollie would give him a run for his money—a match I would pay to watch. I'd throw a hundred bucks on Ollie.

"Damn it, Dad. That's why I said you need to come here."

"I've said it before and I'll say it again. I ain't ever gonna leave here, goddammit. Now stop asking me!"

I snickered at the feisty old wolven before getting us back on topic. "Do you know who it was?"

"Her name's Naomi. She said it was urgent for her to talk to Sage. She left a card with her number."

Since I'd heard her name being mentioned multiple times around the campfire, I went on red alert. Sage had killed Naomi's brother Sorin during the war. Unfortunately, not until after he had Luka taken.

"Naomi? What the fuck could she want?"

Drag shrugged at my question.

"Can you text me a picture of the card?" I asked Ollie and he huffed.

"You know damn well I don't know how to use that cellphone my son gave me."

Drag released a hard breath. "Can you just tell me the number, Dad?"

"Shit, son. Let me get my glasses."

"Wait, is Libby working?" I asked. I sure as hell didn't want to wait the ten minutes it would've taken him to find his glasses.

"She's right here, doing prep work."

"Can you put her on?"

Ollie mumbled something, then shuffling sounds came through the phone before Libby's tender voice said, "Hello?"

"Hey. Can you text Winnie a pic of the card my dad has, please?"

"Of course, Drag."

"Thanks, sweetie."

"You're welcome. Here's Ollie."

The phone shuffled again before the call ended.

"I guess he was done talking." I laughed, and Drag's face told me he was unamused.

A minute later, my phone beeped with a text from Libby.

"We can't call Naomi until we get more burner phones."

Drag nodded, agreeing. "Another reason to head into town tomorrow."

We strolled back to the campfire and filled the others in on the news.

CHAPTER 3
SAGE

*T*hirty-six.

It might seem like a low number compared to others, but it's one I won't forget. It's how many people died because of me. Despite not being solely responsible, I blamed myself. Even if my society had betrayed me.

I had been scorned by Venom . . . by my own fucking father.

He sent his people to a slaughter without a care. When the fight at the Save location first happened, I thought they were attempting to take as many vampires as they could to VRC, but after gaining some runaway Venom members, I quickly realized that wasn't true.

After killing Sorin, I went into a fit of rage before falling into an almost catatonic state. Drag insisted I hide out at his hidden camp deep in the woods. Vivi escorted me here while the rest of my friends stayed behind to help the mortuary guy deal with the dead bodies.

During their clean up, my friend Jimmy came out of hiding. He approached Peach and asked her to get in contact with me. Since I'd lost both my phones, I was unreachable—and completely okay with it. The last thing

I wanted to do was to communicate with anyone. Not until Luka was safe and in my arms.

Peach called Vivi, informing us of Venom members needing a place to hide, and asked what we should do with them. Of course, Vivi said we should kill them, per the norm. As Vivi stood there waiting for an answer from me, I shrugged and walked away. It may be cruel, but in my current state, I didn't give a fuck.

Marcus, Peach, Ravage, and Drag took it upon themselves to decide for the good of everyone. Now we have three former Venom members staying with us, not counting me and my friends. Initially, they mostly stayed in their cabins at night. After a while, they began socializing, gradually forming friendships with the supernaturals.

My friend Jimmy had been one of the former Venom members, and even if he was a little weird to converse with, he was a good guy. And since he was a computer nerd like Winnie, they seemed to become friends pretty quickly. He would wave anytime he saw me, but let me be, unlike some others around here.

The other two were women, each with different personalities.

Nellie was usually blunt with her words, not caring who they affected. She got on my nerves.

Randi was a sweet girl, but extremely shy and quiet.

Both of them avoided me like the plague, not even making eye contact when they saw me. And I was perfectly okay with it. I had no desire to talk to my friends, let alone them.

Even though I hadn't participated in conversations, especially the ones about what happened the night of the war, I regularly listened. More than once I heard the ex-Venom members say their objective had been to capture as many vampires as they could to break up Save, which is a group of vampires and wolven sworn to protect their species from hunters like me. Or, like I used to be before I knew what we were doing was immoral.

After my father realized I was a traitor, his goals changed. The mission shifted from capturing us to killing anyone they could, except for Luka. He was to be un-harmed. When someone figured out Marcus and his brother Zeke helped Erik, Lyric, and myself escape, my father added us to the list. The field crew were told we were *all* traitors and needed to be brought in for interro-gation.

My dad even went above and beyond, sending them pic-tures of us—including one of Luka, which I'm assuming he stole from my phone.

One might think my father's sins were what brought me here, but honestly, my sins did. I knowingly betrayed him just like he did me.

I played the game as best as I could, I just didn't win.

"Can we even trust this woman?" Lynx asked, bringing my attention away from the pine trees.

What woman?

My painful thoughts had kept me from hearing the beginning of the conversation.

Everyone living here usually gathered around the fire every night to talk about random things. But at least once a night, someone would bring up the rescue mission to save Luka and Strike. A mission which I'd eventually given up on. This didn't sound like that.

Maybe I didn't hear *everything*.

"I don't know," Ravage responded. "What do you think, Drag?"

The fire crackled, the sound of a log being dropped into it ringing through the night.

"She may have valuable information, and we don't have any other leads. You know her, Marcus. What's your opinion?"

"I think it's worth a shot. Sage may not come out of the state she's in if we don't."

I whipped toward the crowd of people. "I can hear you, you know?"

"We don't care if you hear us," Winnie spat, hopping up from his seat and pointing at me. "We know you miss Luka, most of us do too, but you need to get your shit together so we can get him the fuck back."

The expression he wore told me he was still angry about his bike, and I needed to tread lightly.

I averted my gaze and glanced around the campfire. Most of the people looked at me with sympathy, like April and Peach, and others blatantly avoided my eyes, like most of the ex-Venom members. But not Winnie and Marcus. They stared me down, ready for the battle.

They had both been on my ass the past few days, and after what I did tonight, it was probably going to get worse. One way or another, they were going to make sure I didn't shut down any more than I already had.

Not wanting to fight or converse anymore, I just shook my head. "Shut up, Winston."

He snickered. "Winston? Still hate me, I see, and even after I healed you." An arrogant grin spread across his face, and it made me miss Luka.

I fought back tears, determined not to let them fall in front of people. I'd been getting good at that. "Whatever," I mumbled, before turning back around.

Every night, something inside of me pulled me toward the forest. I stared into the darkness, hoping Luka would magically walk out of it because he *somehow* managed to escape and make his way back to me.

Obviously, I was delusional. We had no clue of his whereabouts or whether he was dead.

I hadn't told anyone, and I hated myself for this, but I'd given up on believing Luka was still alive.

"You can be pissed at me all you want, Sage, but unlike most of these cowardly people around here, I won't give up on you," Winnie ranted. "And after that shit you pulled earlier, I'm not going to tiptoe around, worried you'll break. I don't give a fuck. I'll continue to give you hell until the fiery girl I know comes back."

Was I *that* bad? Were people afraid to talk to me? Afraid I would break? Possibly, but without Luka, life meant nothing to me anymore.

"Leave her alone," Lyric interrupted. "She misses Luka."

She was constantly defending me, and I knew kindness and love motivated the act, but it further proved my already unstable image.

I whipped my body back around. "I don't need you to defend me, Lyric."

With unhuman quickness, Winnie had me by the waist before I even realized he moved, and within seconds, my body plummeted into icy water. The cold stung my skin as I sank to the bottom. After a second of contemplating if I wanted to drown and end my suffering, I pushed my feet against the muddy lake floor and hastily made my way to the surface. The air rushed into my lungs, my body forcing me to suck in a hard breath.

"What the fuck!" I screamed, wading to the edge of the lake. "Are you trying to piss me off?"

Winnie flung his arms out. "Please get mad. Please fight me! Do something other than stand there staring into the woods, eat soup, and wither the fuck away!"

When I stood up in shallow water, a shiver ran through me, and I was unsure if it was from the chilly night air or from his words.

I averted my eyes and they landed on a lily pad clinging to my shoulder before I plucked it off. "This was unnecessary."

"You think? It seems fitting to me since water lilies are a symbol for resurrection and rebirth in many cultures."

Winnie's face was stone-cold when my gaze met his again. Colder than the lake I stood in.

"I'm still alive, Asshole. I don't need to be resurrected!"

The way he narrowed his gaze on me, I knew his words were about to hurt. "Are you sure about that, Sage? Because it seems like you died when they took Luka."

Even though I expected his meanness, because apparently being kind to me hadn't worked, his words *still* hit me like a boulder. An aching pain settled in my chest and tears filled my eyes.

Winnie said nothing, instead shaking his head, his own eyes brimming with emotion before he turned away.

Peach came to the edge of the water, extending her hand with a kind and compassionate face. "Come on, Kid."

Kid.

Knowing that's the nickname she used for Luka made my chest hurt even more as I trudged my way toward her. She pulled me from the lake, and I did everything in my power to push back my emotions.

"Thanks."

Embarrassed and pissed, I stomped off toward my cabin, and when I entered, I slammed the door shut, slouching against it.

Every emotion that ever existed bubbled in the pit of my stomach, slowly crawling up my chest, looking for an exit. I took a deep breath, blowing it out through pursed lips.

Water dripped from my clothes, each drop landing on the floor like a sympathy of misery. Cold air washed over my body, sending shivers through me and puckering my skin.

I was about to go get cleaned up when Chewy rubbed on my legs with his purr on high before he pulled away, seeming confused by my wetness. I bent down and patted his head for a second, my teeth chattering.

"I'll cuddle you when I get out of the shower," I promised him before I stumbled to the bathroom, flipped on the light, and shut the door behind me.

Pulling Luka's T-shirt over my head, I dropped it on the floor, and more sadness filled me. I'd almost died getting it earlier and it was the last one that still smelled like him. Now it stunk of lake water. I removed his sweatpants next before glimpsing my reflection.

The dark wooden mirror over the sink became my enemy as it revealed my true self. The woman staring back, now a stranger. A lifeless meat sack with no will to live.

My once-full face appeared somber, hollow. Dark circles hugged my eyes like the night sky hugged the moon. It looked as if I hadn't slept in weeks, which was true. Between thoughts of Luka and nightmares, sleep had been almost non-existent for the last five months.

My lip quivered when my eyes trailed down my naked body, which didn't look like mine. Born a thicker girl, I'd never been ashamed of my figure, but this body mortified me . . . scared the shit out of me. I appeared unhealthy, with pale skin devoid of any pink undertones.

Lifeless. I looked lifeless and in only a short amount of time.

The speed at which something can change a person is truly remarkable. The value of my body, of myself, was now measured by a single word—time. Even though the length of time can vary, its nature remains indefinite. Time is never-ending. Even after death, it continues to exist, not caring if you don't anymore.

My whole life I chased time, ready for the day when I turned sixteen and began my training to become a vampire hunter.

Amaranthine is what the Vampire Research Center named the infectious microbe that causes humans to have immortality and regeneration. With Venom and VRC working together, the goal was to find a cure for vampirism to rid the world of vampires. And of course to save humans, because we couldn't have detrimental propaganda fed to us without a solid reason for its importance.

Since my family had managed Venom for generations, I was proud to become the president once my father retired. But even if I wasn't going to inherit Venom, being born into the secret organization made the feeling of being proud inevitable. It wasn't an emotional mask I wore only when my father was around. My mind, my body, my entire soul came pre-installed with it.

At eighteen, I proudly got a tattoo of a snake and flowers to symbolize my heritage, but unlike time, pride *isn't* indefinite. When you die, you take it to the grave with you. If someone doesn't strip it away first . . .

My sharp ribs were visible beneath my inked skin, leaving me feeling the opposite of prideful.

Knowing my friend Deren died because of me made shame cling to me the way my wet T-shirt had.

Since I'd killed Venom members who were unaware of the lies they were being told, remorse unpacked its bags, now living in my brain.

And because Luka's abduction was also my fault, guilt shrouded my heart, sucking on my soul like a leech needing blood.

My pride was gone.

Time had taken it.

The same way Venom took Luka from me.

He was my friend.

My lover.

My soulmate.

My everything.

Somehow, he had become the person I had lived for without me even realizing it, and without him, I had no reason to be breathing.

The tightening in my chest finally became too much to contain and small sobs worked their way out of me. I wrapped my arms around myself, finally letting go of my emotions. Tears fell hard and fast, now allowed to drop freely without fear of judgment or sympathy.

Back in October, freedom to make my own choices had been my only unspoken goal.

But what good is freedom when you're chained to emotions, lost in your own self pity?

The depression was like mud, seeping into me, stealing my air . . . slithering into my soul. The darkness had taken every bit of me I had left.

The cage of despair I'd built for myself was lonely, but being around people somehow seemed worse.

Eventually, I turned the shower on and stepped into the stream. My tears continued to flow while I shampooed, cleansed, and conditioned. At some point, I curled into a ball inside the porcelain tub, allowing the hot water to beat against my skin until it ran cold—cold as the lake.

This was the one good cry of the day I allowed myself to have. After this, I refused to let any more emotions control me until the next day.

With barely any will to live, I peeled myself off the bottom of the tub and dried off. After throwing on whatever sweat pants and T-shirt I found, neither of which smelled like Luka, I noticed the time. I had approximately three minutes before my self-proclaimed therapist knocked on my door, like she did every single night.

I headed into the living room and paused next to the old rickety end table until I heard footfalls against the wooden porch. Knowing it was Steph, here to ask me if I wanted therapy *again*, I yanked it open.

"I don't need . . . oh." I got quiet, surprised by the person visiting me.

"Can I come in?" April asked, her beautiful blue eyes brimmed with tears.

"I'm not in the mood for—"

The blonde-haired beauty pushed the door farther open and stomped past me without a care.

"I don't need an intervention, April."

"I'm not here for that." She stopped next to the couch with arms crossed. Her sympathetic face filled with pain and it didn't seem like it was for me. "Before the battle, your mom was my best friend. Now I have nobody other than you and Zeke. He's comforting, but I needed a woman to talk to."

Worried she'd rope me into a conversation I didn't have the energy for, I swallowed my words, then nodded.

"I wanted to tell you I started my period because I knew you would understand."

My chest became heavy again because I understood exactly what she meant.

April and her husband Zeke had been trying to have a baby for many years. Every month she would show up at my mom's house with a bottle of wine and tear-stained eyes. They would cry, talk, and laugh together. They were each other's rock the way Lyric and Erik were mine. And even though I felt heartache for her, my emotions threatened to consume me, leaving no room for anything else.

"I'm sorry," I whispered softly, hoping the two paltry words would comfort her.

She blinked, tears rolling down her pale, blotchy face. "It's okay. I feel it's for the best, especially since Zeke and I are fugitives now."

"You aren't fugitives." I stumbled into the kitchen, trying to avoid feeling anything, but unfortunately, she trailed behind me.

"Since we left Venom, we—"

"Don't say that name in my house." Grabbing a bowl from the cabinet, I opened a pack of ramen and poured the contents into it.

With no emotional energy left, I refused to meet her eyes, instead placing my hands on the gray laminate countertop and staring at the dry noodles. "Anything else you need?"

April let out a snicker, which had a slight hiss to it. "Well, I guess not."

Her footsteps were louder leaving than they were when she came in. I closed my eyes tight, bracing myself for what was next.

The small cabin rattled when she slammed the door shut.

My chest tightened again, emotions trying to claw their way to the surface. Taking a deep breath, I slowly blew it out through pursed lips, smacking them back down.

Nope. No more crying until tomorrow.

After eating my dinner alone, I went to bed—and by which I mean, I laid in the dark for five hours thinking of Luka.

Winnie was right, I had died when they took Luka . . . or at least my soul had withered away.

Or possibly Sorin shot me in the head, I died for real, and now I'm stuck in emotional purgatory.

CHAPTER 4
WINNIE

We needed to go into town for food and medical supplies, and Drag tasked me with making a list of necessities. We also had to get burner phones so we could call Naomi and see what the hell she wanted. I tried not to expect anything, but a huge part of me hoped she had information on Luka. But despite that possibility, I was apprehensive of letting Sage talk to her. If Naomi didn't have any info, Sage may shut down even more.

Lyric came out of the bedroom, bringing me from my thoughts when I noticed she was wearing my favorite blue T-shirt that said, "Old School Hacker" that had a cassette and scotch tape on it. "That's my shirt."

"And?" She ignored me, grabbing her white sneakers off the floor.

"You weren't even born then. You probably don't even know what it means."

"It's comfortable, though. And cute." She slid her sneakers on, then squatted to tie them. "Oh, we need a bunch of tampons. April started her period, therefore mine came early, and so did Kimber's. I'm sure the rest will be next."

I lifted a brow. "Oh, shit."

Lyric stood with tightened brows. "What? Do you have a problem buying tampons, Winston?"

"Of course not, babe. I was just concerned with all you women being together. If you ladies finally synced up periods, the wolven are gonna go nuts every damn month."

Her cute little nose scrunched up the way it did when she was confused. "The wolven? Wouldn't the vampires go nuts because of the blood?"

I laughed before I wrapped my arms around her, pulling her in close. "It doesn't work that way. I'll explain later. What size tampons do you want?"

"Get different sizes and some multi packs. I like options." She gave me a sweet and beautiful smile, making my dick harden.

"You're so damn sexy." I slid my hands down to her ass and squeezed, her skin warm through her black leggings.

"Stop getting excited, Winston. I told you I'm on my period."

"Good thing I'm a vampire. Blood doesn't scare me." I winked, and she pulled away with a laugh.

"Eww. Stop that."

I sighed because I wasn't kidding. Blood hadn't bothered me before I became a vampire, and now it just aroused me. "What are you doing today, mama?"

"Peach and Kimber are taking me over to the other camp. One of Drag's sisters had a baby and we want to go see it. It's a girl!"

The look on Lyric's face was sweet, her eyes glistening with excitement and innocence. It had been a very heart-warming moment . . . until it wasn't.

A realization hit me, causing my chest to tighten. Since I couldn't give her kids, she would never have a full life with me.

"Cool," had been the only thing I could bring myself to say before I gulped back the random feelings.

She shimmied her arms into her jacket, not noticing my discomfort. "Can you get those noodles Sage likes and some soup? That's all she eats, remember?"

"I'm not buying her any more garbage. She needs to eat something else."

"Winston." She glared at me, her hands going to her hips knowing damn well I wouldn't be able to resist her cuteness.

"Fuck. Fine. I'll get the shit."

"Thank you." She gave me a quick kiss before turning away, and I watched her perfect ass as she left.

Sage and her fucking soup.

I couldn't tell if eating it was a comfort thing or because it was quick to make. Either way, it annoyed me.

Wondering if Sage needed anything else, I decided to head to her cabin and ask. If she spoke to me, that is. If not, she could do without.

Tough love was what she'd been getting from me this past week, and it was all she'd continue to get.

Grabbing my leather jacket, I tossed it on and emerged from my lodge. The night air had a chill to it when I stepped off the porch. Glancing up at the bright full moon, my mind drifted to Lyric and the feelings I had.

Did she want kids?

We hadn't been together long, so why was I even thinking about it? About her happiness? I hadn't ever wanted kids of my own, so if she wanted them, I didn't know what I would do . . . especially since I couldn't give them to her. Letting her go so she could have a normal life didn't seem like an option, but I would do anything for Lyric. If breaking it off with her was for the best, I guess I'd have to.

"What are you doing?" Erik asked, bringing me back to reality.

"Looking at the moon." I grinned while showing him my fangs because I knew he hated it.

His eyes expanded before he cleared his throat. "Can you get me some things while you're at the store?"

"Sure, bro. What do you want?"

Erik shifted uncomfortably, and I wondered what embarrassing thing he needed from the pharmacy. He cleared his throat again. "Umm, condoms."

"Did Kimber run out?" I asked without hesitating.

"What? Why would . . ? No. I don't know. I—"

"We all know you're fucking." Ready to let go of the secret I'd been holding for months, my grin broadened.

"Whatever, Winnie. You don't know shit."

I wanted to milk this out. Make it hurt. "We absolutely—"

"We can smell your lust," Lynx interjected from behind me. "Every time you're horny, we know."

I turned toward the tawny-skinned vampire, a scowl on my face. "What the fuck! You knew I'd been dying to tell him."

"You took too long. It was getting annoying." She pushed her short purple hair behind her ear and gave me a sweet smile.

With a confused expression, Erik's eyes bounced back and forth between us. "What are you talking about?"

"Erik," Kimber called out, and his eyes darted to her. "Let's talk."

She strolled off toward her cabin, and Erik glared at me before following her.

I looked back at Lynx. "You're evil."

"I do what I can." She winked a pretty brown eye before walking away.

With a sigh, I headed to Sage's cabin and just as I stepped onto the porch, April stopped me.

"She's not in there. She went for a walk when the sun started setting."

Typically, one of the wolven would follow her discreetly, but I knew Kimber was talking to Erik, and I was about to leave with Drag, Demi, and Heston. Afraid she would go outside of the magical wards that kept us from being visible to the world, I asked, "Did someone go with her?"

"The shifters were busy, so Marcus intervened. He refused to let her go by herself, so she said he could go with her if he didn't talk to her."

I snickered.

Sage makes up the rules now.

"Thanks, April." Even without Sage here, I decided I would check to see if she needed anything. I opened the door before April stopped me again.

"Hey, Winston. Can you get me some girl things from the store?"

I looked over my shoulder back at her. "I've got tampons on the list. Anything else?"

She crossed her arms, her eyes saddening. "I don't know if you can get eight hundred milligram Ibuprofen, but I have endometriosis and it helps. If not, Aleve or any kind of pain reliever. The pain is almost unbearable this time of the month."

Shortly after we arrived at this camp, I'd quickly figured out that April struggled with infertility. I didn't know much about endometriosis, but if it's painful, I wondered if vampire blood would be a better option.

"I'll see what I can do."

"Thank you. Oh, and can you get honey buns? They're Zeke's favorite."

"Yes, ma'am." After unlocking my phone, I pulled up the notes app and cataloged what everyone wanted.

"What?" Erik's voice bellowed through the night sky. You didn't need to be a vampire to hear it coming from the cabin close by. "Everyone knows when I'm horny?"

Even if I didn't get to tell him, that shit was still funny. I laughed as I entered Sage's door, stopping in the living room, and scanning the area.

Everything seemed untouched. All the pillows on the couch were in perfect position and the TV remote was in the same exact spot when we first came here. An inch of dust seemed to have moved in, now living on top of everything.

Knowing how much of a clean freak Sage used to be, this wasn't like her. She may have been staying here, but she wasn't *living* here. With the way she shut down, she wasn't living at all.

I headed into the tiny kitchen and opened the fridge and found nothing but a barren wasteland. I foraged through a bunch of cabinets and they were the same. Only one pack of noodles and a couple cans of soup laid upon the almost empty shelves. With a sigh, I slammed the last one shut.

My jaw clenched as I headed down the hallway, stopping at the bathroom first. I checked to see if she needed any toiletries and cataloged them.

Frantic meowing screeched through the cabin, getting my attention. I stepped into the hallway and followed the sound down to Sage's bedroom. Her cat, Chewy, scratched at the door, wanting out. I opened it and he twirled between my legs while purring in victory.

"Did she accidentally lock you up, buddy?" Reaching down, I stroked my hand down his soft fur before he took off.

When I went to shut the bedroom door, an orange medicine bottle on the dresser caught my attention. Deciding to investigate, I headed toward it and yanked it up.

Marie Adams. Serovenomine. Take one tablet daily.
"What the fuck?"

I knew Sage's alias for Venom had been Marie, so that hadn't concerned me. But with the bottle being empty and weeks overdue on refill, I worried it might be something she needed but had run out of. I pulled out my phone and did a Google search and got no results.

The wood planks on the front porch creaked, alerting me someone was about to enter the cabin. I stuck the bottle in my pocket and headed out of the bedroom, shutting the door behind me. I turned into the kitchen moments before the front door opened.

"Thanks for letting me walk with you, Sage," Marcus said, and she didn't respond.

The front door shut and she let out an exhausted sigh. Her footsteps made the floors of the cabin creak as she headed toward me.

"Hey," I said when she came around the corner, startling her.

"What the fuck, Winnie! You almost gave me a heart attack."

"Sorry." I shut a cabinet door and finished pretending to log items in my notes.

"What are you doing here?"

I held up my phone for her to see. "Taking inventory. We're heading into town for supplies."

"Oh." She trudged past me and grabbed a cup from the strainer, filling it with water from the faucet.

"Do you need anything?" I asked, getting her to engage in conversation.

"Chewy needs food." She sipped her water while staring out the window framed by pale blue curtains that hung above the kitchen sink.

Even though I already knew why Luka's dog didn't stay here, I figured it would be a way to get her to converse. "Where's Annie?"

She downed the rest of her water and set her cup back in the strainer. "Peach has him. He doesn't get along with Chewy."

"That sucks. Anything you need from town? Food, drinks, meds?" *A swift kick in the ass.*

"I need soup and noodles."

My jaw clenched more as I attempted to keep a calm demeanor. "That shit will kill you."

"Good."

It was like red hot lava burned through me when she silently strolled out of the kitchen. Needing to get her to talk, I shoved my phone in my pocket and headed down the hall after her.

"Hold up."

Sage stopped by the bedroom door and turned toward me. "I don't feel like talk—"

"I don't care what you feel like!" I shouted, causing her to scowl at me.

"Did you come here to be an asshole?"

"No. I needed to take inventory and ask you a question." I let the anger drop from my face, hoping to get through to her with kindness, at least for this next request. "It's kind of important."

She sighed and then shook her head. "Hurry. I have things to do."

What the hell can she possibly have to do? Hide?

With a deep breath, I finally asked what I knew would either piss her off or motivate her. Hopefully, the latter of the two. "Ollie called yesterday to alert us that Venom was searching for you at the bar."

"I don't give a shit about them anymore." Pushing the bedroom door open, she entered and I followed.

"There's more."

"Of course there is." Sage plopped down on the bed, and with the look she had on her face, I realized she was going to shut me out soon, so I decided to rip the bandaid off.

"It was Naomi."

Her eyes darted to me in anger, which I was grateful for. I would take that emotion over none.

"That bitch took Luka!"

"She wanted something and I'm not sure you'll want to do it."

Sage glared at me with tightened brows. "Like what?"

"Don't freak out but . . . she wanted you to call her and—"

"Not fucking happening."

"She may have information on where VRC is located. It could help us finally find Luka."

She hopped up from the bed and started yanking clothes out of the closet. "I have to shower."

"Seriously, it's one fucking phone call."

"I said I'm not doing it."

She threw some clothes on the bed and headed out of the room with me right on her ass.

"This could be the best lead we—"

"I said no!"

Sage slammed the bathroom door in my face, and a low growl left me.

My heart sped up as pure heat coursed through me, making tiny veins scatter across my cheeks and forehead. I had to resist the urge to kick the door down and threaten her until she gave in.

If she didn't want to call, I figured it would be worth a try if I did it myself. One way or another, I needed to save Luka and no one, not even Sage, would get in my fucking way. With a few deep breaths, I calmed my rage, and the veins subsided.

Once outside, I glanced around and my eyes landed on Stephanie. Remembering she used to be Sage's therapist at Venom, I headed toward her, hoping she would know about the medicine.

"Can I talk to you?"

The tall, brown-haired woman turned toward me with a smile. "Of course, Winston."

I pulled the medicine bottle out of my pocket, handing it to her. "Do you know what this is? I Googled it but couldn't find anything."

She squinted, reading it. "Serovenomine is used for multiple things. Mostly anxiety and depression. You won't find anything online because it's made by the Vampire Research Center."

My brows shot up my forehead. "VRC makes antidepressants?"

"They do, amongst other things." She handed me the bottle back and narrowed her curious gaze on me. "Why are you asking?"

"I was worried it might be something Sage needed."

Steph let out a hard breath, a look of defeat plastered her face. "I already brought it up to her months ago because I knew she would need a refill way before now. She said she was fine. I respectfully disagreed with her and she kicked me out of her house."

I rolled my eyes, contemplating heading back into Sage's cabin and kicking her ass. "Of course she did. Where can I get more?"

"You can't, Winston. Not unless you have access to a high security pharmacy run by Venom. But if you want to help Sage, there are other medications you can get which are comparable. They won't contain the same ingredients as Serovenomine but people have been surviving for centuries without vampire blood."

My eyes bulged, a sudden coldness hitting my core. "Those pills have blood in them?"

"Well, yes. The Vampire Research Center makes a few different products that contain vampire blood to help out the Venom members."

I immediately wondered if Sage would benefit from vampire blood straight from the vein, which was more potent than anything VRC could extract. But quickly discarded the thought since I gave her blood last night and she was still in a mood.

"But there are pills that will help Sage?"

She nodded. "You'll need a prescription, though."

"Drag has a deal with a pharmacy. We can get whatever we need without one."

"Oh! Let me get a pen then and I'll write some names down."

"A pen?" I chuckled, handing her my phone. "Type them in my notes."

While I watched her fair-skinned fingers slowly hit each letter, I started to wonder if she actually was a vampire. Good thing I don't age. It seemed like a lifetime passed before she handed my phone back.

"There you go."

"Thanks, Steph."

I let out a couple of piercing whistles to signal my friends it was time to leave. A minute later, Drag, Demetrius, and Heston appeared.

"Let's go." Drag headed toward the parking lot and we followed.

Since I was going to be with my friends for a while, I decided to put Sage out of my head for now and enjoy the evening.

We approached a new black F-150 Raptor that Drag had bought. With pure excitement and a hint of jealousy, I smacked the ass end of the truck. "This is much nicer than your beat up one."

His old truck still worked after the battle, despite being dented to shit from the Venom crew crashing into it repeatedly. We now used the beater to haul stuff.

"I figured it was overdue." Drag slid into the driver's seat and Demetrius hopped in the back.

As I made my way to the passenger side, Heston slung the door open. "Shotgun!"

"Fuck, bro." I hated sitting in the back.

I opened the rear passenger door and Demi patted the seat. "You wanna cuddle?" he asked in a thick Irish accent.

"Only if you're in wolf form. I like my men furry."

Demi laughed at my sarcasm, then I jumped in.

"Do you think we have enough room in the bed?" Heston asked. Or I should say, the Seat Stealer. I had half a thought to flick him in the back of the head.

Drag pointed out the window and my eyes followed. "We got them."

Marcus, his brother Zeke, and Peach were in one of the vans Venom had left behind. Figuring they might come in handy, we had brought most of the vehicles back here after I removed all the tracking devices on them.

"Sweet!" I drummed on the back of Heston's seat, making him let out a grunt of annoyance. Since he stole the front, I was gonna bother him the whole ride. "Let's get this show on the road."

CHAPTER 5
SAGE

*N*aomi. A name I never wanted to hear again in my life. She conspired with her brother Sorin and it resulted in Luka being taken. Now that she was my enemy, I was shocked Winnie would even consider me calling her.

There was *nothing* that bitch could say I wanted to hear. Luka was dead and she was now trying to get to me. Unsure if she wanted to take me back to my father or kill me, I wasn't playing her games either way.

Once I heard Winnie leave, I came out of the bathroom and threw on the clothes I'd laid out. I didn't have the energy to take a shower. Honestly, I usually took them before bed anyway, and I wasn't ready for my daily cry yet.

When I came out of my cabin, the night air was crisp, the moon bright and full. I didn't make eye contact with anyone, heading straight to my spot. I knew Winnie had gone into town with Drag and a few others, so most of the people who would bother me weren't around.

As I took up my roost in the woods, I heard Vivi ask Kimber if there was a portable speaker she could use. Within minutes, music blasted into the darkness.

With a sigh, I glanced over my shoulder to see what the hell they were doing. Vivi and Jimmy were chatting as they passed a bottle of whiskey back and forth in front of the blazing bonfire. There were two other humans with beers in their hands.

My gaze swept over Nellie and the overly-processed bleached hair that came to her shoulders. She was short and medium built with bronzed skin you can only get by using fake tanner. Jimmy took a liking to her, but she was someone I couldn't stand, even before the war. She was one of those people who liked to gossip about others and be everyone's friend, and it made me want to punch her in her big ass nose. I refrained back when we were in Venom together because not only would I've gotten an infraction, but I would've also been yelled at by my dad. But if she pissed me off out here in the middle of nowhere, New Mexico, I wouldn't hesitate to kick her ass.

My eyes bounced to Randi who was rail-thin and tall. Her complexion was fair and had a pink undertone to it. She'd rarely talk but I did once hear her say she'd prefer working the night shift because she burned super easy in the sun. She was modest in her appearance, mostly wearing long sleeve shirts and slacks, even on warm summer days, and her hair was a dull brown she'd always kept in a bun. We weren't friends before we came here but she had always been nice to me.

When Vivi caught sight of my staring, I quickly turned away, avoiding eye contact.

"Sage! Come drink with us! It'll make you feel better."

"No, thank you," I murmured softly, aware that she could hear me due to her impeccable vampire hearing.

How the hell can these people celebrate when we've lost so much?

"Come on. It'll numb your feelings!"

As I stared into the woods, numb feelings didn't sound like such a bad idea, especially if I didn't have to socialize with anyone. In theory, I could take a few shots before returning to my spot.

Fuck it.

Vivi squealed in excitement as I strolled toward them. I kept my eyes on her, completely avoiding the others when I approached. She held the bottle out to me, and I took it, not even checking the brand before taking a swig. The alcohol made a fiery path, running down my throat and landing hard in my empty stomach. I took another big drink before handing it back, a small cough leaving me.

"That tastes like shit."

Vivi tilted her head, eying me like I was a zoo animal on display. "How are you doing?"

"I'm fine," I lied effortlessly, like I'd been doing for months.

"Are you sure?"

The sincerity in her voice along with the sadness in her eyes made me avert my gaze to the bonfire. A pooling of emotions swirled in the pit of my stomach as I watched the flames flicker. Vivi was one of the few people who understood exactly what I was going through, yet I didn't know what to say to her.

How can someone express the depths of emotion without looking like a lunatic?

What was I supposed to say?

That I'm exhausted.

Exhausted from the constant thoughts occupying my brain, each talking louder than the other as if they're determined to win an imaginary race.

Maybe I could say I'm furious.

Furious I let myself be fooled into thinking I was an impervious gladiator, when in reality I was more delicate than a candle flame fighting against the winds of a storm.

Or how about showing them I'm angry?

Angry I opened a sliver of my heart and allowed myself to care for someone, unknowingly setting myself up for failure.

I could simply express that I'm feeling sad.

Sad after realizing the hand dealt to me would never be higher than the one the house holds.

Perhaps I should tell them I'm broken.

Broken into a million sharp pieces when the one person who owned the glue was probably dead.

I shouldn't say I'm jealous.

Jealous of the people who still felt peaceful during a gentle rain when it no longer soothed my weary soul.

What about saying I'm lonely?

Lonely because I refused to let anyone occupy my time while buried deep in the dark, depressing grave that was once my life.

But I can't say those things, right?

Because that would not only make people empathetic but also uncomfortable; therefore, my emotions would stay hidden beneath the heavy barricades I'd created until the fragile glass of my soul shatters, sending shards in all directions, striking anyone in their path.

An icy breeze puckered my skin when it came through and changed the direction of the bonfire, the flames now swirled toward me. I took a step forward, moving in closer, and the fire licked at my pants, ready to engulf my entire existence.

"You can't get that close." Vivi tugged on my shirt, pulling me back a foot, leaving the fire without a victim. "Are you sure you're okay?"

Unable to look at anyone, afraid they would see the emotions my eyes held, I never turned around. "Like I said. I'm fine."

My words were empty. Hollow. Meaningless.

I had lost my society, my family, and the person I loved the most.

I was *not* fine.

Far from it, actually.

I watched the flames flicker for a few minutes before someone tapped me on the shoulder. When I turned around, Randi handed me the whiskey without saying a word. I graciously took it with the plan to only have one or two more drinks . . . or until my emotions were numb.

Time was non-existent as we emptied the bottle of whiskey before Vivi grabbed another. I lost track of how much I'd drunk, but my worries felt insignificant now. I wouldn't say it made me happy, but it did what Vivi said.

I was numb . . .

The alcohol had completely taken over my senses, leaving me with a fuzzy brain. I looked around and noticed Vivi was the only supernatural person in the vicinity.

"Where did Kimber go?"

"Winnie sent her and Erik to a cell phone place or some shit."

"There's usually more people out. Where's everyone else?"

Vivi shrugged unconcerned. "Some went with Drag and Winnie on a supply run, the others went to see Drag's new niece."

No chaperones.

Only me, her, and three ex-Venom members who wouldn't dare reprimand me for anything, which made it a perfect night to not give a fuck.

"Pony" by Ginuwine came over the speaker and I threw my hands in the air. "Turn it the fuck up!"

Jimmy gave me a look of concern before he turned the sensual music louder. Vivi began swaying her hips, having fun dancing her ass off. I wanted to enjoy myself as well, so I stumbled toward her and joined in.

We passed the bottle of liquor back and forth between us, dancing away our worries.

CHAPTER 6
WINNIE

Music blared through the night sky as I stepped out of Drag's truck. I assumed the people here were letting loose and having fun, which was something they needed. It had been rough.

We managed to get all the food and supplies on the list. Hoping to also make her feel more like herself, I got some medicine for Sage, and knowing she loved music, I also bought her an Alexa and a music subscription.

Lyric's natural scent hit my senses, alerting me she was nearby. My gaze shot in the direction it emanated from and found her heading toward me, radiating pure happiness.

After giving her a quick kiss, I lowered the tailgate so we could unload the supplies. "How was your visit, mama?"

Her amber eyes sparkled. "Amazing! She's beautiful, Winston. You have to go see her."

Knowing she felt the happiness many people feel around babies, a happiness I couldn't give her, caused a knot in my throat. I didn't have time to respond because Heston tapped my shoulder.

"Are they drunk or . . ?"

Turning my head in the direction he pointed, my eyebrows rose as I caught sight of Vivi and Sage dancing seductively next to the fire.

"For fuck's sake." Dropping the big ass thing of toilet paper I held, I immediately headed toward them, and everyone who had gone on the trip followed me.

Vivi grabbed the whiskey from Sage and took a huge gulp, spilling it down the front of her, and I let out a hard breath.

When I approached, I pointed to the speaker. "Turn it down." Jimmy lowered the music and I glared at my sister. "What are you doing, Viviana?"

"Getting drunk. Want some?" She grinned, holding the bottle out to me, her brown eyes sparkling with drunken happiness.

I shook my head. "No, thanks."

Sage put her hands in the air and twirled in a circle. "Fucking live a little, Winnie!"

Vivi shoved the liquor in my face. "Fucking live, brother!"

The last thing I wanted to deal with was two broken-hearted drunk women.

With more intensity than needed, I forcefully yanked the bottle from Vivi's hands. "You two have had enough."

Sage stumbled to a stop, and her slanted eyes locked on me. "You're a killjoy, you know that? We're just having fun."

Her slurred words made it clear to me that she wasn't going to last much longer. She resumed spinning in circles, and judging by her uncoordinated feet, she was either going to throw up or fall down soon.

I knew one thing, her ass was going to wake up with a hangover and I wasn't going to take care of her.

My chest tightened, and everything Marcus had been teaching me went out the window when I hit my snapping point. "So, you can get drunk but not make one fucking phone call?"

Sage came to a wobbling stop and her bloodshot eyes practically crossed. "And that's a problem for you, Asshole?"

"Yeah, it is!" I screamed louder than I intended.

"It's not your problem!"

"No, but you giving up on Luka *is* my fucking problem!"

The pounding of her heart rang in my ears over the music and her angry expression melted away. The pain she had been holding back exploded out of her emotional floodgates.

"He's dead, Winnie! That's why I gave up! He's fucking dead!" She fell to her knees, covered her face with her hands, and started crying.

Fuck.

We knew Sage had been going through some shit, but none of us knew she thought Luka was dead. Mainly because she refused to talk to us, but it still didn't keep me from feeling like an asshole.

Not wanting to see her cry, I dropped my tough love act and kneeled next to her.

CHAPTER 7
SAGE

The fear and sadness I kept contained broke off the leash and was now on the loose. The pain hit me like a stab to the heart, making me fall to my knees. I threw my hands over my face and muffled cries bounced off my palms.

Someone kneeled by my side, and warm hands slid around me. "Come here." Winnie turned me into him and even though I was mad at him, he had been right. I'd given up on Luka.

Needing comfort, I laid my cheek on his chest and gripped his shirt tightly as I panted through hard sobs. "He's dead and I don't want to live without him. I can't."

"Oh, Sage." Lyric reached her hand out for me but Marcus grabbed it, stopping her.

"Don't. She needs this."

"But he's not dead." Winnie tried to keep a calm voice, but it cracked a little with emotions, causing me to realize I hadn't been the only one hurting.

"You don't know that." I sniffed back snot so it didn't run down my face, and had a half a thought of wiping my nose on his shirt. "Deep down, I know he's dead."

Winnie ran his hand down my back, soothing me. "Your body says otherwise."

Either my emotions were *too* out of control to understand what the hell he was talking about or I'd had way too much alcohol because I was confused. "What do you mean?"

"Look at me, Princess." Winnie's use of the nickname Luka gave me had my gaze darting up to him with such quickness it made me slightly dizzy. He smiled, knowing he had *finally* gotten my attention. "Did Luka explain what a lenxus is?"

"No. There wasn't much time. Everything happened so fast. I only know what I've heard you guys say."

"Then you know it's a bond between a vampire and their mate. You've also heard us talk about the blood bond part of it. How vampires don't want to feed on others."

I nodded, wiping away tears.

"Well, there's more than that. The lenxus bond also comes with a feeling, a tugging. You feel as though you're being pulled to them."

"It's like an invisible rope," Peach added. My eyes drifted to her saddened ones, and the world moved quickly in the background. "You can feel the tug it has on you."

More confusion filled me, trying to comprehend the conversation. "I don't feel any rope."

"Yes, you do," Winnie said, bringing my attention back to him. "You've been standing in those woods waiting for Luka for months. It may not feel the way you think it should, but it's there."

Peach kneeled on the other side of me and brushed her hand softly down my hair. "And believe me, when it's not, you'll know. There's this hollowness in you, like you love them, but don't remember why. You know it's something you *used* to have. Like a faint childhood memory, but a chunk of it has been taken away. A chunk of *you* was taken away. I think that's what has to happen when a bond is broken. If it didn't, you wouldn't be able to breathe . . . or live."

Peach stood and wiped the tears from her cheeks, and Marcus stepped in close, wrapping his arms around her from behind. It was that moment I finally realized why she had been so kind to me during this whole thing, and why she tried hard to close herself off to Marcus. Peach had experienced this type of pain before and didn't want to get hurt again.

She had loved and lost, like me.

"That's how I know Strike is still alive," Vivi chimed in, her voice low. "The pulling doesn't stop. It's like I'm anxious and need to go somewhere or do something. Not much helps. Except lots of this." She held up a bottle of whiskey before taking a swig.

Doubt filled me when I thought about this mysterious invisible rope. "If this bond thing is real, I don't think I have it." I sniffed back more tears and lowered my voice. "I don't think Luka bonded with me."

Peach leaned down and removed the hair clinging to my wet cheeks before wiping my tears away with her thumbs. "I'm the oldest one here and I have seen things you could only *dream* of. Believe me when I say this bond is real and you have it."

A bizarre, joyful sensation overwhelmed me and caused my stomach to turn upside down.

Was it the bond? Or was it hope finally returning?

"Does that mean Luka is . . . alive?"

"Of course," Winnie whispered. "Why else would we be working so hard to find him?"

I wasn't certain, but this new revelation had me wanting to scream with excitement . . . or throw up. Nausea rose from my stomach and danced its way up my gurgling throat. The atrocious sounds that came out of me were indescribable. Good thing Winnie was faster than lightning. He turned me away just as the putrid remnants of alcohol on an empty stomach flew out of my mouth.

After vomiting for who knows how long, it finally stopped. I took a couple of deep breaths, focusing on it not coming back.

Someone held a water bottle out in front of me, and when I glanced up, it was Lyric. I missed my friend, and judging by the tears in her eyes, she also missed me.

"Sip it slowly."

I took the water from her with a nod.

"If I knew you couldn't hold your liquor, I would have gotten a better drinking partner."

"She's human, Viviana," Winnie shouted. "You can't pump her full of alcohol."

Nausea rose and I retched again. Winnie grabbed my hair and pulled it back. I was extremely grateful for him when I vomited.

Once my hurling ceased, Vivi suggested something I hadn't even thought of. "Turn her. Maybe she wouldn't be so moody."

Winnie snickered. "Yeah, that's all we need. Another *you* running around."

Vivi sucked in a deep breath, veins of anger flooding her face. "Fuck you!" She stormed off into the darkness.

"I should check on her." Lyric tried to follow, but Winnie stopped her.

"Don't. This happens every few months. She'll be fine when she wakes up tomorrow. It's her way of coping."

"Last time Winnie pissed her off she drained a cow dry," Ravage said, widening my eyes. "Do you have cows out here, Drag?"

He shook his head. "Thank the forest, I don't."

Winnie moved a hand to my cheek. "You good to stand, Sage Stick? The ground is freezing."

I nodded, and he pulled me to my feet. Humiliation filled me when I noticed the entire camp watching. My gaze met Winnie's with a silent plea.

"The show's over, folks! Go find something better to do."

I was grateful for the "I-don't-give-a-fuck" attitude he had when he shooed everyone off.

My embarrassment quickly faded as dizziness set in. My body swayed and large hands reached out and grabbed me.

Marcus slid one arm behind my back and the other under my legs, lifting me off the ground. "I got you."

As he carried me to my cabin, my eyes unfocused on the night sky, each star a pulsating sparkle which seemed to breathe.

Lyric held the door so we could enter, and Marcus took me to my bedroom and laid me down. Lyric set a trash can next to me before taking off toward the bathroom.

"You're the only real father I have ever had, Marcus." The confession had more tears threatening to consume me. "I love you."

"I love you too." He kissed my head, then covered me with my blanket. "I'll be in the chair if you need me."

Lyric came back and crawled onto the bed next to me before pressing a wet washcloth against my head. "You can go. I got her."

Marcus looked at me, waiting to see what I wanted. I knew my best friend needed this job as much as I needed her to have it.

"I'll be good. Thank you for taking care of me."

Marcus nodded before he left, shutting my bedroom door behind him. The silence of the room left my ears ringing.

"It's too quiet in here."

Lyric said nothing, instead pulling her phone out and putting on thunderstorm sounds, something she knew I loved when I couldn't sleep. She turned the volume down low and set it on the nightstand before laying down next to me.

"I'm sorry for everything, Lyric."

She shifted, her warm hand grabbing mine, her thumb grazing slightly over the back of it. "Blood of the coven, remember?"

I sniffed back tears. "Blood of the coven."

One of the biggest things I regretted was not letting Lyric help me when I needed her most. I knew I fucked up, but I also knew she would forgive me.

Not much else needed to be said for us to bond back together because the blood of the covenant was thicker than the water of the womb.

The sun peeking through the window disturbed my sleep and I regretted not shutting the curtains. My head pounded in protest from last night's activities, so I rolled over and covered it with a blanket. Apparently, alcohol was *not* the solution to hiding my feelings since it heightened them.

My hangover didn't keep the embarrassing drunken flashbacks from racing through my mind, and one crucial memory stood out more than the others.

I flung the blankets off me and sat up.

Luka is alive!

Nausea and dizziness hit me like a ton of bricks, but it wouldn't stop me from reveling in this new information. Vaguely remembering Lyric came to bed with me, I glanced over and saw her sleeping. Needing to find out more information, I let her be and quietly slid out of bed.

The wood floor was cold against my bare feet as I made my way into the hall, gently shutting the door behind me. Despite it being chilly outside, putting on shoes would be a waste of time. I needed to talk to Winnie immediately, so I figured I'd run to his cabin and hope my feet didn't get frostbite.

The living room was darker than normal when I entered it. Stopping at the door, I unlocked it and put my hand on the knob.

"If you open that, I'll be burnt toast."

My head whipped toward the dark shadow on the couch who sounded like Winnie. "What are you doing here?"

"I wanted to make sure you were okay. Plus, I knew when you woke up you'd come looking for me, no matter what the time."

He was right. I had a thousand questions running through my mind but it seemed none of them wanted to come out of my mouth.

Winnie flung his blanket off and sat up. "Come sit with me."

"What did you put over the windows to keep the sun out?" I asked as I gingerly made my way to him and took a seat on the couch.

"Nothing. I closed the steel shutters and curtains."

I shifted and pulled the edge of Winnie's blanket over my freezing feet. "I didn't even notice I had those."

"There are lots of things you haven't noticed lately, Sage."

Before I had a chance to stop them, tears fell. "I know. Sorry."

"Don't be sorry. Like everyone else at this camp, life kind of smacked us in the face. We all have our own way of dealing, ya know?"

I nodded, but I honestly didn't know how everyone else felt or handled anything. I had been so caught up in my own misery, I hadn't once stopped to think about anyone around me.

"To save you the time. Yes. Everything I said last night is true. If you can remember it all."

I let out a light laugh, wiping away tears. "I remember."

"What do you want to know?"

There were a thousand questions pooling in my mind, but as I stared into the eyes of a person I used to call my friend, I could only ask one. "Do you hate me?"

Winnie tilted his head like he contemplated his answer before his eyes softened. "Even if you're a pain in my ass, I don't hate you. You're my family now so I have to put up with you the same way I do Vivi. I'll love and protect you when you need it, but I'll also tell the truth, no matter how much it hurts."

A snicker left me. "Obviously."

"Tell me one thing. Why did you give up on Luka?"

I stayed quiet for a minute while I thought about my answer, and the one I came up with surprised even me.

"I guess because I didn't think I deserved to be happy, so when I found happiness and Venom ripped it away, it devastated me. I would have given up anything to get it back. To get *him* back. But the hours turned into days and then weeks. Now it's been over five months. I kind of just thought I got what I deserved. I also figured my dad would've killed him for being with me."

Winnie's thumb brushed across my cheek, wiping away another tear. "You deserve happiness just like anyone else."

My anxiousness had me dropping my head down while I picked my cuticles. I still didn't believe I deserved happiness, but I wasn't going to open my mouth and mess up the slight progress we'd made mending our friendship.

He sighed as if he could read my mind—I still wasn't convinced vampires couldn't hear people's thoughts. "Are you ready for the hard part?"

Of course, I wasn't because I knew he was going to ask me to call Naomi. Despite the fact I didn't want to, if it helped find Luka, which there was a small possibility it would, I didn't have a choice. "Yeah, I'm ready."

Winnie stood and paced the room, prepared for a battle. "I know you don't want to do it, but you have to take Naomi's call."

"Okay."

"It could be our only . . ." He stopped pacing, his shocked eyes shooting toward me. "Wait, what?"

"I said okay. I'll take her call."

His shoulders dropped, a look of determination sagging off his face. "That was *too* easy. I was ready to fight you." He gave me a fanged smile, making me let out a small laugh.

"I know, but you said Luka's alive and I'm going to take your word for it."

"You don't need my word. Your body will tell you when he isn't. I promise you'll know."

The wood floor creaked and I glanced over at Lyric entering the room.

"Morning, mama."

She flicked her eyes at Winnie before nervously looking at me with a hopeful expression.

I stood, heading around the back of the couch, and she squeaked when I yanked her toward me.

"I'm sorry, Lyric. I shouldn't have shut you out like I did."

"It's okay," she whispered, hugging me back. "Blood of the coven."

"Did you guys start a new cult? Because if so, I want in."

Winnie's joke made us both giggle and release the hug.

He headed toward us and put his arm around Lyric while still eyeballing me. "We have important things to do tonight."

I took a deep breath, slowly releasing it. "We definitely do."

Winnie looked me up and down, his nose scrunching, a look of disgust on his face. "You may want to shower first. You stink."

Lyric laughed when I punched him in the arm before heading down the hall. "I'm going now, Asshole!"

"Atta Girl," Winnie yelled from behind me, putting a genuine smile on my face for the first time in a while.

After showering and getting dressed, Winnie set up my new Alexa and gave me some meds he picked up for me. I researched what they used for and their side effects before I took one.

Since the sun hadn't set, Winnie and Lyric hopped in my shower, and when I heard bangs coming from the bathroom, I rushed outside to give them privacy.

The cold air prickled my skin when I took a seat in the rocking chair on my porch. The sounds of chatter had my attention while a few of the other humans came out of their cabins. With curious eyes, I watched them while sipping on a cup of coffee. Some people glanced over at me before quickly averting their gaze, except for Jimmy who waved. I waved back before shamefully looking away.

Purposely, I had alienated everyone, and it was going to take work on my part to make people comfortable again. Even though I wasn't ready to start socializing yet, one of the few people I would talk to was heading toward my porch.

Marcus beamed with pure radiance, taking the four stairs with one huge step. "This is new."

"I figured I'd watch the sunset. There's fresh coffee if you want some."

"I already had two delicious cups. Peach makes the best pour over."

He took the seat next to me, and I peered at him in surprise. I hesitated on the next question but his grin made me ask, anyway. "Did you sleep there?"

"Yeah, but on the couch." Marcus sighed and leaned forward, resting his elbows on his knees and staring off into the distance with hopeful eyes. "That woman has the mind, body, and soul of a goddess. She'll converse about the world, aliens, magic, recipes . . . anything you'd like except for her feelings. Getting into her heart is like exploring the Labyrinth. I'm uncertain if I'll ever get to the center, but I know it's worth trying." His gaze met mine and he grinned. "But I got coffee."

My whole life I'd waited for Marcus to find someone to love. His genuine care for Peach made happy tears form in my eyes. "Two cups of pour over? She must like you a lot."

"She does. I'll eventually break through her walls once she's comfortable being loved again. I'm taking my time and letting her know her heart will always be safe in my hands."

Peach's past wasn't any of my business unless she wanted it to be. But somehow Marcus's words had a huge impact on me because I also needed to get comfortable being loved.

No matter how scary forming a bond with Luka was, I'd taken for granted the feelings he had for me—and the ones I had for him. If I could take it back, I would. If I could *bring* him back, I would.

A sigh left me when I thought about the bond. Even if I still couldn't feel it, I had to believe it to be true.

"Why don't you go out there and get a little sun before it disappears. You're looking a little pasty, sweetie." With a laugh, Marcus stood, kissed the top of my head, and left.

After I finished my coffee, I decided maybe I did need some vitamin D. When I stepped off the porch, my body wanted to pull me to my normal spot in the woods, but I wasn't going to find sun there. Forcing myself to ignore the pull, I headed around to the side of my cabin. Rocks crunched beneath my low-top Converse as I stepped onto the gravel lot where everyone parked their vehicles.

I stopped and took a deep breath, attempting to quiet my mind. Like every day since the battle, my thoughts were stuck on Luka.

I'd give *anything* to hear the deep timbre of his voice again as my nickname rolled off his lips, or to have his fingers press against my chin and tip my face toward his so I could gaze into his beautiful blue eyes.

Anytime I thought of Luka, I would get more and more depressed, and that was how I lost hope. This time as I reflected on everything, a fire buried deep inside of me sparked back to life. It was the first time in a while I was ready to fight.

The vengeful fire intensified with thoughts of saving him.

This . . . this was who I used to be. Not some weak person sheltering herself from the world and praying for death to swiftly end her suffering. I was a hunter. A soldier. A trained assassin, ready to take on a mission to save the one I love, even if it killed me in the process.

I took a deep breath and released it in a slow stream as I stared into the horizon.

Beautiful orange and pink smears painted the evening sky as the sun fought to stay a few seconds longer. The winter clouds moved fast, attempting to cover up the beauty. Tipping my head toward the sunset as the last bit of its rays shone upon my face, I finally believed Luka was still out there.

CHAPTER 8
LUKA

Three hundred miles away . . .

Screams coming through the walls alerted me they were back, poking and prodding, taking what they needed from us without a care. We were nothing more than lab rats, and they were using every piece of us they could to the highest extent to fulfill their needs.

This had been the same routine since I got here months ago: every three days they'd come in to do their *research*, feed us, and leave.

The blood they offered didn't excite me. After I bonded to Sage, all other blood had become unappealing. The shit tasted like mop water smells after sitting in a bucket for a week. After being forced to drink blood that didn't come from my mate, I had much more respect for Vivi. She had been dealing with drinking it for a year.

Blood bonds suck.

But sacrifice means the destruction or surrender of something for the sake of something else, so I'd never regret my decisions.

I traded a life for a life, a soul for a soul, and I would do it again.

The vile taste was a bittersweet reminder of what I had sacrificed to keep Sage safe, so I appreciated the nasty shit. If my bond with her broke, other people's blood would taste good again. The only thing connecting me to her and the outside world, the bond reassured me of her survival. I wouldn't trade it for the best blood in the world.

Regardless, the hunger hurt. It gnawed away at my insides, burning through my veins, leaving pain and delusions in its path.

They only gave us a small fraction of the amount of blood we needed—enough to keep us alive. It's how they kept us weak. Even if I had enough blood to strengthen me, I couldn't do much in my situation.

The exam table they had me splayed out on had small silver spikes which were buried into my backside, each sharp point stinging. The cuffs on my wrists and ankles that had me spread eagle also contained spikes.

The screams coming from the female vampire in the room down the hall finally stopped. The sounds of her moans now filling the cold air as she devoured her feeding. Which meant one thing: the blonde-haired 'scientist' bitch would be here soon.

As I lay buck naked awaiting my turn, my mind brought up visions of Sage's beautiful face. Her high cheekbones, luscious lips, and perfect hazel eyes—drop dead gorgeous. Sometimes, when I pictured her, it was blurry, and

I was unsure whether the lack of blood or the extreme exhaustion caused it.

My biggest fear was her dying. My second, forgetting what she looked like. Especially since I wouldn't likely see her again.

Click. Click. Click. Click. The sound of high heels resonating through the hallway like a death knell brought me from my thoughts.

Here she comes. Fuck.

Six beeps sounded when she entered her code, then the door unlocked and she sashayed in like she had the best job in the world.

"Morning, Luka." Her cheerful voice had a sweet and optimistic tone to it. Like a song of illusion. A symphony of lies.

Dr. Amy Ishman.

A forty-seven-year-old unmarried woman with no kids, by choice, who earned a Master in Philosophy, a PhD, a Doctorate, among other prestigious awards, and she spent her time torturing vampires for the United States government.

I liked to call her Dr. Cuntface.

And I abso-fucking-lutely hated her.

"As always, Doc, fuck off."

She strolled up to the table and leaned into my view, her blonde hair falling forward, blocking the bright lights and casting a shadow across her face. "As always, this is going to hurt." She grinned before turning away. "You should be more grateful. Few people get to be involved in ground-breaking research."

I snickered, my eyes following her every movement as she grabbed her torture cart, or at least that's what I liked to call it, pulling it over to a metal supply cabinet.

"I mean it, Luka. Because of the virus you carry, we're able to do wonderful things. American soldiers are already faster, stronger."

"How long do you think you can keep this up?" I asked, watching her load the cart with her favorite instruments.

"As long as the funds are there we will stay in business. And with some of the biggest billionaires backing us, I'm certain we'll be around for a long time."

"I mean, how long do you guys think you'll be able to maintain this before someone shuts down the entire operation?"

She dropped supplies on the tray before turning toward me with a scowl. "By who?"

"You're eventually going to piss off the wrong people."

She shook her head, a cackling laugh leaving her. "This research has been going on for over two hundred years. We have had enemies and will continue to have them. Because only a small number of elite members know the locations of the research facilities, we have managed to remain secret. It's impossible for someone to get in here."

Facilities?

I couldn't help but wonder how many they had, then a thought hit me.

"Wait, I thought the government paid for everything."

"They give us paychecks, but only fund the research required for their needs. The rest is thanks to our supporters. They cover the cost of all the other items we make." She closed the cabinet, and the wheels of the cart squeaked as she headed toward me.

With all that research money, they should've gotten new carts.

I was always an asshole on purpose, consistently meeting her answers with more questions. "So, these backers, they don't care to know where the lab is?"

After snapping on a pair of gloves, she picked up a syringe and filled it with a serum. "Of course not. They only care about the products we make."

Remembering the name of the wound sealant Sage had, I mentioned it to prolong our discussion. "Like the Bond-coat?"

"I mean, we sell plenty of that, but it's not even a big item. Face creams and skin tightening serums that keep women looking younger are some of the most popular. Next are the sexual enhancing and stamina pills for the old men who still want to feel like a young stud on the golf course." She rolled her eyes before she continued filling syringes.

"Do they know you're torturing people for these products to be made?"

She tied a tourniquet around my arm and tapped my skin with her fingers. "Not people. Vampires. And no, but they wouldn't care as long as they could get their products."

"That's kind of fucked up, don't you think, Doc?"

"When you have as much money as they have, you don't care about anything other than what you want." She sighed, wiping the bend of my arm with an alcohol swab before finding a vein. "Little poke."

"Then why not turn them?"

"Oh, no. There's no money there, Luka. Once turned into vampires, they wouldn't need us anymore, and we need them to fund us." She filled five vials with my blood before releasing the tourniquet.

After wiping my upper arm with another alcohol swab, she injected me with the first of five shots I got every three days. I had no clue what was in them, and honestly, I wasn't sure I wanted to know.

"But if everyone paid to be turned, you wouldn't need more money."

"We would because the research doesn't ever stop. One day, we hope to cure specific diseases like cancer. The backers fund that too."

Our conversation had my mind reeling about the billionaire backers and the general population as she gave me two more injections. "And if you ever find a cure for cancer, will it be readily available to the public?"

"Someday, Luka. But not anytime soon. Obviously, our backers will be the ones to get first dibs. Plus, we can't cure *everyone* of *everything*."

My forehead creased because I assumed that was the whole reason behind the research. "Why not?"

She snickered, injecting me for the fourth time. "It would really piss off big pharma."

After setting the last syringe down, she pulled a surgical light closer to me. "Only four shots today?" I asked, a blinding pain radiating behind my eyes.

"Yep. You're now in a different phase. We didn't find anything during D942." She picked up a scalpel from the tray before turning toward me. "Are you ready?"

I attempted to stall her as much as possible, and I'd noticed her assistant wasn't with her today. "Where's Bill?"

"You won't see him much for a few weeks because I got him on another project that needs to be finished before the next recognition ceremony. If you ask me, Bill and I both have earned a trophy and a raise for the hard work we've done this year. So hopefully, we get them."

She glared at me, as if she was waiting for me to tell her congratulations.

We had conversations like this frequently, and her willingness to share all of her greatest accomplishments had me wondering if she had a praise kink. Maybe she needed a daddy to tell her how much of a *good girl* she was. Sadly for her, I wouldn't be the one praising her horrendous research, but I was curious as to why she was so open.

"Why are you willing to give up secrets? Aren't you afraid I'll share them with someone if I ever get out?"

A radiant smile spread across Amy's face, her eyes fluttering like I was an innocent child. "No one has ever gotten out of here, Luka."

My thoughts immediately went to Victor and his brother Finneas. They reminded us at least every other Save meeting about how they escaped after being tortured for years by the Vampire Research Center.

"Maybe not in your time," I muttered, not believing her.

She jutted her chin out as if she was a sophisticated queen, and I was nothing more than a mere bloodsucking peasant who was lucky to even be in her world. "Not even before me."

What the fuck?

Deep down, I *knew* Fin was a rat. What I hadn't guessed was the possibility of Victor being one, since he had been the head of the council of Supernaturals Against Venom Elitists for centuries, even before I turned.

Leaning down, she dug the scalpel into my thigh, and I gritted my teeth. "Today, I'm going to be taking samples of your tissue from last week's injections."

I ignored her, my mind still on the outside world.

If what she said was true, no one had ever escaped from a research lab. Not like I had much hope of escaping or being rescued, but my friends were out there with the enemy and I had no way of warning them.

She shaved and sliced for a good two minutes before holding up a pair of hemostats with a chunk of *me* hanging from it.

"That's a good one!" She placed it into a container with solution in it before screwing on the lid.

An hour later, she had violated me until she finally got everything she needed. Then left me with the putrid taste of someone else's blood lingering in the back of my throat.

"I'll see you in a few days. Let's hope this is the one that will finally let me retire to Venezuela." She crossed her fingers and held them up next to her big, smiling face. A face I wanted to rip off. "Bye, Luka."

Six beeps and the door unlocked. Dr. Cuntface's high heels clicked against the white marble floor again as she made her way down the hall. When I heard the door which I assumed left this area click shut, I called out to the vampire down the hall.

"You good, Carmen?" I asked in Spanish, and I'd never been more grateful for Winnie teaching me. She could speak English, but we had no clue if anyone listened in or if they had microphones. And after many conversations, I knew Amy wasn't bilingual.

Carmen whimpered, and my heart ached from the sound. "This is miserable. I don't know how you do it, Luka. I've only been here for a week."

I smacked my lips, wishing I had a sip of water. "Be grateful you're not blood bonded."

"I can only imagine." She sniffed, and I could tell she had been crying. "I don't think I can do this. I'm not strong enough."

"You are more than strong enough. Don't give up. We'll get through this together and get the fuck out of here. I promise."

She became quiet for a few seconds before she responded, "I believe you."

Being a man of my word, honor meant everything to me, but deep down, I had no idea how to honor the promise I made to my new friend.

CHAPTER 9
WINNIE

I was grateful Sage was ready to call Naomi, but she wanted time to burn off her nervousness first by sparring. We decided to set up the call for midnight. Since I had a few hours to kill, I worked on a project I thought about while we were out getting supplies. With high hopes of creating something extraordinary, I had purchased a pair of necklaces.

After inserting a chip into a bezel, I made a spring connection and put a pearl with a flat back on top. Taking the pliers, I pulled the claws of the bezel over the pearl to hold it in place. If it worked correctly when activated, it would send a location alert to multiple phones. Once I was done, I slid it onto a silver chain and held it up.

"What's that for?" Lyric asked, and I grinned pridefully, handing it to her.

"It's a GPS necklace. When you push the pearl, it sends an alert to our phones. I figured Sage may need it. If it works, I'm going to make more."

"Wow. That's so cool!" Lyric turned it over in her fingers, admiring it before her gaze met mine, and she sighed when she saw my glasses. "Why do you insist on wearing those when you have perfect vampire vision?"

"I told you, I used to wear glasses and they make me feel smart."

She snickered, then handed the necklace back before pressing her luscious lips against mine. The kiss was short and sweet, but perfect, like she was.

"I gotta go. I promised Sage I would spar with her before the call."

"You look too beautiful to be sparring." I laid my hands on her cheek and stared into her amber eyes. She was so gorgeous, it almost hurt sometimes. "Have fun, mama."

When she pulled away, her scent filled the air, sending my blood pumping and emotions flooding straight to my . . . my heart?

The scent people released when they were in love was called an *amore*. It differed from the lustful scent they released when they're horny. Her sweet smelling lilacs were now mixed with lemongrass as her amore caressed my senses.

The scent filled my heart with joy and happiness. I gulped down my shock, my bulging eyes locking on hers. "You love me?"

Lyric's face quickly turned confused. "What?"

Setting the necklace on the table, I stood. "I can smell you," I whispered before snaking my hands out and yanking her toward me. "I can smell your love."

"Oh, my god!" She inhaled sharply before clasping her hand over her mouth like it would contain the scent.

I laughed, pulling her hand away. "It's okay if you love me, Lyric."

She nodded. "I know and I was going to tell you, but I was worried about what you'd think. We've only been together a few months."

The nervous expression she wore made me want to ease her emotions. I leaned in and gently kissed her before pulling away. "Thank you for loving me," I said with sincerity.

Her heart nervously pounded in her chest as she peered into my face, searching for something. She inhaled deeply before letting out a long sigh. Judging by the look she finally settled with, it was clear I had said the wrong words.

"It's okay if you don't love me back."

Fuck.

Realizing what I had done, I swallowed the lump in my throat. "It's different for vampires, babe. I won't know until I know. If that makes sense."

"I'm going to go spar." She pulled away and headed out the door, leaving me feeling like an asshole once more.

Fuck seemed to be the only word that shot through my mind daily at this point.

There were only a few women in my life I would even consider loving: my sister, Lyric, Sage, and Peach. I had somehow pissed off three out of four of them in the last twenty-four hours. I made a mental note not to piss Peach off next—I wouldn't live if I did.

Love was a hard word for me to use. It not only came with insecurities, but I felt it meant I'd have to put someone else's needs before mine. Every day I watched the emotional pain both Vivi and Sage went through, and it wasn't something that interested me.

The longer I sat there, the more I wondered what I could do to make this situation better.

Lyric deserved a man who loved her *and* could give her the children she would want someday. I wasn't that man. I was a goddamn vampire.

Knowing I could never completely fulfill her needs killed me inside. And I realized I should have let her go *before* she fell for me. My selfishness had fucked everything up. If Luka was here, he'd be the voice of reason.

With a sigh, I headed outside to find Sage. When I approached the makeshift ring, everyone stood around watching Sage get her ass kicked by Peach. A smug part of me wanted to snicker, but I didn't. My friend had been through enough bullshit, and the last thing she needed was me being unsupportive. Plus, I'd seen her kick ass before, so I knew she wasn't bad at fighting. She just needed to regain her strength.

Sage went after Peach with a roundhouse kick to the chest. Peach caught her ankle and twisted it and Sage fell to the ground. Faster than lightning, Peach was on top of her with fangs bared.

"Match!" Marcus yelled.

Peach rolled off, leaving Sage gasping for air. "Fuck! This sucks."

Peach lowered a hand and pulled Sage to her feet. "Let's take a break. You're a little rusty."

"I feel like I'm sixteen again and new to training. My muscles are already hurting." Sage rubbed her neck with a grimace.

"Muscles stiffen when you don't use them," Marcus said, entering the ring. "You need to get up before the sun sets and stretch and jog. I'll run with you."

"Me too." Lyric handed Sage a water bottle before she locked her gaze on Erik. "We could all use the extra training for the mission. You in?"

He shook his head. "I don't need to jog in the mornings. I spar almost daily."

"Plus, you get that extra special training with Kimber at night," I added, and Erik glowered at me.

"Do you just like to hear yourself talk, Winnie?"

"It's Winston, and yeah, I do." I grinned, showing him my fangs.

Lyric put her hands on her hips and glared at Erik without saying a word.

With that one look, he quickly relented. "Whatever. I'll run with you guys."

"Perfect!" Lyric squealed, back to her sweet self. "I'll ask if any other humans want to join us."

"I made something for you," I said, stepping in close to Sage.

When I held up the necklace, she narrowed her eyes on it. "It's pretty, Winnie, but I don't wear jewelry."

"You'll wear this one because it's important. Turn around so I can put it on you."

Sage hesitated, then turned away, pulling her hair to the side. I slid the necklace around her neck and latched it. She twirled back around and, judging by the look on her face, I knew she would say something sarcastic.

"Did you fill this thing with your fancy vampire blood?"

I smirked. "You wish you were that important. If you push the pearl, it'll send your location to our phones, alerting us that you're in danger. Press it."

"That's cool as shit." She ran her finger over the pearl and mere seconds after pushing it, beeps came from around me. I pulled out my phone as did a few others.

Erik held up his phone. "I got it."

Drag nodded. "Me too."

"Same," Ravage added, before shoving his phone back in his pocket. "How many of those did you make?"

"Only one for now, but I have enough GPS chips from the Venom vans to make more."

"These will definitely come in handy." Ravage moved in close and with gentle fingers, admired the pendant. He smiled before dropping it. "I love a good pearl necklace."

I laughed as did Drag and a few others.

Sage rolled her eyes. "It didn't even take two minutes for someone to make that joke."

"Can I have one of those?" Lyric asked, and I turned my attention to her.

"I'll give you a pearl necklace anytime you want, mama." I winked, making her blush and causing Erik to gag.

"Gross!"

A large sigh left Peach, her expression frustrated. "Listen. I have students to teach. Y'all can either get the hell out of my ring or fight me!"

I put my hands in the air and backed away from her. "I'm good, Peach."

"Me too." Lyric quickly followed, causing me to laugh.

"Bunch of scaredy cats!"

"Only because you're amazing, Peaches and Cream." Marcus's words caused Peach's cheeks to turn pink.

"That I am." She gave him a wink before she turned toward Sage. "Let's go again."

Sage let out a hard breath before retaking a defensive stance.

Even though I wanted to watch Peach give Sage a pounding, I had shit to tend to, so I turned to Lyric. "Can I talk to you?"

"Sure."

She gave me a half-suppressed smile, and I could tell she was still upset by what I *didn't* say. I grabbed her hand and pulled her toward the forest, and even though it was dark, I could still see. Being a human, she couldn't, so I kept her close to me to make sure she didn't trip.

We walked in silence for a while because I didn't know how I would approach the subject. Once we were far enough away for anyone to hear, except for maybe some vampires paying close attention, I stopped and turned toward her, and she instantly shook her head.

"You don't have to do this, Winston."

My mind raced as I wondered what she thought this conversation was about, because I was definitely about to throw her a curveball. "You don't even know what I'm going to say."

A small laugh left her. "You're going to say you should have said something and you're sorry. It's fine. I don't need an apology or for you to tell me you love me when you don't. You'll love me on your own time."

"Actually, I was going to say I'm not sure being with me is what's best for you."

"Excuse me?" Lyric's expression turned pissed off quicker than I'd ever seen before. She pointed a finger at me, and if I wasn't a vampire, I would have been frightened. "*You* don't get to tell me what's best for me! I can make my own damn decisions."

Lyric never cursed, so when she said *damn,* I knew I was about to get my ass whooped if I didn't explain my reasoning. "I can't give you kids, Lyric."

Her anger faded, her expression turning sympathetic. "Is that what this is about?"

"There was a look on your face before and after you went and saw Drag's niece . . . there was happiness there." I swallowed the growing knot in my throat, shaking my head. "One I can't give you."

She placed her palms on my chest. "You are my happiness, Winston. I'm still young and don't know if or when I will want kids, but it won't be anytime soon."

I placed my hands on top of hers and her skin was cold from the night air. "I get it, but this isn't me saying I don't want to have kids and may change my mind down the road. I literally *can't* give them to you because I'm a vampire. You need to think about that."

As I stared into her beautiful face, the sadness in her eyes told me she wanted kids, and one day, we wouldn't be together because of it.

"I understand, but it doesn't stop me from loving you today." A tear rolled down her cheek and I wiped it away with my thumb before she placed her forehead against my chest. "Can't we just be happy for now?"

"That I can do." I ran a hand down the back of her hair and whispered, "Happy for now."

CHAPTER 10

SAGE

My stomach was my nemesis, flipping and gurgling as midnight approached. My hangover had finally faded, eliminating it as the cause. Since I had to talk to the woman who played a role in Luka's abduction, my nervousness had taken over, turning my emotions inside out. Even if this call brought us no leads, my plan was to eat healthier and restart my training because, one way or another, I was going to get my man back.

"This shit is making me sick, Winnie."

"Breathe. You got this."

I shook my head. "It doesn't feel like I do."

"Listen, Luka is my best friend, so I'm just as nervous as you are."

The phone rang, startling me. I glanced at Winnie in a panic, and he stopped his anxious pacing of the cabin. "Answer it."

I sucked in a hard breath before slowly releasing it and hitting the answer button. "Hello?"

"Hey, Sage. I know you don't want to talk to me after what happened to the vampire you were with, but I need to give you an important message."

The sound of Naomi's light Russian accent had my heart racing, anger immediately filling me. "His name is Luka, and you're part of the reason he's gone!" The emotions I attempted to contain made me speak louder than I intended.

"Sage." Winnie's whispering scold had my gaze darting to him. He shook his head, silently reminding me to stay on the mission.

"I'm sorry, I didn't know what Soren was doing . . ." Naomi sniffed back tears.

"Just tell me what you need to tell me so we can get this over with."

She cleared her throat before attempting to sound stable again. "Janene wants to meet with you as soon as possible."

The fact she would use my mother to get to me had me furious. "Do you think I'm stupid enough to fall for your tricks? Fuck off!"

I hit the end button on the phone, causing Winnie to throw his hands out.

"What the hell! Why the fuck did you hang up on her?"

"She said my mom wanted to see me. She's lying, Winnie."

"Do you know for a fact?" The way his eyes narrowed on me had me doubting my decisions.

"Well, no, but—"

"This could be our only chance at finding out where Luka is located and you hung up on her!"

I pushed back my apprehension and thought about the situation.

Could I trust Naomi? Hell no.

Would I risk being murdered to find Luka? Hell yeah, I would, so why did I hang up on her?

"Fuck, Winnie. Should I call her back?"

"Prob—"

The phone vibrated in my hand, ringing again. "It's her. What should I say?"

"Umm, answer it."

With a deep breath, I clicked the phone on. "I'm sorry, I—"

"Sagelynn Argent, did I *not* teach you manners?"

My heart raced at the sound of the familiar voice. The person on the other end was *not* one I'd expected. "Mom?"

"Yes, baby. It's me." Her words cracked with emotion, sending tears brimming my lids.

I hadn't gone more than a week without speaking to or seeing my mother in my life before this. She was my person. One I knew would constantly be there for me. I missed her more than I could ever express.

As I stared at the phone, I pictured her beautiful face with her high cheekbones framed by her dark hair. Her sweet smile and caring nature. I'd missed it.

"Are you still there, sweetie?"

"Yeah," I croaked, trying hard to hold my emotions back. "I'm still here."

"I can't be long, but I need to see you. I can't go any longer without hugging my only child."

Worries of me being captured left me the very second the words fell out of her mouth. The one thing in this world I would bet my life on was the fact my mother wouldn't do anything to put me in harm's way.

"When and where?" I asked.

"Oh. I don't know. I didn't expect you to answer so quickly." She let out a small laugh. Angelic and pure . . . like her.

Winnie cleared his throat, getting my attention. "Tell her to hold on."

"One sec, mom." I hit the mute button. "What, Winnie?"

"I have an address of a place she can meet us at. It's roughly halfway between here and there. I'll drop it to her in a text. Tell her tomorrow night at ten in Las Vegas."

I shook my head, my brows pinching. "Vegas is too far. We'd have to spend the night."

Winnie smirked. "Las Vegas, New Mexico."

Taking the phone off mute, I immediately relayed the information to my mother.

"I'll be there." The conversation went silent since neither of us wanted to hang up. Finally, my mother whispered, "I love you, Sagelynn."

"I love you, Mom."

The call ended and I felt broken again. Lost.

"The next twenty-four hours are going to be the longest ever." A long sigh left me as I wiped a runaway tear. I glanced up at Winnie and he was staring at me. "What?"

Taking a few steps forward, he pulled me in for a hug. "Everything will be fine."

"Why are you being nice?" I asked when he let go.

"I'm going to need a favor."

I narrowed my gaze on him. The look on his face told me I wasn't going to like what he needed me to do. Which seemed to be a familiar scenario lately. "Like what?"

His hazel eyes burrowed into me for a few quick breaths before he said something stupid. "I need you to ask your mom if she knows where VRC is."

"Are you serious, Winnie? You know how dangerous that is! What would happen if someone found out? She could be killed."

"Who's the president of Venom?" he asked, and my brows furrowed.

"You know it's my dad."

"Do you think your dad would ever allow harm to come to your mom?"

Thinking of the answer, I shook my head. "I don't think so. But if you asked me a year ago if I would be standing here talking to my vampire boyfriend's best friend while he's possibly being tortured by VRC, I would have said hell no."

Winnie crossed his arms and leaned back with a grin. "You called Luka your boyfriend."

"What? I did not."

Wait, did I?

"You did."

"Shut up, Pooh Bear."

Winnie's eyes glistened as he gave me a fanged grin. "There's my Sage Stick."

A few hours later, I grabbed a battery-operated lantern and went to find Vivi, hoping she would accompany me on a walk through the woods.

"You want *me* to go?" Her suspicious expression amused me.

"What's wrong with that?"

"You've been so, I don't want to use this word but, you've been super depressed and didn't seem like you liked anyone. Since we were never really close beforehand, I just assumed you would want one of your friends to go."

"I figured we have a lot in common since both our men are locked away somewhere being starved of our blood and . . ." Vivi's expression turned sad and I quickly changed the topic. "Anyway, you're my friend and I thought maybe we can walk, talk, bond, whatever." I bit my lip nervously, waiting for her to laugh at me.

Her cheeks tightened with a smile, which showed off her dimples. "I'd like that."

My brain was in hyper-drive as we headed for the edge of camp. "Can you tell me more about this pulling from the bond? What's it like? And do you know why it's called a lenxus? Is there a specific meaning behind it? Oh, and can you feel it all the time? Can the person you're bonded to feel it? Does—"

"Let me answer the first hundred questions before you stack on a hundred more."

We both laughed and it felt good, considering our situations. But feeling joy while knowing Luka suffered felt weird at the same time.

Vivi didn't hesitate to start answering my questions.

"Like I told you before, the bond is a pulling. It's like I'm one end of a magnet and Strike is the other. No matter how long it's been or how hard I fight it, I can't. My emotions aren't mine anymore. My body isn't mine anymore. It's always looking for him. Begging to be touched, loved, held. He's like some kind of life source now. And . . . and I miss him."

I stopped walking and glanced up at her. "Somehow, I know exactly what you mean."

She may have been smiling but her eyes screamed with the sadness she carried. We started walking again and the smell of the evergreen trees tickled my senses as we entered the forest. Making sure I didn't fall on my face, I turned on the lantern.

"To answer another of your questions, as far as I know there isn't a specific reason the bond is called a lenxus. But to me, it makes sense because it's like we're linked to our mates. I can't feel what Strike's feeling, but I know he's alive. And yes, I can feel it all the time and so can he, unfortunately. I was already a vampire when I linked with him, so I don't know how it feels for you. But Peach said she was human when she bonded to Alvin, and told me after she turned into a vampire it felt similar but much stronger. She finally felt the electricity that happens when we connect to our bond-mates and the vibrations of that connection to their soul."

"She lost him, didn't she? That's why she knows how it feels when the bond's gone. She lost the love of her life."

Vivi stopped walking, and I held the lantern up so I could see her face.

"I can't say much about the situation because I don't know the whole story. But yes. Their bond lasted for over three hundred years and his death nearly destroyed her."

I shook my head, my chest aching for Peach. "That's a long time. I can't even imagine."

"I knew Strike for only a month before we bonded. He was basically a stranger to me, but the bond didn't care. The magic that seals you to a mate has a mind of its own. Or at least, that's how it feels."

Vivi began walking, so I followed. "How long were you guys together before they took him?"

"I met Strike after Luka turned Winnie. Which was twenty-seven years ago."

"How old are you now?"

"I'm fifty-eight."

"So, you were thirty-one when you were turned? And how old was Winnie?"

"Twenty-five. He's fifty-two now and still acts like a damn toddler. He's smart, though. Like really smart. He always had issues in school because he usually knew more than the teachers."

I thought about how Winnie would act in school and giggled. "I could see him telling a teacher he was smarter than them."

"He for sure did. More than once his mouth has got him in trouble. That's kind of how he died."

My feet immediately came to a halt, my eyes going wide. "What happened?"

"I was at a bar one night and some dude kept hitting on me. I ignored it for a while, but the guys he was with joined in and it made me uncomfortable. It was the nineties and back then, people minded their own fucking business. Sometimes, too much. No one in that Podunk town would've batted an eye if those guys would've forced me to leave. So, I called Winnie from a payphone and asked if he could come get me. After a few mins, I went outside to wait, and the guy and his friends followed. They kept flirting and grabbing at me, trying to get me to leave with them. It scared the shit out of me."

Vivi stopped walking for a second and even though I couldn't see her face, I knew how she felt. When Mannie had me locked up, I feared being raped more than I feared dying.

No matter how scary a situation is, that feeling, that fear, is like no other.

I laid my hand on her shoulder, and she nodded before she continued walking. Neither of us had to say anything to understand we both knew what that feeling was like.

"A few people even passed by the front of the bar and said nothing. When Winnie pulled up and saw the situation I was in, he flipped his shit. He jumped out of the car, screaming at them. One of them shoved him and he shoved back. Next thing I knew, he was on the ground. Six guys against one man wasn't fair odds, so of course I jumped in. I'm a scrapper and got some good hits on them, but I got my ass beat. Not as hard as Winnie did. He was beyond bloody and bruised, and I had a feeling he was going to die from the kicks and punches to his head and stomach. But just as I had that thought, three men walking on the opposite side of the street saw it. They didn't hesitate to run over and jump into the brawl. I had never seen people get thrown around with such ease and the only thing I could think of was, I wish I was that strong."

Knowing Luka turned Winnie, I assumed he was one of the men who had stopped to help. After thinking for a second, I quickly figured out who the other two were. "So, Luka and his brothers helped you and Winnie?"

"Yep. They beat the creepy guy and his friends with little effort, causing them to run off scared. Andrei and Luka helped Winnie off the ground, and Strike checked on me. They put Winnie in the passenger seat of his car, and I got in the driver's side. I was about to pull off when the bar owner came out and said he called the police on us. On us! Not the assholes who started it. Can you believe that?"

Even though she walked in front and couldn't see me, I shook my head in disgust.

"Anyway, I told Strike and his brothers to get in and I would take them home so they didn't get arrested. Before I could pull away from the curb, Winnie coughed up blood, and my panic set in. So, I headed across town toward the hospital, hoping he made it, but once we were a few minutes away, Winnie started having a seizure. Luka was sitting behind him in the car, and I could hear him and the others arguing about something, but had no clue what they were talking about. I told them to shut the fuck up unless they could save my brother."

I laughed because I could totally see Vivi doing that.

"Luka made eye contact with me in the rear-view mirror and told me he was going to do something weird, but I was going to have to trust him if I wanted Winnie to live. At this point, I didn't have a choice, so I told him to do what he had to do."

I sucked in a hard breath. "Oh shit. Did he turn him in the car?"

"Yes, and no. The next thing I see is Luka biting into his wrist. He wrapped it around the seat and covered Winnie's mouth with it. Of course, I freaked out and started screaming at him. But Strike grabbed my shoulders and leaned forward, whispering calmly in my ear, promising me Winnie would be okay. And I believed him. There was something about him. Some kind of force drawing us to each other. We felt destined to be together."

"I know the feeling."

"I know you do. The bond is similar to what the wolven feel for their fated mates. It doesn't care what you want."

Vivi stopped and pointed to the ground. "Watch out. There's a fallen tree."

I held my lantern down and made sure I didn't trip as I went around it.

"Anyway, Winnie stopped seizing and went still," she continued. "Almost too still, but I could tell he was still breathing. The guys were in discussion in the backseat, saying things like, 'if he turns, he'll kill her,' and 'he's gonna need blood soon.' And I didn't know what any of it meant. Strike gave me directions to their place, but by the time we got there, Winnie was gone."

"Were you scared?" I asked.

"More than I had ever been at that point in my life. When Luka yanked Winnie out of the car and took him in the house, my human vision barely caught it. That was the first time I realized these guys weren't human. Andrei ran after Luka, leaving me alone with Strike. My ass was out of the car and ready to follow, but Strike was in my face. He told me everything was going to be okay, but if I went into the house, I could be hurt. He's an amazing guy who always had a way of calming me. I think that's why I fell for him so quickly. He just knew me."

Vivi inhaled deeply before releasing it.

"After Winnie came back to life, the guys had no choice but to let me in on their little secret. Luka promised to teach my brother how to be a vampire, and they went out feeding a lot. With Winnie being the only family I had left, and scared of being left behind, after a week of hanging out with them, I wanted to be a vampire, too. Not to mention I wanted the kind of strength where no one would ever make me feel too uncomfortable to sit in a bar. When I asked, everyone refused to turn me. They said it shouldn't be something you want, it should be something you need. Well, I disagreed with them. It only took me another week of threatening to stake them all, including my brother, while they were sleeping before Strike gave in, deciding he would be the one to do it."

"Is it common for someone to be bonded to their origin and their mate?" I asked, completely fascinated with the magic system of supernaturals.

"Actually, everyone's bonded to their origin. It's called a sentinel bond. It feels different from the lenxus bond one has with a mate. If you have both bonds with the same person, it's called an ardent."

Feeling like I needed a dictionary, or possibly an encyclopedia on vampires, I didn't even attempt to remember everything she was telling me.

Vivi stopped walking and took a seat on a fallen tree. I did the same, plopping down next to her.

"Can you explain the difference between them? Sorry if I'm asking too many questions."

"It's fine. I did the same thing to Strike when I first found out about vampires. I loved annoying him, and I secretly think he loved being annoyed by me." She smiled but it melted off her face rather quickly. "The lenxus is a mating bond. It gets you in your feels. Makes you want to kiss, hug, fuck, and protect your mate at all costs. The sentinel bond someone has with their origin is about loyalty. You have an attachment to the person, almost like they were one of your birth parents. You love them like family. If you fall in love with your origin and the bonds combine, it's like magic. I can't even explain it."

"I don't want to sound like a nerd, but this shit is cool."

"If you think vampire statistics are cool, you should talk to Drag about the wolven. Theirs is the coolest."

"I've heard them say some things about it. It fascinates me."

"We better get back before someone thinks I killed you."

Vivi hopped up, and I did the same with a laugh. "Why would they think that?"

"I may have told Winnie I was going to murder you in the woods because you got us in trouble with him."

I laughed again, and for the first time in a long time, it felt good.

CHAPTER II

LUKA

Blood gives vampires their strength. Being the only thing that sustains us, we rely entirely on it for survival. It fills our muscles, our bones, and our veins with power. It fuels our bodies in ways a human can't even imagine.

Blood can also be our weakness. Our kryptonite. Like a car without fuel, a vampire becomes nonfunctional without enough blood—devoid of energy, power, and eventually life.

With minimal blood, our muscles go rigid, causing sharp pains to shoot through them. Our brains become clouded with only hunger. And after a while, when the hunger is too much to bear, the anger sets in leaving us dangerous to even the people we love.

That was the state I was currently in. Complete vexation.

Pure, unadulterated fury.

Click, click, click, click.

The doc's high-heeled shoes hammered in my ears like the beat of a drum at a funeral. Every time they tapped against the white marble floor, I wanted to rip her throat out and drain her dry. Visions of me bathing in her blood wavered in my mind as she made her way to her rolling cart.

Am I in hell?

Abso-fucking-lutely.

I glared at Dr. Cuntface, watching her scroll on the computer, skimming through research data.

Amy glanced over her shoulder at me with an eager expression on her face. "I got great news on my research today, Luka. One step closer to Venezuela."

"Only great for you."

I thought how satisfying it would be to shove my thumbs in her eyes when she rolled them.

"It's great news for everyone when we have a medical breakthrough."

I snickered. "The doctor says to the lab rat."

With a heavy exhale, she rose to her feet. She had her blonde locks tied up in a high ponytail today, and it annoyed me watching how much it swayed when she made her way toward me. Between that and the sound of her heels, I clenched my teeth to keep from screaming obscenities at her.

She stopped next to the table with tight brows, which caused a big fat crease on her forehead. The egotistical part of me wanted to remind her she made an anti-aging cream using vampire blood, so maybe she should think about using it for herself . . .

"How can you not have any concern for healing others? Or children, for that matter? How can you not care about them?"

"I do care about human disease and would donate blood or anything you need for research, but on my time. Not like this."

She crossed her arms. "That's not how it works."

"Fucking obviously!" I snarled through gritted teeth.

Her eyes darkened, narrowing on me. "Did you scream at me?"

After enduring months of torture with barely enough blood to keep me alive, I'd reached my breaking point. If it were possible, I'd rip her throat out to keep from hearing her talk.

My anger took over, causing the sensation of veins being filled with blood to scurry across my face. A large hiss left me, my hungry fangs elongating at the thought of draining her dry.

"I'm fucking tired of listening to you run your mouth about how *amazing* you are while ruining people's lives! Ruining my fucking life!"

She showed no emotion while I had my first meltdown since being here, but inside those evil blue eyes was a small twinkle. A darkness brewing which said if I didn't shut the fuck up, I was going to regret it.

She uncrossed her arms and raised her hand, pulling the examination light closer to me. "Say you're sorry."

"Fuck you, cunt!"

Her eye twitched for a split second at my insubordination before she quickly regained her composure. "I don't appreciate the tone."

She flipped the light switch and instead of the super annoying bright light she regularly worked with coming on, torment silenced me.

The UV light sent searing pain through my eyes and I closed them tight. The horrendous smell radiated into my nostrils seconds before a loud scream broke free from my throat, drowning out the sound of my sizzling flesh.

What felt like an eternity later, she turned off the light and the pain stopped.

Dr. Cuntface let out a huff. "Next time, choose your words carefully."

"Leave him alone!" Carmen screamed so loud it echoed through the halls. The frantic tone of her voice indicated that she had been crying. "What's wrong with you people?"

"Stop talking," I told her in Spanish. "They want you to react. Don't give her the satisfaction."

"What did you say to her?" Amy asked.

Peeling my eyes open was similar to pulling the lid off a Pringle can. Every tiny piece of skin stuck together when I painfully ripped them apart. "None of your fucking business!"

Her nostrils flared this time, and I knew the light was coming back on, so I slammed my eyes shut again, bracing myself for the pain.

The flip switched, and my screams echoed throughout the room, the smell of burning flesh filling my nostrils once more.

Despite the unbearable torment, I knew the value of enduring it. Anything was worth knowing Sage was safe.

The doctor flipped the light off and I gasped for air. With a lack of blood in my system, my wounds were healing at an extremely slow rate.

She made her way to the door, her high heels clicking against the floor. "I hoped you were different . . . not like the others." After putting in her code, she took a deep breath and let out a disappointing sigh. "I guess I was mistaken."

The door shut with a click. Small sobs filled my ears as they left Carmen. I stayed quiet, hoping Amy wouldn't bother her. When her walking stopped, and the beeping started, I knew she'd entered her code into Carmen's door.

Shit.

"Stay strong," I said loud enough for Carmen to hear, but not the doc.

Minutes later, Carmen screamed, now being punished for sticking up for me. My chest became heavy and I closed my eyes tight, attempting to drown out the sounds of her pain.

My brain went to the only comfort I had. Sage.

I thought about her beautiful face.

Her dark hair.

Hazel eyes.

Sensual voice.

A single tear stung when it exited my eye and rolled down my burnt face.

I was far from a godly man. After my parents were taken from me long ago, I stopped believing in heaven and hell. To me, earth was the only place where hell actually existed. People resorted to immoral actions to gain an advantage or sometimes just for fun.

As visions of Sage played in my mind like an old VHS tape rewinding itself over and over, I started believing in heaven.

CHAPTER 12
SAGE

Twenty-four long and treacherous hours later, I sat in the front seat of Drag's truck, staring out the window as we went south on Highway 518. The anxiety and nervousness this mission gave me were overwhelming, so I was grateful when I realized the new meds helped a little.

The last thing I wanted to do was ask my mother to help me find Luka. Especially since she thought she was only coming to see her daughter. She would be blindsided by my request. I felt bad, but we had no other leads. If we wanted to save Luka and Strike, she was the only possible answer.

"Ya good over there?" Drag's question brought me out of my internal monologue.

"I'm nervous."

"Obviously. Your heart rate keeps speeding up."

I glanced over my shoulder when I heard Lynx speak. "Sorry."

The purple-haired vampire gave me a kind smile, then squeezed my shoulder. "It'll be okay."

Since my other friends were busy with what I didn't know, Drag roped Lynx and Demi into this mission. Since I was only going to meet my mom, I figured I would be fine going alone, but *apparently* it wasn't safe—or so Marcus said. But since I made him worry enough lately, I gave in and let him arm me with two wolven and a vampire.

Drag turned up the radio when the song, "Cover Me Up" by Jason Isbell came on. I wasn't big into country music, but listening to the words had my eyes filling with tears. I turned my head back toward the window, continuing to think about Luka.

The drive seemed to last forever, even if it was only an hour and a half long. Not far off the highway in the city of Las Vegas, New Mexico, Drag whipped the truck into a gravel parking lot.

"This is the place."

I looked up to read the sign. "The Branded Steer? That's a weird name for a restaurant. Aren't all steers branded?"

Drag put the truck in park and turned off the engine. "It's because they only serve meat from animals raised on their farms."

My gaze drifted from the neon sign to Drag. "How do you know?"

"The owner is a good friend." He gave me a smile, which made me suspicious of his words before he quickly changed the subject. "You know the plan. If anything happens, push the button on your necklace."

Trying to build up the courage to go inside, I took a deep breath and slowly blew it out. A hand landed on my shoulder again and I glanced into the backseat.

"You got this." Lynx's demeanor was sweet, but it didn't do much to calm my nerves.

"Thanks."

Mustering as much strength as I could, I exited the truck and made my way toward the restaurant door, my heart racing. The smell of greasy food hit me when I pushed it open. Looking for any signs of threat, my eyes darted across maroon booths filled with people.

"Sit wherever you want," a waitress said, hurrying past me, her hands filled with plates of food.

It had been such a long time since I heard the sounds of clinking silverware and chatter, it seemed foreign to me.

A glass shattered in the distance, making me jump. A part of me wanted to run, but I had stopped running from my problems. Saving Luka was crucial and this was our sole chance for a breakthrough.

With a deep breath—and a small reminder I was a badass—I moseyed through the crowd of people, making my way to the back. I had nearly given up hope when a waitress moved to the left, revealing my mom sitting at a table alone. The air caught in my throat as I'd forgotten how gorgeous she was.

The child in me wanted to run and jump in her arms, let her caress my back and tell me everything would be alright, like she used to.

Forcing myself to walk at a slow pace, I fought back tears and cautiously made my way over to her. I stopped five feet from her table and my heart filled with a love I thought I'd never feel again as I watched her nervously fold a napkin into a perfect crease.

When she saw me, her hand went over her mouth for a split second before she cleared her throat and righted her face.

"I missed you," she whispered when I slid into the booth across from her, her eyes glistening. Her hand went to the middle of the table and I clasped it in mine.

"I missed you too."

We let go of each other and my mom wiped the tears from her cheeks before handing me a menu.

"What's good here?" I asked, peeping at the variety of steaks and burgers, before doing an eye sweep of the room. My body being on high alert made it challenging to focus.

"I have no idea, Sa . . . umm, Marie, but our waitress is the sweetest person I have ever met. I already ordered you a sweet tea." She glanced past me. "There she is now."

"I see your guest has arrived." The voice was familiar—*too* familiar. My eyes widened as I looked up into Vivi's brightly smiling face.

"We haven't had time to look at the menu yet, Carol. Can you give me and my, umm, niece a minute?"

Carol?

Glancing at Vivi's name tag, it indeed said Carol.

"Sure thing." Vivi's smile stayed as she set our drinks down and walked away.

"I told you she was nice. And her dimples are so adorable." My mom grinned while she gushed.

Knowing how ruthless Vivi was behind those dimples sent shivers through my body.

An adorable killing machine.

After a few minutes of trying to decide what I wanted, Vivi came back, and I picked something simple to eat. "I'll have the small soup and salad combo."

"Which salad and which soup?"

I hadn't picked what kind because I had a thousand questions.

How did she get the uniform? The Carol nametag? The job? Does she even know what she's doing?

But I was mostly concerned with my food being incorrect.

"Caesar salad with chicken noodle," I mumbled, then handed her the menu.

"I'll take the same, but with a chef salad," my mom added.

Vivi wrote on a pad like she was a professional server. "Got it." She continued to smile, strolling off.

"How are, umm . . ."

I knew my mom was asking about Lyric and Erik, but was afraid to say their names. Anyone could be watching or listening, making everything we say potentially dangerous. I wasn't worried about me, but I would kill for her, so I kept as vague as possible.

"They're good. They said to tell you hi."

"I miss them." Tears brimmed her eyes as she cleared her throat. She reached her hand back to the center of the table. "I also miss my baby."

Grabbing her hand once more, I squeezed it, reassuring her everything would be okay.

"How have you been?" she asked, her other hand clasping mine in between hers.

"I've been fine."

My mom's soft eyes turned worried. "I didn't want to say anything, but you seem to have lost weight, sweetheart. Do you have food where you are?"

A large sigh left me. "I'm fine. I'm working on feeling like myself again."

"That's good. Anything I can do to help? Do you need money?"

My teeth bit down on my bottom lip while I decided if now was the time to ask the dreaded question. Realizing the situation wasn't going to go away unless I did, I leaned over the table and whispered, "I need to know where VRC is."

"I can't believe . . ." She released my hands, furiously shaking her head. "How can you ask me that? You know if your father—"

Vivi set my mom's salad down, interrupting our conversation. "I hope you're hungry. I accidentally ordered the wrong size salad for you, but I only charged you for the small."

"Thank you, Carol." My mom sighed as she picked up her fork. Her stare met mine in disbelief. She pressed her lips tightly together, her eyes scolding me for asking.

"And here's your burger." Vivi laid my plate in front of me and my mouth fell open.

"That's not what I—"

"It's fine, Marie." My mom gave me a look which said I shouldn't complain. She was the biggest supporter of anyone working for tips since she had done it as a teenager.

I was also a huge supporter, but I knew damn well Vivi did this on purpose. Probably trying to get some decent food in me.

My eyes narrowed on her as I gritted my teeth. "Thanks."

"You're welcome. The busser will be here in a second with your soup." Vivi's smile was pure arrogance when she strolled off.

I contemplated kicking her ass later, but I was certain she could take me without looking . . . and probably while chugging a bottle of whiskey.

I sighed and picked up a fry from my plate. After popping it in my mouth, my gaze drifted to my mom. "Are you going to tell me?"

She fiercely stabbed her salad before looking up. "Tell me this first. Why do you need to know?"

I swallowed down my fry, and my nervousness, and attempted to be vague. "They took someone close to me."

"You're talking about that person. Luke."

"It's Luka. And how do you know?"

"Nicole told me." I immediately recognized Naomi's code name and wondered what else she told my mom. She took a bite of her salad and chewed it while she bought herself time to think. After swallowing and taking a sip of her tea, she let out a hard breath. "I need more information before I can help."

"I'm going to go there," I stated in a low voice, causing her brows to furrow.

"To save him?"

Another shadow caught my eye, and I realized I had stopped watching my surroundings. When I looked up, my mouth dropped open.

What the fuck?

"Here's your soup, ma'am." Winnie set a bowl in front of my mother before staring at me. "It's the last of it. There's *no more* soup for you, miss."

The dominatingly cocky grin Winnie had on his face made me want to punch him.

"Thank you," my mom said, breaking our eye contact.

"You're welcome." Winnie gave her a charming smile before leaving.

"The wait staff here is impeccably nice. And very good looking, might I add."

I rolled my eyes and sighed. "Back to our topic. Yes, I'm going there."

I picked up my burger and took a bite. It had been so long since I had any real food, I almost forgot how much I used to enjoy eating. The deliciousness made me forgive Vivi pretty quickly.

"They will capture you, or worse." She leaned in and lowered her voice. "They could kill you."

"I'm not going alone." I took another bite, savoring every second before I realized Winnie was right. I wasn't living. I was only eating to survive.

"Why do you have this desperate need to go?" she asked in a stern voice, seemingly irritated with me. "Why, Marie?"

I took a swig of my tea, then scanned the room. No threat. Not like I had to worry much with Winnie and Vivi here. I couldn't help but wonder if Drag was in there washing dishes. "It's not important. I only need—"

My mother smacked her hand on the table, bringing my full attention back to her. Her voice was low, but firm when she said, "You look me in the eye right now and tell me exactly why you feel the need to go save this man. And I won't ask again."

A shadow brought my attention away from her gaze. "Let me refill these." Vivi held a pitcher, topping off our iced teas.

"For fuck's sake." I threw my napkin down as frustration filled me. "Because I need to save him, Mom!"

She sucked in a breath as she glanced nervously at Vivi. "Marie, we can talk—"

"She knows who I am. Her name isn't even Carol."

Mom's mouth dropped open as she looked up at Vivi. "What?"

"They have my mate. My husband, so to speak," Vivi said with a sadness in her voice. "If you don't tell us, I may not see him again."

"My god, Sage. How can you ambush me like this?"

I reached across the table and grabbed her hand. "Please, Mom. If you love me, you'll do this one thing for me. You have to. If you don't, I'll die. I'm already dying. I can't live like this. I have to find him." The pain I contained had my voice cracking, and my mother's expression saddened.

"Then tell me why."

"I, umm . . ." I shook my head, unable to say the words I needed to.

"Because she's in love with him," Vivi blurted, and my mom sucked in a hard breath.

My head fell forward and I squeezed my eyelids close as an aching pain filled my chest.

"You fell in love?" my mother asked, and I said nothing. "Sagelynn Juniper Argent, you look at me right now."

Hearing my full name, my tear-filled eyes shot up. My mom didn't use it often, but in the times she did, I sat up a little straighter.

"Is this true? Do you love Luka?"

"I do," I croaked out with fear of disappointing her.

That's what I was afraid of, I realized. I didn't want my parents to be ashamed of me, disappointed in me. Or worse, I didn't want to fail them. Especially my mother.

"I'm sorry, Mom." Tears slowly rolled down my cheeks as I stared at her, waiting for the disapproval to become apparent.

"Why are you sorry? For falling in love?" she asked, and I nodded. "Oh, honey. Don't ever be sorry for that."

"I didn't want to disappoint you." I bit back tears.

"That is such an impossible thing. You couldn't disappoint me if you tried. In fact, I'm prouder of you than I have ever been."

Confusion filled me, and I shook my head. "Why?"

My mom glanced up at Vivi as she hovered. "Can you give us a second?"

Vivi nodded and strolled away.

My mom took in a deep breath and let out an exhausted exhale. "You have become the woman I have wanted to be my whole life. You go after what you want, and you stand up for what's right. It's more than I have ever done in my life. I've known for years about the government's *real* involvement with VRC and Venom. You hear things when you're around enough. Especially when no one thinks you're listening. But I do. I'm hearing everything I'm not supposed to." She looked away as her thoughts took over, sadness washing over her face.

"I don't want you to do anything that could get you in trouble, Mom."

She let out another large sigh. When her gaze met mine again, a look of pure happiness radiated across her face. "I can't believe my daughter is in love."

"I regret not telling him," I whispered. "Now he's gone and doesn't know."

Her eyes sparkled. "Luka knows, baby. Believe me. The person you fall in love with always knows."

My emotions broke free, sending silent streams down my face.

My mother grabbed her cloth napkin and wiped her dampened cheeks. I took the opportunity to do the same.

After clearing her throat, she leaned over the table and whispered, "White Sands Missile Range."

The location of White Sands was south of where I was currently staying and a place I visited as a child. "What?"

"VRC is somewhere close to it. I'm unsure where, but I may be able to help. But it will involve, um, Nicole."

Partnering with the woman I watched put Luka into a Venom van was the last thing I wanted. But I had no other choice. And even though I didn't trust Naomi, my mom did . . . and I feared for her life.

CHAPTER 13
WINNIE

It had only been three days since Sage met with her mom. Every night after that, I'd talked back and forth with Naomi on a burner phone, until we'd hit a dead end. Needing to find the VRC location, I made a possibly deadly decision.

"Are you sure that's what she said?" Sage asked as she dug in the fridge for a snack.

As I sat at the computer in my living room, I could feel Lyric's gaze on me, but I kept my eyes fixed on the screen, weaving a web of lies. "Yep."

"It just doesn't make sense." She shut the fridge and came back into the living room. "If she has information, then why didn't she give it to you?"

Concern for her mother filled me just as much as I assumed it worried her. I hoped we weren't getting played by Naomi. Even though it was a possibility, I had limited options.

"Like I said before, she wants to meet up with us. And don't get excited about seeing your mom. Naomi said she's coming alone."

"Then I am too."

Knowing Sage would figure out something was up if I didn't play along with the lies I fed her, I made sure I seemed irritated. "You're not going alone, and if I have to bring Marcus in on this conversation, I will."

"Whatever, snitch." She sighed before plopping down on the old tan couch and pulling the top off a yogurt container.

"This is serious, Sage. You're public enemy number one right now. You can't be doing shit alone when you have a team of people willing to support you. It's unsafe. Not to mention, stupid as fuck."

"Winston is right. We should go with you," Lyric chimed in, and I was grateful—Sage was more likely to listen to her than me.

Thanks to Jimmy telling Nellie that he would be manning the computers while I went on a mission to meet Naomi, Sage hadn't been the only one I'd lied to. My girlfriend had also found out, and they both had questions.

If I come back from this secret mission, they're gonna be pissed.

"When do we leave?" Sage asked with a mouthful of yogurt.

"Once I get back from town, we'll call Naomi and set a time to meet up."

I stood and slid on my leather jacket, then leaned down and kissed Lyric goodbye. When I pulled away and saw her excited smile, shame burrowed its way into my chest.

"You and Erik have fun."

Lyric thought I was taking her brother to the store to get some personal items I'd forgotten to pick up on our last trip. She said it would be a great bonding experience.

"You two have fun on your girls' day." Worried my dishonesty would show, I headed for the door.

Once outside, I went three cabins down to find Marcus, Jimmy, Erik, and Peach huddling on the side of it, waiting for me.

"Did you get out easily?"

"Yeah, Marcus. They believed everything I said. My girlfriend probably won't trust me after this."

Peach squeezed my shoulder. "It's best neither of them knows about this. Lyric will just worry all night, and you know Sage will insist on going."

Knowing what we were about to do was incredibly dangerous, I let out a long breath. "Just make sure you keep them out of my cabin for as long as you can, Peach. Lyric is familiar with what I do. If she catches Jimmy hacking, she'll know something is up."

Peach nodded.

Marcus gave me a bro shake before pulling me in for a half hug. "You two be careful."

"Don't worry. I'll keep the blood bag safe." I gave Erik a fanged smile, and he let out a sigh of annoyance before heading to the driver's side of one of the Venom vans.

He looked nervous, attempting to buckle his seatbelt as I hopped in the passenger seat.

"If you die, do you want me to turn you?" I asked. His eyes were wide when his head whipped toward me. "Don't look so shocked, bro. I'm dating your sister, and I actually care about her."

Erik let out a frustrated sigh. "I mean, it sucks we even have to have this conversation. I don't particularly want to be turned into a vampire today, but if I die, your ass better bring me back."

"That would make me your daddy," I said with a wink.

Erik made a grossed out face before starting the vehicle. "Shut up, Winnie."

"It's Winston."

An hour later, we were pulling up to a black Venom van exactly like the one we were in.

"This bitch better not be betraying us or I'll kill her."

Erik nodded. "Same."

Noami seemed nervous when we got out and strolled up to the vehicle she leaned against. "Hey, Erik."

His face stayed blank as he went straight into business. "Do you have our things?"

"They're in the back of the van."

"If this is some trick, you won't survive." My hand went under the back of my shirt where I pulled out one of my custom Springfield 1911s before raising it to her chest. Erik mirrored me, pulling out his Glock 19. I nodded my head toward the van's passenger door. "Open it."

Naomi did as I ordered. Erik kept his sights on her as I peeked inside, finding the front of the van empty. "Clear."

Erik nodded his head toward the back of the van. "Go first."

Naomi took a deep breath, stress consuming her face, before leading us to the rear end. We kept target on her as she opened the back van doors. The inside had a bench down each side and contained nothing but a box and a gray blanket.

"I told you I was alone," Naomi muttered. "Can I give you the stuff now?"

She didn't wait for me to answer, instead opening the box. I peeked inside and two creepy-ass wooden masks peered up at me.

"Those are the ceremonial items I was telling you about on the phone, Winston. Erik knows our customs."

When Naomi called me and said she couldn't get into a system without throwing an alert out, I spent an hour going over different ways to get around it. During the conversation, I realized she may be great with computers and some software, but she didn't know shit about actual hacking. Being the idiot I am, I said it would be best if I could do it myself.

Another hour later, I had pulled Erik in on the plan, then the others so they could make sure Sage and Lyric didn't find out. Now I was about to enter enemy territory with nothing more than some creepy fucking mask, a girl who didn't fight much, and Erik. At least he could throw a good punch.

I cocked my gaze toward Naomi. "Our friends will kill you if you—"

"Yeah, I know. If I betray you, I'm dead. You've said it over and over. If we don't get on the road now, we're going to miss the ceremony, and this whole thing will be pointless."

She stared at me, waiting for me to confirm. A huge part of me was concerned about this stupid idea we had come up with, but backing out wasn't an option.

I put my gun back in my waistband holster and pulled a cloak from the box, throwing it on. Erik did the same. When I reached for a mask, Naomi stopped me.

"You can't wear that one. The guy it belongs to is closer to Erik's size. Wear this one."

"You said everyone has their own masks and most people can tell who they are by their designs. So, whose masks are these?" I asked.

"The one you have belongs to my cousin Alex. The other—"

"You brought someone else in on this?"

Naomi clenched her brows. "No. You told me I couldn't, so I didn't. Like I was saying, one is my cousin's. He wanted a night off, and I said I would cover for him by making it look like he logged into work. He doesn't know anything."

Erik suspiciously looked down at the mask he held. "And how did you get Duncan's?"

Naomi tightened her lips, a shameful expression on her face. "I gave him the flu. Well, not literally. But he's incapacitated at the moment and probably won't be leaving his house or the bathroom anytime soon. Once the time comes, I'll mark him present for attendance and then tell him I covered his ass so he won't get another infraction. He'll be grateful since he's on thin ice already."

"You gave someone the shits? A girl after my own heart." I slapped the side of the van with a laugh. "Start her up. I gotta grab my shit."

"I stashed a plastic tote about a hundred feet into the woods." Naomi pointed to the side of the road. "Just make sure when you make it back to your van, that you leave these masks in there."

I nodded and she headed to the driver's side and Erik took the passenger seat. I went back to the van we arrived in and grabbed a small black bag before hopping in the back of Naomi's vehicle.

Once on the highway, we drove for a while. Naomi eventually took an exit and a few turns onto some back roads before pulling over.

"Cameras start a mile ahead. Get in your positions."

Erik squeezed in between the two front seats and headed toward me. We both stared at each other for mere seconds before Naomi cut in.

"Hurry up. You know there's a tracker on this vehicle."

I squatted down, then situated myself until my back rested against the van floor, leaving enough room for Erik to lie down next to me. Grabbing the blanket, I spread it out over our legs. Before pulling it over our heads, I turned my face toward Erik. "I know you want to know how big my cock is, but refrain from getting me excited until after the mission."

"Geezus, Winnie. Do you ever stop talking?"

"Quiet. Both of you," Naomi said sternly before she pulled away and I finished covering us up.

We took unpaved country-ass back roads, and every little bump shook the van, causing my gun to dig into my back. Naomi had said she would give us a sign when we were about to enter the gates. When she let out a couple of coughs, I knew we were at Venom's base headquarters. My heart thundered against my ribcage, reminding me how dumb of an idea I had planned.

The brakes squealed slightly as she pulled to a stop.

"Hey, Naomi! How have you been?"

"I'm good, Rick. And you?"

"I've been great. Maybe you can come by after work and we can hang out for a bit." The man's voice got louder, and I assumed he had leaned into the window.

"We can do more than hang out," Naomi said, and my brows rose. "How does six sound?"

"Perfect. See ya then."

The sound of a kiss filled my ears before the van pulled a few feet forward. After a couple of beeps, I heard the gates opening. The van moved again, taking a couple of turns before it stopped. Naomi cleared her throat, causing Erik and I both to sit up. When my eyes landed on her, she had a tablet in her hand, typing away. She cleared her throat again, indicating that she had disabled the cameras in the parking area before she hopped out of the van. Erik took a deep breath and slid the van door open.

When I got out, I noticed we were on the bottom level of a parking garage, and as we made our way through it, I appreciated the lack of people. Once on the elevator, we took it up to the first floor, stepped off, and headed right.

Naomi cleared her throat again seconds before pushing something on her tablet. Lights positioned on the walls roughly ten feet apart flickered and screeching alarms blasted through my sensitive ears.

CHAPTER 14
SAGE

An excited look adorned Peach's face as she dropped three duffle bags next to four wooden saw horses.

"What the hell are we doing out here?" I asked.

"Practicing!"

My brows pinched as I thought about all the reasons this was a bad idea. "We're going to spar in the middle of the forest?"

Peach handed Lyric and I both a leather knife holster. "We're not fighting. Strap these on."

I fastened mine onto my right thigh and adjusted it, and when I looked up, Peach held out two daggers.

"Those are genuine Argentium silver, and you can kill vampires and wolven with them. Which is good since we don't know who Venom is working with. Just make sure you both keep them strapped on you as much as possible."

I took one from her and turned it over in my hand, admiring the beautiful markings on the handle.

Next she pulled a glow-in-the-dark target out of her bag and hung it on a nearby tree. "I want each of you to practice throwing them at that target."

Lyric went first with Peach correcting any mistakes she made. Even though we'd trained in throwing stakes, daggers, and knives, it had been a while since either of us had practiced. I went next and after a while, it seemed almost natural again.

"That's enough. Let's move on to shooting." Peach dug in her bag and handed Lyric and I both ear plugs. After pulling out some water bottles, she lined them along the saw horses. I held up the lantern I was holding to get a better view.

"You know me and Lyric only have human vision, right? We won't be able to see the targets to shoot them."

Peach ignored me, instead screwing the lid off a bottle. She dropped something into it, replaced the lid, and gave it a shake causing the bottle to light up like a glow stick.

Lyric squealed. "That's cool! I did something similar once for a science project."

"Ravage showed me how to make them. He's a genius with anything relating to science." Once Peach finished making twelve bottles glow, she dug back in her bag and handed us each a gun. "I'm assuming you both remember how to use these."

Lyric said nothing, instead turning toward the bottles and quickly shooting two before dropping the gun to her side with a smile. "I remember."

"Good job, Lyric!" Peach took the lantern from me and nodded her head toward the targets. "Your turn."

I raised the little Glock 43 and stared at it. "The last time I held a gun, I killed two people."

Peach rested her hand on my arm, soothing me. "You did what you had to do just like they were doing. Life isn't always fair and sometimes, we're dealt sucky cards. It's an evil game but someone has to be the dealer, and if you don't keep playing the game, then you'll never win a round."

I let out a hard sigh before eyeballing the targets. The bloodshed I had caused was all I could see as I stared at them, and I shook my head.

"I don't know if I'm ready for this."

"Marcus said if you don't practice, then you can't go on the mission."

My head whipped back to Peach. "Are you serious?"

"And I agree with him. Don't take this the wrong way, but you're no good to anyone if you can't protect yourself. It would cause a weakness to the group because someone would need to constantly watch your back. And what's the purpose of saving Luka and Strike if multiple people die in the process? It's not fair to value one life over another."

Peach's words settled in me, accelerating my breaths. She was one hundred percent right. If something happened to one of my friends because they helped me save the man I love and his brother, I would be in worse shape than I already was.

The fire inside of me flickered again, building higher. Without hesitation this time, I raised the gun and took aim. My instincts took over, my muscle memory doing the work for me when I quickly took out four targets.

"Wow. Great job," Peach exclaimed. "I guess you really want to go on this mission."

"No person or thing will stop me." I looked down at the small 9mm gun. "Except maybe this. It's not my normal style. Do you have anything else?"

"I like the 43. Do you want to trade for my 19?" Lyric held out her gun, and I shook my head.

"Do you prefer a 1911?" Peach asked. "I have a Kimber in the bag. Not Drag's sister." Peach grinned teasingly and Lyric giggled. I shook my head again. "I also have a Luger, another Glock, a Sig, a musket, and a Flintlock back at the cabin."

"How old are you?" Lyric asked, and I laughed.

Peach ignored her. "Oh, I also have a Beretta."

If I had been born a dog, or a wolven, my ears would have shot up. "Is it an M9? That's what I normally use."

"It is. It's custom and has sights. It's up to you if you want to use it."

Lyric took the Glock I had, and Peach stuck the other back in the bag before pulling out the Beretta and handing it to me.

It was black with gorgeous walnut pistol grips that had the Beretta insignia, a larger circle with three arrows and three small circles inside of it, engraved into them, and had a custom slide.

The weight in my hand felt familiar, easing me. I practiced for a while, and truly began to feel like my old self, but hopefully a better version.

After we exhausted our targets, we headed home.

"Do you want to head over to see Drag's niece?" Peach asked as we reentered the camp. "You haven't seen her yet."

"I'm not big into babies."

Peach's brows rose as a shocked look took over her face. "You don't like babies?"

Lyric shook her head. "Sage has never liked them."

"What do you expect? They cry and poop a lot. I'll stick to my cat." I grinned nervously at the two women who stared at me like I was a foreign object. "Umm, but I'll go with you guys."

Peach let out a small laugh. "It's four miles, so let's drive."

She led us to the side of a cabin where a brand new Jeep Wrangler awaited. It matched the color of the one I'd left at Venom the night of the attack, but this one had four doors.

My heart palpitated in excitement that I hadn't felt in a while when I ran my hand down the smooth sting-gray coat of paint. "Whose Jeep?"

"Isn't it beautiful?" Peach asked as she opened the driver's door and gestured her hand. "Check it out."

I slid into the seat, the smell of a new car filling my lungs. "This is so nice! Mine was the basic factory model, but I still miss her."

Peach held out the keys to me. "She's all yours."

My eyes bulged, my mouth falling agape. "You can't buy me a car, Peach. I can't accept it."

"I didn't. He did." She pointed toward the passenger side and when I turned to look, Marcus opened the door, grinning as he slid in.

"Do you like it?"

"Marcus, I—"

"Before you go saying I shouldn't have done it, like you have some idea on how much money I have, don't bother. I have plenty of funds. So much so, when I cleared out my bank account after the battle, I didn't know what to do with it all. I had been looking for the perfect one for a while, and I actually paid cash for it. That's how much money I have, Sagelynn. And you can drop the shocked look off your face because we aren't taking it back. Not only are you going to need it for this mission, you're the closest thing I have to a child. Plus, I do what I want."

My gaze left Marcus and went to the smooth leather steering wheel beneath my hands. "Why do I need this for the mission?"

"I've been helping Winnie map out White Sands and everything around it. Jeeps are perfect for off-roading. If something happens, you can flee in it."

I whipped my face back to Marcus. "If you think I'd leave you if something happens, you're delusional."

He laughed before his face turned serious. "If we get caught and have to flee, those vans we have might not make it far in the sand. You'll have to take as many people as you can in this thing and run. That's why we got the four-door."

My mind reeled with different scenarios as I counted out the seats versus how many people would be going. "There's only five seats. Even if we stick two in the trunk area, that's only seven. There's nine of us once we find Luka and ten if we find Strike."

"Luka and Erik will have to take the front since they're bigger. Winnie, you, Lyric, Lynx, and Strike will have to fight over the back seat or trunk."

"Wait. That's only seven. What about you, Ravage, and Zeke?"

"We're the elders. We'll figure it out."

"First thing, you're only forty-one, so you aren't *that* old. Second, we aren't leaving you, so come up with a better plan."

"I agree with Marcus," Peach said through the window.

I rolled my eyes and sighed. "Of course you do."

"This is a worst-case scenario, Sagelynn. Everyone else has hesitantly agreed to the plan."

I put my elbow on the door handle and leaned my face against my fist. "It's a stupid plan, Marcus."

"And what do I always say?"

I side eyed him while reciting his words from memory. "It's better to have a stupid plan than no plan at all."

"Exactly."

"You guys done?" Peach asked. "We need to get going before it gets too late."

Marcus looked around me, locking gazes with her. "I'll miss you, Peaches and Cream."

Peach smirked, but behind her blueish-green eyes was a glimmer of passion. "Get out of the car, Marcus."

"Yes, ma'am!"

"You can sit in the front, Peach," Lyric said, opening the rear door and sliding in.

"You ladies have fun." Marcus had pure adoration plastered on his face as he held the door for Peach, and my heart melted. His smile was wide when he shut it.

"Listen, I know it's not my business, but Marcus is a great guy."

Peach's head turned toward me. "I know. And it's literally impossible to ignore how amazing he is."

Lyric leaned in between me and Peach, her excitement contagious. "For the record, I think you guys would make a perfect couple."

Peach nodded before turning her gaze away from me, and I pulled out of the parking lot, heading toward the other campground.

CHAPTER 15
WINNIE

The alarms were still sounding as we hastily went down the hall. A few people ran past us in a panic, none of them even making eye contact. Naomi's plan worked exactly like she said it would. Now we could roam the building for a few minutes without being noticed.

After rounding a corner, we stopped at a door and Naomi placed her fingerprint on the scanner. Even though she planned everything to make sure the room was empty, she peeked her head in to check before stepping inside.

It felt like Christmas when I entered the room and fixed my eyes on the row of computer monitors lining the back wall. Each of them running programs like access control, intruder alert, and a couple I didn't recognize, but could easily figure out their function. The left wall held over a dozen screens with CCTV monitoring, which seemed to cover almost every square inch of the compound. To my right more screens displayed maps with hundreds of flickering dots, each pinpointing the whereabouts of every Venom member, some of them in residential neighborhoods. Below the screens was one of the biggest server racks I had ever seen.

Naomi tapped her tablet again and the alarm quieted before a man's voice came over her watch. "What's the status?"

She held her wrist up and clicked the button on the side. "I had the Ultra Mech Program I designed running when I wasn't here. I'm trying to work out these kinks and hit a snag. Sorry."

"That's the third time this week, Naomi. You need to get those bugs fixed asap before President Argent gets pissed."

"I will, Daniel."

"The ceremony is about to start. Hurry up and get down here."

"Copy. Over."

Naomi turned toward us with an arrogant smile on her face. "The other times were also on purpose. Just making sure my lies are solid."

"Can we talk in here?" I asked in a hushed voice.

"Yep. I activated a blocker that will scramble the audio in the building for the next fifteen minutes, so when it's played back, you'll only hear static. They'll assume it's a glitch from my fake failed program."

I narrowed my eyes on Naomi. "I don't understand how you can do all of this amazing shit, but can't get through a few security steps."

"I'm trained on this equipment. I know how it works and what messes it up. I'm not good with things I don't know. I'm a security specialist, not a hacker." She took a deep breath, a small bit of self disappointment lining her face. "We have to hurry. Follow me."

She headed to the back right of the room and went to the last computer in the row. "This is the one. I'll grab the other things while you set up."

After removing my hood and mask, I pulled out some USBs from my pocket, then took a seat.

While there is frequent discussion about addictions to drugs, alcohol, gambling, and sex, people rarely acknowledge the addictive qualities of hacking. The self-gratification of being able to break into an almost impenetrable security system was immeasurable. But the keyword was *almost.* I hadn't once found something I couldn't penetrate and hopefully today wouldn't ruin my winning streak.

After quickly finding the USB port, I slid the first one inside, my hands itching to feel the tap of the keys. I cracked my knuckles and stretched my fingers, ready to annihilate any security blocking my digital path.

The keys were cold from not being used when I laid my fingers on the keyboard. "Don't worry, girl. Daddy Winston is gonna warm you right up."

"Who the hell are you talking to?"

I glanced up at Erik who had his mask on his head, allowing me to see his confused face. "The computer. Hacking isn't about luck. You have to bond with the equipment. Let it know who's in charge. Once good and primed, you penetrate it with force and it'll open right up."

"You're such a weird nerd."

I grinned with pride. "I know."

Turning back toward the monitor, I pulled up the command-line interface and worked as fast as I could.

Ten minutes later, I had copies of some files, passwords, and any programs Venom had ever used.

"Done."

"Did you plant a virus in their system?" Erik asked.

"Hacking isn't really about planting viruses or typing out a bunch of shit like you see in the movies. It's about identifying weaknesses in the system. In this case, it was easier to get the info I needed by stealing it. It would've been a lot harder if I had attempted this from my computer."

"You're a damn genius."

I snickered at Erik's remark. "Nah, bro. I'm just highly trained."

"We gotta go." Naomi headed toward the door and stopped. "When we're done getting the info we need, can I join you guys?"

My brows rose as I nervously twisted the gauge in my right ear. I had no idea how Sage or anyone else felt about bringing on another person. Especially another Venom member who could possibly have an ulterior motive.

"Um, we'd have to discuss it with everyone at the . . . with everyone." I almost said at the camp, but I didn't want to give her any information.

I might be trusting Naomi to get me in and out of this building alive, but I wasn't sure how much I actually trusted her with the lives of others.

She nodded with a slight look of disappointment on her face. "Fair enough."

I stuck my shit back in my pocket and slid my mask back on before Naomi opened the door.

Back in the hallway again, the plan this time was to try and get through without an alarm since everyone would be down at the meeting. We were almost to the elevators when an odd smell got my attention.

The aroma that lingered in the air was an intriguing mix, not quite like any single creature, but a fusion of wolven, vampire, and witch. A paranormal trifecta. I clenched my teeth and flared my nostrils, desperately trying to locate the source of the overpowering smell.

We made up signals on the ride to the compound, so I rubbed the nose of my mask, letting Naomi know something alerted me. She pushed her hair behind her ear, a sign that she acknowledged.

Once we rounded a corner, there stood a bulky man in a dark green cloak, holding his mask in his hand. When Naomi saw him, her heart sped up, causing her to slow her steps. Erik and I took that as a sign and did the same.

The man's head seemed mechanical when it slowly turned in our direction, like he could feel our presence. For a moment, his eyes narrowed like he was figuring something out before he looked at Naomi and grinned with pure confidence. "Are you headed down to the meeting?"

"Yeah," she said with a smile as fake as his.

"Good. We can catch up. I haven't seen you in months." The man took a deep breath through his nose and his nostrils flared before he tilted his head toward me, his face deadpan. Even if I was unfamiliar with the species he was, I could tell he knew I was a vampire. "What's up, Alex?"

Not knowing what Alex's voice sounded like, I gave the dude a nod of my head.

The elevator beeped, then the doors opened, breaking the suspicious eye contact he had on me. When he stepped on and his back was to us, Naomi took the split second opportunity and hit a button on her tablet, causing the alarms to sound again.

"Damn it!" she yelled over the screeching sirens. "This stupid new program is going to get me in trouble. I have to go fix it. We'll be right down."

The guy nodded, but the look on his face said he didn't believe her. After pushing the button for his desired floor, he locked his hazel eyes on me again and they stayed there until the doors closed. The scent grew weaker, leaving no doubt it emanated from him.

Naomi turned the alarms off again, and a man's voice came over her watch.

"Damn it, Naomi!"

"I'm so sorry, Daniel. I may not make it to the meeting after all."

"Stop messing around. End that program and get down here."

"Copy. Over." Naomi pushed the button on the elevator, and we waited for it to return. After we entered, she hit the button for the parking garage, and one for the floor she was going to. "You two go ahead and grab those boxes from the van. I'll head to the hall. Meet me there when you're done."

That was our signal that she was abandoning us, and we had to get out on our own, which was going to be tricky since we couldn't take the van, but Erik assured me he had a plan.

Once off the elevator, he led me through a dark parking garage. We weaved in and out of the black vans before coming out a door in the back. The air outside was crisp but warmer than it had been this week.

We headed across the compound and the layout and spacing of the large brick buildings reminded me of a college campus. We stayed as close to them as possible, hiding in the shadows instead of walking the streets. With perfect night vision, I was able to see numerous cameras and floodlights Naomi had disabled.

When we were close to the back fence, Erik stopped next to a manhole. "Help me with this," he muttered low.

Even though I wouldn't need his strength, I assisted him in removing the cover off a sewer drain. He nodded his head toward the hole, telling me to enter. I shook my head no. He repeated his actions, and I once again shook my head.

"There could be snakes down there," I whispered.

Erik's eyes bulged under his mask before he let out an exasperated sigh, lowering himself into the hole. "Close the lid on your way down."

After a few seconds of wondering if I could jump an electrified fence with barbed wire on top—which sounded much safer than snakes in a sewer—I followed him into the hole, pulling the lid on behind me.

Once my feet landed in a half a foot of standing water, my skin crawled. "Seriously, bro. There better not be snakes."

"You're a damn vampire. How are you scared of snakes?" Erik asked as I eyed the water for creepy crawlers. "Wait, don't you have a snake tattooed on your arm?"

"I got that because it was cool. And I'm not scared, I just don't like them."

"Sure, Winnie." He trudged through the sewer, and I hoped he knew where he was going as I followed.

"Who was that dude by the elevator?" I asked, wondering why he smelled the way he did.

"That was Benjamin Argent. Sage's uncle. Why?"

"Fuck," I whispered, and Erik came to a stop, causing me to almost run into him.

"What's the problem?"

I lifted my mask to the top of my head. "There was something weird about him. He knew I was a vampire, he could smell me. And his scent was weird. Like a mix of different species or something. I don't know, dude, but something is definitely up."

"He's an asshole, but as far as I know he's human." Erik continued walking, rounding the corner to the left.

"Believe me, he wasn't."

When we finally reached the end of the drainage system, we stopped at a ladder and I went up first, pushing the cover off. Once I emerged, the entire area looked desolate. Nothing but land beneath my feet, trees, and empty spaces as far as my vampire eyes could see. I turned around to see how far we were from the Venom base and . . . it was gone.

"What the fuck," I mumbled as Erik crawled out of the hole. "Where did the headquarters go?"

"What are you talking about, Winnie?" Erik got to his feet and scanned the area. "It's too dark, so we probably can't see it."

"Bro, I can see much further than you. It's gone."

Erik removed his mask before his gaze swept the darkness once more. "That's weird. I can't even see the lights from the windows."

An odd feeling came upon me and I realized why. "Shit. Because it's cloaked." I yanked my cell from my pocket, dialed Drag's number, and put it on speaker.

"You guys okay?" he asked after only one ring.

"We need to be picked up and taken back to our van. We're sitting ducks out here. I'm sending you the location now." I shared our GPS coordinates to his phone. "We need to get as far away from this place as possible, so we'll start walking until we find a road."

"Did you get the info we needed?"

"I got more than that, Drag." I looked back toward the direction where the compound should be standing and a creepy feeling went down my spine again. "The entire Venom headquarters disappeared after we left the property without the person allowed to enter. So, you know what that means."

"Venom's base is cloaked?"

"Yep. Those fuckers are working with witches. Now we know why no one has ever found any of their locations. Which means VRC is probably cloaked too. There's more, but I wanna talk to you and some of the older vamps about it when we get back."

"Alright, I'm on my way." Drag hung up.

"I can't see anything out here, Winnie."

"It's Winston." I pocketed my phone and turned toward Erik. "Use your phone light, but keep it low to the ground. I can hear vehicles, so we need to go this way."

Erik flipped his flashlight on and we headed for the highway. "You said Venom's cloaked. Is that the same as the wards we have around the camp?"

"We have both. The cloaking spell conceals a place and keeps anyone from seeing it even exists. The wards are the invisible line surrounding it. The two different spells can be used separately or in unison." I pointed to the right of me. "Look at where the Venom base was, do you feel that creepy feeling?"

Erik turned his head toward where the base should be. "I do. Feels like the land is haunted or something."

"That's the wards. Certain warding spells can make people feel uncomfortable, so they won't go near them, and others can be used to keep supernaturals out. Since I was able to cross, I'm surprised Venom didn't use one of those."

Erik's forehead tightened. "If Venom has magical wards like the camp does, how did we get in at all?"

"When a resident permitted inside of the wards allows someone in, it appears visible to the newcomers. So, when Naomi guided us across the barrier, the wards considered us safe."

"So, anyone inside our camp could bring enemies in?"

I stopped walking, bad thoughts filling me. "Technically, yes."

"Maybe we should consider who we keep there."

We started walking again and I began to wonder about the wards. I knew neither the shifters nor vampires would do anything to harm our community. The humans were the only ones I was unsure of.

Lyric and Sage were both safe in my book. And after spending some time with them, I was sure Erik and Jimmy were trustworthy. But Nellie and Randi were frequently on my watch list. Even more now.

CHAPTER 16
Sage

After we got to the second campground and exited the vehicle, we headed onto a porch with a woman pacing back and forth, trying to soothe the baby in her arms.

"Hey, Dani."

"Hey, Lyric." The woman nodded her head toward Peach with a smile before her gaze traveled to me. "You must be, Sage. My name is Danika Montoya, but you can call me Dani. Dragos is my brother and has told me so many wonderful things about you."

I furrowed my brows, wondering who the hell Dragos was, but as my eyes drifted over her brown hair and fair skin, it finally clicked. She looked like my friend. "Do you mean Drag?"

She laughed as she swayed her hips, soothing the fussing baby. "Drag is his nickname. Do you know where he is? I'm not trying to be rude, but I'm panicking here."

"I saw him leave with a couple others right before we came here," Lyric said. "But I didn't ask where they were going."

"We have an issue I need to discuss with him." She pulled the blanket back, revealing the face of a pink infant with red hair. "This is Scarlet. She's a wolven baby and I don't know what to do with her. Her mom, Tilly, used to be a part of our pack before she left with her boyfriend James who was from Ironclad."

Living in New Mexico my whole life, I'd never heard of a city called Ironclad before, so I assumed maybe it was one of the surrounding states. "Where's that city at?"

"It's not a city. Ironclad Claws is the name of the pack. Their alpha is a dickhead, so I don't blame James for leaving."

My brows rose at the fact the packs had different names. It irritated me knowing I'd missed a lot of information during my depressive months.

"Tilly and James were on their way to check out a new apartment they were going to settle down in," Dani continued. "They were the only vehicle on the road when he lost control of his bike and wrecked. They both died."

"Oh, no." Lyric threw her hand over her mouth, her emotions engulfing her face.

A heaviness filled my chest and I laid my hand softly on it. If a supernatural creature like a shifter could die in a motorcycle wreck, then my human ass could have easily died.

"They were both so young, especially for wolven." Dani shook her head, her eyes wet with emotion. "Kaysa, one of the females in Ironclad, was the one who had my brother-in-law call me. Since the alpha of that pack doesn't have a luna to make decisions, it was up to him. Knowing Galen's a dick, I knew the answer would be no, but Kaysa asked anyway. Galen said they had enough members to feed and James shouldn't have left his pack to become a Freepelt, which is a nomad wolven."

"And a luna is a female alpha?" I asked. I had heard it said before during discussions, but I wasn't positive.

"Yes, and most of them sit on councils, contribute to food swaps, run activities, and anything else the pack needs. Everyone always talks about how strong an alpha is, but lunas are the true leaders of any pack. The alphas know this, and it's the reason most of them choose a luna at a young age. If Galen had made Kaysa a luna when he was supposed to, none of this would be a problem because the decision would've been hers."

Another baby in the distance began wailing, and I assumed it was Dani's newborn daughter. A few seconds later, a good-looking man with shoulder-length blond hair popped his head out the door. "I think she needs to eat."

"I'll be right there, Lane." Dani sighed, then turned back toward us. "That's my mate's brother. They're both from the Shadow Hounds in Arizona. By the way, he's single if any of you ladies are looking."

"Do you want me to take the baby to the other camp for a while?" Peach asked, completely avoiding her statement. "I know you have a lot on your hands."

"The unmated wolves don't mind alloparenting at our camp, but they don't like taking the kids over there."

"Well, Aunty Peach doesn't give a shit what they like. Come here, little one." Peach took the baby from Dani, admiring her beauty.

"I have plenty of breast milk right now, so I pumped extra for her. I usually donate it. I'm glad my over-productive boobs came in handy."

Lyric brushed her hand over the baby's red hair. "She's so beautiful. But isn't she cold out here?"

"Wolven babies don't get cold as quickly as humans do. She also screams when I go inside." Dani let out a long sigh, her shoulders sagging. "If I didn't already have two kids and a newborn, I would raise her in our pack, because without one, this baby will know nothing about our culture or her true potential. After I talk to Drag, maybe we can come up with a way for us moms and dads to co-parent. I don't know what else to do. Everyone here is raising young children, but she needs to be raised in a pack."

The door popped open again, and this time Lane had a look of panic on his face. "Dani, this baby is trying to feed from my chest and I don't have milk like you! Plus, I think she needs to be changed." Lane scrunched up his nose, and Lyric giggled.

"I have to go. Thanks, Peach. I'll have Lane pack you a bag with everything she'll need for now. Just bring her back when you get tired."

Dani took off into the house, and Lyric turned to Peach. "Are you wanting to keep her?"

"No. I love kids and I might adopt one someday, but I'm too busy fighting for the equality of vampires right now to raise a baby."

Lyric and Peach both took turns admiring Scarlet with happy squeals and awe sounds. I stood there with my arms crossed afraid someone was going to hand her to me. She was definitely cute, but I sure as hell didn't want to be responsible for something so tiny and fragile.

A few minutes later, Lane came out with a car seat and a diaper bag. "Do you want me to stick these in your car, Peach?"

"That'd be great. Thanks, Lane."

Peach headed toward the Jeep and we followed, Lane falling into step with me. He was very handsome and after seeing him up close, I couldn't help but realize he looked similar to the main character of a popular motorcycle club TV show.

"I haven't met you before. Name's Lane."

"Sage. Nice to meet you."

A knowing look fell upon his face. "Oh, you're Luka's woman."

Before my twenty-fifth birthday, I would've cringed at that term, but now, it only made me feel lonely. "I guess I am."

"Luka's my friend so I'll refrain from flirting with you." He gave me a gorgeous smile before opening the Jeep door.

After he installed the car seat, Peach strapped the baby in, then her and Lyric said their goodbyes to Lane and entered the Jeep.

"It was nice meeting you, Lane." I put my hand out to shake his, but he took it instead, gently kissing the back of it before letting go.

"I wish you all the luck finding the one you love."

The kind gesture made me feel like he was a genuinely nice guy. It also made me want to play matchmaker.

"There are a few girls back at the camp that may tickle your fancy, or however you say it."

Lane laughed, then shook his head. "I was kidding about flirting with you. I'm sorry if I came off as a creep. I know you've had it rough lately, so I said it to break the tension that was in your face and maybe make you feel a little better. It's weird to say aloud because only a few people know but I'm actually in love with someone else. I do appreciate the offer to help me *tickle my fancy,* though."

"Shit. I'm sorry. Dani said you were single, so I didn't know."

"She's always trying to fix me up." Lane pushed his blond hair behind his ear and nervously glanced at the cabin before turning his attention back to me. "You're pretty good at keeping secrets, I hear. Can I tell you something?"

"I mean, at this point, I feel like I know so many secrets I probably can't remember them all, so go for it."

"I'm not sure you'll even know what this means, but I actually found my fated mate."

I sucked in a hard breath.

After living at Drag's camp for months, I heard a lot about the wolven and their fated mates. Sometimes, destiny chooses the person they fall in love with. They can't run from it or control it unless they're rejected by that person. It's similar to the blood bond a vampire has with their mate. I also heard how much of an honor it was to bring your mate and present them to their pack, so the fact that his sister-in-law didn't know, confused me.

"Why haven't you told Dani?"

"That's the secret part. My fated is also a promised luna, which is a woman who's obligated to marry an alpha male due to hierarchy and family ranking. Most of the packs don't follow the old ass tradition anymore, but the one she's in still does."

"That's horrible. How does she feel about the situation?"

"She, umm . . . she doesn't know because I'm too scared to tell her."

"Wait." I shook my head and put my hands up. "Heston told the humans back at camp that both wolven know the instant a fated mate thing happens. Each person has to agree or reject the bond, or something like that."

Lane laughed. "The *fated mate thing* is called a pairing, and the bond is called a nexus. Wolven have to claim their mate to seal the nexus. But for some reason, her being promised to another wolven is blocking her from feeling our bond. I talked to some elders about it, but it's a situation no one's ever heard of happening before. And personally, I would never reject a fated mate. Which most of the wolven I know wouldn't unless they see an immediate issue. Possibly if there was a huge age gap or they're in love with someone else. Otherwise, I don't really see why anyone would reject someone. At least not after the feelings that surged through me when I met her."

Lane's pupils dilated as he stared off into the distance, his yearning expression thickening the air. "When I looked into her eyes for the first time, it was like she was the electricity that lit up my senses that were shadowed in a house I didn't even know was dark. "

I stared wide-eyed, unable to comprehend *that* feeling. "I wish I could say I understand, but I didn't have that with Luka. I never felt any kind of electricity or connection click into place. Not like the ones I've heard the wolven talk about."

Lane put his hand on my shoulder and gently rubbed his finger back and forth. "It's because humans can't feel a lenxus bond. If you had paired with a wolven, you would've sensed the nexus, but since you bonded to a vampire, you won't experience it the same way he does because you're still human. He won't even feel the full strength of the lenxus until you're turned into a vampire."

I pulled my shoulder away from him in confusion . . . or possibly irritation. "Who said I would turn?"

"If you don't turn, then you *are* the person who rejects their mate. It's sad, but I'm just being honest."

"I . . . umm." My breaths became fast as I swallowed down the words at the tip of my tongue, unable to process the twenty different thoughts running through my head.

Will Luka feel rejected if I stay human? Will he stay with me when I get old? Do I want to be a vampire? Do vampires still have periods?

Because if not, I may quickly decide to change because the cramps I had were killing me.

"You'll make the right choice when the time comes, Sage."

The baby in the car let out a wail and Lyric tapped on the window, rushing me.

"You better go. It was really nice meeting you. I hope you save your mate from the eternal hell he's in."

"And I hope you save yours," I whispered, my heart hurting from the sadness glistening in his eyes. I couldn't help but put my hands out for a hug that he gracelessly accepted.

He released me and opened the car door. "Take care, Sage. Hopefully next time I see you, we'll both have our mates with us."

Lane waved to my friends before he shut the door.

We headed back to the other camp, and I drove incredibly slow because having a tiny baby in the car made me nervous on top of the overwhelming thoughts of me rejecting Luka.

In the past, I had passing thoughts about being turned into a vampire, but I'd never really considered the possibility of it happening or the issues that came with it.

As we were getting out of the vehicle, one of the ex-Venom members came strolling up to me. I hadn't said more than two words to her since she came to live here, so I wondered what she wanted.

"In case you're wondering, the guys aren't back yet, but Drag and a few others went to go get them, so they got out of there without being injured."

"What are you talking about, Nellie?" I asked, confused by the random topic.

"Oh, I thought you knew about the mission. Winnie and Erik are safe, so it's all good."

"What mission? What's she talking about?" My attention went to Peach, and her face confirmed that someone had deceived me.

"Winnie and Erik went to get some much needed information."

"And where did they go?" Lyric asked. Her face showed a torn expression, alternating between anger and worry. "Because if my brother and my boyfriend both lied to me, someone is getting their ass kicked tonight."

"To the Venom compound," Nellie blurted, and panic soared through me.

"What the fuck? Why?"

"If they aren't dead already, I'm going to kill them." Lyric pulled out her phone and started hitting buttons. Whoever she called didn't answer. After the second time of trying to call someone, her gaze shot to me. "Neither of them is answering."

Nellie placed her hand on Lyric's arm, comforting her. "They're fine. Jimmy told me Winnie's plan and apparently it worked because they're headed back now."

"Jimmy knew about a new plan and we didn't?"

Nellie shrugged at Lyric's question. "Probably because he's in your cabin hacking. Winnie had him setup in case he needed him to get them out of a sticky situation. I seriously thought you both knew."

Lyric got quiet, her lips tightening into a thin line. Knowing her for as long as I had, I immediately recognized her angry face. Without saying a thing, she turned on a dime and headed toward her cabin.

"Sorry." Nellie frowned, then walked away.

I looked at Peach. "Are you going to fill me in on everything?"

"Yeah. Let's go inside." She pulled the car seat from the Jeep, and I grabbed the bags, then followed her into her cabin.

Marcus sat on the brown couch with a laptop on his lap, his face popping up with a smile. "Hey, ladies. How was your . . ." His wide eyes locked on the car seat Peach held. "Whose baby is that?"

Peach nodded her head toward me. "She knows about the mission, Marcus."

"You knew too and didn't tell me?" I asked in a tone harsher than I had ever used with Marcus.

He gave me a look of sympathy. "It was for your own protection, sweetie. I knew you would want to go and we couldn't risk that."

"Why not? I could have helped them, but instead of giving me the option, two of my friends entered a heavily guarded compound alone!" I took a deep breath, attempting to control my anger. "Did everyone betray me or just you two?"

"You aren't ready to go on any missions."

A fire coursed through my veins as I stared into Marcus's brown eyes. "I am ready!"

His empathetic expression changed to one of a commander. "You're out of practice and malnourished. You would've been a liability."

Pain settled in my chest from his words.

A liability. That's all I am right now.

"Whatever." I stomped toward the door and flung it open. Despite being highly pissed, I chose not to slam it because I didn't want to startle the baby.

Once outside, I angrily paced the parking lot, waiting for Winnie and Erik to return. The longer I waited, the more I realized Marcus was right. I wasn't ready to go on a mission. My body had become weak because of my own actions and I was now dealing with the consequences from it.

Disappointment in myself had to be one of the worst feelings.

The night air had gotten chilly, so I went inside my cabin and waited for them to return. When a car door slammed, then another, I knew they were finally back.

I headed outside and ran straight for the black van Heston, Drag, and Demi stood next to.

"Where are they?" I asked Drag, but before he answered, another van pulled into the gravel lot.

"We're going to do a perimeter check," Drag said before he and the other wolven began to shed their clothes.

I had seen enough of their naked bodies, so I turned and glared at the other van as Winnie parked it.

Drag and his pack darted past me, heading toward the woods and my focus went to Erik getting out of the van first.

"You could have been killed. What's wrong with you?" I asked, and he shook his head, saying nothing.

Winnie killed the engine and stepped out with an apologetic expression. "I asked him to go, Sage Stick. Don't be mad at him."

"You be quiet, Asshole. I'm mad at you too. You could have gotten—" He held up a USB drive so close to my face my eyes practically crossed as I focused on it. "What is that?"

"I may be able to find the location of VRC now. Are you still mad?"

Disbelief or shock, I wasn't sure which, hit me, and my heart skipped a beat. I took the tiny drive from his hand and stared at it like it was some magical key to another world. If the location to VRC was really on this USB, the chances of us saving Luka doubled . . . tripled in size.

"How mad is Lyric?" Winnie asked, bringing me back to reality.

"I don't know if you know what she does when she's highly pissed off, but she's quiet."

"Fuck." He yanked the USB from my fingers and headed toward their cabin.

I immediately turned toward Erik. "Is it true? Can he find VRC now?"

He shrugged, leaning onto the side of the van. "Winnie said it's a huge possibility."

"I'm glad you're alive. Even if you are an idiot." I pulled him in for a hug and when I let go, his face seemed confused. "What?"

"I know you, Sage. And I know how you really are when you're mad and this ain't it. Why aren't you yelling at me?"

"I was pissed at you both for a hot minute, then Marcus called me a liability."

Erik made a hissing sound through his teeth. "Ouch."

"Even though it hurt to hear him say I wasn't ready for missions, I knew he was right. I'm going to have to bust my ass to get my strength back."

Erik gave me a smile containing the pity he felt for me. "You're still fast and you have great instincts, so you'll get there pretty quickly."

I took in a cleansing breath, letting it out on an unconfident huff.

Will I?

CHAPTER 17
WINNIE

Drag and his crew had picked me and Erik up on the side of the highway and drove us to the van we'd left when we met Naomi. We stashed our masks and cloaks in the tote like she'd requested, and after filling Drag in on some of the things we'd found, we followed them home.

On our way back, Jimmy called and alerted me that Lyric and Sage knew where we'd gone, and Lyric had very politely kicked him out of our cabin. He explained he didn't snitch directly to them, but since he and Nellie were now a couple, he'd figured it would be okay to tell her about the mission, and she was the one who told them.

Seriously, I didn't even tell my girlfriend, so I had no idea why he'd thought it would be okay to tell his.

Despite my frustration with Jimmy, my primary concern was Nellie and I questioned *why* she'd shared information with Sage and Lyric.

Is she a teenage girl stuck in a woman's body? Or she is purposely starting shit?

Either answer to my thoughts pissed me off, but I had no room for my anger when I needed to be focused on my groveling.

When I stepped through our cabin door, Lyric sat on the edge of the couch and said nothing as she glanced up at me, her face unreadable.

I did notice her constant joyful smile had disappeared because of my foolishness. I had murdered her happiness, smothering it with lies and severe commitment issues.

Fuck.

"I'm sorry, mama. I didn't have a choice. We needed info and I was the only one able to get it."

She dropped her head down, looking at her hands that were nestled between her thighs. "Winston, I . . ."

"It's okay. You can yell at me. Tell me I'm an asshole and I messed up."

Tears had welled in her eyes when they met mine again. "Actually, I was going to say that maybe you're right. I'm not sure that us being together is what's best for me, either." She stood, grabbed a duffle bag off the floor, and slung it over her shoulder. "I'm staying with Stephanie for a while."

She walked past, and I placed my hand on her shoulder trying to halt her so we could talk. "Hold up."

Her sudden wrenching away shocked me, as it was something she had never done before. "Don't."

"What happened to *happy for now*, Lyric? That doesn't exist anymore?"

Her heart raced as she looked over her shoulder at me. "You damaged our happiness when you lied to me."

And without another word, she left the cabin. I stared at the door, wondering if I should go after her and maybe show her some kind of grand gesture.

Could I be a gallant knight with a sword, riding in on a white horse when I feel more like an antihero?

Should I pour my heart out to a woman I haven't fallen in love with yet?

My feet wouldn't move, locked onto the wood planks of the floor, and maybe, just maybe, this was for the best.

The last time a girl broke my heart I was still human. I hadn't really let anyone else get close since then, and for good reasons. Between my heartbreak, Peach's, Vivi's, and Sage's, I had seen too much—felt too much.

Obviously, it always ended in disappointment.

The woman that broke my heart had cheated and repeatedly lied to me.

I despised liars.

Had I done the same to Lyric? I would never cheat, but had I accidentally broken her heart by lying?

I suppose I did.

But my intentions were to protect her. I didn't want her worrying about us for hours, or worse, trying to stop us from completing the mission because that wouldn't have happened.

Am I laying down a double standard?

I plopped down at the computer desk and propped my feet up on it.

Even though I felt like Lyric should have been my top priority, saving my best friend from rotting away in a research lab had always stayed at the top of my list. Maybe that made me an asshole, but it felt nearly impossible to make everyone happy at the same damn time.

Sometimes, I believed things happened the way they're supposed to. This was a sign I needed to let her go so she'd have a normal life with a man that could give her love and a family—give her the entire world.

Because in my mind, she deserved someone better than me.

Not long after Lyric left, Sage showed up, wanting to know what I found. I told her it would take me a while to go through the files and to check back when she awoke. Even though I should have said something about her uncle, I didn't have enough mental energy to tell her.

After Sage left, I uploaded the files from the USB and hit the digital jackpot with the information I found. Not only did I have the coordinates for the closest VRC location, I also found six more facilities.

Venom attached Luka's name and an identification number to a location only three hundred miles from here.

Unfortunately, I couldn't find Strike on any of the lists. But I wouldn't reveal that information to my sister or anyone but Ravage for now.

I awoke with the sunset, and before I even had time to take a piss, Sage came knocking on my door, wondering if I found any info yet. I quickly filled her in on everything, and before we even talked to Drag or the others, she had me making hotel reservations—the first step in our new plan.

"There are only two bedrooms available, but there's two beds per room. If we want more, we'll have to wait three weeks."

Sage's head popped up from her phone. She had been staring at the map of the area by VRC for twenty minutes. "No more waiting. Luka's been in there long enough, thanks to me. We have to go now. I'm not making him wait any longer."

"Alright. We'll have to bunk up." I clicked confirm on the screen, reserving our rooms before a hard sigh left me.

Four days. We only had four days to get our shit together before we left on a mission that could cost some of us our lives. Sage hadn't been training long enough and Lyric wasn't speaking to me. These were only small weaknesses in our system, but weaknesses nonetheless.

Leaning back in the chair, I clasped my hands behind my head, my stare going to the ceiling. I yawned, exhaustion from last night hitting me. After sleeping next to Lyric for months, it felt weird being in bed alone this morning. It took me over an hour of laying there thinking about her before I finally dozed off.

"Did you have trouble sleeping alone after Luka was taken?" I asked, without looking at Sage.

"Um, that's a random question."

"Lyric is so pissed at me for going on the mission she slept at Steph's, and I had trouble sleeping without her in bed."

"I didn't really have that issue because Luka and I never got the chance to be in a real relationship. But I have had trouble sleeping every night since he's been gone. I have a lot of nightmares now. Some of them are about me killing people, but most of them are about Luka being tortured."

Sage got quiet and besides the hum of my PC, her racing heart was the only sound filling the room. I knew she was in deep thought about what kind of torture Luka had been getting for months. Worse torture than my girlfriend being mad because I lied.

"Only a few more days," I mumbled, breaking the silence. She didn't respond, making my stare drift to her. "You hear me, Sage Stick?"

"What if he hates me, Winnie?" She bit her lip before dropping her head down, picking at her nails.

"That's literally impossible."

Her hazel eyes met mine, glazed with emotions. "I couldn't save him and he probably hates me for it."

The last thing I wanted was for Sage to go back to hiding from the world. I dropped my hands from my head and sat up. "Luka decided to sacrifice himself for you and he couldn't possibly be mad at you for it. You need to let that shit go."

Sage snickered, a playful expression on her face. "Or what, Pooh Bear? Are you going to yell at me?"

"No, but I might throw your ass in the lake again."

"I would like to see you try, Asshole."

We both laughed as I hopped up from my chair. "I gotta freshen up so we can fill everyone in on what I found. I have some other info you're not gonna like."

"Of course you do." Sage stood from my recliner and headed for the door. "I'll see you out there."

Since I didn't have time to shower, I quickly brushed my teeth because I had morning breath, but primarily in case Lyric decided she wanted to talk to me. If we made up, I wanted my breath to be fresh when I devoured her mouth.

Once outside, I went straight for the circle of people gathered around the bonfire. Lyric had taken a seat next to Erik, and she glanced at me before quickly averting her eyes. I snickered and surveyed the surroundings, pondering where to find a seat, as it definitely wouldn't be next to her.

As I took in the many faces, I noticed some people were still missing. I also realized this seemed to be our group's thing . . . like a supernatural council that allowed humans in.

"We should make our own organization," I blurted. "Like Save, but with humans."

"Would you like to fill us in on the conversation you were having with yourself, son?" Ravage asked.

"I mean, Save kind of fucked us over, but we have enough people to start our own group. Plus, some of the older members, like you or Peach could lead the council for the vamps, Drag for the wolven, and Marcus for the humans."

Ravage barked out a belly laugh. "You better watch your mouth, boy. Peach will rip your balls off for calling her old."

"I'm being serious, dude. It's kinda like we already started one. We just haven't appointed positions like we had in Save."

"What does Save mean again?" April asked with a curious look. "Zeke always kept me out of Venom and vampire politics, so I knew very little until I came here."

"Save stands for Supernaturals Against Venom Elitists. It's an organization that actively protects vampires and wolven from being used for research. Or that's what they used to do before we found out some of them were traitors."

We hadn't completely cut ties with Save. We currently had Lane and Laren attending meetings and monitoring things, but it was a need-to-know basis. For now, none of the ex-Venom members, other than Lyric, Sage, and Erik, needed to know because we had to do what was best to protect our spies.

"Why do you guys call Venom members elitists?" Nellie asked, causing my attention to drift to her.

"Because Supernaturals Against Venom Cultists doesn't quite roll off the tongue as easily."

Her brows clenched at my sarcasm before her eyes narrowed on me. "And why do you call it a cult? Just because we're inducted into the society by giving blood doesn't make us a cult."

Us?

Since being here, the ex-Venom members had referred to the society in the third person, as if they left it behind. But this bitch looked me right in the face and said, "us."

Even though the hairs on the back of my neck were standing up, alerting me of a possible intruder, I refrained from breaking her neck in front of everyone. Peach would yell at me for not getting more info first, April would probably cry out of shock, plus I might actually feel bad if I was wrong.

Probably not.

My back stiffened and I glanced down at Ravage. His expression told me he had the same feelings I did.

Not wanting to be suspicious, I lowered my ass onto the log next to him and leisurely leaned my elbows onto my knees. "Because that's exactly what they are, or at least that's what they portray. Cultic behavior causes vulnerability in its members, or so I've read. Once individuals participate in it, it can impact their critical thinking and emotional processing. That shit allows cult leaders to have complete control over their members. Consider this, would Venom be able to function without the masks and cloaks?"

"Absolutely, it could," Erik answered, before looking toward Nellie. "The cult shit seemed normal until Winnie and I had this same conversation right after we came here. It's easy to get caught up in the society when you're raised to believe you're doing the right thing. Now it all makes total sense. We were brainwashed to follow the leader."

My gaze went to Sage since her father was the *actual leader* of the Venom society. She stared at me, then quickly glanced at Nellie, and when her eyes met mine again, I somehow knew she had caught on.

"Not to mention they pay for housing, cars, and still gave us a paycheck," Steph added. "Which sounds nice, but it's another way to make the members dependent on them. They would give us the world as long as we obeyed."

"Is that what this meeting was about?" Nellie interrupted. "Us starting our own society? I thought you found VRC information or something."

Ravage stood rather quickly, and I did my best to keep my cool. "That's what we were going to discuss, but there's a storm on the way, and there's too many of us to fit in one cabin. We can discuss it later. Everyone better head inside soon." Without another word, he strolled off into the darkness, and I knew our meeting was being relocated.

Peach turned toward Marcus, laying her hand on his knee. "I need to get the baby from Kimber and Vivi. I told them we wouldn't be long. Not that they wanted to give her back, anyway."

"Baby?" April's eyes sparkled as she scooted to the edge of her seat. "Whose baby do you have, Peach?"

"Oh, she's a sweet little thing. Do you want to come meet her and I'll fill you in on how I got her?"

"I would love that."

Peach peered over at Sage. "I think I left one of the baby's bags in your Jeep. Can you bring it to me when you're done here?"

"Sure. I gotta pee first, then I'll bring it over." Sage rose from her seat and gave Lyric one look.

"I want to see the baby again," Lyric said as she stood.

I didn't know how they always knew what the other thought or wanted, but it fascinated me.

Peach, Marcus, April, and Zeke took off, and I turned my attention to Drag, hoping he understood the lie I was about to tell. "Do you still want me and Erik to help you at your sister's place?"

Drag hopped up without hesitation. "Yeah, and we better get there before it gets too late. She'll kill us if we wake their baby."

I glared at Erik, and it took him a few extra seconds to catch on and stand. "I'm ready when you guys are."

We followed Drag to his truck and when I went to get into the passenger seat, Ravage appeared next to the door like a magician.

"I don't think so." He opened the door and slid into the front seat.

With a sigh, I hopped in the back. "Where's Lynx?"

"She's back at the tattoo shop, keeping things running for me. She'll be back in a few days."

Ravage hadn't tattooed me in months and I really needed some ink therapy, but we had too much going on for me to worry about myself.

Pulling my phone out, I sent Peach a text letting her know what we were doing.

Winnie: *Going to Dani's. Bring Sage and Marcus.*

I hesitated a second before adding another name

Winnie: *And Lyric.*

Peach: *Be there after we pack up the baby.*

"What's going on?" Erik finally asked when Drag pulled out of the lot. "Why didn't we have the meeting about what we found last night?"

Ravage turned his head toward us. "Because we're pretty sure we have a rat living here."

Once at Dani's cabin, I stood in the middle of the room and quickly filled everyone in on the VRC locations and about Sage's uncle smelling weird so I could get some honest feedback before Sage got here.

"Do you think he's some kind of hybrid?" Lane asked, sitting on the brown leather couch. Since he'd been working with us, and Dani knew about it, they had both listened in on our conversation.

Drag let out a hard breath from the matching recliner across from Lane. "I've never heard of a hybrid of all three species before. It seems unnatural."

Erik was leaning against the wall with his arms crossed when he snickered. "And you guys are all natural?"

Dani cackled. "I like you. From what Kimber tells me, you seem like a good guy. You're Lyric's brother?"

Erik nodded. "Yes, ma'am."

"She's sweet as pie. I like her a lot." Dani's gaze wandered to me, and the way they narrowed, made my skin crawl. "Don't fuck that up, Winnie."

Little did she know, I already had, so I completely avoided her statement. "All I'm saying is at first I could smell each species individually, but then they blended together somehow, which made my nose confused as shit."

"And if that's true," Dani said, her eyes wide, "then Sage is a witch and doesn't know it."

"I've known Sage and Ben my entire life and I've only known them as human. But I did notice how weird Ben acted last night. His actions were mechanical. Almost like he was purposely slowing them down."

"I noticed that too, but it made sense to me because that's what we're trained to do in the beginning."

Erik stared at me with a look of confusion. "What do you mean?"

"When you become a vampire, you're filled with overwhelming energy that you aren't used to, so our origins teach us to slow our movements. Mainly because it consumes too much energy and that would require us to feed more often. And feeding isn't as easy as it seems without a mate, so we have to conserve. Most of us usually only move super fast if we have to, or in my case, if I'm pissed off. Ben looked like someone that was new to it. Like someone who recently became a vamp and that's why he seemed mechanical. Or at least, that's my theory."

"It's a good theory, son," Ravage said from the kitchen adjacent to the living room. After taking a big swig of his beer, he set it on the counter. "Maybe we can visit Shayla tomorrow evening and see what she has to say about it."

I scrunched up my nose, not wanting any part of visiting the witches.

The baby began fussing and Dani picked her up from a bassinet, then retook a seat in the recliner next to her brother. "I don't like this, Drag. It's giving me a bad feeling. Are the spells strong?"

"They aren't due to be re-cloaked until mid-summer. But if we go to Shayla's, I'll ask if there's a way they can add an extra layer of protection." Drag's attention went to Lane. "Did you and Laren find anything at Save tonight?"

"Not much going on. Viktor is still letting Finneas lead every meeting."

Every one of us believed that Finneas was the one working with Venom so they knew where vampires were, making it easier for them to capture or kill them. But considering Viktor had all but fallen off the face of the earth, I was unsure if maybe we'd accused the wrong brother.

"When is that shit going to be done?" Dani asked, rocking the baby. "I don't trust those people enough for my brother-in-law to be hanging out with them."

The crunch of tires filled my ears as a car pulled into the driveway. "Shit, they're here," I said before heading toward the door. "Don't anyone mention anything about Save yet."

Once everyone exited the Jeep, Peach was the first through the door as I held it open, with Marcus right behind her.

I rolled my eyes when Vivi came in, her expression telling me she knew about me fighting with Lyric.

"You're a punk." She punched me in the arm when she went past, then went over to stand by Dani and the baby.

Sage strolled in next, her eyes going wide at the room filled with people before she seated herself on the floor.

Last was Lyric who nervously looked at me before saying, "Thank you."

I shut the door. "No problem, mama."

We locked eyes and for a split second, I wanted to grab her and smash my lips against hers.

"What's up, Marcus?" Lane shouted, breaking the intense gaze I had on Lyric. "How've you been?"

"Much better since I get to see your sexy ass." Marcus laughed, taking a seat by Lane before pulling Peach down next to him. You couldn't take Marcus anywhere without him making best friends.

Since the cabins weren't very big, Lyric squatted onto the floor with Sage and I remained standing.

My hands were jittery, which surprised me since nervousness had never really been an issue for me. But as I looked around the room full of people I loved and admired, I had a feeling that some of us weren't going to make it to the end of this war. Especially after knowing there was some kind of triple hybrid species.

Tribrid? Trispecies? Evil trinity of hell?

I took a deep breath, attempting to keep a calm demeanor before locking eyes with Sage and blurting, "Your uncle's a freak."

CHAPTER 18

SAGE

'**W**hen words can't be spoken, one must rely on the body.'

That was the first thing my professor in my Nonverbal Communication lesson told us students, and I was grateful Venom required us to take the class. Not only had I been taught how to use tactical hand signals and eye contact as a way of communication, but also how to understand a person's body language.

In most social situations, I'd never really used the skill, but as we sat around the fire waiting for Winnie to relay information, I noticed the shift in his demeanor and his back stiffening. I immediately focused on his body, wondering what threat he had observed.

Over the years, Lyric and I had mastered our own version of nonverbal communication. It was easy since we were trained, but even easier because we knew each other very well.

When Ravage's mannerisms also changed, I gave Lyric the "look" to let her know something was happening. Though I was unsure of what alerted them, I didn't care. I trusted Winnie with my life. And when I finally realized it was Nellie, I was furious—and secretly hoped I was the one that got to kill her.

Once Ravage confirmed the meeting was over, everyone started dispersing in different directions. Lyric followed me toward my cabin, but instead of going in, we snuck around the side of it and rounded the back, heading into the darkness.

Peach lived only two cabins down, so we arrived at her place pretty quickly. The outside light was off when we stepped onto the porch. I slowly cracked the door open and we slid in.

"What are you doing here?" Vivi asked before I even shut it.

She was sitting in a large green upholstered recliner, holding baby Scarlet. Standing on one side of the chair was Kimber who wore a confused expression, and on the other side was someone I wasn't expecting to see.

Laren locked her heated gaze on me, not even attempting to hide her hatred. She had been the wife of Luka's brother, Andrei, before I staked him in an alley on my induction night.

The first time she'd met me at the Save church, I had slightly feared for my life. Ultimately, Laren had told me the only reason she wouldn't kill me was because she wouldn't do to Luka what I did to her. At the time, I was unsure what she meant, but I'd eventually figured it out.

When I had killed Andrei, I had unknowingly also killed their bond. After seeing the pain both Vivi and

Peach carried, and learning more about the feelings that came with a bond, I felt even worse about my heinous act.

Even though she'd visited the camp every few weeks since I'd been here—why, I didn't know—she never came within twenty feet of me. I wasn't sure if it was because she struggled to keep the promise of not killing me and didn't want to tempt herself, or if it was the mere fact that she couldn't look at the person who ruined her entire life.

Either way, I didn't blame her.

Laren drew her glaring away from me and tramped into the kitchen.

"The meeting was stopped," I mumbled. "I don't know what—"

The door opened, hitting me in the ass, and I quickly moved aside so the others could enter. Peach and Marcus came in first with April and Zeke right behind them.

April sucked in a slow gasp when she saw the baby. "Is that her? She's so little."

"Would you like to hold her?" Vivi asked.

April approached slowly, her eyes wide and curious. She reached her hands out and one set of loving hands gently passed Scarlet to another.

Pure joy took over April's expression as she instantly became nurturing, slowly swaying her hips. "She's the most gorgeous baby I've ever seen." Her hands were slow to move, gently pulling the baby's pink cap back before cautiously running her hand across her red hair. "Does she have a name?"

"Scarlet," Peach answered. "I'm tending to her for a bit until we figure out what to do with her."

April looked up, her brows pinched. "What do you mean?"

"Her parents are . . ." Peach shook her head, unable to relay the sad story.

Sadness filled April's eyes before they went back to Scarlet. "I'll happily help with anything this precious baby needs."

"Vivi, can you grab the car seat?" Peach asked. "We have a private meeting at Dani's."

"But I just got her to sleep."

"I can watch her," April interjected, her eyes filling with a fierceness I'd never seen from her before. "I'll protect her. I promise."

Peach and Vivi locked eyes, and after a few seconds, Peach nodded and Vivi got up from the recliner. "You can sit here. She just ate, so you should be good until we get back."

April slowly lowered herself into the chair before waving her husband over. "Come look at how beautiful she is."

Zeke was tall, so it only took him a few strides to get to them. "Hello, little one."

It was an amazing sight, him towering over April and the baby with more admiration in his eyes than the world could possibly hold.

And . . . at that moment, even if Scarlet wasn't theirs, April and Zeke became the parents they'd always hoped to be.

Emotions swirled in my chest and I drew my gaze toward Lyric to keep from feeling them, but it didn't help. She happily wore her emotions, wiping a tear from her eye.

"Are we ready, Peach?" I asked, needing to leave a room filled with too much parental love when I missed my mom . . . and even my dad.

"Yeah. Laren, are you coming?"

I held my breath as I awaited the answer, hoping to not have to ride with a vampire who hated me.

"I'll stay here with April, in case she needs anything."

"Me too," Kimber added. "You can fill us in when you get back."

Knowing that April had her very large husband, a vampire, and a wolven staying with her made me feel confident leaving her and the baby here with a possible traitor lurking in our camp.

Peach checked outside and no one was around, so we piled in my Jeep and headed to Dani's place at the second camp.

Winnie held the door open as we entered, and my eyes went wide with the amount of people in the room.

To my right, Erik leaned against the beige wall by the hallway, his arms crossed snugly against his body, and Ravage was in the kitchen drinking a beer, his normal radiant smile absent.

To the left, Drag and Dani were sitting in matching recliners. Her expression worried as she rocked the baby. Lane was on the brown leather couch across from them and gave me a nervous smile before turning his attention elsewhere.

"What's up, Marcus?" he shouted. "How've you been?"

"Much better since I get to see your sexy ass."

I ignored the men being men and took a seat on the floor, leaving a space on the couch for Peach and Marcus. A few seconds later, Lyric sat next to me, and playfully nudged her shoulder into mine. When my gaze met hers, I could see the yearning she carried for Winnie. I nudged her back, bringing a small smile to her face.

The room quieted and the air surrounding us seemed to thicken, becoming stale. Not in an unclean sense, more like there were lots of secrets and worries about to be thrown around like confetti, but in a wearisome kind of way.

Attempting to stay calm, I focused my attention on Winnie since he was always chill, but that was a horrible plan. His hands were shaking as his eyes darted around the room, bouncing across each person before they landed on me.

"Your uncle's a freak."

My anxiousness got pushed aside by confusion. "What are you talking about?"

"We saw Ben at the Venom compound," Erik said, uncrossing his arms, his posture stiffening. "Winnie thinks he's not human anymore."

I opened my mouth but memories of feeling inadequate had stolen my words.

Despite him being my uncle, Ben and I had never developed any true familial connection. Being the younger of the two brothers, he was second in command in the Venom society, below my dad in rank. Like some leaders, Ben issued orders with no respect for us, yet demanded our obedience, especially from me, as if he were royalty.

During my childhood, he'd say my father failed their bloodline since he'd never had a son, and other hurtful things within earshot. He'd also say that he should be the one running Venom in the future, not me. Whenever it happened, my dad would casually brush it off and switch to a different topic.

The moment I turned sixteen, I was determined to win my uncle's approval. I trained harder than anyone else and even attempted to shrink my personality to fit into a tiny box just to make him happy. My hard work was in vain since Ben continued to hate me.

By the time I'd reached eighteen, I stopped caring what he thought of me and began to stick up for myself. Obviously, my tendency to speak my mind along with what he called "disobedience" led to frequent arguments and created tension during family events.

About two years ago, my uncle decided to step down, pushing Marcus into second in command, and Sorin into third rank. According to my mom, Ben had left because he moved to a Venom location in another state, stepping down to a fourth rank commanding officer position, which never made sense.

Why would someone so power hungry want to be lower ranking?

I'd never fully understood why he made that decision or why he hated me. I was just grateful that he was gone . . .

Until now.

Lyric nudged me, reminding me to answer Erik, but fear had halted my words, and I slowly shook my head. "What?"

"When we snuck into Venom—"

"I heard what you said, Erik, but what the hell is my uncle doing here?"

Winnie dropped one knee to the floor, making eye contact with me. "Listen, I can't answer that question, but I can tell you something bigger is going on. VRC is making some kind of super hybrid or something. Your uncle smelled like a vampire and a wolven blended into one, which is something Ravage said he'd never heard of before."

"Me neither," Peach added. "And I've been around the longest."

"And I might as well rip off the bandaid, Sage Stick. He also—"

"What?" I asked again, since apparently my brain took a leave of absence.

My uncle was back and possibly some kind of supernatural creature? Anything Winnie had to say after that, was completely irrelevant.

Winnie's forehead pinched. "Are you okay?"

I turned my head toward Drag. "Can someone make a wolven or are they only born?"

"Born. But it appears that VRC has possibly figured out how to convert a human into a wolven. I can't help but wonder if he can shift."

"I . . ." I shook my head again, attempting to remove the fear eating at me. If my uncle hated me when we were both human, I couldn't imagine what he'd do if he was a supernatural.

Lyric rubbed her hand down my arm and whispered, "Slow your breaths."

I needed time to process everything I'd learned, so I gave Lyric one of our looks, letting her know I was in no condition to continue this conversation at the moment.

"Can we talk about the possible rat for now?" Lyric asked, and Winnie nodded.

"I don't know if anyone else has noticed some odd things about Nellie, but I sure have."

Winnie pulled on his gauged earlobes as he explained his concerns with Nellie. As everyone weighed in their opinions, I tuned out their words as thoughts clouded my head.

Do hybrids exist? And if so, are they stronger than normal vampires or wolven? Did Venom make them? Is my dad one? Did Ben turn so he could kill me? Does he want to kill me?

The internal questions were rapid, each one adding to our already extensive list of potential dangers, keeping me from staying calm.

Once I'd found out Luka was alive, my only goal had been to save him, and all would be right in the world, but with hybrids mixed into the equation, that looked more and more impossible.

The world will never be safe, I realized. *I need to broaden my goals beyond just my happiness.*

Our mission to infiltrate VRC and rescue Luka wouldn't be enough. We needed to retrieve classified files to uncover the truth about Venom and the VRC's secret activities.

CHAPTER 19

LUKA

Dreams can be an escape from reality. A happy place where love and romance dance beneath the trees, and anything you've ever wanted shows up to fill your brain with misleading pleasure.

It can also be a place where fire and pain hold hands, infiltrating your body while darkness takes over, turning your beautiful dreams into nightmares . . .

"Stay with me, Luka. It's almost over."

Fighting.

Screaming.

Pain.

"We should pull back on the experiments and give him more blood, Doctor Ishman."

Am I dreaming? Delirious? Dead?

"I've been doing this research for fifteen years, Bill. I know what I'm doing."

Hunger. So much hunger.

"His heart rate has accelerated tremendously. He can't take much more of this!" The man's voice sounded panicked . . . scared. "What's the point of this if he dies like the rest of them?"

"Fine!" the woman screamed, her tone angry. "Give him one more teaspoon of blood."

Something cold and metallic slid into my mouth, prying my jaws apart. A splash of blood hit my tongue and I gagged at the rotten egg flavor. The metal was removed and I pursed my lips, spitting it out, and wet droplets fell onto my chin.

"He refuses to eat, Doctor Ishman. What do we do?"

"We're going to have to sedate him, Bill."

Dreams. So many dreams.

CHAPTER 20

SAGE

A couple of days have passed since we discussed Nellie potentially being a spy for Venom. Since then, we held meetings in private, excluding her, her boyfriend Jimmy, and the quiet Randi from the discussions.

It hurt leaving Jimmy out, but everyone was concerned he would tell Nellie things, and that's the price you pay for dating a blabber mouth, I guess. As far as Randi goes, I didn't know her as well as Jimmy, and after the suspicions with Nellie, I was keeping my eye on her too.

Since we only had two days before we infiltrated one of the VRC locations, I'd woken before the sun set so I could practice.

Currently, all three of the ex-Venom members along with a few other humans and wolven were standing on the sidelines watching Marcus whip my ass.

"Come on, Marcus," Nellie cheered, and fiery anger flooded me.

I whipped my head toward her, taking my attention off Marcus for a mere second and a fist landed on my face.

Pain radiated through my teeth as blood filled my mouth, forcing a vexed scream from me. "Fuck!"

"You shouldn't have looked away," Marcus teased.

"I would have never been off my game like this." I spit out the metallic wetness, then looked back at Nellie. "Don't you have some place else to fucking be?"

"Sage!" Marcus reprimanded, dropping his defensive stance.

I ignored him, locking my heated gaze on Nellie until Jimmy stepped in front of her, blocking my view.

"Let's go eat breakfast. I'll make those pancakes you loved so much."

He took Nellie's hand, pulling her toward his cabin.

"Are you okay?" Randi asked in a sweet voice. "Do you need a bottle of water or something?"

I shook my head because all I wanted was for her to stop staring at me like I was about to spontaneously combust.

"She actually does need some water." Marcus's tone was calm and collected, but I had a feeling once we were alone, it wasn't going to be. "Could you grab a couple room temperature ones from my cabin, please?"

"Sure. I'll be right back."

Randi walked away and Marcus's gaze went to everyone else. "Could you guys give us a minute?"

"We need to do a perimeter run," Drag said, nodding his head toward the woods, and Heston followed him.

"It's about time for Scarlet's next feeding," April said, admiring the little one in her arms before her eyes went to me with kindness. "Good luck, Sage."

Once Zeke and April left, and no one else was around, Marcus didn't hesitate to tear into me. "What the hell is your problem?"

Thoughts of failing this mission swarmed through my mind. "I'm too damn weak for this. I'm going to get myself or someone else killed!"

"Hey, hey! That's enough of that shit," Marcus snapped, his brows tightening, his finger pointed at me. "I don't *ever* want to hear you say anything like that again."

"It's true, Marcus!" I dropped my chin to my chest and rubbed my hand across the back of my neck, attempting to relieve the tension.

"Look at me."

Marcus had taught me almost everything I knew about fighting, and the last thing I wanted to do was disappoint him.

"Look at me, Sagelynn!"

Even though I was unready for the lecture I was about to receive, I pushed back my anger and forced my gaze upwards.

"Have you forgotten who you are?" he asked, his question confusing the shit out of me.

"Umm. I'm—"

"You don't need to tell me because I already know who you are. You're a trained killer and a strong woman, not just intellectually, but physically. The only reason your body isn't acting like it right now is because you're malnourished. You went through some traumatic shit, Sage. And now that your soul has had some time to heal, your body needs to catch up. The only thing stopping you from being who you are is your fear. You're giving it power to control you. Once you decide to dominate that fear, the easier this will get. And the more you stand there sulking and complaining, the longer it's going to take. Now stop whining and get your damn fists back up!"

None of the training Marcus gave me compared to the value I gained from his lectures. He had many great attributes, but his words of encouragement along with his motivation to do better . . . to *be* better, were always my favorite.

Marcus raised his fists, going back into a fighting stance, and after a few shocked blinks from me, I realized he was right. I mirrored his posture because regardless of how much I loved him, I was ready to kick his ass.

After training, my nervousness continued to consume me. A thousand scenarios of what could go wrong during our rescue mission occupied the space where my brain once was, the agonizing thoughts buzzing through my head faster than lightning.

Attempting to calm myself and to tackle my fear, like Marcus said, I slipped away undetected to go for a walk.

Even though the sun had barely begun setting, the canopy of pine and oak made my surroundings dimmer, so my eyes were on the hard, cold ground below my feet as I stumbled through the brush of the forest.

At the edge of the treeline, I emerged into a field and my gaze went to the sky lit up with orange and pink hues before they went wide in surprise, my feet coming to a sudden stop.

Not paying attention to my surroundings had never been a weakness of mine. Today, I failed to spot the three women in front of me until it was too late.

The light still clinging to the horizon lit their faces, revealing them a mere four feet away. Not comprehending how the magical wards worked, I held my breath, worried they would . . . see me? Smell me? Sense me?

The woman on the left was eager as a small child, squealing with excitement. Her bare feet slammed against the grass and her white sundress flowed behind her like a symphony of fabric as she chased a butterfly with nothing less than pure joy.

The temperature had to be only around fifty degrees when I left the camp, but with the sun setting it had dropped even lower. I wondered how she wasn't freezing since I wore jeans, a T-shirt, and a leather jacket, yet my cheeks and hands were ice cold.

The woman on the right wore a black leather, strapless jumpsuit with what I thought was a scarf around her neck but it turned out to be a large ball python. Her expression was joyous as she peered down, affectionately stroking its body.

The one in the middle was the tallest of them, with wavy copper hair, and when she locked her attention on me, her cheeks tightening with a smile, I realized I had wandered outside the wards.

My hand instinctively went to the dagger Peach had given to me, which was fastened to my thigh, flipping open the leather strap that secured it.

"Don't," she warned. "We're faster and stronger than any weapon."

Suspicious of the fact that three women were wandering in the middle of the woods, I didn't heed her advice. Instead, I yanked my dagger from its sheath.

Before I had a chance to decide if I needed to use it, an unseen force slammed into my body, knocking me onto my back and expelling the air from my lungs, causing me to gasp.

Now pissed off, I sprang to my feet with efficiency and raised my dagger again, ready to plunge it into the woman in the middle.

She flicked two fingers in my direction and another invisible wall hit me, shoving me backwards as if I was light as a feather.

The back of my skull bounced off the cold, hard ground, sending sharp pains through my head.

My body alerted me to stop, but I ignored it, instead scrambling to my feet slower than before, my sore, over-worked muscles also screaming for me to retreat.

When I raised my dagger this time—because apparently getting knocked on my ass twice wasn't enough to stop me—instead of being thrown backwards by some mysterious power, my entire body locked in limbo.

She had frozen me in place like a heroic and possibly idiotic statue.

While I could still breathe and move my eyes, my body was completely unresponsive. Every muscle I had appeared to be no longer owned by me and I finally panicked.

"What the fuck!" At least my vocal cords still worked, even if it didn't matter since scolding them to death wasn't a power I possessed.

My mind reeled with possibilities of what the hell was going on. Was I dreaming? Perhaps sleepwalking? Or were these actual witches?

The woman in the middle gave me an empathetic smile, her fair skin seemingly unfazed by the frigid weather. "You shouldn't be outside of the wards. Anyone could see you."

"My butterfly is gone. It's gone!" the butterfly-chaser belted out.

"It's okay, Cece. We'll find you another." The one in the middle appeared to be the leader when she stepped forward and raised her freckled hand, grazing the back of her finger down my cheek. "You are exquisite, my silver."

"Beautiful silver, beautiful silver," the one I now knew as Cece chanted. She looked similar to the copper-haired one touching me, except she had fewer curls and more freckles sprayed across her pink cheeks.

"Yes, sister. The silver is beautiful." The leader laid her hand flat on my cheek and tilted her head in an admiring manner.

The third woman had umber-colored skin with a radiant golden undertone. Her eye and lip makeup were dark, giving her a beautiful yet mysterious look. "Shayla, can you step aside? Archibald wants to meet her."

"Be my guest, Delaney." Shayla dropped her hand, taking a few steps back, and the third woman replaced her.

Delaney held her hand out and the snake slithered out from under her black hair, crawled down her arm, and wrapped himself around her wrist. She raised her arm so he was eye level with me, and I held my breath as he flicked his tongue on my cheek. I may not be afraid of snakes, but I sure as hell didn't want one kissing me.

"Archie likes her, Archie likes her," Cece chanted excitedly, then pulled her dress up and spun in circles.

Delaney lowered the snake, turning her attention to Shayla. "The wolves are on their way. Time is up."

"I know, sister. We shall not fret, the alpha is with them."

A twig cracked a split second before a gray wolf prowled in from the right side of me, and after spending months seeing them, I immediately recognized the wolf to be Kimber. Heston, a lighter gray wolf, circled in from the left. Both of them issued low warning growls that made the hair on the back of my neck stand up.

Drag had been the biggest of the wolven I had seen so far, and I was grateful when he darted right up between me and the trio without hesitation. He shifted back into a human and my gaze accidentally landed on his naked backside before I let out a regretful sigh.

"Release her." His commanding tone surprised me, but didn't faze the women.

"What is the point of us cloaking your camp if you can't keep your people inside of it?" Shayla flicked two fingers toward me again and the death grip on my muscles lifted, leaving me feeling like jelly had replaced the stone. "Sorry we had to use magic on you, silver. But your fast-acting demeanor could have injured one of my sisters."

I pulled my arms into myself, rubbing the numbness away. "What the hell is going on?"

Drag snapped his fingers at me, his eyes relaying a warning, as did his reprimanding. "You be quiet. Your ass shouldn't have even been outside the wards."

Every interaction I had with Drag assured me he was a gentle and caring man, so his unusual abrasiveness caused my mouth to fall open.

"Shocked silver. Shocked silver." Cece laughed, then smiled innocently at me.

Drag ignored us both, turning his attention back to Shayla. "What are you doing here?"

"You missed the Winter Solstice festival without a call, Dragos Oliver Montoya. And when you didn't show up for our quarterly meeting, my sisters and I became worried. When I spell-checked you, I observed a bright light surrounding your presence. Not being able to contain our excitement, we came to see the star with haste." Shayla's eyes drifted to me and the sparkle shining in them was almost unreal. "She is the silver who will end the war. The prophecy we have been waiting for."

"The silver prophecy departs for odyssey, but destiny will veer if the course is not clear," Cece sang.

"You need not worry, sister. Destiny is on course and shall stay that way if everyone involved fulfills their responsibilities." Shayla stepped in close to me again. "Please sheath your dagger."

I looked at Drag for confirmation. He nodded, so I slid my blade back in its holster.

Shayla took my right hand in hers and I felt a small electrical spark. "Your light shines bright, my silver. Do not let the blood of your blood dull your blaze. You must fulfill the prophecy."

I blinked repeatedly, making sure I wasn't dreaming. "I'm sorry, but I'm not involved in any prophecy."

"Is your name Sagelynn Juniper Argent?"

Knowing only a couple people knew my middle name, I glanced around before I hesitantly answered. "I am."

"Then you are an Argentum, are you not?"

The word she spoke was one I'd never heard before. "Argentum?"

"Your surname means silver in Latin. Do not confuse it with Argentium silver, which is the material used to make your dagger and other weapons around the camp."

"I know what Argentium silver is, but you have the wrong person. My last name is Argent. Like you said."

Shayla grinned proudly. "Yes. Yes, it is."

I waited for more information to come but she mindfully said nothing, and the other women she was with were also silent.

Ravage appeared astonishingly fast, causing me to suck in a hard breath.

"That's a name I haven't heard in years." Smoke from a bit of sun hitting his face steamed into the air before he took a few steps back, going under the canopy of the trees. His expression as it healed told me this conversation was about to get interesting. "Argentum was the original surname for your family before they shortened it in the eighteenth century. The same year they renamed the VEM society to Venom."

I was about to ask him what the hell he was talking about when Lyric and Erik came sprinting up, gasping for air. Drag held up his hand, letting them know I was safe and they halted whatever plan they had to save me.

"You are the one, the silver. The witch to end the war," Shayla said, bringing my attention back to her. "It will take you many, many moons to finish the battle of fang and foe, but with help from your coven, you will prevail. I have envisioned it."

Shayla's words left me bewildered. I blinked a few times, my gaze lingering over the freckles near her right temple, if connected, they'd form a star. She had big, almond-shaped eyes which were neither blue nor green, but somehow a perfect blend of each.

She was mystical. Unlike me.

Considering I had no magical powers, her accusations of me being a witch had to be false. I tapped my finger on my thigh as I waited for more information, and once

I realized she wasn't going to give me any, I glanced at Ravage for clarification.

"She's telling you she's a seer and has the capability of predicting the future. They're witches."

Although I had already realized what they were, the words being spoken aloud sent shock flooding through me. Despite my knowledge of vampires and werewolves, the idea of witches existing seemed unbelievable, and I found it even harder to accept that I might be one of them.

Shayla released my hand and took a step back. "I speak the truth of prophecies long forgotten. You are the silver to end the war."

The trio raised their hands in a V shape, palms toward the sky, closed their eyes, and spoke in unison.

"Fangs and silver destined to unite.

Foe becomes friend under lover's light.

A new creature has formed, strong and mystique.

No spelled silver shall make it weak.

A family unfolds as the blood moon cries.

With fangs bared, together they rise.

Death will come when swords clash.

The fires burn bright, leaving nothing but ash.

When silver strikes, the snake will fall.

Only a new era of union will bring peace to all."

Their eyes popped open, the last of the sunset glittering across their faces.

I shook my head, bringing myself out of my unrelenting daze. "But I'm not a witch, nor am I in a coven."

"Your genesis bloodline has birthed witches for centuries. The magic in your body is so strong, you formed a coven at age nine, which is extremely rare for such a youngling." Shayla's gaze drifted to Lyric and Erik before it came back to me. "The siblings were your first two members and have lovingly stayed by your side through all weather. You three live by Blood of the Coven. It has come out of your mouth for many moons."

"Many moons, many moons," Cece repeated.

"I must have heard it somewhere," I mumbled hesitantly, not sure if I believed my own words.

"No, my darling, the magic is in your blood. The ancestors spoke to you. They knew that you would need an alliance to succeed, otherwise you wouldn't fulfill the prophecy. Your ancestors are always forthcoming when you call upon them. They have helped you on numerous occasions when invoked."

Her words only caused more confusion for me. "I don't understand what you mean. I don't even know how to call them."

"Give me your hand and I'll bestow an example."

I reluctantly placed my hand out in front of me, palm side down. Shayla flipped it over, placing her index finger in the middle of my palm before drawing slow circles, her eyelids drifting close.

"You and my fanged friend went into battle at your apartment. On your third encounter with him, you fought valiantly, but he hesitated, almost costing him his life, which would have ended the prophecy. The silver hit the ground and you unknowingly called upon your ancestors while seeking it. The moonlight glistened upon the silver, unveiling it, but not before your ancestors made sure your cat paused the battle long enough for you both to cool off. You know the rest."

Shock hit me when Shayla explained something no one but myself would've known. The night I fought Luka in my apartment, the moonlight had revealed my stake to me, and I'd never told anyone because it seemed coincidental.

"Your senses tell you things often, yet you ignore them because you haven't tapped into your true power. After you dismissed your instincts, someone took you hostage and tortured you. Thankfully, my fanged friends saved you."

My heart beat uncontrollably when I realized I had thought Mannie was creepy both times I met him. I should have listened to my gut feeling.

Shayla's eyelids popped open and I sucked in a gasp when I spotted a nictitating membrane covering her cornea. She blinked and the third eyelid swept back into the corner, revealing her catlike pupils. Two blinks later, her eyes were back to normal.

"Those aren't the only incidents. I can continue if you would like."

My words had disappeared, running off to hide from the fading sunset like I wanted to. The abundance of emotions swirling in me only twenty minutes ago was nothing compared to what I was currently feeling.

My thoughts went into four different directions before coming together and forming one ridiculous image: the long pointy nose, big black hat, cauldron-stirring witches I had seen in cartoons.

But these witches weren't like that. They were beautiful, mystical, eloquent, and completely unfazed by the cold air that slapped my cheeks.

I wasn't beautiful, mystical, or eloquent, and I was pretty damn sure I was only minutes away from freezing to death.

How can I be a witch?

"The silver is tongueless!" Cece shouted with a concerned look. "Tell her more. Tell her more."

Shayla tilted her head, her tender expression easing my anxiety. "Would you like me to explain the role your bloodline has to play?"

I noticed the witches spoke in a specific manner, which I found pleasing to the ear. Me, not so much. "Um, sure."

"There are others living here who also need to hear this, Dragos. It's a long story, may we have a sit?"

"Come on up to the camp," Drag said, nodding his head toward the trees.

In an instant, he shifted back into his wolf form and stood next to me, the top of his head lining up with my shoulders. His sky-blue eyes stared into mine like he was telling me something.

"Does he want me to pet him or what?" I asked, and Ravage barked out a laugh.

"He's telling you to follow him. Without a mate, he has no Luna, so the Alpha wolf has to lead the way."

I sucked in a hard breath at a secret I didn't know. "Drag's an alpha?"

Ravage smiled, showing me his fangs. "Indeed, he is. A damn good one, too."

After thinking about it, it made total sense. Drag's sister needed him to decide about the baby when we were there. He'd also organized the food runs, handed out orders, and fulfilled both of the camp's needs.

How did I miss the signs?

Being heartbroken had made me oblivious to the world around me.

Drag turned away and everyone followed, except for Ravage who stayed behind me like he was my protector.

Lyric fell into step next to me and offered solace by holding my hand. Erik approached me from the other side and briefly rubbed my shoulder.

As we walked in silence, I remained unsure about my true identity as a witch, but I knew without a doubt that Shayla was right about one thing.

I had a coven who loved me.

CHAPTER 21
SAGE

Once back at camp, Drag trotted off toward his cabin, as did Heston and Kimber, and I assumed they were getting dressed. The rest of us took seats around the already blazing fire. Everyone chatted away as I sat there waiting for some kind of sign from the universe that I was a witch.

Twenty minutes later the sun had set and the rest of the vampires came out of their cabins. Of course, Winnie strolled right up with a glare on his face.

"What the fuck did you do now?"

I shrugged, avoiding his question.

"She wandered outside the wards and tried to attack us," Shayla informed him. "Luckily for her, we aren't enemies. The silver must be protected."

Winnie took a seat across from me, shaking his head. "Why the hell would you attack three strong-ass witches?"

"I didn't even know witches were real until a half hour ago."

Winnie cocked a brow. "The magical wards that we tell you almost every day to stay inside weren't any kind of hint at all?"

I threw my hands out. "I thought it was a wolven thing. Maybe they marked their territory or something."

"What did you think they did, pee a circle around the whole damn camp?" Winnie asked, and I blushed from embarrassment because that was precisely my thought.

"Circle of pee. Circle of pee." Cece bursted out laughing before letting out a happy sigh. "The silver is silly."

Drag and the other two wolven came back fully clothed, and I was grateful. I think I had officially seen every part of his and every other person in his pack's bodies at this point.

Shayla sighed with a dissatisfied look on her face. "We're waiting for two more, Dragos. Everyone must hear the story since all have a part in the war to come."

"They're right there." Ravage nodded his head to the left.

I looked in that direction and my heart fluttered with excitement as Marcus and Peach headed toward us, hand in hand, with Luka's dog trotting ahead of them.

Annie came up to me first, wagging his tail and excitingly licking my hand as I tried to pet him. He left quickly, making his way around the circle, happily greeting everyone.

"It has been moons, Heather Nicole Matthews. I hope you're faring well."

Peach dropped Marcus's hand and held hers out to Shayla. "Nice to see you again."

"Your name's Heather?" Erik blurted before I had a chance to.

Peach ignored him, instead taking a seat with Marcus sitting next to her. When he slid his hand between her thighs and she smiled, I did a little happy dance inside.

Delaney sauntered around the bonfire with effortless grace, observing the numerous faces around her. "It's fabulous to see fang and foe working together." She stopped in front of Winnie who was bug-eyed as the snake curiously poked its head toward him.

"You know me and Archie aren't friends. He hates me. I can feel his threatening eyes staring at me like I'm prey."

"Don't be silly, Winston. Archibald would never harm a friend without my command. The fear you contain for snakes is what feels threatening."

Winnie squirmed in his seat and I grinned at the fact he was afraid of snakes. "Can you put him away, please?"

Delaney let out a sigh. "As you wish."

Within seconds, the large snake melted into her skin, turning into a golden tattoo wrapping around her arm from bicep to wrist. Me and pretty much every human around sucked in a gasp.

"What was that?" Nellie asked.

"Winston is frightened of Archibald, so I dismissed him for now."

Before any of us had a chance to ask more questions about the amazing magic we saw, Shayla clapped her hands twice, getting our attention. "It's time to begin."

She strolled up to the bonfire and waved her hand over it. The flames crackled, spitting higher, and a proud smile spread across her face. She waved her hand again and the fire went back to normal.

"The year was 1642 when vampires were scarce and unknown to the world. An apothecary in a small town had a patient with a rare blood disorder and technology wasn't advanced enough at the time for any proper testing. One day, this man attended his weekly visit with normal coloring and an abundance of energy. He seemed completely cured, stupefying the doctor. During an examination, the physician found a bite mark on his neck. Which you know, Sagelynn, fades with swiftness."

Everyone's eyes stared in my direction, knowing Luka had fed from me, and my insides shriveled. But no matter how embarrassing, I was grateful for the knowledge because I had noticed the bites fade within hours when we were in Vegas. When I asked Luka about it on the car ride home, he said it had something to do with vampire venom, but he didn't elaborate on it. He wasn't much of a talker when it came to certain topics.

"Do not feel embarrassed, my silver. Without the lover's light, none of us would be sitting here."

"What happened next, Shayla?" Drag asked, taking the attention off of me.

"When the doctor questioned the man about the mark, he told him he was newly married and his wife had gotten overzealous in the bedroom. The truth is the woman was a vampire who had fed from the man only an hour prior to the visit. Unbeknownst to the doctor, vampires everywhere were feeding off humans to survive, unaware they were bloodletting, in a way. When they feed through the vein, it purifies human blood and temporarily eases blood-related illnesses. This doctor began his investigation and eventually discovered the secret vampires and their magical properties. With the help of his patient's wife, the doctor's research progressed. It eventually led him to discover the healing properties of blood for common abrasions, later finding it could even heal fatal wounds.

"The townsfolk inevitably discovered what the doctor was doing, causing one man to start a society called the Vampire Eradicating Men. VEM for short. His name was William Argentum and your ancestral grandfather seven generations ago. He called vampires an abomination and ordered them to be executed, along with the doctor. Thankfully, the doctor, his patient, and his vampire wife skipped town, never to be heard from again.

"William was still angry over the existence of vampires and with his new group formed, they were ready to kill them all. A woman named Hester, who's your seventh generation grandmother, was his wife. Being the most powerful witch, with one of the brightest lights ever to be seen, she was called upon by William and some elders to cast a spell to protect humans. Together, Hester and her coven mastered the incantation for wards, sealing the small town with the invisible ring. The town remained visible, and humans could come and go as they pleased, but vampires, wolven, and witches, amongst other beings, were now barred from entering."

I wondered what other creatures could possibly exist when movement caught my eye. Jimmy had his hand raised.

"Do you have a question?" Shayla asked.

"If the wards keep supernaturals out, then how are these guys here?" Jimmy asked, pointing to the vampires and wolven sitting around.

"That's a great question. There are many types of incantations and some are more intricate than others," Shayla said as she circled the fire pit, stopping next to Drag before placing her hand on his shoulder. "The one my sisters and I used for this camp has multiple effects. The first part is a cloaking spell. It prevents anyone, supernatural or human, from seeing the existence of the camp, and Drag is the only one who can sanction new-comers since he is the land owner." Shayla removed her hand and continued circling. "We enhanced the barrier to include a danger spell. If a non-resident comes near the wards, which are set far and wide, they will feel a sense of dread, making them want to run as far away as possible. The wards will also allow anyone living here to leave and reenter naturally, including supernaturals, unless Drag says otherwise."

"So, witches are supernatural?" Jimmy asked.

"Technically, no. Although witches are mere humans who possess magical abilities, the wards perceive us as dangerous, so we cannot enter. Not unless our magic is used to cast the spell or we receive an invitation from a permanent resident or land owner, depending on the incantation used. However, witches are able to feel warding spells from miles away."

Jimmy's eyes widened under his glasses. "That's really cool!"

"Wards of many, wards of plenty," Cece chanted. "It's cool. It's cool."

"Indeed, sister." Shayla gave Cece a seemingly loving look before returning to her story. "With the town now safe, the group went out on their first hunting mission. An *unsuccessful* one. They realized the vampires healed too rapidly to be killed with any normal weapon, so once again, they turned to Hester for guidance. Steel and iron were common materials used in weaponry, so the coven infused magic with it during the forging process, binding it to a sword. The members of VEM tried slaying a vampire and failed once more. After more manipulation, Hester realized the spell bonded best to pure silver. They made another sword and managed to terminate a vampire using it.

"During the altercation, they realized the silver hadn't harmed the vampires to the touch. The swords only injured or killed the vampires when they penetrated their bodies. They forged more weapons, like daggers and short swords because they were easier to wield. Since the heart seemed to be the swiftest way to kill them, eventually stakes became the common defense for hunters. The only complication they had with the silver was the spells would eventually wear off. But with a coven of strong witches by their side, it hadn't become a problem yet. These new advanced weapons eliminated many vampires, leading the rest to conceal themselves from the world. Over time, the humans stopped believing in what they could not see and vampires became folklore.

"In 1717, the society renamed itself as the Vampire Eradicating National Organization of Malice and shortened your surname to Argent. Everyone believes that was the year when the society had formed. A few decades ago, the master blacksmith of Venom had limited access to witches, because most of us didn't want to be involved in the war against vampires. With the spells wearing off and no casters to help, it left them in a challenging situation. Hoping it would prolong the magic, a distant relative of yours helped with the process of making Argentium silver. It's close to your original surname but with the letter I in it."

"Yeah, I kind of figured that out," I mumbled sarcastically.

Shayla cocked a brow, an amused smile pulling at her cheeks as she glanced toward the other two witches. "The silver is snarky."

"Snarky silver, snarky silver," Cece rambled. "The light still shines bright, so do not let it deter us, Shayla."

"I shall not, sister. I find it rather refreshing that someone other than you speaks their mind so freely."

Winnie snickered, side eyeing me. "Shit. Sage always says what she wants. It makes me want to punch her most days."

Shayla's gaze wandered to Winnie, a whimsical expression beautifying her face. "Winston Javier Rodriguez, as a fanged friend of mine for many lunar years, you shouldn't comment on the loose lips of others when yours are never tightly wound."

Giggles and stifled laughs came from everyone's mouth but Winnie's. The look on his face said he wanted to retort with something evil, but wouldn't.

"All I'm saying is Sage can be annoying as hell, but she's cool in my book."

Shayla smiled, turning back to me. "What the fanged one is attempting to convey is that he loves you like a sister."

Winnie huffed, crossing his arms over his chest and leaning back. "Yeah, an annoying little sister."

"I love you too, Pooh Bear." I gave him a mischievous grin, then winked.

One side of his mouth cocked up with a smirk, but the gleam in his eyes told me he was glad I said it.

"Pooh Bear!" Cece squealed, clapping her hands. "A pot of honey for Winnie, that's funny!"

Winnie sighed heavily. "It's Winston."

"His name's Winston. It's Winston." Cece frowned, then flicked her gaze to Shayla. "He says that a lot."

Shayla let out a small laugh before clearing her throat. "Back on topic. I disclosed the story to tell you this. All of you have a role to play with the battle of fang and foe," she said, turning her back to me and glancing at Jimmy. "Yes, that includes you, James Christopher Thomas."

I leaned to the side, peeking around Shayla so I could see Jimmy, whose eyes were wide under his black-framed glasses.

"I didn't say anything," he muttered.

"You did not have to speak the truth. You feel useless among the strong, causing your light to be dim, but you must remember this. You shall not need fists to fight a battle when you have brains stronger than most metals."

Jimmy's brows rose before his expression turned prideful. "Thank you. I think."

"The rabbits they run but cannot hide when the light of destiny is on your side," Cece sang.

"Yes, sister. The rabbits are running now, but soon they will reveal the truths of their sciences and once they do, everyone should prepare for the long battle which is to come."

"Can you explain what that means, exactly?"

No one answered my question. Instead, the three witches moved in unison as they circled the fire. With palms raised to the sky, they closed their eyes. The flames from the fire shot high, blue sparks shining bright as they spoke in unison . . . again.

"Fangs and silver destined to unite.

Foe becomes friend under lover's light.

A new creature has formed, strong and mystique.

No spelled silver shall make it weak.

A family unfolds as the blood moon cries.

With fangs bared, together they rise.

Death will come when swords clash.

The fires burn bright, leaving nothing but ash.

When silver strikes, the snake will fall.

Only a new era of union will bring peace to all."

Once they dropped their hands, the flames went back to normal.

Shayla turned, meeting my eyes. "Do you understand now?"

"I think."

"Shall we repeat it?" Delaney asked, and I shook my head.

I sure as hell didn't want to hear it a third time. "That's okay. I understand."

"Then we shall be off after I say my goodbyes." Shayla stepped up to me and took my hand in hers. "The one you love has suffered tremendous damage and he will need more than your blood can give. Be patient, be kind, and be strong." I took her words as more confirmation of Luka being alive. My heart raced and tears formed as she smiled. "Your new eyes will see the beauty this world has to offer."

Shayla dropped my hand and headed toward Winnie, and he shook his head. "You know I prefer not to know my future."

"Very well."

Next she went to April who was holding Scarlet. Shayla pulled the blanket back from the baby's head before gently placing her hand on it. "She is so happy in your arms." Shayla slid her hand onto April's forearm. "When the day arrives and you're exhausted, completely questioning your choices, remember it's normal for mothers to experience stress. The love you hold for her is pure. Unstoppable. It may have not been said aloud, but fate has decided it. Scarlet is yours and you are hers."

April's lip quivered. "Thank you."

Zeke stiffened when Shayla turned toward him and took his hand. "Your child may not resemble you nor April, but will carry the proud Alexander name. Don't fret, Ezekiel. You'll be an amazing father to many children." His face was in full-blown shock when she let go.

Shayla moved on to Lyric who wasn't sitting with Winnie tonight, and had a nervous expression on her face.

"Don't fret, little one," Shayla said, her voice kind.

Lyric hesitated, then slowly raised her hand to Shayla.

"Lyric Sofia Muldova, you shall receive the love your kind soul deserves. Even if it does not come from the one you want. Decisions have to be made before I can tell you more."

Lyric sucked in a breath and looked at Winnie with concerned eyes. Without saying a word, he stood and headed toward his cabin.

I questioned whether genuine happiness could exist if the most passionate couple I knew couldn't find a way to fix their lives.

Shayla strolled up to Peach who had her hands clasped together. After a long sigh, she relented. "I've never liked this, but you know I can't resist."

Peach raised her hand and Shayla took it. "The value you put on yourself is much lower than anyone else sees. Especially him." Shayla nodded her head toward Marcus. "You have prevailed from many trials in your extremely long life, this I know. You should not box out love because of it. If fate is not tested, then he'll never break your heart."

Shayla turned her attention to Marcus with a huge smile that quickly turned concerned when she took his hand. "Marcus Henry Alexander, you, my dear, are a force to be reckoned with. You are a perfect trifecta, physically, intellectually, and emotionally strong. Those three traits rarely meet to form such greatness. It's unfortunate the road ahead is unclear. Depending on the decisions of others, your path can diverge in two different directions. For the sake of the prophecy and everyone involved, I hope *he* chooses wisely. A soul like yours is too rare to lose."

She dropped Marcus's hand and I witnessed a glimpse of something I'd never seen from him before—fear. My stomach twisted as concern filled me.

Shayla moved on to Vivi who happily held out her hand. "Viviana Jade Rodriguez, my sister, my friend. Your pain will not end as quickly as you desire. Until then—"

Vivi yanked her hand away and bolted out of her seat, heading toward the woods, and a heaviness weighed on my chest.

"I do not understand why you insist on reading her," Delaney uttered, holding out her hand. The golden snake tattoo returned to its original form and slithered up her arm, wrapping around her neck. "You always have the same results."

"Her light has faded, a sister no more."

Shayla turned toward Cece, her face calm. "We have had this discussion, sister. Viviana being fanged doesn't exempt her from our coven responsibilities. As a born witch, even in fanged death, she is *still* family."

My brows rose, a million questions trampling my thoughts.

If Vivi is a witch, is Winnie one too?

Are they called male witches?

Mitches?

Oh my god, is Winnie a Warlock?

"Still family, still family," Cece whispered, bringing me out of my overthinking brain. "I love her."

"We all do," Shayla said with a concerned expression that dropped when she made her way around the camp.

A few people declined to be read, like Drag and his entire pack, and I wondered why. Randi also rejected Shayla, but Nellie hadn't.

"Natalie Elaine Shimwell, beware of the dark clouds who are leaving you unsafe in your current position. Choose a new direction or choose death."

Fear took over Nellie's face and it took all my strength not to jump up, call her a rat, then kill her. Since Drag was the alpha, I glanced at him for confirmation and he shook his head. A long sigh left me, and for once, I kept my damn mouth shut.

Shayla stopped at Jimmy with a curious expression. "There are nine figures for the house. Seven will lead the race with nine on its tail, and snake eyes come in last. The two shall not pass the other three, but five shall follow it along with six."

Jimmy's eyes were as wide as mine, neither of us having any idea what the hell she meant. He quickly pulled out his phone, and I hoped he was taking notes as Shayla turned her attention toward me.

"You must stay safe, silver. You cannot complete the prophecy if your body lays cold in the ground. Take the offer."

"If you are not fed, you will be dead," Cece sang. "Take the offer."

"Do not be stubborn," Delaney said, holding Archie up to her face. "Take the offer."

I started to open my mouth and Shayla waved her hand. "We are done."

She lifted the hem of her dress and strolled toward the darkness with her sisters behind her.

They departed so quickly, I didn't have time to ask the thousand questions that swirled through my head.

My gaze went from their retreating shadows to the bonfire, my mouth hanging open. I rubbed my eyes, attempting to once again make sure I wasn't dreaming.

What just happened?

How can she tell me I'm a witch who might die, then disappear?

Everyone began to converse about what Shayla had told them, and I zoned out, only hearing muffled voices.

My twenty-fifth birthday was only eight months ago, and since then I'd fallen in love with a vampire, betrayed and escaped my society, became so depressed I'd wished I was dead, got slapped back to reality when I found out Luka was alive, and had been told I came from a long line of witches.

What the fuck else can happen?

CHAPTER 22
WINNIE

A fire burned inside of me as I paced the creaky wooden floors of my cabin. I wasn't mad at Shayla or Lyric. I was angry with myself. If I had told my girlfriend the truth, I could be out there enjoying everyone's company—enjoying her company. Then Shayla had to stick her nose in our damn business and make things worse.

Seriously, though. What the fuck do witches know? Not shit, that's what. Okay, maybe they know more than me, but that doesn't mean they should go around telling people.

A tap on my door halted my furious thoughts, and I stopped next to my desk, using my senses to see who it was. "Come in, Marcus."

The door squeaked open and he stepped inside, the look on his face telling me it was lecture time. "It still creeps me out that you can smell me."

"I can smell everyone." I slammed my ass into my computer chair, leaned back, and crossed my hands behind my head. "What's up, bro?"

"I was letting you know the witches left."

"Good," I spat, and Marcus narrowed his eyes.

"What's going on with you and Lyric?"

I snickered, then let out a hard breath. "Nothing."

He cocked his head to the side. "Doesn't sound like it's nothing."

"She's pissed at me because I lied to her about the mission!" A hundred emotions went through me at once and I flung myself from my seat. I began pacing again, my hands flying wildly as I spoke. "But you know I didn't have a choice, Marcus. We have to do whatever we can to find Luka and Strike. We have enough to worry about with my friends being tortured and everything else going on, and now I have to worry about someone else being happy? Well, what if I don't want to? What if I was fine only worrying about myself? This is why I didn't want a *real* relationship. Because of shit like this. Then Shayla had to stick her nose in and put more doubts in Lyric's head, and that's gonna make it worse. Just because she can see the future doesn't mean she should go blabbing it! That witch needs to stay out of my business. I fucked up my relationship and *I* will be the one to fix it, if I decide that's what I want!"

As I stopped pacing and glanced at Marcus, he appeared as if he had witnessed a toddler having a meltdown. "Feel better yet?"

"Not really, but it's whatever." With a huff, I retook my seat at the computer desk. "I'm just a traveler with a lifetime pass on the hot mess express."

Marcus crossed his arms and leaned back in a relaxing stance, wearing what I liked to call his "dad" face. "When was the last time you fed?"

My thoughts flew in multiple directions. "Shit. I don't know. Over a week ago, I think."

"Maybe you should eat."

"I doubt Lyric wants me feeding from her right now. I'd have to drink one of the blood bags."

"Then go get one from the fridge." Marcus uncrossed his arms and headed toward the door.

"Wait. You're not going to give me any words of encouragement?"

He glanced over his shoulder, his deep brown eyes locking on mine. "There are times we have to lie to protect the ones we love. It doesn't mean the lies didn't hurt them in the process. Give her a sincere apology."

"That's it? That's your deep Marcus wisdom?"

"Sometimes it's the simple things that make the most sense."

I scowled. "What the fuck does that even mean, bro?"

"Get your ass off the hot mess express and figure it out." Marcus smiled his pearly white teeth like he had all the answers in the world but wouldn't give them up for free, then left the cabin.

I stared at the door for a few seconds before letting out a sigh. Marcus was right about one thing. I needed blood.

A part of me wanted to ask Lyric if I could feed off her. Knowing if I did it would lead to sex, my mind spun with images of her beautiful naked body. I decided it wouldn't hurt to at least mention it.

The music was louder than normal as I headed out the door and toward the people gathered around the fire. Most of them were sitting on logs or in lawn chairs, but Kimber, Vivi, and Nellie were dancing.

"I see a nosh pit forming," I said, approaching Heston and Demetrious.

Demi scrubbed his hand across his short red beard. "Nosh? Like food?"

"Yeah." I pointed to the people swaying to the music. "It's what I call dancing humans. Like a mosh pit but tastier."

Heston laughed. "Nosh pit. Now that's fucking funny."

I took a seat by him and leaned my elbows onto my knees. "What's been up with you guys? Enjoying the night?"

"Aye. And enjoying a drink under the full moon," Demi said, his Irish accent thicker than normal. He held up his glass, never looking away from the dancing people. "These ladies are gonna be knackered from throwing shapes all night."

I stared blankly. "What the fuck does that mean?"

Heston scoffed. "He means they'll be tired from dancing. But I'm not going to complain. I'm enjoying the view from here."

The music turned to "After Dark," by Tito and Tarantula, and an image of Salma Hayek dancing in a movie entered my brain.

My focus diverted to Lyric when she joined the other women, now dancing seductively next to the fire. I couldn't help but lock my gaze on her body as she rolled her perfect, curvy hips. She was an amazing dancer, just as good as Salma, and I had to forcefully pull my eyes off her.

I glanced around and almost everyone here was watching the women. Knowing Lyric had the attention of other men caused a fire to fill my chest, my jaw clenching.

"Whoa," Heston groaned before sniffing the air. He cocked his head to the side and glared at me. "Salty and smoky. I never thought you'd be a jealous man."

I flexed my fingers repeatedly as I lied. "I'm not."

"You know damn well wolven can smell emotions, Winnie."

Ignoring Heston, I looked back at Lyric. Normally, she braided her hair on both sides, but tonight it cascaded down her back in loose waves. She turned slightly, her eyes catching mine, and they locked like magnets, pulling our souls together, not allowing either of us to look away.

She sensually moved her body to the music, running her fingers through her dark chestnut locks. The way she swayed her hips sent blood rushing to my cock and it hardened.

I leaned back slightly, pushing my hand against the front of my jeans, begging it to stop.

The more it throbbed the more I wanted to throw her over my shoulder and carry her back to the cabin caveman style.

The aroma of sweet lilacs radiated off her and hit like a ton of bricks, almost causing me to fall off the wooden log I was sitting on.

"Damn," Demi said in a low tone. "These scents are gonna kill me."

More like I'm gonna to kill you.

Jealousy continued to build within me, resulting in a low growl escaping my throat. Looking at Demi and Heston, my mouth fell open and my fangs involuntarily extended, a loud hiss leaving me.

"Winston!" Ravage yelled in his *"stop fucking around"* tone. "I may not be your origin, but he's not here to keep you under control. Handle your shit, boy, before I handle it for you."

I tightened my jaw, my stare traveling to him.

Ravage glared back, completely unfazed by me. Being a burly vampire who was much older than me, I knew damn well he'd beat my ass.

A few seconds later, I took a deep breath, attempting to push down my feelings before I relented with a nod.

When my gaze went back to Lyric, she tilted her head, seemingly concerned. Not being able to take it anymore, I jumped up and headed toward her.

"Are you okay?" she asked, and instead of answering, I grabbed her hand and pulled her away from the bonfire, heading straight for the forest.

Once far enough away, I stopped, releasing her from my grip.

"Why are we here?"

"You can't do that, Lyric!"

Clouds filled the night sky, creating a darker atmosphere than usual at three in the morning. Even though she had difficulty seeing me, my vampire vision allowed me to see her confused expression.

"Do what?"

"Dance seductively next to a bonfire in front of a bunch of vamps and wolves who can smell the lust radiating off you from a damn mile away let alone ten damn feet!"

Her face angered. "What do you expect, Winston? Just because I'm mad at you doesn't mean I don't want you anymore. You think I'm supposed—"

Without hesitation, I laid one hand on the back of her head, the other on her lower back, and yanked her toward me, the rest of her words got sucked into my mouth when it locked on hers.

In the heat of the moment, our hands grabbed and pulled at clothes, hair, anything in the way of our lust. I slowly backed her against a tree, my mouth still angrily consuming hers.

She slid her hands up my shirt, running her gentle fingers across my abs. I sucked in a breath and her lure seeped into my nose, filling my lungs with a much needed dose of what I'd been missing.

When she dropped her hands to my pants and unbuttoned my jeans, I grabbed her wrists, halting her. "What are we doing?"

Her chest rose and fell quickly, panting for air. She shook her head, pulling her hands out of my grip. "I don't know, but it's frustrating."

"What do I have to do to fix this? Do you want an apology?"

She shook her head again. "I . . . I don't know."

My eyes traveled over her face. Even in the darkness, it was beyond beautiful.

"I'm truly sorry I lied to you. I really didn't have a choice."

"I just . . " She trailed off, her heart drumming loudly in my ears. "I miss you so much and I don't want to fight with you anymore."

"I miss every piece of you." I raised a hand and ran a thumb across her bottom lip before trailing it down her face, onto her throat, and not stopping until I got to her breast.

Her sweet lure was stronger than it had ever been, causing my dick to throb.

"You smell delicious." I placed a hand against the tree to hold me up as I leaned in, brushing my lips against her neck. "Do you want me to make you come, mama? Is that what you want? Is that what you *need*?"

She let out a breathy whine through her nose and I took it as a yes. I glided my tongue over the smooth skin of her neck before gently sucking it. Her blood pumped fast against my lips, elongating my fangs and causing them to scrape her skin.

"You missed your feeding yesterday," she said, her tone sultry and seductive. "Are you hungry?"

"More than you can imagine," I whispered into the dip of her neck.

Moving my hand across the smooth curve of her hip and down to her thigh, I yanked it up. Her core was warm when I pressed my cock against her.

Lyric's lustful scent became stronger, taking over my senses. I was ready to give her everything she ever wanted when a twig snapped in the distance, switching my brain to red alert.

Of course, it could've been an animal out here in the middle of the woods, but when I glanced in the direction of the sound and saw a soft glow, I knew it was a person.

The faint sound of buttons being pushed fell upon my ears.

Someone had a cell phone.

I dropped Lyric's leg and lifted my finger, pressing it against her lips, letting her know to be quiet. "Stay here."

Nellie's natural scent forced its way into my nostrils.

No fucking way.

Moving as fast as possible wasn't something I did often because it drained my power and required me to feed more frequently, but I was ready to kill the rat.

I bolted toward her, coming up from behind.

"Hey. It's me," Nellie whispered a mere second before I yanked the phone from her ear.

She slung around and I held it in front of her face, bending it in half, causing the glass to shatter. She let out a blood-curdling scream and ran away from me. But I was right behind her, forcefully pulling her into a chokehold.

"Who were you calling?" I asked, and she tapped my arm repeatedly, barely able to breathe.

"Winston!" Lyric shouted, racing toward us. "Let her go."

"I can't. I'm interrogating her."

Nellie clawed at my forearm and just as I was about to snap her neck, Ravage appeared in front of me.

"You can't question her if she's dead, boy!" He tugged at my arm, causing me to let go of Nellie. She ran toward the camp, crying heavily.

Lyric sighed and went after her, leaving me with Ravage who asked, "What the hell is going on?"

"She was making a phone call. Our damn secrets are probably being shared with Venom!"

"And instead of sitting back and listening, you scare the shit out of her?" Ravage shook his head the way he always did when disappointed, and turned away.

I followed, hoping it was finally time to kill the rat.

Back at camp, the music had ceased and all eyes were on Nellie, tears streaming down her cheeks as she clung to Jimmy.

"Why did you do that to her?" Randi asked, stomping up to me with a scowl on her face. "She was calling her mother because she misses her. We all miss our families but you keep us locked up here like we're animals."

That was the most I'd heard the woman talk since she got here, and now, I wish I hadn't. "You can leave anytime you please," I growled, then stepped in close. "Or I can swiftly end your suffering."

"Goddammit, Winston!" Ravage hollered, and I threw my hands out.

"That bitch was in the woods probably calling Venom and everyone wants to point fingers at me like I'm the fucking bad guy," I pounded my fists against my chest, "when I'm the only one taking action while you assholes sit around and watch!"

"I gave her permission to call," Peach said, bringing my heated gaze to her. Her eyes darkened, and it was rare to see Peach actually angry. "You need to go feed. Right damn now!"

"You heard her," Ravage added with a glare.

My blood boiled as I pointed at Nellie. "When she betrays us, and I guarantee she fucking will, everyone will be apologizing to me!"

I took off fast, flames flickering within me as I approached my cabin. Upon entering, I forcefully shut the door and resumed my restless pacing.

The fusion of my uncontainable anger and months of frustration resulted in a scream tearing from my throat. "Fuck! Fuck!"

How can no one else see a rat?

I wished I'd taken two seconds out to see Sage's expression, because I knew damn well, she also believed Nellie was betraying us.

The rage continued to bubble in me, and I took a deep breath, attempting to control it, but it had gone too far. I tore my T-shirt off and balled it up, squeezing it tightly like it was my enemy before tossing it aside.

There were only a couple of things that had the power to soothe me now. Either sinking my fangs into a vein while having mind-blowing sex or hacking into someone's security system. Considering I'd possibly angered Lyric further, I'd have to opt for the latter.

Plopping my ass into my computer chair, I pulled up the programs I had running on my PC, and after clicking around on a few things, I quickly realized hacking wasn't going to help me tonight.

Shit.

Exasperated, I slung myself back into my chair and scrubbed my hands over my face. Deep down, I knew I needed blood and angry sex, and if Lyric wasn't going to give it to me, then I guess I'd have to find someone who would.

My body required a fangster—a human willing to trade sex for a vampire bite. And if I wanted to find one and get back before sunrise, I had to leave town now.

Yanking my motorcycle keys from the coffee cup on my desk, I stood, shoved them into my pocket, and headed into the bathroom. After cleansing my face, I reapplied some deodorant and added a few sprays of cologne to my chest.

As I smoothed out my hair, I eyed myself in the mirror, ensuring I was desirable enough to fuck. Tattoos of flowers, skulls, and snakes covered my arms and chest, and my throat had a large moth inked on it. I grinned, knowing some women found it irresistible.

My gaze went to the stubble on my face before landing on my hazel irises and I immediately thought of Lyric. Her big doe eyes were almost the same color as mine, but had more yellow in them. I'd always felt their color was a flawless reflection of real amber. Of course, they were completely gorgeous too, set below long lashes and perfectly arched brows.

Does it count as cheating if your girlfriend ends the relationship but still loves you?

Lyric's face remained etched in my memory, making it impossible for me to answer my own question with any response other than yes.

A woman had broken my heart by cheating on me and I'd never do that to Lyric. If that meant not sleeping with anyone else until she moved on with her life, then so be it.

The wind left my sails as I headed to my desk and threw the keys back into the coffee cup. With a sigh, I retook my seat and leaned my elbows onto my knees, dropping my head into my hands.

Attempting to reach a place of calm, I took some long deep breaths, relaxing my body. As I inhaled my fifth breath, a hint of Lyric's natural scent entered my nose, then my porch creaked.

I lifted my face toward the door and before she could knock, I said, "Come in."

She slid smoothly inside, the scent of the bonfire mixed with alcohol clung to her, hiding some of her natural scent. She softly shut the door, then nervously leaned against it. "I was just checking on you."

She locked her eyes on me, awaiting my response.

Her stunning features were impossible for me to not notice, including her tousled chestnut hair from where I had my hands in it earlier. Even messy, it somehow made her even more beautiful. My gaze left her face, traveling to her perfect breasts with pebbled nipples visible under a blue crop top. I wasn't surprised she was braless since she rarely wore one unless sparring. Her leggings were low cut, allowing her flat stomach and belly button to peek through, and at her waistband was a tiny bit of her favorite pink laced panties.

Flashbacks of the first time I saw her wearing them filled my brain. I remembered it like it was yesterday, but really, it was the night I fucked her on the kitchen counter. I swallowed the lump in my throat, shoving the memories aside.

That beautiful body is going to be the death of me.

Not being able to stare at something I wasn't sure I could have, I dropped my head, looking at my clasped hands. "I'm fine."

"Nellie had permission to call her mom. Peach and Ravage decided to allow her so they could eavesdrop and possibly gather more information. Plus, they aren't really prisoners."

I snickered, thinking about the ways the situation could've been avoided. "Maybe Peach and Ravage should have involved us in their plans and I wouldn't have choked her. Or maybe we should've interrogated her as soon as we thought she was a rat so I could've killed her already."

"In case you were wondering, she's fine, but she's scared of you now."

I didn't respond to Lyric as I thought about the situation.

When I saw Nellie crying, I felt slightly bad, and I mean slightly. Only a small fraction, almost unnoticeable, and definitely not enough that I wouldn't do it again.

With her potential alliance to Venom, everyone's life in this camp was in constant risk. If killing her would've saved completely innocent people who'd been dragged into this shit show, like April and baby Scarlet, then Nellie's death would've been justified.

Does that make me a villain?

The room stayed silent for what felt like eternity before the wood floor creaked. "I forgive you for lying," Lyric said, moving toward me. "I know you did it to protect Sage, because she would've insisted on going, but she wasn't ready for any missions. She's barely ready now."

I nodded, still avoiding her eyes.

"And you being the kind of person who risks pissing off his girlfriend to save her best friend's life . . . makes me love you even more."

Now in front of me, she laid her soft hands on my cheeks, forcing me to gaze upwards. Her hooded eyes conveyed everything she wanted as she peered down at me.

"And it's okay if you don't love me, Winston, because like we said before, we can be happy for now." I opened my mouth to say something, but she moved her hands to my shoulders, shoving me farther back into the chair. "I know you want me and that's enough."

She lowered herself onto my lap and I let out a light moan. "You have no idea how bad I want you, mama."

"Yes, I do," she whispered seductively only inches from my face. "I can feel how bad you want me."

Lyric was so mesmerizing I hadn't even realized my cock throbbed, pressing hard against my pants, until she pointed it out.

With a sexual power I'd barely seen from her before, she grabbed my wrists and forced my hands to clasp her breasts. "Touch me, fuck me, feed off me. Do whatever you want. As long as we're together, I don't care."

She rocked her hips forward, eliciting a small moan from us both. The frantic need to be inside of her swirled in my groin and I slid my hands to the bottom of her crop top, pulling it off her. Lyric's breasts perfectly matched her body with larger brown nipples and areolas. I couldn't resist sucking one into my mouth, and she let out a whimper, digging her nails into my shoulders.

Her lure was strong, the sweet lilacs seducing my senses as much as she was, causing my balls to ache. Unable to endure it any longer, I let go of her breasts, only for her to immediately seize my hands, pinning them against my chest.

"Keep them there."

I lifted a brow. "But you told me to do whatever I want."

Lyric laid her finger over my lips, shushing me.

Despite being the possessive one in our relationship, I was completely accepting of her taking charge of my body. My heart, on the other hand . . . wasn't ready to be released to her yet.

She slid off my lap and kneeled in front of me before removing my black and white Adidas, tossing them to the side. Her fingers moved elegantly as she trailed them up my legs like she was on a stage playing piano in front of a million people, not stopping until she got to my groin. She slowly unbuttoned my jeans and lowered the zipper, causing my dick to twitch, dying to be set free. Moving her hands to my side, she pulled on my pants and I lifted myself to expedite their removal.

Her soft breasts pressed against my thighs as she leaned in and took my shaft in her hand. I had the best view ever, barely breathing as I watched her slowly kiss and lick her way up my length until she reached the head of my cock. She sucked it into her mouth and I hissed in a breath through my teeth.

The warm wetness made my muscles tense and my hands instinctively went to her hair, but before I had a chance to tighten my fingers into it, she swatted at my thigh.

My hands trembled and I needed somewhere to put them other than my chest, so I clutched the edge of the chair tightly, holding on for dear life as she took me completely in. Her cheeks hollowed out and the tightness of the hold she had on me caused a tingling sensation in my lower abdomen.

"Fuck, mama. You need to stop."

Even though I was dying to come in her mouth, I desperately needed to be inside of her, so I suppressed my orgasm for a few more seconds before she finally released her grip, leaving me completely breathless.

She used my thighs to push herself off the ground, then took a few steps backward. Her moves were sensual and slow as she peeled off her leggings, revealing those beautiful, pink lace panties. I wanted to grab her, yank her forward, and rip them off with my teeth, but since she was in charge now, I kept my hands to myself.

Tucking her thumbs into the edge of her panties, she slid them down her smooth legs and when she stood, her perfect pussy was in my line of sight. But what caught my attention was her pubic hair or should I say lack of it.

The last time we'd had sex a few days ago, Lyric had complained about not being able to go into town to get waxed. But from the looks of it, she'd managed to perfectly groom herself. Not too short, not too long, but exactly how she liked it.

Then I realized she'd planned this entire evening out in advance.

Not only had Lyric shaved, but she also wore her hair down, had on a sexy outfit, and danced in front of a bonfire all to get my attention. Little did she know, I didn't need her to do anything for me to want her. She'd completely mesmerized me since the day we met by merely existing.

With the way her hooded eyes gazed into mine as she stood shamelessly naked in front of me, she could fuck me blind for all I cared.

"If you don't get your sexy ass over here, I'm going to have to disobey your commands and take matters into my own hands."

She laughed as she stalked forward, then planted a leg on either side of the chair and slowly lowered herself onto my lap. My cock slipped smoothly between her soaked pussy lips, causing us both to moan.

"Damn, you're wet."

I lifted my hands to touch her and she slammed them onto my chest. "I said to keep them there."

"Holy fuck, I'm the luckiest man in the world."

She tightened her lips, her eyes conveying the power she now held. "Do you hear me, Winston?"

I had no clue how I was supposed to answer her, so I said the first thing that came to mind. "Umm, yes, ma'am."

She pushed herself onto her knees and reached between us, sliding my full length inside of her. Her cunt was warm and tight, the walls clamping onto me. I secured my fists against my chest, forcing myself not to move as she laid claim on my dick.

With the grace of a goddess, she moved her hips slowly at first, drawing moans from us both. For a while I stared at her, enjoying the change in her facial features when the pleasure took over. I don't know what awakened the sexual lioness she'd become, but it enthralled me.

Gradually, she increased the speed of her movements and her breaths became ragged. My fingers were almost numb when I clenched them tighter against my chest, restraining myself from touching as her orgasm drew near. Sweat droplets formed on her chest and the sound of her heart thundered faster in my sensitive ears.

"Oh shit," she panted out, her pussy muscles tightening around me. "Touch me now."

Finally.

I grabbed her hips and assisted her as she rode out her ecstasy. Her loud moans softened as she sucked in deep breaths, her muscles relaxing. She melted into my embrace, emitting small whimpers as her wetness flowed onto me.

I caressed her back, giving her a moment to recover before I said, "Now it's my turn."

Holding her tight, I stood and pushed the chair to the side, then turned around and sat her on the edge of my desk. I dropped my thumb to her swollen clit, circling it as I slowly moved inside of her. With a moan, she firmly grasped my shoulders, her nails piercing my skin.

While entangled in our ecstasy, groaning and gasping for air, I had an epiphany. I know . . . horrible timing.

Although my feelings for Lyric hadn't developed into love yet, we were about to embark on an immensely perilous mission tomorrow—one I wanted her to survive. And she would . . . if she fed from me.

"Drink my blood," I panted out in between breaths.

"Wh . . . what?"

"It'll make you strong for the mission, but if something happens, you might turn."

She pushed on my chest, halting my movements.

Our eyes locked, my heart thumping in my ears as I awaited her answer.

"Is this your way of saying I love you?" she breathed out.

The act of sharing vampire blood during sex was a highly sensual and intimate experience—one I was dying to have with Lyric—but if she got killed, she'd turn. And that was more important to me.

"This is my way of saying I care for you so much, I don't want you to die."

With a sudden force, she grabbed my face and passionately kissed me as she grinded against my cock. We continued fucking and when I knew we were both close to losing ourselves in the paroxysm of pleasure, I pulled my lips from hers.

"Is that a yes?"

She stared into my eyes before finally whispering, "Absolutely."

I pulled my dick out of her and lifted her from the desk, setting her on the floor. "Bend over, mama."

"Is your blood going to taste bad?" she asked, turning around.

"You won't even notice the flavor through the raging orgasm you're about to have when I bite you."

She bent forward, placing her hands on the desk to keep herself steady, gracing my eyes with a perfect view of her beautiful ass. "Those are my favorite."

Even though she couldn't see it, I wore a proud smile.

Our sex life was already perfect in my eyes, but this was about to take it to a whole new level. I spread her ass cheeks, lined up my dick, and slid it into her juicy pussy from behind. After a few thrusts, I lifted my right wrist to my mouth and pierced it with my fangs.

Blood trickled from me as I curled my arm around Lyric's head, putting my wrist in front of her face. "Don't suck yet," I said, tapping the vein in her neck. "Not until you start coming."

Leaning forward, I aligned my fangs with her vein and sunk them into her skin, causing her to gasp. Her delicious blood pooled into my mouth as her pussy pulsed around my cock.

"Oh, god," she screamed, before she fastened her mouth onto my wrist, gloriously sucking blood from my body.

Each swallow I took sent pleasure swimming through my veins, pushing me higher and higher through the realm of ecstasy. My balls tightened, my orgasm taking over my body as I released her vein. A loud moan conjured from the pit of my stomach, ripping itself from my throat before warm cum shot from me.

My breaths came out ragged, my heart rate at an all-time high and I slouched forward, laying across her back, my dick softening inside of her. "Are you okay?"

"Uh huh," she whimpered, and I chuckled.

"Let's get cleaned up."

I withdrew my cock from her, and she attempted to get up, but she was in full-blown vampire venom ecstasy.

"Happy for now," she whispered, her eyes glistening as she wobbled.

I grinned, wiping the blood on her chin off with my thumb. "Happy for now."

Knowing she could barely walk in this condition, I scooped her into my arms and carried her to the bathroom for a hot shower before we went to bed early. We had a huge mission tomorrow, and I really hoped revenge tasted as good as the blood on my lips.

CHAPTER 23
SAGE

Last night was definitely one for the books in terms of weirdness. When the witches left, everyone, except for me, felt a sense of euphoria. Some were talking and others were dancing around the fire, while I quietly observed. Winnie almost killed Nellie and I secretly wished I'd been the one to choke her before the party finally ended with everyone returning to their cabins shortly before the sun came up.

Since we were leaving for the hotel in only a few hours, I'd awakened before the sun set, showered, and packed my bags. A shaky breath left me as I descended my cabin steps, not ready for what I was about to do next.

The minute I stepped off the porch, heading to Peach's, Lyric yelled, "Sagelynn, wait for me."

I whipped around and put my hands on my hips, squinting as the sun glared in my eyes. "Hurry up. I'm not standing here all day."

"I have something important to tell you." She bolted toward me with a huge smile, which dropped when her brows pinched. "Where're you going this early?"

"Peach's."

She cocked her head and I noticed her hair was extremely messy.

Sex hair.

"Is she even awake? There's still an hour before it gets dark."

"She said she always gets up before the sun sets." I nervously bit my lip and Lyric crossed her arms, eyeing me.

"Save yourself the trouble, Sage, and tell me the secret now because you and I both know you'll cave later."

A rush of warmth flushed my cheeks as I determined whether I should disclose the truth. But she was right—I would tell her, eventually.

"After Winnie dragged you off into the woods, I'd mentioned to Peach about how nice it would be to have one of those immune booster injections we used to get weekly from Venom. You know, the ones Ravage said had vampire blood in them."

Her head tilted, eyeing me suspiciously. "And?"

"Peach mentioned consuming vampire blood would produce a similar outcome, possibly better, for one to two weeks."

Lyric leaned in closer to me, her eyes narrowed. "What else?"

I huffed because we both knew I wasn't saying the *whole* truth. "Then she offered to feed me, and I accepted, but she also said if I die with her blood in my system that the chances of me coming back as a vampire are very high."

She uncrossed her arms, her back stiffening. "How high?"

"Like ninety-nine percent."

"Oh." Lyric got quiet for a second, her eyes trailing over my face as if she was reading my mind. "So, let me guess. You're worried Luka will be mad at you for not saving him sooner, or because he gave himself up to save you. And then you'll die, actually become a vampire and you'll have to spend eternity pining over the only man you've ever really loved, and that's too much shit to worry about at once."

"I, uh . . . " I looked toward the ground, kicking the dirt beneath my feet. "You really should charge people for psychic readings."

Lyric laid her hand on my shoulder, bringing my gaze back to her. "Stop worrying about what *might* happen in the future and make the best decision for today."

I snickered, rolling my eyes. "Do you really think it's that simple?"

"I know you're mocking me, but it genuinely is. Make the best decisions your brain will allow you to make today and deal with tomorrow's problems tomorrow."

As I stared into Lyric's beautiful hazel eyes, I couldn't resist the urge to make her happy. Although it would take a lot of work on my part to get myself into that type of mindset, her advice somehow made sense.

"Then I choose to become a vampire if I die. At least, for today."

Lyric squealed before pointing toward Winnie's cabin and lowering her voice. "Good, because I drank his blood last night and he didn't tell me about the ninety-nine percent thing. So if it happens, I don't want to spend eternity without you."

My mouth fell open and my eyes widened as my thoughts took a hard right, bringing up memories of a stress ball I once had. It looked like a dog's head and when I squeezed it, the eyes bugged out. The thing gave me the creeps, so I avoided using it, but I was certain that's exactly how I appeared at that moment—an overly compressed stress ball.

"Wh . . . wh . . . " this new information made me fumble on my words, "when were you going to tell me?"

"Actually, that's why I stopped you. I was going to talk you into drinking Winnie's blood again, since you did it after you wrecked his bike, just in case. But the problem solved itself." She clapped her hands excitedly, like we were now *blood brothers* or something. "I gotta go get these tangles out of my hair, shower, and still pack. I'll see you when you wake up."

Lyric strolled off, leaving me feeling dumbfounded.

After she'd left the party last night, I'd figured she and Winnie had made up, especially after seeing the sex hair she was sporting, but I hadn't banked on them becoming partners for life. I mean, I know she wouldn't have to stay with Winnie for eternity, but she'd have to deal with him for it because he'd be her origin.

That's why I decided to take Peach up on her offer. She was a friend, someone I could trust, and not someone I was dating. Not that I assumed Luka and I would break up, but if there's one thing life has taught me, it's that everything had an expiration date.

It technically wasn't my business if Lyric wanted Winnie to be her origin, but I was still worried about my friend getting her heart broken . . . or dying and becoming a vampire.

I let out a heavy sigh and made my way toward Peach's cabin, praying that none of us were making harsh decisions out of fear.

An hour later, I'd drank Peach's blood, taken a forty-five minute nap, and the sun had set. My phone beeped and it was a text from Winnie telling me it was time to go.

With a deep breath, I grabbed the one bag Winnie allowed me to bring, tossed it on my shoulder, and made my way outside. I shut the door behind me and when I turned around, Vivi was standing on my porch.

"Winnie's still not budging. He insists I have to stay here to help Drag protect the camp." She rolled her eyes. "I know he's only leaving me behind because he's afraid I'll mess up the mission."

"Even though I'd love for you to go with us, I do actually feel better with you staying here." I lowered my voice. "Especially with the concerns of a certain spy."

"I would like to be here if anything goes down, so I agree with that, but I'm not going to guarantee I won't drain her of every ounce of blood if she pisses me off. One less mouth to feed I guess."

Vivi shrugged and I laughed.

"I'll be jealous if you get to."

"Are you ready?" Ravage asked as he and Drag walked past my porch, and I nodded.

"Shit, I gotta go."

Vivi stood in silence for a few seconds, not knowing what to say before she sighed, opening her arms. "Give me a hug, in case you die."

I attempted to keep the surprised look off my face as I stepped into her embrace—and even though I'm not big on hugs, I really hoped it wasn't our last.

"I will do my best to find Strike," I whispered, pulling away.

"I just know you guys are going to find them both and once the brothers reunite, they'll be an unstoppable force."

Back in October, Mannie had tortured me for only a few short hours, yet the impact it had on me would last my entire life. I feared it would happen to Luka and Strike, and I lacked the courage to tell Vivi there was a high possibility that both of their personalities might be different after being imprisoned. Especially Strike, who'd been captive for over a year and a half.

A small smile pulled at my cheeks, locking away my concerns. "I'll see you when we get back." My stomach twisted as I headed toward the parking lot. Winnie was standing in front of my Jeep, groping Lyric, and I hollered, "Get a room."

Winnie broke the suction he had on my friend's face and cocked his head toward me. "I hope you finally shaved. Luka won't know what to do with that forest you've been growing."

I halted myself so fast, my bag slid off my arm.

With a fanged grin, he showed an unmistakable aura of arrogance, and I wanted to punch him. "I'll take that as a no."

I slang my bag back onto my shoulder. "Shut up, Winnie."

Lyric smacked his arm and I giggled, heading toward the back of my Jeep. After tossing my bag in the trunk, I hopped into the driver's seat and gripped the steering wheel, my thoughts running rampant.

When's the last time I shaved?

I'd gone so long without Luka, I'd completely stopped taking care of myself. After thinking about it, I deduced it to be a day or two before Venom took Luka, which was the end of November. It was now May and . . .

Oh my god! I haven't groomed in six months!

When we find Luka, he may not recognize me through the leg hair I'm sporting. A deep sigh escaped me as I pondered something else.

Not once had I thought about sex since that night. I was a big advocate for self pleasure, and I hadn't even masturbated, which was way less frequent than my normal once to twice a week.

The passenger door opened and Lyric gracefully slid in, her brows drawing together. "Why do you have that look on your face? Oh crap. You really didn't shave."

I shook my head. "If my life was equivalent to my leg hair, then it's been a long, dark ride."

Lyric giggled, then placed her hand on my arm. "It's okay, Sage. Maybe you can do it at the hotel."

"It's not just that." I turned in my seat so I could face this problem head on. "I haven't thought about sex since Luka. Not once. I haven't even touched myself. Is my vagina broken?"

Lyric's facial expression became worried and I thought it was adorable she cared so much about my womanhood. "Oh, I don't know. I really hope not."

The rear passenger door opened, letting in a slight breeze as Winnie got in. "I hope not either. I don't think they make a cream for that."

I tightened my lips. "We already said you're not riding with us."

"I have to. I won't be able to hear the girl gossip over the roar of the engine, plus that van smells like fish."

A shiver rolled through me thinking about a fish market my grandmother used to take me to when I was little. I always hated the smell. "Eww, why?"

"Heston, Demi, and Lane caught a bunch of catfish and brought them back. Drag's gonna clean 'em, then Laren and Kimber are gonna fry them up. I'm only slightly jealous that I won't be here to eat them, but at least I get to kill people. Hopefully."

The other rear door opened and Lynx got in with a sigh. "Go ride with the boys, Winnie."

"It's Winston."

"Get the hell out before I—"

"Geezus, Lynx. Fine." Winnie opened the door with a scowl, slamming it on his departure. A grin replaced his angry face as Lyric rolled down her window and he leaned in, kissing her goodbye. "I'll see you there, mama."

Ravage pulled up next to us and honked the horn. "Damn it, boy, get your ass in this van!"

Winnie snickered, then squinted his eyes at me. "Drive like a normal person for once, Sage Stick. I'd like my woman to arrive safe and sound." He tapped the side of my Jeep and backed away, pointing into the backseat. "You're evil, Lynx. Pure evil!"

"Winston!" Ravage screamed and we laughed as Winnie bolted to the sliding door on the side of the van.

I started the car, meeting Lynx's eyes in the rear-view mirror. Ravage had assigned her the preparations, and I really wanted to ensure we didn't leave anything behind. "Did you get everything on the list?"

She held her hand up, ticking off her fingers as she spoke. "Kimber and I packed weapons, ammo, handcuffs, and a cooler filled with blood bags. Winnie said he has all the instructions Naomi had planned stored in his head. He also brought some stuff he said we needed. So, we're good to go. With all that shit in the van, hopefully Ravage doesn't get pulled over or someone will be eating a cop for dinner."

I attempted to ignore that possibility and wiped my clammy hands onto my jeans before re-gripping the steering wheel. This was the moment I'd been waiting for and my twisting stomach was going to constantly remind me the entire drive.

Ravage pulled out of the parking area and I followed suit. In approximately five hours, we'd arrive at a hotel near White Sands Missile Range and sleep one day before we embarked on the riskiest mission any of us had ever done.

CHAPTER 24

LUKA

Reality used to be a term for describing something real, not the magical aspects of an occurrence. But when reality becomes blurred by medicine-induced hallucinations, it's difficult to differentiate between what's actually real and what's merely a dream.

A small sliver of sunlight had barely cast its ray onto the world below while I relaxed in a rocking chair on my front porch, its warmth now eager to embrace the awakening plants and animals after a chilly fall night.

"Luka?" Sage whispered, and I shifted my gaze toward the sound of her heavenly voice. Despite her tousled hair and sleepy appearance, she looked more beautiful than ever.

"Good morning, my love."

She stifled a yawn before wiping the sleep from her eyes. "What are you doing out here?"

Wondering myself, I glanced down at my favorite Star Wars mug in my hand, then to the horizon ahead of me. "I'm drinking coffee and watching this beautiful sunrise."

She dipped her head down and picked at her nails, a behavior she often did when anxious. "You can't be out here. Come back to bed."

My gaze traveled down her body and I smiled at the T-shirt that extended to her mid-thigh. "You look sexy wearing my clothes."

"You can't be out here, Luka."

I turned my head, inspecting my surroundings before my brows pinched. "I'm sitting on the porch of the house I own, so why can't I be?"

"You need to come back. Come back to me."

My forehead tightened, more confusion settling in me. "How can I come back when I never left?"

"Come back, Luka. Don't die on me!" she screamed, seconds before a sting radiated across my cheek. She had slapped me, yet I never saw her move.

Her strange actions puzzled me, her words contradicting her composed manner. "Why would I die, Princess?"

"Give him more blood! Force him if you have to."

My chest tightened as she shouted nonsensical words. Needing to comfort her, I attempted to place the mug down on the small marble-top table next to me, but my fingers refused to let me release it. In my attempt to stand up, I found myself unable to, an unknown force mysteriously locking my knees.

"Luka, please!" she screamed, but this time it didn't sound like Sage anymore. The hauntingly familiar voice sent shivers down my spine.

The sun's rays brightened, making it unbearable to keep my eyes open. Despite my attempt to close them tightly, something pulled my lids back, forcing me to stare directly into the intensely bright light.

"Bill, his pupils are dilated. Inject him with the serum now!"

"But it could kill him, Doctor Ishman!"

"If we don't do it now, he will die anyway and our hours of research will be for nothing!"

Someone released my eyelids and my entire world went black. I frantically felt around, looking for my girlfriend.

Sage! Where is Sage?

Gray pulsing shadows floated around me, each one attempting to steal my breaths before engulfing me, revoking my license to live.

My heart began to slow, the dark void taking over my senses.

An icy coldness washed over me, sending a chill through my veins and slowing my movements until I . . .

disappeared . . .

from . . .

existence . . .

CHAPTER 25
SAGE

We got to the hotel around three am last night. Ravage grabbed some food for us, and we chowed down while going over the plans once more. Lyric and Winnie crashed in my room. Lynx slept in the bed with me. Marcus and Zeke took the other room, and I don't think Ravage ever went to bed. My emotions were so high, I'd barely slept a wink myself.

Now, the fear of dying lingered in the air before I even had my coffee.

The mission we'd been preparing for had finally arrived, but strangely, I felt completely unprepared. A small bit of worry mixed with a high dose of anticipation tickled my nervous stomach as I sat on my hotel bed, listening to Ravage go over the plans one last time before we left.

He stood in the middle of my room, cracking his knuckles. "I'm going to explain the rules again. If anyone finds Luka, you feed him a blood bag, but only for thirty seconds at a time. And whatever you do, don't let him feed from you. If he's been starved into submission, which I'm sure he has, then he won't be able to stop. He'll drain you completely dry."

As I wondered why Strike hadn't been mentioned, Ravage's eyes locked onto me, and I instinctively recoiled from his penetrating stare.

"You hear me, Sage? You can't let him feed from you. Once his fangs pierce you, you'll be useless, and he'll drink until you die."

Everyone in the room glared at me as if I had fire shooting out of my asshole or something.

Erik leaned against the wall, his face telling me to just agree.

Zeke sat in the only chair in the room, his fingers laced together, pressed under his chin, his expression unreadable.

Lynx's forehead wrinkled, a look of concern on her face.

Winnie dropped one knee to the beige carpet, his eyes conveying he wouldn't believe me even if I did say yes. And he was correct. If my only option was using my blood to save Luka, I'd happily die.

Marcus crossed his arms, leaning back in a relaxed way. "Sagelynn, answer Ravage."

I kneaded my knuckles into the top of my thighs and Lyric laid her hand on top of one stopping me. The gentle touch assured me I could do this.

Taking a cleansing breath, I nodded. "I understand. If I feed him, I die."

"What about Strike? Do the same rules apply?" Lyric asked, her questions mirroring my previous thoughts.

Ravage's eyes shifted toward Winnie, indicating he had some undisclosed information.

"Just tell us, Pooh Bear."

Winnie rotated the plugs in his gauged ears, something I noticed he did when nervous. "No one can tell my sister because she'd kill us, but I went through every Venom file I obtained and Strike wasn't on the list. I even checked under his real name, Daniel Draven."

The news hit me with an overwhelming force. I tightened my fist and pressed it to my lips, my heart fluttering in my chest.

Vivi had convinced herself that we would safely rescue her man, but now the probability of that happening was very slim, and it pained me knowing she'd have to continue with her suffering.

As I wondered why Winnie hadn't disclosed this information to her, I suddenly realized the answer. The prolonged separation from Strike had an intense, emotional impact on Vivi and was the main reason Winnie and Ravage didn't want her doing this mission. Without hesitation, she would set fire to VRC or do anything else she deemed necessary to locate Strike.

And I didn't blame her. If they had said I couldn't come, I would have stolen another motorcycle and been waiting at the hotel when they arrived.

Winnie passed out small earbuds for communication, then dug into a black duffle bag. He pulled out a handful of badges, and only handed them to the humans. "These will get you past security. Remember not to use anyone's real name while we're in there."

He handed me mine and I clipped it on my black T-shirt. "Where did you get these?"

"I picked them up from Naomi yesterday," Ravage stated, a huge grin engulfing his face. "When Winnie described what she looked like, he'd forgotten to mention how sexy she was. And tall. I'm six five and it's rare to stand next to a woman only a few inches shorter. Made me want to rip her clothes off."

"Maybe her head, but not her clothes," Winnie said, eyeing Ravage.

"I don't think she's a threat to us, son. But if she is, we'll know. The truth always reveals itself." Ravage glanced at his vintage silver watch and I immediately wondered how old it was . . . and how old *he* was. "Get armed. We're leaving in twenty minutes."

After he left the hotel room, I moseyed over to the other bed lined with guns, picked up my Beretta, and slid it into the holster hanging from my hip. I was used to back carrying so I hated it, but it was how normal Venom guards carried, and since I was pretending to be one today, I'd have to play the part.

In an attempt to conceal my identity, I had already pulled my hair back tightly into a small bun at the nape of my neck and donned a breton cap, which was one of the few approved hats for Venom society members.

I tucked my black T-shirt into my black Venom-issued tactical pants before sliding on the matching jacket. "Where did you get all this stuff, Pooh Bear?"

"Also, Naomi."

I furrowed my brows. *Naomi is being awful helpful.*

"You and Erik were lucky to be a part of the field crew," Lyric said, racking her gun and sliding it into her holster. "You guys could wear whatever you wanted to blend in with civilians and we had to dress like this every day."

Winnie pulled Lyric close to him. "I think it's sexy, mama. You're like an adorable Rambo."

Lyric squished up her nose and I laughed. "I'm going to see if it's still raining. I'll meet you guys outside."

When I went to leave the room, Marcus stepped in front of me, placing his hands on my shoulders and leaning into my face. "You can do this. I have faith in you." He pulled me into a hug and whispered, "I love you, Sagelynn."

"I love you, too."

He let go and moved to the side, opening the door for me. I left the hotel room, my mind flooding with the lies I told as I took the elevator down.

Well, I guess they weren't technically lies. I only said I understood Luka would kill me if I fed him, not that I wouldn't do it.

Upon entering the lobby, a heaviness settled in my chest, a foreboding sensation growing in the core of my being. Although I knew how strong and trained my friends were, there was a trickle of fear warning me something horrible was going to happen. I wasn't sure if it was from my anxiety or because I had supposed witch abilities. If I did, now would be a good time for them to kick in.

Outside, I found Ravage under the hotel awning, leaning against the building, smoking a cigarette. "I think those things have a surgeon general warning. A man of your age should know better."

He tipped his chin toward me, sporting a fanged smile. "Your sarcasm must be the reason my boy fell so hard for you."

A thunderstorm had rolled through, chilling the air, so I zipped my jacket closed. "And here I thought it was because I tried to kill him."

He took a long drag, pursed his lips, and blew it out on a nod. "I see you know a quick way into a man's heart. With and without a stake."

I smiled before letting my thoughts take over. "Vivi and Peach said that I knew Luka was alive because of the pulling. Do you think I can use that to help find Luka?"

"It doesn't work like that. Vivi spent months attempting to use it to find Strike. You have to get really close before it alerts you. It's weird and extremely unreliable." His eyes hollowed, his expression turning grave as he dropped the cigarette to the ground, extinguishing it under the toe of his large black boot. "You do know there's a good chance Luka won't be the same person he was when he went in there."

I crossed my arms and leaned against the building, kicking my foot back and pressing it against the wall. "I do, and I'm ready for it."

"Caging a man like that, well, it'll completely change him. He may be callous. Completely emotionless." Ravage shook his head, almost as if he knew exactly what Luka was going through. "Shit, the little bastard might fool us all and come out completely unfazed."

I giggled. "One could only hope."

He ran his hand along his thick, dark beard and there was a sparkle of fear in his eyes. The kind of fear that only comes when you truly love someone. "His changes may affect his ability to love you the way you deserve."

I nodded, turning my attention to the flickering lamp post in the parking lot, the drizzling rain dancing under the glow of the light. Typically, I loved thunderstorms, but this particular one seemed orchestrated to slow our progress. "I know. And it's something I'll have to deal with."

"I hope you also understand that if it does happen, you deserve what's best for you, even if it means letting him go. It's okay to move on and live your human life knowing there was nothing you could have done."

I swallowed down my uneasiness, tilting my head toward him. "I don't think I can do that."

"You owe it to yourself to at least try. The only one you should be living for is yourself. Everyone else in your life is just a bonus."

Ravage looked away and I stared at his side profile, realizing he'd been through something similar in his life, but *he* was the one who had to leave. It may have been a long time ago, but the pain he had endured stayed with him like a birthmark. It would never be buried, clinging on like a reminder of his failures.

Something I was very familiar with.

He glanced at his watch and let out a long sigh. "It's time to go."

"How did you do it? How did you leave?" I asked, and he locked his dark eyes on me.

"You're an exceptionally perceptive girl. It must be the witch's blood running through your veins." He walked past me, heading toward the van.

"That doesn't answer my question, Ravage."

He stopped, letting out a hard sigh. "Moving on was never an option for me. I chose to remove myself from the situation. That's all." He glanced over his shoulder, his gaze on me. "I know you're strong enough to do the same if you have to." Without another word, he hopped in the driver's seat of the van.

I squeezed my eyes shut and clenched my lips to prevent them from trembling.

Though I was never one to stay in an abusive relationship, if Luka had transformed into a different person, a heartless one, I doubted my ability to leave him.

The hotel door opened and my friends came out, and as I watched each one head toward our vehicles, I once again prayed to whoever was listening to keep watch over them.

If anyone has to die, please take me.

Lyric stopped next to my Jeep and waved me over. "Come on, Sagelynn."

I pushed whatever fears I'd carried with me like unnecessary baggage aside, took a deep breath, and headed to meet the witches.

And hopefully rescue my man.

CHAPTER 26

WINNIE

The rain finally stopped and we were five miles away from the bottom of the mountain when my phone rang. "Hello?"

"Technology is not my strong suit. Magic, on the other hand, is a completely different narrative."

My forehead clenched at the familiar voice. "Shayla?"

"I sense you are close. My sister shared our location with you. Everyone must get out of the vehicles for this. I look forward to seeing you there."

The phone went silent and I released a hard breath. I hated the way the witches were always so vague about things.

When I pulled up the location Shayla sent and realized it was only a few minutes away, I wondered why they'd changed the plans because, from my understanding, we were meeting them closer to VRC.

"What's up, son?" Ravage asked from the driver's seat.

"That was Shayla. She said to meet her at this location and we all have to get out of the cars. Take a left up here."

Ravage turned onto a dirt road surrounded by trees, and I texted Lyric, letting her know the extremely vague plan before I asked, "Do you know what we're doing, Ravage?"

"Shayla said she had a plan but couldn't say more until we got here. Something about other witches seeing her actions before she did them."

I raised a brow, wondering if she knew the witches who had spelled the wards surrounding the Vampire Research Center.

Three miles ahead, Shayla stood on the side of the road, gleaming in the headlights of the van, and as Ravage parked, she strolled off toward the trees.

"Where the hell is she going?" I asked no one in particular, opening my car door.

Zeke, Marcus, and Erik got out of the back of the van just as Lyric, Sage, and Lynx exited the Jeep.

Lyric slid her hand into mine, intertwining our fingers. "What's going on? Why are we meeting them so soon? It's another thirty minutes away."

I shrugged, pulling her behind me as we followed Ravage.

Under the canopy of the trees stood Shayla, dressed in a long black cloak, her two witch sisters who matched her attire, and a stranger.

"Hello, ladies." Ravage strolled right up to Shayla, took her hand gently in his, and kissed the back of it. "To what do we owe the pleasure?"

"Alfred Johnathon Kingston, you never fail to amuse me." Shayla pulled her hand away and I chuckled at the fact she used what Ravage liked to call his government name.

"Alfred?" Sage questioned, her brows pinched. "That's less badass."

Ravage snickered. "What do you know, girl? There were kings named Alfred." He shook his head, staring at the stranger hiding in the shadows five feet behind the witches. "Who is she?"

"Come forth, my dear."

The woman did as Shayla instructed and stepped into the moonlight. She didn't have a matching cloak, but she had a book tucked under her arm.

"Hi," she murmured low, her cheeks reddening as she nervously pushed her mousy brown hair behind her ear.

She looked to be in her late twenties and had a casual appearance. The long brown skirt hanging to her ankles and the knit top so high it almost covered her collarbone reminded me of those shy students in school who'd rarely speak and aced every test.

"This is Crystal Blue Waters. She's new to our coven and needs the experience."

The newcomer nervously glanced between us. "You can call me Blue."

"Were your parents wanting to get you beat up as a child?" I asked with a smirk.

She pulled the book from under her arm and grasped it tightly between her hands while she simply said, "Sprecta."

It felt like a boulder hit me, smacking against the front of my body and knocking the wind from my lungs before I flew backwards, landing on my back.

I jumped to my feet, fangs bared before Lyric even yelled, "Hey!"

Sage pulled her dagger out, going into a defensive stance.

The newcomer smiled, cocking her head. "You can't really bully a witch."

"Put your fangs away, son," Ravage commanded more calmly than he normally did before glancing around at our crew. "All of you take a damn breath."

"Blue is a Book Darling," Shayla stated with a wave of her hand. "Unlike my other sisters, her powers require her to use spells. She is here to practice with us."

Ravage crossed his arms. "And what are we doing out here, Shayla? I thought we were going to meet closer to VRC."

"I said the edge of the wards and we are here. Beyond this is dread and gloom for any human and no entry for supernaturals." She glanced at each of us from head to toe. "Lovely attire. Not only must you look the part on the outside, you must be suitable on the inside."

"You are not residents, you are not lords, you must be safe to cross the wards," Cece sang, and my brows rose.

"So, what you're saying is, you're going to make it to where we can enter?" I asked, and Shayla nodded.

"This shall not halt you much longer."

The four witches circled us. Shayla, Delaney, and Cece raised their hands to the sky, and Blue Book Bitch, as I now called her in my head, gripped her book tightly and chanted a bunch of words, none of them sounding familiar.

This went on for about a minute before the witches relaxed, and Shayla said, "It is done."

"We appreciate you taking the time to do this," Ravage expressed and Shayla smiled.

"Before you go, we must tell the silver some important things." Shayla stepped up to Sage, taking her hand. "I can sense the blood in you. We are delighted to see you took the offer like we suggested. Heather has powerful blood. You are safe with her."

Sage's eyes bulged as Shayla revealed her secrets. Of course, Lyric had already informed me about Peach feeding Sage her blood, so I wasn't surprised.

Delaney walked past me, heading to Sage, and I was glad she didn't have the damn snake out. "Listen to your instincts, my silver. Less is more."

"Less is more, less is more," Cece chanted. "Small raindrops bring back life while large rivers will end it."

I snickered, annoyed by the vagueness of the witches and the amount of time being consumed. And probably because I got knocked on my ass. "Are we done yet?"

"The sun will be our enemy in the morning and we'll be racing it." Ravage held his hand out to the new bitch. "It was nice meeting you."

"Likewise." She shook it with a smile before turning to me and tilting her head. "Blue Book Bitch is an awfully long nickname for me. You should think about shortening to BB. It rolls off the tongue easier. Kind of like Pooh Bear."

My mouth fell open and Cece bursted out with laughter. "Blue Book Bitch is an exquisite nickname!"

"This is why I don't like witches." I shook my head, and turned toward the car.

"It was nice meeting you," Blue called out from behind me, and I ignored her. "Sorry I knocked you on your ass!"

Once back in the vehicle, I slammed the door shut, seething.

Fucking witches.

Ravage entered the van, started it up, and we continued driving toward VRC. We were only a few miles away when he pulled over again to stash Sage's Jeep.

We got out and waited for the ladies to join us, conversing about the only two bulletproof vests we had, leaving the other humans unprotected.

"This one will only fit Erik," Ravage said, handing him a vest before turning toward Marcus and Zeke. "And you two can fight over this one."

The brothers stared at it, Marcus shaking his head. "I'm not taking it."

"Me either," Zeke stated. They both crossed their arms and glared at each other, being stubborn as fuck. Even though the brothers looked similar, this was the first time they'd appeared to be real siblings.

Erik took off his jacket and held it out to me. "Can you hold this?"

I rolled my eyes and yanked it from him, still seething over the witches.

Erik slid the body armor over his black T-shirt, and latched the sides, leaving them loose. Marcus stuffed two IV bags filled with blood under the vest, hoping to get them past security. The rest of the blood stayed in the cooler in case one of us vampires needed it after the mission. Erik pulled the fasteners tighter and I handed back his jacket.

"Are we all supposed to wear ballistic vests?" Sage asked, strolling up with Lyric and Lynx behind her.

Ravage let out a hard sigh and clicked his tongue. "Naomi could only get two and since there's five of you humans, I left them in the van figuring y'all could fight over who got to wear them. But since finding out you and Lyric both ingested vampire blood, your chances of survival are pretty high. So I gave one to Erik because it wasn't big enough for Marcus or Zeke. And that leaves one more, but neither of them will give in and wear the damn thing."

"Like I said, I'm not taking it," Marcus stated firmly. "Zeke has a wife and a baby waiting for him. He needs to wear the damn vest."

"You need to not tell me what to do!"

"We don't have time for you two to be arguing, but he's right. You have a family that needs you." Ravage handed the second vest to Zeke who scowled when he took it, his deep brown eyes locking on Marcus.

"If you get killed, I will never stop blaming myself, even though you're the one being an idiot." Zeke took his jacket off and slid on the bulletproof vest with a huff.

I'd never been nervous about much in my life, but my chest tightened as I reentered the Venom van, taking a seat on the left bench along the wall, right behind the driver's seat. Lynx sat next to me at the end of the bench closest to the door, and Ravage across from us, right in the middle.

Naomi had acquired three pairs of Venom-issued hand-cuffs lined with spikes around the inside and made of genuine silver—one of our few weaknesses. I'd woken before the sun rose and sawed the tips off so they wouldn't actually injure us, but would give the illusion the guards had properly restrained us.

Erik went to handcuff a pair on me, but I stopped him. "Hold on, bro."

Wanting for us to look as legit as possible, I elongated my fangs and raised my two first fingers to my mouth, piercing them. I smudged the blood from my fingertips onto my wrists to make it look like the spikes actually punctured my skin.

"That's genius, boy." Ravage said, then he and Lynx followed suit.

Erik latched the cuffs onto my wrists before fastening another pair around my ankles, securing me to the van.

Lyric squeezed in between the two front seats and laid a kiss on me before taking the driver's seat.

Sage looked over her shoulder from the passenger seat, eyeing me. "Fucking bloodsucker."

I cocked a brow. "What the hell was that for?"

"I'm getting into my part as a Venom member again. I was using Erik's persona before he went rogue."

I laughed and Erik scoffed, taking a seat between me and Lynx. Marcus and Zeke quickly hopped into the back with us, shutting the door behind them, then they took their respective spots on either side of Ravage.

"Alright, mama. Get us there safely."

Lyric flashed a nervous smile at me in the rearview mirror, started up the van, and began ascending the mountain. We were only a quarter of the way up when she turned onto a rather sketchy road that ultimately led us to a dead end, causing her to slow down.

"Don't let up on the gas," Ravage said, leaning forward and peering through the front windshield. "It'll seem like you're going to run into the side of the mountain, but Shayla told me the entrance will unveil itself once the second set of wards recognize us as safe."

With the mountain rapidly approaching, my eyes remained fixed on it, awaiting the entrance to show. "This is sketchy as fuck. Are you sure about this?"

Before Ravage could answer me, the side of the mountain flickered as if the sun shone on, then the illusion dropped, revealing a half moon shaped entrance.

"Holy shit."

"They have cameras," Sage whispered, and I barely saw a few dim light fixtures clinging to the cave walls before I sat back.

Lyric rolled the window down.

"Paperwork?" a guard commanded, his voice old and husky.

Sage handed Lyric a folder and she passed it along to him.

"You got three bloodsuckers at once? Great job. Pull on through, following the signs directing you to dock three, and give Randal your folder. He'll escort you to decontamination."

"Yes, sir."

Lyric continued on the smooth road of the cave for about three minutes before she stopped again.

"Back it in," a man said, sounding a little younger than the last guy.

She did as instructed, turning the van in a curve before putting it in reverse. When she stopped, the guard was immediately at her window.

"Paperwork?"

She showed him the folder and this guy took it.

"Badges?"

Lyric and Sage both handed their badges off. He scanned the backs of them with a handheld scanner, then passed them back.

"Let's get them inside. Dr. Ishman has rooms set up for them."

Lyric and Sage hopped out of the van, came to the back and opened the rear hatch. Sage unlocked the small metal cabinet by the door and took out an AR-15, handing it to Lyric before taking one for herself. They took a few steps back, one on each side of the rear of the van, and readied their guns on their shoulders, locked on us.

Making the conscious decision to effectively embody the role of a prisoner, I fully immersed myself in my weak, angry character, and glared at them.

"Passenger side first," the guard said, his overly confident smile pulling at his pale pink cheeks. His crooked teeth were stained yellow and his beard was short and patchy, barely covering his chin, which was too small for his wide face. He had pointy brown eyebrows that reminded me of Jack Nicholson, and I had an odd craving to watch the Shining.

Zeke kneeled down, unlocking the ankle cuffs for that side of the van, then grabbed Lynx's arm, escorting her out.

"Get your grubby hands off me, you prick!" she yelled, flawlessly playing her imprisoned vampire role.

The guard looked her over, seemingly confused. "She must be really old, resisting the silver that easily." I held my breath, worried he'd inspect her wrists. Instead, he reached into his pocket and pulled out what looked like pepper spray. "Open your mouth."

"Screw you!" Lynx spat, and the guard lifted his hand, spraying the shit into her eyes, and she screamed, gasping for air. He took the opportunity to squirt the substance into her mouth and she shrieked again before her body slumped into Zeke.

What a fucking douche canoe.

I glanced at Sage, and judging by the look on her face, she was about ten seconds away from putting a bullet into the back of the guard's head.

He flipped the canister into the air and caught it with a smile. "Nothing like some liquid silver to calm them down."

My heart thundered, my gaze locking with Ravage across from me, and I wasn't sure what question my eyes conveyed, but he slightly shook his head.

Looking back at the guard, he scanned Zeke's badge, then said, "Get the rest out. We don't have all damn day."

"Yes, sir." Marcus grabbed Ravage, escorting him out next. He stayed quiet, and honestly, I couldn't blame him. After what the guard did to Lynx, I changed my weak and angry role to weak and quiet. I wasn't about to fuck around and find out.

Erik undid my ankle cuffs and gripped my arm, yanking me to my feet. Now out of the van, I glanced around at the large cavern in awe as the guard scanned Erik's fake badge.

Once done, he swept his gaze over us three captives. "These look good. Dr. Ishman will be thrilled. My name's Randal. I'll be escorting you through the process even though some of you already know the procedure. It's just how Doc likes to do things. Follow me."

As we made our way up a long concrete ramp, it almost felt like we were about to be hanged. Our three fake guards had us vampire prisoners in the middle, Zeke carried Lynx, and Sage and Lyric walked on either side of us. Randal stayed a few feet in front of Sage.

The ramp led us toward the majestic mountain rock walls, damp and cold with a sizable white bay door nestled within a meticulously carved out hole.

"I'm sure you're familiar with the decontamination room," Randal said, swiping his card on a security pad on the right side of the door and the light hanging above it turned from red to green. "That's where we're going first."

To my surprise, next to the security pad a small window slid open, revealing a keypad, letting me know they'd implemented a two-step security system. The guard proceeded to input a passcode, and I paid close attention.

207948.

I repeated it in my mind multiple times because I knew after I took down that asshole and confiscated his identification, I would require that pin.

Air compressors sounded before a mechanic hum replaced it, the large metal door sliding up into the mountain. We entered a hallway, empty and long, without a single person in sight. The atmosphere felt heavy, devoid of any warmth or vibrancy, making me think I was about to get an anal probe. The stark white walls, impeccably polished marble floors, and fluorescent light fixtures further intensified the clinical impression of the space.

"Ms. Jones," the guard said, using Sage's fake name, falling into step with her. "When I scanned your badge, I noticed this is your third time here. Have you seen the new updates to the facility? The doc had everything renovated a few months ago. Now our atmosphere is 'clean and pristine', her words, not mine. Everything is so white, it gives me headaches. Even the chairs in the break area and the beds in the private sleeping rooms."

He smiled, nudging Sage's arm with his, and I realized he was flirting with my best friend's girl. I glared at his brown hair, ready to put a bullet into him.

"I haven't, actually. Didn't the walls used to be beige?"

My eyes bulged, knowing it was a risky move for Sage to lie.

Randal smiled, turning his head toward her. "You have a great memory. But they weren't actually beige. They were white, but it had been so long since this place was painted, they'd become discolored."

At the end of the corridor, we went right and Randal turned his attention toward Lyric.

"I noticed you were new to this position, Ms. Cox. Since you're unfamiliar with the building, let me explain. This is the outer ring of the lab where everyone comes to get decontaminated. The entire facility works as a hive, the seven inner rings contain different departments like hematology, immunology, surgical pathology, you get the point."

"This is an amazing experience, sir. One I'm truly grateful for."

I cocked a brow at Lyric's extremely fake demeanor. The guard seemed to enjoy it, sporting a smile. I really hoped he didn't make a move on her. I'd hate to have to kill him early and ruin this mission.

Randal stopped in front of a door, scanned his card, and entered.

Erik, still gripping my arm, pushed me in first and my mouth fell agape. There were shower heads positioned along the backside of the wall, with no dividing walls separating the cleansing stations. On the rack to my right, I noticed long animal control poles adorned with silver wire collars hanging from them. My ass cheeks tightened immediately when I saw boxes of gloves and lube on the counter to my left.

"Latch the two men by their ankles over there," the guard said, pointing to a wall with chains attached to it, spiked handcuffs at the end of them. "We'll start with the foul-mouthed woman first."

Sage pulled the detector I'd given her out of her pocket and pressed the button as Randal continued to bark orders. "Each guard is in charge of their prisoner. One by one you will do body cavity searches, shower them, and then—" The machine beeped, clearing the area of any cameras or microphones, and Zeke's fist immediately landed on Randal's face. He melted to the ground, out cold.

I grinned. "Nice."

"What a dickhead," Sage said before putting her scanner away, eyeing the room. "This place is fucked up."

"I hate it here," Erik said, moving fast, uncuffing my wrists.

I rubbed them before turning toward Randal, ready to break his neck when Lynx stopped me.

"He's mine," she moaned. "I need the blood."

Marcus released Lynx's cuffs, then helped her hobble over to the guard. He knelt down with her, holding her steady as she pierced Randal's neck. She took forever feeding, and I realized she'd drained him dry, which was good, one less person in our way.

By the time she was done, we were all ready to move to the next step in the plan. I stripped off my flannel button up, revealing my solid black T-shirt and Venom-issued windbreaker. Under the light jacket, I had my dual chest holster, containing both of my custom Springfields, so I zipped it to conceal them. Next I pulled off my baggy jeans, which had Venom-issued pants underneath them. Digging into one of the large pockets, I yanked out my fake badge and clipped it on my shirt. Knowing it wouldn't give me the same security clearance as Randal, I quickly grabbed his badge and shoved it in my pocket in case I needed it. My back holster had Luka's Sig in it. I pulled it out to make sure there was one in the chamber, before I moved the holster to my hip, and slid the gun back in.

Ravage and Lynx had also shed their street clothes, each of us now looking like Venom guards before we left the decontamination room.

"Everyone got their earbuds in?" I asked, and each person nodded, before glancing around nervously at each other, knowing there was a possibility some of us might not make it out alive.

"Let's go team," Marcus said, opening the door.

Since he and Zeke had been high ranking in the Venom society, they walked ahead of us, taking on fake leadership roles as we casually sauntered the halls like we knew where we were going. Thanks to Randal explaining the setup of the building, we ignored any door we saw, knowing the rooms wouldn't have anything useful.

We were at the end of a long corridor that had a large door that said HIVE, the exact place we knew we needed to be. I pulled Randal's badge from my pocket and tapped it onto the security pad, then waited for the keypad window to open. After I typed in his code, the door unlatched.

Each of us stood in silence, fully aware that a potential threat could be present and we might have to engage in combat the instant we stepped into the Hive.

Marcus pushed the door open and I did my best to keep my eyes from going wide. The walls and floors were the same bright white as the outer ring of the building, but the smell of disinfect mixed with chatter, beeping machines, ringing phones, and people made it all feel like I'd just walked into a hospital.

To the left was a large reception desk where two men in lab coats stood talking. They both glanced at us and then continued conversing as if we weren't a threat.

The blonde woman sitting behind it had on a silk blouse with a floral pattern covering it and a phone to her ear, shuffling through a folder.

She peered up, catching sight of us. "I'll call you right back." After hanging up the phone, she sprang to her feet. "It's about time." She came from behind the desk, straightening her pencil skirt as she beelined straight for Marcus. "Do you really need this many people?" Her gaze darted over each of us before she huffed, then shook her head. "I guess you do since there's seven of you, one for each department. Sorry, I'm on edge. Charles said he'd send someone down yesterday and it never happened. Follow me."

I had no clue who Charles was, but I really wanted to thank him.

She turned into a hallway on the left, and as we walked it there were windows on both sides revealing rooms filled with lab personnel. None of them even looked up from what they were doing as we passed.

Halfway down the corridor, a hum of computers filled my ears like a sweet sympathy of relief.

"All of these new updates are jacking up our programs and interfering with our progress." She flung the door open and stepped in, revealing a large area filled with desks and people, all who looked too busy to care. "Which one of you is taking this one?"

Marcus instantly pointed to me. "He is."

We all had roles to play, and mine was to find the security room, work alongside Jimmy to dismantle the entire building, and steal as many files as possible in the process, so this opportunity was perfect.

"Great. I'll show him where to set up. Do you need me to escort you to the next area afterwards?" the receptionist asked, peering up at Marcus, giving me a perfect opportunity to slide Randal's badge into Sage's hand.

"I appreciate the offer, but I'm familiar with the layout, ma'am," Marcus said so genuinely even I almost believed him.

"Thank you. I appreciate all the hard work you guys do."

The receptionist strolled into the room and I took two seconds to glance at Lyric. She gave me worried eyes as Marcus shut the door, leaving me behind.

CHAPTER 27
SAGE

Winnie slid a badge into my hand and I quickly pocketed it before the door closed. We followed Marcus off with no clue where we were going. I was grateful Lyric and I had both stashed our rifles in the decontamination room, thinking they'd be too obvious to carry when we no longer had prisoners. I wasn't used to carrying one like she was and the damn thing was heavy.

My mind reeled with thoughts of everything that already happened today, including the witches. If I wasn't a hundred percent convinced they existed before, I was now.

No one other than Marcus, Lyric, and Peach knew I'd ingested vampire blood. Well, and Winnie. I could tell by the look he had that Lyric already told him. I hadn't meant to keep it a secret, there was just too much going on for it to qualify as a topic of conversation.

The last time the witches told me to take the offer, Peach had offered me her blood the same night. I had accepted it without even considering the witch's words. Now I was going to hang onto every damn one of them.

Less is more. Small raindrops bring back life while large rivers will end it. What does that mean?

Although uncertain of their importance, as we walked the pristine white establishment, I had a feeling those words would come in handy.

We came to an area with a large sign that said Public Health in black lettering. Marcus scanned his badge and it opened, then he locked his eyes on Lyric, nodding his head to the side. I swallowed my nervousness as she disappeared alone through the door, grateful she had an earbud.

We passed doctors, nurses, a janitor, and even a couple guards and not one person gave us a second look. We stumbled upon a designated space for the study of hematology and Ravage scanned his badge, entering the section alone.

Like Randal, the whiteness of the area gave me a slight headache as we moved on. I was grateful I'd been walking the woods back home every day and was used to it because the halls in VRC felt never-ending.

Another five minutes had passed when I read the next sign: Anatomical Pathology. While I had limited knowledge on the subject, my gut twisted, my instincts strongly indicating this area was mine.

I didn't wait for Marcus to give me the go-ahead before I slapped my badge onto the security pad and entered, leaving everyone behind, praying for their safety.

The door slowly closed behind me as I stared into another damn white hallway with no one in it. I inched my feet forward, taking casual strides until I came to a fork in the road. The white sign on the wall had black letters with names of the areas and arrows pointing the way.

Straight in front of me was Cytopathology, Surgical Pathology to my left, and Forensic Pathology on my right, and for some reason, that was the one that kept replaying in my brain.

Forensic Pathology it is.

The hallway was short with a large double door at the end, reminding me of ones I'd seen in hospitals. I tapped my badge and the security pad stayed red, then beeped.

This must be a higher clearance area.

Retrieving Randal's badge from my pocket, I slapped it against the security pad and a small window to the right of it opened, revealing a keypad.

Shit.

I pushed the button on my earbud and whispered, "Winnie, I need that code."

Silence.

I tapped again. "Marcus?" No answer. "Can anyone hear me?"

Unsure why my earbuds weren't working, I yanked my cell from my pocket and when I went to text Winnie, I saw three little dots, alerting me he was already sending me something.

Winnie: 207948. I can hear you. Don't know why you can't hear me.

A small hint or worry filled me as I pocketed my phone and punched the numbers into the keypad, causing the doors to open with s swoosh.

Each muscle I had began to tremble as I stepped into the new area. This mission had been nerve-racking and the thought of getting caught lingered in the back of my mind the entire time I'd been inside VRC, but I was unsure why my body decided to alert me of something now.

The corridor I entered was empty of any lingering personnel. To my right was an alcove, a fifteen-foot-wide area containing metal racks filled with medical supplies. To my left was another recessed area with two vending machines, one with snacks and one with drinks, and a small white table with two matching chairs.

The hallway ahead of me was shorter than the others, with four doors on each side of it and led to a dead end. My gut instincts pulled me to the right side first, so I decided I'd check the rooms there, then go down the left side and end up back where I started. A perfect way to clear an area.

The first room I came to I went to tap my badge and there wasn't any security panel for badges, only a keypad. I typed in the only code I had and to my surprise, it unlocked. Not wanting to look suspicious if someone was hanging around, I barged in like I belonged there.

The room was empty of people, the walls the same bright white as the rest of the facility. On the left side was an empty metal platform bed with enormous lights hanging above it, reminding me of a surgical room. To my right, a rolling pedestal with a laptop on it, the screen dark.

In the back right corner was a large cabinet and I moseyed my way toward it. I flung open the door, expecting something shocking or dreadful and found pure white scrubs sitting on the shelves. I rolled my eyes at the amount of white this place had, then shut the cabinet.

One last glance around, then I headed back into the hall and entered my code for the second door. It unlocked and I pushed it open, not surprised the room looked exactly the same as the other. I sighed, shutting it and moving on.

The pulling of the bond twisted my stomach as I stepped up to the third room. My breaths became choppy, my heart speeding along with them. I shoved the feeling aside, brushing it off as nervousness before entering my code.

The door unlocked and my hands felt stiff as I rotated the handle, pushing it and stepping inside

Despite the eerie resemblance to the other rooms, this particular one had an icy chill as if death himself lingered in the corner, ready to claim a soul.

And this . . . this disgustingly white, cold ass room . . . wasn't empty.

A shiver of dread jolted down my spine and my body betrayed me, locking itself in limbo. Being the only part of me able to move, I narrowed my eyes, focusing on the naked man in front of me.

Empty skin clung to nothing but bone, the sight of him causing my breath to hitch, refusing to enter my lungs. Once my brain realized the man on the table looked like a skinny version of Luka, time stood still. Nothing in this world existed as silent cries ripped themselves from my throat, coming out in muted sobs.

Panic coursed through every cell of my body, the heaviness in my chest suffocating me—my windpipe tightened, the air around me threatening to take my life instead of sustaining it.

Needing desperately to hear his heartbeat, I lifted a foot, ready to bolt toward the table, but the fear was like a poison that now owned my stiff, uncooperative bones and muscles.

This can't be him. He can't be dead.

Still unable to budge, my gaze locked on his torso, waiting to see if it moved, pleading for him to still be breathing. When his chest expanded a slight bit, my fight-or-flight response kicked in.

And I was ready to fight.

My entire body trembled when I forced myself to take a step into the room, the door swinging shut as I stumbled my way toward the table. My unwavering gaze darted over his body, taking in his features, and a shocking pain burned its way into my heart.

This person looked like Luka, yet it didn't. He was frail and thin—nothing but literal skin and bones. The wounds covering him weren't healing and it didn't take me long to realize they'd starved him.

My frantic eyes landed on the very recognizable goat skull tattoo in the middle of his chest. A tattoo I had once run my fingers across.

This . . this almost lifeless soul . . . this tortured man . . . was Luka.

Terror coursed through me and I grabbed his shoulders, shaking him, his skin ice cold against my palms. "Luka. Luka."

His eyelids drifted open and I sucked in an audible gasp that staggered into my lungs, choking me. His once beautiful eyes were empty, hollow. The blue irises were now pale, almost white, and surrounded by bloodshot veins.

"You're here . . . again," he mumbled, his cracking voice barely above a whisper. "Not . . . real."

"I swear, it's me," I cried out, begging for him to believe me. Perhaps, after many months of pleading for this moment to happen, I'd attempted to convince myself this was real.

"Dreams. Many . . . dreams." His incoherent words made no sense to me.

I leaned into his ear, being as quiet as possible. "You just need blood."

If I had any chance of getting him out of here, he needed to feed now and I had no idea where Erik was with the blood bags.

I tapped my earbud, knowing my team could still hear me. "I found Luka in Forensic Pathology. I need blood now."

Not sure if anyone would be able to find me quick enough, I slid my hand into the top of my T-shirt and pulled my necklace out, pushing the pearl which would send my location to my friends.

As I waited for them to find us, I searched for a way to release Luka, and noticed his arms and legs were tightly secured with large metal cuffs. His bloodstained wrist caught my eye and I ran my finger along one, pulling the skin taught. Silver spikes lined the inside of the cuffs and were digging into his flesh, and when I noticed that the bed he laid on also had spikes covering it, digging into his backside, my stomach twisted in knots.

I took a breath and shoved my emotions back, keeping my tears from falling—or maybe, I was keeping myself from falling apart.

I scanned the area, looking for blood . . . a chainsaw . . . a miracle . . . anything to help me. Other than Luka's shiny bed, the room contained nothing more than a laptop on a rolling pedestal, a cabinet, and a cart with . . .

I froze.

Upon the rolling cart laid a metal tray filled with surgical instruments. Memories of Mannie and his tray covered in torment goodies flooded me, causing a tightness to settle in my chest. Luka had saved me from being tortured to death that night and I needed to do the same for him.

"Sage . . . safe." He let out a groan that conveyed his pain, and despite Ravage's warnings, I knew what I had to do.

I had to feed him.

I pulled back his lip, inspecting his teeth, and his fangs weren't visible. Even if I tried, he wouldn't bite me.

"Fuck," I whispered to myself before yanking a surgical blade from the tray, hoping it cut smoother than the dagger strapped to my thigh.

The edge of the table he laid upon didn't contain spikes, and I prayed the five-inch strip of flat steel was enough for what I was about to do.

With a deep breath, I crawled onto the cold table and straddled Luka, keeping my knees on the edge so the spikes didn't injure me.

"Not real . . . dream girl." He blinked his pale blue eyes repeatedly as if he was swatting a fake version of me out of his head.

I mustered enough strength to control my intense emotions, and took a deep breath, slowly exhaling as I lifted the sharp scalpel. My hands trembled intensely and the blade shook too, as if it was an extension of my body. My eyes locked on the silver sheen, the sharpness scaring me, yet ultimately commanding my respect.

"Please don't kill me," I whispered, unsure if I was talking to Luka or to the scalpel.

This was going to either be the best or the worst decision of my life.

Ready to do what needed to be done, I laid the blade across my wrist, took a deep, shuddering breath, and . . . a door slammed shut in the hallway, halting my actions.

Needing to hide fast, I scrambled off Luka to the side of the bed closest to the wall and hunched down on the floor out of sight. Being a solid platform, unless someone walked behind it, they wouldn't see me.

My heart raced at the sound of six beeps from the security pad before the door opened. Someone entered the room and high-heeled shoes tapped against the marble floor.

"Dream girl," Luka whimpered.

"Is Sage visiting you again?" a woman asked, and I held my breath at the sound of my name.

"Not real."

"At least you get to see her in your head." She giggled, and it sent furious anger to the depths of my soul.

After the sound of her digging in the cabinet stopped, the wheels of a cart squeaked as she pulled it across the room.

"Dream girl."

"Yeah, yeah, I know. Dream girl." Another giggle, then more shuffling sounds.

Not being able to hold myself back anymore, I popped up from the side of the table and had the scalpel to her throat before she even knew I was there. She sucked in a large breath when my other hand went to her blonde hair and gripped it tight.

"Drop it," I said through gritted teeth, and she immediately let go of the scalpel she held. It hit the side of the table and bounced off, the metal on metal sound another reminder of my torture.

Her eyes locked on mine. "Sage, I'm presuming. Luka said you'd come for him."

"Where's the blood?" She didn't answer, but I caught sight of her hand slowly moving toward her pocket. "You try anything and I'll slit your throat."

"We don't keep blood supply on this floor in case—"

I dug the scalpel into her skin, making blood roll down her neck in a light stream. "Tell me or your blood will be feeding him." My words came out in a low growl.

"He talks about you. Dreams of you."

She attempted to delay the inevitable by distracting me, but I wasn't gonna let it happen. "Shut the fuck up."

"You can kill me and save him. Do whatever you need to do, but it won't stop us, Sage. We will get what we need. We never fail to do so."

Pure hatred filled me when I took in her features. She was a pretty woman, middle-aged, with light skin, thin lips, and a perfect nose, and the only thing I could think of was how badly I wanted to *fuck it up* with my blade.

"I told you to shut your damn mouth!" My voice echoed through the room, and I reminded myself to stay quiet or risk getting caught.

"From what Luka says, I know you're a smart girl. If you understood what we were doing here . . . ahhh."

I dug the blade in a pinch more. "Where. Is. The. Blood?" My teeth were hurting from the amount of clenching I had to do to keep from slicing her wide open.

"We can cure cancer in children, Sage. Think about that!"

The door in the hallway slammed shut again, and my eyes darted toward the sound, which was a big mistake on my part.

Dr. Blood Stealer lifted her fist and punched me in the face, but unfortunately for her, I was used to taking *way* harder hits.

Gripping her hair tighter, I yanked her toward me.

She started to scream for help, but the sound came out in a choking gargle because I shoved the blade into her throat.

Oh, fuck.

Warm blood poured down my hand, momentarily stalling me.

Someone entered their code into the door, sending me into a panic.

To ensure Luka's safety, I did what was necessary and shoved Dr. Bitch's neck into his face, forcing him to eat. He took a small gagging gulp before turning his head away.

"Luka, feed." I held her there until the door unlatched and began to open.

With nothing but fervor flowing through me like high octane gasoline, I propelled my body forward, plowing into the guard with my shoulder. He fell backwards with a grunt, his head bouncing off the marble floor with an eerie cracking sound, and I landed on top of him.

Raising my fist, I halted it in midair when I noticed his face void of life. I quickly jumped to my feet and saw blood pooling under his head, so I grabbed his wrist, checking for a pulse. If he had one, it was too faint to find with my fingertips. He was dead and no longer a threat to me.

Turning back toward Luka, I hoped he'd fed and regained his strength, but the doctor had slumped onto the floor, lifeless.

I stepped up to the table and peered into his eyes.

"Dream girl."

Knowing he was only going to drink my blood, I looked around until I found the scalpel I'd dropped during my attack, yanked it up and held it to my wrist as I replayed Ravage's warnings in my head.

You can't let him feed from you. Once his fangs pierce you, you'll be useless, and he'll drink until you die.

"I'm sorry, Luka. I don't have a choice. I love you."

With no time to waste, I laid the blade across my wrist and sliced it open. Tiny droplets of my blood dripped onto the steel bed, the sound reminding me of raindrops . . .

Less is more. Small raindrops bring back life while large rivers will end it.

I gasped at the witch's words.

The raindrops were my blood. If I gave him a little, it would give him life. If I gave him a lot, it would take mine.

Ravage had said if Luka's fangs pierced me, I'd be useless from his venom and he'd drain me dry. He never said I couldn't *give* Luka my blood.

Holy shit.

I finally knew what I had to do.

With a deep breath, I placed my wrist close enough for Luka to smell my blood but not bite me. His nostrils flared, sniffing the air before his head whipped toward me. With a hiss, he opened his mouth and his fangs elongated.

Hoping to feed him and survive, I hovered my wrist above his lips, letting my blood drip into his mouth.

With every drop, his tongue trembled, then slowly became pinker. But his body still wasn't healing. He needed a lot more than a few tiny drops of blood.

I decided maybe I could control the situation. As long as he didn't sink his fangs into me, he could get blood faster from sucking on my wrist.

Being cautious as possible, I moved in closer, pressing my open wound against his lips, and thankfully he latched on without piercing me.

He furiously sucked, and with each ravenous gulp moans of pleasure left his nose. I did what Ravage said and counted to thirty seconds in my head as he drank, making sure he didn't go into bloodlust. When I finally had to pull away, he groaned, and I felt terrible.

Having successfully fed him and now needing a bandage for my wrist, I took a step back from the table, sliding in something wet. When I glanced down, my eyes widened.

Against the stark white, beautifully polished marble floor, a pool of blood surrounded the doctor. The old me would've had a panic attack from the sight of it. The new me only had one thought.

All this blood is going to waste while Luka is starving.

Deciding I wasn't going to let it go unused, I quickly grabbed gauze and tape off the cart and bandaged my wound, then stepped up to the body. I shimmied my hands under her armpits, attempting to pull her up, and pieces of her kept slipping out of my hands.

In every movie I'd ever seen, people lugged around dead bodies like they weren't heavy. Dr. Bitch was only a hundred and twenty pounds soaking wet, which was sixty pounds less than me. I should've been able to lift her with ease, but her muscles had no firmness, making it near impossible. It was like trying to scoop water with a fork.

"Sage. You're really here."

My breath caught at the sound of Luka's voice. "I'm coming, baby," I whispered breathlessly, and then hoped he was too delirious to remember. I'd never called him that before . . . and it was slightly embarrassing.

After pulling and struggling for a few minutes, my arm muscles and lungs burned with the fire of Satan, causing me to almost give up. Using the last of the strength I had, I yanked her up as far as I could. She started to slouch, so I shoved the front of her chest against the table, using her boobs for leverage. Her head was hanging and I cringed when the blood seeping from her neck dripped onto my favorite boots.

Grabbing her wrist, I threw it in front of Luka's face. "Drink."

His eyes widened. "Did you kill her?"

"Yes, and your wounds haven't healed, so you need more blood. Now drink."

Sadness filled his expression and he shook his head. "It's not your blood."

The doc began to slip and I stuck my knee under her body to help hold her up. "If you get mad, you can feed."

"No." He tightened his lips into a line.

"Luka, if you don't get mad and drink this goddamn blood, I'm going to end up on a table next to you."

"I can't do it. I've tried."

Frustration filled me, sending anger pouring out of my mouth. "She was about to cut into you. Think about all the shit that you went through and drink the fucking blood!"

Luka's eyes met mine, locking onto them as if I was the only thing in the world that mattered. Each breath he took came harder, faster, before the tiny veins of his face came alive, rippling beneath his skin.

His mouth fell open and he sucked in an angry breath, letting it out in a hiss. It was hard to witness the hungry desperation he had when his fangs throbbed like they were begging for food. I pushed the doc's wrist against his mouth and he didn't hesitate to pierce her skin.

Assuring he didn't overfeed and go into bloodlust, I once again counted the seconds in my head. Each gulp he took brought life back into him. The dark circle under his eyes faded away and his pale skin regained its color. Another few gulps and his ribs weren't as sharp and protruding as they previously were.

Once I got to thirty seconds, I pulled the doc's wrist away, letting her dead body tumble to the floor, splattering even more blood on my boots and now my pants.

A growl vibrated in Luka's throat, and I knew it was from starvation, not him being angry at me.

I laid my hand across his chest, right on his goat skull tattoo, and rubbed my thumb across his cold skin. "It's okay. You're safe."

After a few ragged breaths, the veins in his face slowly stopped pulsing. "Fucking kiss me," he whisper yelled, the relief his voice conveyed making it hard to deny him.

Standing on my tippy toes, I smashed a quick kiss against his lips. Unfortunately, time was important, so I pulled back and wiped the doctor's blood from my mouth.

Gross.

Finally safe to free him, I looked at the cuffs, not knowing where or what to touch without injuring him further, or possibly myself.

"Luka, how do I get these off?"

"The computer. Dr. Cuntface controlled the lengths of the spikes for my wrists and the table from some kind of software."

What the fuck?

Knowing she had the power to control how much pain Luka felt ignited a fire within me, and I wished I had a shot at killing "Dr. Cuntface" a second time, I'd make the pain last longer.

I headed toward the laptop and clicked the enter button to bring it out of sleep mode.

"Shit. It's password protected." Turning my head toward Luka, he had a look of contemplation.

"Try Venezuela. It's where she was going to retire. But all caps. She once told me she hated small letters."

What a fucking psychopath, I thought as I typed V E N, then second-guessed myself on the proper spelling of a word I rarely used.

"How the hell do you spell it?"

"V. E. N—"

The security alarms sounded and a red light in the upper right corner of the room flashed, sending panic coursing through my body.

"Hurry!"

"E. Z. U. E. L. A."

I finished typing, hit enter, and hoped for the best.

It unlocked and I was relieved for a split second until I remembered how much I suck at computers.

There were multiple programs and spreadsheets already open, and I had no idea what any of them were. I clicked on a few different ones with no luck. "I don't know what the fuck I'm doing here!"

Gunshots rang through the hallway and whomever was out there would be here any second. I swiftly swiped the blade off the ground and hid behind the door, which remained ajar due to the dead guard.

The person's shadow cascaded across the marble floor before they entered the room. I lunged forward with my blade held high, and Winnie grabbed my wrists, halting me.

"Easy, killer."

"Winnie, I need you!" I dragged him toward the computer and frantically pointed at it. "This controls everything on Luka's bed. Can you get into it?"

Winnie sniffed the air, then glanced at Luka before laying his hand on the mouse, and my heart raced as he opened up a couple programs, clicking around.

Luka's bed made a ticking sound from the spikes lowering, then the huge metal cuffs opened up, releasing his hands. Before I even had a chance to run to him, he was already in my face.

Making sure this was real, I placed my hands against his bare chest and his strong heart beating against my palms assured me he was alive.

A whimper conjured in my throat and burst out, my heart attempting to mend itself, as Luka placed his hands on my cheeks and peered down at me. His eyes . . . his beautiful perfect eyes were bright blue again, darting across every inch of my face like he had trouble believing this was reality.

"I didn't think I'd ever see you again, Princess."

My nickname rolling off his lips was better than all the music in the world. A sweet serenade of love and devotion, and nothing less than pure magic.

Before I could respond, Winnie interrupted my three seconds of peace. "Copy, Jimmy." He turned toward us, a wary expression. "We gotta go, now."

Luka's hands dropped from my cheeks before he headed to the cabinet, quickly grabbed a set of scrubs, and handed them to me. "Hold these."

I wondered what the hell I needed to do with them as he grabbed a second pair, sliding the bottoms on.

"There are others being held captive here. Release all the beds and unlock the doors."

Winnie scoffed, shaking his head at Luka. "We don't have time to save them all."

"Release them so they at least have a chance!" Luka's voice rang loud over the still blaring alarms.

Winnie hesitated for mere seconds before he turned back to the computer. My eyes went to Luka, watching him put the scrub top on, and I couldn't help but notice his body was back to normal size.

By the time Luka adjusted his shirt, Winnie had finished.

"All the doors are open, and just so you know, I think this is a bad idea." Winnie clicked his ear piece. "Kill the damn alarm, Jimmy." A second of silence as Jimmy answered. "Yeah, I know we'll lose some of it, just do it anyway. We gotta get the fuck out of here so I need those doors opened too."

The alarms stopped, leaving my ears buzzing in the quietness.

Luka grabbed my free hand and I tucked the extra scrubs close to my side. We stepped around the dead guy before entering the hallway.

"Carmen?" Luka called out.

Not hearing a response, I wondered who he sought as he dragged me down to the last door and opened it, pulling me inside. I glanced over my shoulder into the hall at Winnie and he shrugged, shaking his head.

"Carmen?" Luka repeated.

As I worried about him possibly still being delirious, a naked girl with thick curly hair stood, appearing from behind the table. Her skin was a deep, warm taupe, her eyes dark brown, conveying the worry she had as her gaze bounced between us.

"Luka?"

"It's okay. These are my friends." Luka let go of my hand, taking the scrubs from me and handing them to Carmen. "Put them on and follow us."

"Incoming," Winnie hollered, and I went to peek my head into the hallway to check on him and I'm glad I didn't get far enough. Bullets flew by right after Luka yanked me away from the door, shutting it all but a sliver.

I pulled my Beretta from my holster and pushed him aside.

Laying my back flat against the wall, I kept my gun pointed to the ground as I peeked out the crack, barely seeing Winnie in the dark room across the hall. He held up two fingers and pointed in the direction the bullets came from.

I inched the door a little more and saw two guards armed with AR-15s, slowly making their way toward us, checking every room.

Since the guard on the opposite side of the hall was ahead of the other guard, he would approach Winnie's room first.

My gaze went back to Winnie and he pointed to him, held up one finger, pointed to me and held up two fingers again, then he ducked down into the shadows.

I took his sign as I was supposed to take out guard number two.

Never have I felt more grateful for the training I received from Venom—a tool I would use to beat them.

Remembering my breathing techniques, I slowed my breaths and waited patiently for the guard to walk into Winnie's room. As soon as he did, anguished cries filled the air.

The other guard swiftly approached, pointing their gun into Winnie's room, and I took quick aim, shooting him in the back of the head.

My once steady breaths were now coming fast and hard.

"Give me the gun." Luka softly placed his hand on my shoulder and I shrugged it off.

He'd already done his job saving me, it was my turn to protect him.

"He's not the first person I killed today and won't be my last. Our window is closing. Let's go."

Winnie stepped into the hall the same time we did, and Carmen followed closely behind as we headed for the door.

CHAPTER 28
Luka

My perception of reality had become distorted, hindering my ability to realize if I was really being saved by my friends, each of them dressed as Venom members, or if I was merely having another hallucination. Then I laid my hands against the warm skin of Sage's cheeks, the taste of her sweet blood lingering in the back of my throat, and knew they'd really saved me.

We stepped out of Carmen's room and Winnie handed me my Sig P226 Legion, the only love of my life before I had met Sage. I'd barely had time to reconnect with her before Sage grabbed my hand, yanking me down the hall toward the door, protecting me like a little badass. I uselessly stared at the back of her head, my feet moving without me even trying, begging for her to turn around. All I needed was one more glimpse of her beauty.

She dropped my hand when we stopped at the door, turning her head toward us, the side profile of her face beyond perfect. "What's the plan?"

"Kill anything that looks like a threat," I said, my body running on pure adrenaline. Holding up my gun, I turned toward Winnie. "Did you put one in the chamber?"

He nodded, shedding his Venom jacket, revealing his chest holster, and I eyed both of his beloved custom Springfield 1911s.

"Do you have any more guns on you?" I questioned, and his eyes locked on mine before he realized why I'd asked.

"Fuck," he huffed, yanking a gun out and handing it to Carmen. "It's ready to go. Whatever you do, don't leave it behind or I'll kill you."

Carmen's eyes widened. "I don't know how to use this thing."

"Point toward the center mass of a person and pull the trigger," Sage said. "Just try not to shoot one of us."

"Hold on. I have to answer them." Winnie clicked his earpiece. "No, I haven't seen him, but Luka and Sage are with me." There was a moment of silence. "Copy." Winnie let his hand fall away, locking gazes with Sage. "Lyric is at the front door and Lynx is with her. She went and got the Jeep, and Erik and Zeke just entered decontamination. Ravage hasn't answered and Marcus took the farthest route, so he's going to be a minute."

Sage's worry showed in her eyes as she twisted the handle and opened the door, then peeked out. "Clear."

The three of us worked as a unit, making our way through the hall, peeking around every corner with Carmen behind us.

It didn't take long for us to make it out of Anatomical Pathology with no altercations or any people in sight before we stepped into the hall leading to Hematology.

"This is where we left Ravage," Sage said.

A screaming woman wearing white scrubs, with three others on her tail, ran straight up to Winnie, not even noticing who was with him. "Where are we supposed to hide?"

"Um." He glanced around, then tipped his head. "Go into the bathroom and don't come out until it's been at least twenty minutes and it's quiet."

"Thank you, sir!" She frantically ran toward the bathroom with the others behind her.

We quickly passed through the area as more medical staff ran around, some of them finding places to hide, while others kept asking Winnie and Sage what to do.

Ravage was nowhere in sight until we entered the Public Health area.

He was in a standoff, being shot repeatedly as he fought his way through six guards. One lifted a crossbow, aiming it at his back and Sage took aim, shooting the guard in the chest twice as Winnie and I simultaneously took out the rest of the guards.

"Thanks." Ravage slouched against the wall completely covered in blood. I counted at least seven wounds as he caught his breath, healing quickly. "I'm glad these aren't silver," he said, picking a bullet out.

Once he was ready, he fell into step with us as we continued on, making our way through each area, killing anyone who was in our way. I didn't bother counting the amount of bodies we were leaving behind.

We had finally made it to the main area of the Hive and cleared it when my first wave of exhaustion hit me.

Sage stopped by the exit and said, "This door goes to the intake and decontamination area, which leads outside. We need to make sure everyone is out before we leave. Do you have updates on everyone's location?"

"I did a few mins ago," Winnie answered, shaking his head, his eyes worried. "Everyone is out but Marcus and he's not answering."

"We can't leave anyone behind. I have to go back." Sage turned away, the sound of her heart thundering loudly in my ears.

I grabbed her arm, halting her. "*We* go back. We go back together," I said, and her eyes searched my face before she nodded.

Each of us took a second to reload before we headed back toward Public Health. Clearing the hallway as we went.

We'd finally come upon the main door to the next area and right when Winnie went to pull the handle, it opened on its own. Each of us raised our guns, quickly halting ourselves as Marcus limped through it.

"Whoa, shit," he whispered, the smell of fresh blood filling my nostrils. I glanced down at his hand holding onto his side. He had taken a bullet to the abdomen.

"Marcus," Sage yelled, relief in her voice. "I'm glad you're okay. Follow us toward . . ." Her words trailed off as she finally noticed his wound. "No, no, no!" She ran to him, throwing her hands over it.

"I'm okay. It's just a flesh wound."

Ravage locked eyes with me because we both knew by the sound of his heart, it wasn't a flesh wound.

"Can one of them give you blood?" Sage asked, and Marcus shook his head.

"There's no time for that, plus I wouldn't be able to walk because of the euphoria. I'm too heavy to be carried, so just get me to my brother, please."

Ravage put one of Marcus's arms over his shoulder, and I put his other over mine before sliding my hand across his backside into something wet. A hard breath left me when I realized the blood came from another wound on his lower back.

I met Marcus's eyes and he shook his head, telling me to shut up. He either didn't want Sage to know or he didn't want to be a vampire. Possibly both.

My heart hurt, my chest heavy with each step Ravage and I took, assisting Marcus with seeing his brother one last time.

Winnie and Sage led the way, clearing any threats, and Carmen stayed to the side, unsure of what to do until we finally made it to Decontamination.

That was when the second wave of exhaustion hit, my eyes unfocusing, the white walls making me dizzy.

The hall was the longest I'd ever been in, clear of any dead bodies or people. We took a few twists and turns before stopping at the exit.

Winnie tapped his badge and the door beeped, the light staying red. "Fuck!"

"Let me try," Sage said, tapping her badge, and the door beeped again.

Winnie put his hand to his earbud. "Jimmy, we're at the entrance and can't get out." Silence. "Have you tried—"

Gunshots flew down the hall toward us and Ravage and I moved in unison, attempting to get Marcus out of the way. A bullet hit me in the lower right side of my back and I hissed.

Winnie and Sage immediately stepped around us and shot toward the threat, and Carmen followed suit.

"We're clear," Winnie said before clicking his ear piece again. "Hurry up. We're sitting ducks here!"

Winnie's eyes darted to mine and he realized the same thing I had. Marcus's heartbeat slowed tremendously, almost stopping.

The door clicked, then made a whooshing sound when opening.

We finally made it outside, and our friends stood guard next to the Jeep and a black Venom van, surrounded by more dead bodies.

We were only ten feet away when Marcus coughed up blood, spewing it down the front of him.

"Marcus!" Zeke ran toward us in a panic. "Why haven't you given him blood?

"No blood," Marcus choked out, before going limp.

"No!" Sage screamed, the piercing sound vibrating to my core.

"Zeke, grab his feet!" I commanded, and he did, making it a lot quicker to get Marcus to the van.

It took the strength of Zeke, Ravage, Winnie, and myself to hoist him into it. That was when the exhaustion settled in my bones.

"Load up!" Ravage yelled.

Lynx jumped in the driver's seat of the van and Lyric in the passenger. Winnie and Zeke got in the back, and Sage stood there, staring at her hands.

Ravage shoved Carmen in the back seat of the Jeep and hollered, "Grab her, boy, and come on."

I did what Ravage said and pulled Sage toward her car. "I'll drive."

After pushing her to the passenger side, she handed me the keys. I ran and opened the driver's door, and stopped.

Sage had her gaze locked on the van.

Damn it.

CHAPTER 29
SAGE

My father figure, my dad, was bleeding to death, refusing to feed off any vampire, and all I could do was stare at my blood-soaked hands as they trembled.

Luka stood on the driver's side of the Jeep, his eyes locked on mine. "Get in the car!"

My gaze went from him to the van when Zeke screamed, "My brother is dying!"

Glancing back at Luka, I had to make a hard decision. *Get in the van with Marcus, who may be dead before I see him again, or go with the man I love. Shit.*

"I have to go with Marcus! I'm sorry." I sprinted toward the van just as Winnie was about to shut the door.

He held it for me until I jumped in. Lynx slammed the gas and I almost fell out the back, then Winnie pulled me inside before shutting the door.

"Someone do something," Zeke screamed.

Squeezing past him, I kneeled next to Marcus, my eyes meeting Winnie's with a pleading question.

He shook his head. "I can't do it, Sage."

"You can't or won't?"

"It's too late now. He'll turn and he'll be pissed because he doesn't want this. He said it repeatedly and even refused Ravage's blood at the hotel before we even left!"

"You have to," I whimpered, and then the words Shayla said to Marcus played in my head.

For the sake of the prophecy and everyone involved, I hope he chooses wisely. A soul like yours is too rare to lose.

"Oh my god, Winnie. Shayla said he would die if *he* didn't choose wisely. She meant you. You're the one who *has* to choose to save him."

"If he wakes up with humans around, he'll kill all three of you. And he doesn't want to be a vampire. Is that not enough for you?"

"Please," I whispered, my voice lowering, tears rolling down my cheeks. Peering up at him from the floor, I picked up his hand, and caressed it between mine. "He's my dad."

Winnie's jaw clenched as he stared into my begging eyes before ripping his hand away. "Fuck you, Sage! Zeke, get the damn blood bags out of the cooler. You, go up there with Lyric."

"I'm not leaving his side until he opens his eyes."

"Goddamn it, Sage!" Winnie screamed, making the hairs on the back of my neck stand up. Small purple and blue veins popped up on his face, sending goosebumps across my arms. He opened his mouth and bared his fangs with a hiss. "Do what I said!"

I forced back my need to help and, for once, I did what I was told. Squeezing past them, I lowered my ass onto the edge of the passenger seat, next to Lyric, but kept my body facing them in case they needed help.

Winnie put his wrist up to his mouth and bit into it, leaving blood on his chin.

"What the fuck are you doing?" Zeke asked frantically.

"Turning him into a vampire," Winnie answered, halting his wrist at the brim of Marcus's mouth. "Unless you say otherwise. He's your brother."

Zeke's panicked eyes went from Winnie to me and back again. "Do it! Save him."

Winnie pressed his wrist against Marcus's mouth. "Babe, I'm going to need you to switch seats with Lynx. We're going to need more vampire strength back here."

Lyric slunk past me and the van slowed as she took over driving.

"Should I pull over and—" Gunshots sounded from behind us.

"Don't stop, we're being chased." Winnie removed his wrist from Marcus's mouth. "Hold his legs, Zeke, and try your damndest not to give in. Because if this works, he's going to try and kill us all."

"If you thought he was strong before, he's going to be a literal god if he transitions," Lynx added. "When people are already strong, they—"

A large growl filled the van, almost deafening me.

"Zeke, grab the blood," Winnie yelled.

Zeke removed one hand as he reached for a blood bag, and Marcus flailed, flinging Lynx and Winnie off like they weighed nothing.

Marcus lunged for Zeke, grabbing him by the shoulders. Winnie put him in a choke hold and Lynx grabbed onto Marcus's arms, but he was much stronger.

He flung her off like she was only a bothersome mosquito, then did the same to Winnie. They both responded quickly, hurling themselves on top of Marcus, pinning his back to the van floor. He snarled, revealing his newfound fangs, the sight leaving my heart racing.

"I can't feed him the blood and hold him down," Winnie shouted, then his eyes met mine.

I was ready to bolt out of the seat, my fingernails dug into it, barely holding me in place.

He shook his head, let out a hard breath, and finally relented. "Fuck. Don't get killed or Luka will kill me!"

I leapt to my feet and dove for the blood bag, barely having it in my hands when Marcus thrashed again, sending everyone flying.

The bag got knocked from my hand and I fell flat on my ass. I desperately went for the bag again and as soon as my fingers grasped it, a wave of absolute terror washed over me.

Marcus snarled inches from my face and I froze.

He grabbed my shoulders, fangs bared, and leaned in for the kill.

With the blood bag gripped tightly, I did the only thing I could do. I turned my head and at the last second, slid the bag in between Marcus's fangs and my neck.

He bit into the bag, sending blood pouring down the front of me.

The trio pulled Marcus back and he yanked the bag with him, furiously sucking on it.

Now free of his grasp, my body trembled.

Loud moans of satiety filled the van as Marcus squeezed the blood bag, savoring every drop. Winnie had another up to his mouth before the first even dropped from his hands.

When Marcus had almost finished the second bag, Winnie yanked it away, pulling Marcus into his neck.

Panic soared through me when Marcus bit down without a second thought.

"What the fuck!" I screamed, ready to plow into Marcus, until Winnie put his hand out, stopping me.

"Sealing the sentinel bond."

Holy shit.

Everything happened so fast, I hadn't even contemplated my own actions let alone who Marcus's origin would be. Not only had he refused Ravage's blood, but I knew that and still forced Winnie to turn him. Afraid Marcus would be furious with me, I swallowed hard, my throat feeling like it was full of sand

After a few seconds of moaning and groaning as Marcus hungrily fed, Winnie laid his hands upon his shoulder and whispered, "The darkness shall not command thyself. Thou shall command it."

I had no clue what that saying meant, but apparently Marcus took the words to heart. He pulled back, sucking in shuddering breaths. "What the . . . what happened?"

Tears rolled down my cheeks as I stared into his big, brown, bloodshot eyes. Not worrying about my safety, I fell into his arms.

"I'm sorry. I couldn't lose you." Every emotion I had poured out of me as I begged for his forgiveness. "I'm fucking selfish and I don't care. Please don't hate me. I couldn't live without you. I can't. I would die. You're the only dad who loves me."

Marcus's arms went around me, pulling me in tight. "It's okay, Sagelynn. I just think I'm in shock."

I let go of the hug and placed my hands on his face, more tears dampening my cheeks. "I'm glad you're alive."

Marcus nodded before he glanced over at Zeke who stared wide eyed, wiping away tears. "Welcome back, brother."

Glancing up, Lynx was also wiping her eyes, and to my surprise, so was Winnie.

The sound of gunshots brought us out of our panic states. Venom still chased us and we were too frantic to notice.

"Winston!"

"I got them, mama. Just keep driving." Winnie pulled a gun from his waistband. "Zeke, get behind Marcus and Lynx. He's practically bullet proof now. Sage, go up front."

I didn't hesitate to listen this time because I had finally learned that people do things because they care about you. Sometimes, they're actually right in situations and I hate to admit this, but I'm stubborn and occasionally wrong.

I slid into the passenger seat, slouching down as far as possible in case bullets came into the van.

Everything got loud as Winnie opened the rear door and started shooting toward them. Then I heard metal on metal slamming together, before the sound of crunching trees.

"What the fuck was that?"

"Um, the threat has rolled down into a large ravine," Winnie said, and I peeked into the back.

"Then why do you have that face on? Are they okay?"

"They are, but Luka used your Jeep to push it there."

He grinned nervously and I sighed, sitting back in the seat.

It was sad to have my Jeep damaged but with us all making it out alive, well, most of us, I was beyond grateful.

The ride back to the hotel seemed to take forever. My gut twisted with an overwhelming desire to reach Luka. I needed to touch him, see his face, and feel the warmth of his body before I knew everything would be okay.

When Lyric pulled into the parking lot of the hotel, I jumped from my seat, heading into the back, and squeezed past everyone sitting on the benches.

The van hadn't even stopped when I flung the back door open and jumped out, praying I didn't eat concrete.

The instant my feet touched the ground, Luka threw the Jeep in park and bolted out, sprinting toward me.

No one else in the world existed when our bodies smashed into each other like two stars colliding. He ripped me off the ground and I hung onto his neck, my legs wrapping around his waist.

"I'm so sorry," I whimpered into his neck, tears staining his shirt.

He held on tight with one hand, rubbing my back with the other. "What could you possibly be sorry for?"

Every muscle I had trembled against his warm body and the tighter he hugged, the more I never wanted to let go of him. "For not saving you sooner."

"Hey, hey. It's okay. You broke into a highly secured research center for me. A guy couldn't ask for much more out of a mate."

I pulled back, my watery eyes meeting his. "I'm your mate?"

"Of course you are, Princess. Our bond is eternal. No one will ever separate us again."

My breaths were fast as I leaned in, gently pressing my lips against his, a sense of peace flooding through me.

"Get a room!" Winnie hollered, and we broke free.

I laughed while crying and Luka sat me on the ground. "I'm really tired. It's like I've slept forever, but somehow haven't slept at all."

Peering up into his eyes, I took his hand in mine. "I have a warm bed for you to sleep in."

Once our group had exited the vehicles, we made our way to the back of the hotel, our silence speaking volumes. Winnie managed to get us into a private entrance and I was grateful. Our blood-soaked clothes told the tale of our night, and I prayed no one lingered in the halls at five am because it was a story we weren't willing to reveal.

Despite appearing normal, Luka's eyes had a slightly distant look as we stepped into our room. He went straight to the bed and stared at it.

"Let me clean you up first." I slid my hand into Luka's and pulled him toward the bathroom, stopping by the door. "Winnie, can you find him some clothes?"

"I'm on it."

I shut the bathroom door and helped Luka shed his once white scrubs that were now splattered with the reminders of the lives lost.

"I'm too tired to shower, Princess."

"Okay, but the sheets here are white so we have to at least get the blood off you."

Luka nodded, his eyes slowly blinking as if he was forcing himself to stay awake for me.

With a heavy breath, I turned on the sink and once the water was warm, I ran a washcloth under the stream, then added some soap.

He stood silently, staring into nothingness as I briskly cleansed him, noticing his naked body still had some scars on it.

Winnie came back with his clothes and slid them through the door. After I helped Luka get dressed, we returned to the bedroom. He stood next to the bed, staring at it like it was a foreign object before he finally laid down and let out a long breath.

More worry filled me as I took a seat at the tiny table by the window, and by the time I removed my boots, Luka was asleep.

"We're really going to have to clean this place up before we leave," I said, stifling a yawn. Exhaustion had hit me hard, pulling at my eyelids. "There will be so much DNA evidence."

"You don't worry about that, Sagelynn. I already set my alarm to get up early," Lyric said, bringing my slanted eyes to her. "You go shower first, then Winnie and I will once the water is warm again."

I nodded and grabbed a long T-shirt to wear to bed before stumbling into the bathroom. Each piece of clothing I shed became a strain on my heart. Blood covered my hands, my legs . . . my entire body. I made sure I completely avoided the mirror. I didn't need a picture-perfect, horrific memory engraved into my brain of what my body looked like in the aftermath.

With a deep breath, I turned the shower on and slid in. As I quickly scrubbed the blood from my body, I thought about Marcus. I really needed to talk to him and make sure he wasn't upset with me. But that was a problem for tomorrow.

CHAPTER 30
WINNIE

There was an odd scent coming from Luka when we found him that worried me, and when he went to sleep before the sun had risen, my concern intensified. I took on the responsibility of staying awake all day, closely monitoring him and guarding against potential attacks.

In the bigger room, Marcus and Zeke shared a bed, and Lynx got the other one to herself while Erik slept on the pullout couch.

Sage fell asleep, but woke up constantly, making sure Luka remained by her side. Lyric slept on and off, and since we didn't have a couch, Carmen slept next to her. Ravage diligently checked on us every thirty minutes.

I swear the dude doesn't sleep.

He had called Peach to let her know we'd found Luka, everyone who'd gone on the mission was safe, and he'd explain the rest of the details when we arrived back home. He also detected the peculiar odor radiating off Luka and suggested we return to the camp immediately for Drag to examine the scent.

The next evening when the sun was still high in the sky, I had already packed everyone's bags and helped Lyric clean up the room. Knowing Luka *always* awoke when the sun set, I'd patiently waited at the foot of his bed.

When darkness came, and he didn't even stir, my concern turned into panic, and I immediately grabbed Ravage, dragging him into the room.

"Why is he still sleeping?" I asked, stopping at the foot of the bed next to Sage, and pointing to Luka.

Ravage's eyes were uneasy as he went to his side. His gaze raked across Luka's body before he reached down, placing his hand on his chest. Then he sniffed the air and turned his head toward us. "He's gone through a tremendous amount of torture and needs time to heal."

"I can feed him again if it'll help," Sage suggested, her arms crossed and her face somber.

I glanced back at Ravage as he headed toward us, and judging by the look on his face, a feeding wasn't the answer.

"I don't think blood is going to fix him, Sage Stick."

She turned toward me, her brows pinched. "What do you mean? I thought you guys needed blood to regenerate or whatever."

Ravage slid between us and clasped a hand on each of our shoulders, his sad eyes staring at Luka. "Unfortunately, being a vampire doesn't change who you are as a person or how emotions work. His body has healed. It's his heart and soul that haven't."

My chest tightened, and I bit back my feelings.

Even though Luka was an arrogant, strong dude, they'd tortured him until he broke. His soul was exhausted and needed time to decide if it wanted to live or not. And even though I'd just dealt with a similar issue with Sage and her depression, I felt helpless.

"I wasn't in there nearly as long as he was," Carmen said, pulling at the front of the pink crop top Lyric gave her. "But the things I had to endure while I was . . ."

Sage shook her head. "Nobody should have to go through that."

Ravage dropped his hands from us and turned toward Carmen. "You don't seem as bad as Luka. How long were you in there?"

"Only two weeks. They gave me just enough blood to keep me alive, but not too much, so I'd stay weak. I was hungry when we got back, but I only drank half the blood bag Lynx gave me, so I wasn't really starving like Luka. He told me I was lucky not to be bonded to anyone, that the blood they gave him was disgusting. The blood tasted good to me and I devoured every drop they offered."

"He starved because of our bond?" Sage whimpered, taking a deep breath and blowing it out through pursed lips.

"Not entirely," Carmen answered. "Dr. Ishman didn't focus nearly as much on me as she did Luka. She was constantly putting him to the test, experimenting with things she never did to me. It was like she was searching for something specific in him. I couldn't see what she was doing to him, but I could hear it. Hear his screams."

Carmen shook her head, tears brimming her lids. "The more she tested, the more he refused the blood they gave him, and the weaker he got. He was to the point where he just kept spitting it out at them and I could hear them complaining about it."

Sage dropped her head, tightly shutting her eyes, and I knew she'd had her fill of the conversation, so I stepped in. "We can just load him up and go home. Maybe he'll heal better the further we get away from this place."

"That's a good idea, boy," Ravage said, moving toward the door, stopping with his hand on the knob. "You help Sage get him to stand. I'll get Zeke and Erik to help me load the vehicles."

Ravage left and I kicked the bed Luka slept in. "Hey, asshole. We're going home with or without you."

Luka didn't move and my forehead creased, concern filling me.

Sage punched me in the arm and I completely lost my train of thought. "What the hell."

"Stop being an asshole, Winnie. You're only doing it so you can hide your feelings."

I stared at Sage, my mouth agape. "That's the pot calling the kettle black."

"You two are mirror images of each other. Both guarded as fuck, " Lynx said, before turning her attention to Carmen. They'd been chatting since we woke up. "So, where are you from?"

"Bullshit. I'm not guarded," I said to no one in particular, but mainly to myself.

Deciding to show the love I actually felt for Luka, I drowned out the sounds of their chatter and stepped up to the side of the bed, placing my hand on his shoulder, shaking him lightly.

"Hey, bro. If you don't get up, we're leaving your ass here."

"Geezus, Winnie." Sage snickered, heading to the other side of the bed. She laid her hand on his arm and whispered, "Um, Luka, we have to go home now."

He didn't move and I tilted my head at Sage. "We can just carry his ass out the back entrance."

She nodded, straightening her spine. "Good idea."

"What is wrong with you two?" Lyric asked, pushing me aside. "All you have to do is let him know he's safe and be kind with him."

Lyric laid her hand on Luka's chest, and leaned into his ear, her voice low. "Hey, it's Lyric. You're safe now, but you have to wake up so you can go home and sleep in your own bed. It's nice and warm and quiet. You'll be safe there. No one will ever hurt you again."

She stood, and I scoffed. "I kicked the bed and that didn't even wake him up, and you think . . ."

Luka squirmed, his eyelids drifting open before he whispered, "What?"

"Told you," Lyric said, smiling proudly. "We're taking you home, Luka, so you have to get up and get in the car. Okay?"

There was a distant look in Luka's eyes when he nodded, then slowly crawled out of bed, heading into the bathroom.

Twenty minutes later, we managed to get him in Sage's Jeep. She drove and I sat in the back with Lyric. We stayed mostly quiet the entire ride home because Luka fell back asleep and none of us wanted to disturb him.

Ravage had the rest of our crew and Carmen with him and said they were stopping to get food at a drive thru. Since none of us were hungry, we continued on and arrived at the cabin first.

The moment Sage parked and got out, Kimber came running up. "Is he okay?"

"He just needs some rest," Sage said, helping Luka out of the car and leading him toward her cabin.

Kimber sniffed the air, her expression suspicious. "Luka smells different?"

"Yeah. I noticed that when I first saw him. I talked to Ravage about it last night. He also said he smelled off. He was waiting for Drag so they could discuss it. Where is he?"

"We just got back from helping Lane and so much shit happened, and Drag was upset so he took off through the woods in a panic. Heston and Demi are with him. I stopped by my cabin to throw some clothes on."

My brows pinched. "What happened?"

Kimber let out a puff, anger taking over her expression. "Right as the sun was setting, Lane called, requesting backup because he and only a few others were up against Galen and the entire Ironclad pack. Well, when we got there, my stupid ass brother—"

"Where's Strike?" Vivi screamed, cutting Kimber off, running toward me. "I can't smell him. Why isn't he with you?"

The panic coming from her was heartbreaking, and I was afraid to tell her the truth. I forced my tightened throat to relax, my eyes softening.

"He wasn't there, sis."

"You're lying!" She shoved me hard enough to make me stumble backwards, her face contorting with anger. "You left him."

"No, I didn't."

"Go back and get him!" She shoved me again before baring her teeth and letting out a large hiss.

"I swear to you, Viviana, he wasn't there."

Stepping in as close as she could, veins rippling across her face, she shoved me against the Jeep, and I grabbed her shoulders to hold her back.

"He has to be. Go back and get him."

"Stop. Leave him alone." Lyric pulled on Vivi's arm, attempting to "save me" and my sister turned on her.

Vivi forcefully shoved Lyric onto the gravel parking lot, causing herself to fall on top of her, then let out another large hiss. She was less than a second away from sinking her fangs into Lyric when I yanked her off.

Vivi went flying backwards, landing on her ass before swiftly getting to her feet and approaching me again. "Go back, Winston!"

Kimber jumped in front of Vivi and got shoved away, but shifted into a wolf mid-fall and landed on all four paws, going right back into the fight, growling and snarling.

Vivi lunged for me again and Kimber latched her jaws onto her arm, slinging her to the ground.

My sister jumped right back to her feet, not stopping.

I didn't want to, but I bared my fangs, warning Vivi she was crossing a line. "He wasn't there and nothing will change that!"

"You have to go back," she whimpered, tears welling in her eyes, shattering my heart.

Peach ran up to us, then gently grabbed Vivi's arm, getting her attention. "He wasn't there, sweetie. There's nothing more we can do right now."

"Not true. Not true." Vivi stepped in close to me, her hands secured tightly on her chest. "Please, Winston," she begged. "Please go get him."

"I'm sorry," I croaked out, attempting to contain my own emotions. "He wasn't there, Viviana. I swear to you."

Crying was something I'd rarely seen my sister do, and never in front of anyone else. It surprised me when she let out a loud wail, tears streaming down her reddened cheeks.

Attempting to calm her, I pulled her into a hug. She punched and squirmed, fighting me off. "Stop. Leave me alone."

I ignored her requests and held on until her body eased into mine, small sobs vibrating her chest against me.

"Why is this happening to me? I just want him back."

"I know, sis. We would have saved him if he were there."

I loosened my hug slightly and she took the opportunity to yank herself from my arms before storming off and screaming, "Ahhhhh," the haunting sound echoing through the woods as she disappeared.

I took a breath and wiped away the dampness on my cheeks, glancing at Peach. "I can't deal with her right now. Not this time. I got too much shit on my plate."

"I'll take care of her. You guys get some rest." Peach disappeared in a flash and I turned to check on Lyric.

"Are you okay, mama?"

"Yeah. It's not my first time getting knocked down by an angry vampire." She pulled on her left shoulder before massaging it. "Is she going to be okay?"

I shook my head, memories of the night Venom captured Strike flooding through me. Vivi had lost her shit then, but somehow, this felt even more severe. "I really don't know."

Kimber shifted back into a human, crossing her arms in front of her now naked body, a scowl on her face. "Here comes the asshole."

My focus went to Drag, who was completely naked as he approached, with Heston and Demi's bare asses following closely behind him.

"This is fucking crazy," Drag spat, stopping in front of me with a panicked expression. "I don't know what to do. Why now? And why her? It's like the universe hates me."

"What are you talking about?" I asked, making sure to only make eye contact. My gaze tended to drift to naked people, even the unattractive ones.

Drag put his hands on his thighs, leaning forward, and heavy pants left him as he completely ignored me.

I glanced at Heston, hoping to get some kind of hint to the situation.

"He found his fated mate," he muttered, and my eyes bulged, my mouth falling open.

Even though my emotions were stuck on my sister and Luka, it was nice having some good news for a change, so I forced a smile. "It's about time, bro. Congrats."

"Congrats? Congrats?" Drag flung his body back into a standing position, his face angering as he flung his arms out. "I can't even be with her. She's barely an adult!"

I cocked a brow. "Who the hell are we talking about?"

"Aluna," Kimber said, glaring, seemingly pissed. "She's from Galen's pack. And for the record, she's twenty-four and super sweet. He's lucky to even have her."

"She's twenty-four?" Drag put his hands on the side of his head. "You've got to be kidding me."

I tsked, furrowing my brows. "That sounds like an adult to me."

Drag smacked his hairy chest. "I'm thirty-three! I can't entertain a child when I have responsibilities to this pack."

"She's not a child!" Kimber yelled, clenching her fists. "And you won't have to worry about that after what you did to her. The poor girl probably has a broken heart, thanks to you."

"What did he do?" I asked, ready for some tea. Shit, I was ready for some popcorn so I could sit back and watch the show. It was nice being on the sidelines of the drama for a minute.

"He rejected her!" Kimber shouted, throwing her hands out, her boobs separating. "Who rejects their fated mate? My brother, that's who. And you should have seen Aluna's face, Winnie. She just stood there, all teary-eyed, and he didn't say a damn thing."

"I didn't reject her. I just walked away so I can think about things."

"We have traditions, Dragos. Ones you completely neglected to do. So, call it walking away or thinking about it all you damn want, but you rejected her, you asshole!"

Kimber stomped off and I glanced at Drag.

"Shut up, Winnie!"

I threw my hands out. "I didn't even say anything."

Drag stared at me because, although I didn't state it, he knew exactly what I was thinking. He shook his head and trudged off toward his cabin.

For years now, I'd followed him to every witch festival or party he wanted to attend in hopes of finding a fated mate, or at least a luna to help him lead his pack, each of them ending with him being sad. And now that he had a fated mate, I couldn't understand why he didn't feel relieved, other than the obvious age gap. But nine years wasn't a lot. Shit, I was twenty-five when I turned, but had been on this earth for fifty-two years, and was dating Lyric who was twenty-six.

I tilted my head, wondering if I was technically dating an older woman.

"How's Luka and Vivi?" Heston asked, bringing my attention to him. "We heard the screaming."

Not knowing what to say, I shrugged. "I don't know, bro."

"They'll be fine, I'm sure," Lyric said with a fake smile that didn't back her words. "We just have to be patient and kind."

"Keep your eyes above their waistline," I teased and she smacked my arm.

"Winston, stop." She blushed, tilting her head toward her feet, and I couldn't help but stare at the side profile of her beautiful face.

The only thought occupying my mind was the overwhelming concern I had for her while we were infiltrating VRC. I could finally imagine the pain Sage went through when they took Luka.

I loved her so much, I would have totally lost my shit without her.

Oh fuck. My lips parted, my mind stalling as if it was running on Windows 98 and attempting to use dial-up.

I love her?

The beating of my heart against my chest was so intense, I thought I was going to die. I quickly closed my mouth when Peach strolled up, her face unreadable.

"Unfortunately, I was unable to locate Vivi this time. She's becoming a pro at covering up her scent. I'm sure she'll show back up in a couple days."

"She always does," I agreed with a deep sigh that encapsulated the magnitude of shit I'd been piling on my plate.

"The others are back," Heston said, sniffing the air. "And they got a new person with them."

"That's gonna be too many damn people seeing my willie today," Demi said, putting his hand over his crotch. "We're gonna get our knickers on."

I laughed as Demi and Heston beelined toward their cabins.

A minute later, Ravage pulled into the parking lot and Peach turned her attention in that direction. "Why does Marcus smell like . . ." Her mouth fell open. "Oh my god!" She bolted toward the vehicle, and Lyric and I followed.

The van door slid open and Marcus stepped out. I hadn't talked to him since he turned and I wondered if he felt our sentinel bond like I did.

"What . . ." Peach choked on tears, placing her hand on his chest. "What happened? Are you okay?"

Marcus grabbed her cheeks, yanked her closer, and smashed his lips onto hers.

It was so hot and passionate, after a while I felt like we needed to leave them alone.

"Where's April and Scarlet?" Zeke asked when he exited the van.

I shrugged. "I haven't seen them since I got back." Zeke took off and I turned back to the free live make-out show and wondered if I should be selling tickets. "Okay, dude. Let the woman breathe."

Marcus pulled back, flashing me a pearly white smile. "Sorry, daddy."

I put my hands up, waving them. "Whoa, bro. Since I'm your origin, you can call me dad, but never daddy. That's Lyric's job."

"Eww," Erik said, making a gagging sound. "I don't need to know what my sister calls you."

"Winston! Stop telling people stuff like that or they're going to believe it."

I cocked a brow at Lyric because she *had* called me daddy on multiple occasions.

She pulled on one of her braids, her cheeks reddening. "I'm going to go check on Sage."

"I'm going with her," Erik added.

They left and I eyed Marcus. "Are you mad at me or are we good, bro?"

"I'm not going to lie. I was pissed at you last night because I told you how I felt before the mission. But after the shock wore off, I was really glad to be alive. Then the more I thought about it, the more I realized Peaches and Cream wouldn't be able to block my love anymore since I'll be around for a long time."

Peach smiled. "You're the only one allowed to call me that."

"Don't I know it." Marcus gave Peach another long kiss before he pulled away, his face confused. "What's that delicious scent? It smells like fresh peaches mixed with a hint of coconut."

I sniffed the air and didn't smell anything. Then my mouth fell open as I gaped, pointing at Peach. "Your essence smells like peaches! That's how you got the nickname."

"Shut up, smartass."

"What's an essence?" Marcus asked, her brows straining.

"It's like the human's lure and your amore combined, but only for vamps and wolves," I said, grinning from ear to ear. "Once two supernaturals bond, no one but their mate can smell their scents."

"Oh, my," Marcus growled, pulling Peach into him. "I want to taste your essence."

"If you'll excuse us." Peach took Marcus's hand, yanking him toward her cabin.

I let out a whistle. "Get it, boy!"

Lynx and Carmen were the only ones standing with me and faced each other, still chatting.

"Haven't you run out of things to talk about yet?"

Carmen laughed. "It's nice having someone who cares. Everyone seems nice, so far."

"Ha," I scoffed. "If you would have been here five minutes earlier, you could have watched my sister try and kill me."

Carmen's eyes widened.

"Vivi knows?" Lynx asked with a frown.

I nodded. "She took off into the woods again."

Lynx let out a hard breath before asking Carmen, "Anything you need? A drink or something?"

Carmen pulled on her shirt, like she'd been doing since Lyric gave it to her. "Coverage would be nice. Crop tops aren't really my thing."

Lynx pushed an errant strand of purple hair behind her ear, her smile flirtatious. "If you want, I can get you some better clothes to wear and show you around."

Carmen leaned into Lynx with the same exact expression. "I would love that."

I cocked a brow then made myself a bet they'd be getting it on soon.

They walked away, still chatting.

With everyone gone, I finally had a second to ponder my thoughts on my current relationship situation.

My heart had deceived me, leading me to fall in love with a woman who was truly flawless. A normal man couldn't ask for anything more, so what the hell was wrong with me?

The longer I contemplated my fears, the clearer the answer became and I realized I was never afraid of Lyric breaking my heart. Although it would hurt, I was strong enough to handle it.

Protecting *my heart* wasn't the problem. Protecting hers was.

Since the day I met her, I'd mentally and emotionally stuck her in a box in my head. I referred to her as perfect or an angel on numerous occasions. It was hard not to do when she had a tender, sweet, and honest soul. She was also a woman I couldn't give kids to. The thought of me causing any damage to her or causing her to miss out on what her life could have been with a human, terrified me to the core.

A familiar scent creeped into my lungs, interrupting my moment.

Fuck.

I whipped around and there stood Shayla, hands clasped in front of her.

"Take me to Sagelynn, please."

CHAPTER 31
SAGE

Once I got Luka into my cabin, he wanted to go straight to bed, intensifying the knot of concern in my gut. He fell into a deep slumber within moments, and I stood silently at the foot of the bed, watching his chest rise and fall with each labored breath.

Lyric and Erik's arrival prompted me to finally venture into the living room. She told me about Vivi freaking out, though I'd heard most of it. Then proceeded to tell me about Drag finding his fated mate and how he rejected her.

"Kimber was so mad at Drag. She said he didn't follow their normal traditions and now I want to know what that is," Lyric said, finishing her story as I made one of the few things I knew how, iced tea.

"That's sad."

I wasn't sure how the nexus bond felt to the wolven, but if it felt anything like the lenxus I had with Luka, I felt horrible for the girl.

I had just stirred sugar into the pitcher when the door opened. Glancing into the living area, my eyes widened. "Shayla?"

"Hello. We need to speak. May I have a seat?"

"Uh, sure. Give me one second." I put the lid on the pitcher and quickly washed my hands.

"That tea smells delicious," Winnie said, strolling into the kitchen like he didn't just bring a witch into my house. "Can I have some?"

"What is she doing here?" I whispered, drying my hands on a towel.

Winnie shrugged, grabbing a glass from the cabinet. "I don't know. I hate witches."

I glared at him before tossing the hand towel on the counter and flipping him the bird, then headed into the living room.

Shayla had taken a seat next to Lyric on the couch and Erik had scooted himself to the edge of the recliner across from her, ready to bolt.

"I'm going to take off," he said, standing. "Kimber is upset, so I want to check on her."

He said his goodbyes and quickly left the cabin.

"How have you been?" I asked, awkwardly standing in the middle of the room, crossing my arms over myself.

"Faring well. And you?" Shayla clasped her hands together, settling them on her lap and it reminded me of my mother.

"I'm good. Would you like a glass of iced tea?"

"Although it sounds pleasing, I tend to stay away from sugary substances." Shayla wrinkled her freckled nose, then glanced around as if she looked for something specific. "I see everyone made it out alive. I'm glad the loose-tongue one made the right decision. The prophecy is right on track."

I tightened my lips to suppress laughter, yet a slight tinge of concern gathered in the depths of my stomach since I had yet to have a private conversation with Marcus.

"Do not worry, my silver," Shayla said, bringing my attention back to her from staring at the wood floor—I hadn't even noticed my mind had wandered off. "The strong one loves and forgives. He is the trifecta, unlike anyone else. His new eyes will see the beauty this world has to offer. As yours will soon."

I snickered, my face contorting of its own accord.

"Is something funny?" Shayla's facial expression remained refined and polished.

Unlike mine.

"It's just . . ." I looked upward, shaking my head as if attempting to pull thoughts from my mind. "You say the 'beauty of the world' like it's just everywhere, yet all I've seen for months is hate, and lies, and blood, and tears, and . . . and . . ." I took a deep breath, blowing it out through pursed lips, attempting to control my emotions. "And everything evil. People I love have died, endured torture, or been forced to turn into a vampire. There's no beauty there."

"The stars guide us along treacherous pathways, my silver. The choice to walk or stumble upon those paths is entirely yours to make."

I threw my hands up. "Then why did they choose to have Marcus get killed in the first place?"

"While the stars may offer guidance, our choices harbor the capacity to alter the predetermined trajectory of destiny. At times, it may be challenging, and occasionally, it is effortless."

That did not answer my question.

I rolled my eyes, a jagged breath leaving me as I suppressed a laugh. "If fate controls everything, why doesn't it just prevent evil, then?"

"There must be wicked things in order for people to learn and adapt. If true evil ceased, time would halt and the earth would no longer exist." Shayla raised her hand, waving it slightly. "The absence of moisture is dry. The absence of anger is calm."

I blinked, awaiting more of an answer, but she said nothing. "I kind of understand, but without evil the world would be perfect."

"Nothing is perfect, my silver. Some flowers are big and stunning, while others struggle to bloom."

I drew a long, heavy breath before releasing it in a sigh. "I understand the concept, but it doesn't make sense. The reasoning behind it all just baffles me."

"The lack of carnivores would lead to an imbalanced ecosystem, with herbivores prevailing and overpopulating the world. Earth would not be able to regenerate quickly enough to meet the demand for the amount of plant matter consumed. Then comes the extinction of flowers, bees, trees, and eventually life."

"But the magic—"

"There are no *buts*. Only balance. The realm of magic, like everything else, operates under the guidance of rules." She placed her hand over her heart. "The consequences will be harsh if I do not use my magic wisely."

I slid my butt onto the edge of the recliner and leaned in. "Like what?"

"If I were to disclose the answers to the universe now, you would have no lessons left to learn."

I darted my eyes to Lyric, and she raised her brows, telling me she had no clue what to say . . . and I was on my own.

"But—"

"There are no *buts* in the stars," Shayla said, rising from her seat with more grace than a queen, heading toward me. "Give me your hand."

At this point, I would take any info I could get from a witch, so I did as she said, holding my hand up in front of me.

Shayla grasped it, her brows furrowing.

"Your uncle is a powerful force now. Given that he shares the same bloodline as you, he will prove to be a formidable opponent. He is not a witch, a vampire, nor a wolven. He is a precise amalgamation of the three. A tercet among men."

My eyes expanded, my jaw unhinging to the point of no return. "My uncle's a witch?"

Shayla dropped my hand, glaring at me like I was an imbecile. "I have entertained you enough, my child. Good night."

She strolled to the door with ease and left my cabin, leaving me completely bewildered.

"Winnie," I screeched, jumping to my feet and pacing the small living room, my thoughts running rampant. One of them landed on the possible lies I was told.

Winnie finally weaseled his way out of the kitchen where he was hiding. "I'm glad she's gone."

My heated eyes darted to him. "You told me my uncle smelled like a vampire and a wolven. You never once said witch."

"I tried to tell you that same night, but you shut us out. Then the next day you met the witches and I *assumed* you'd figured it out. You know, because you're an Argentum witch and you and your uncle both have the same damn blood."

"I was busy with the one million other thoughts in my brain." With a huff, I slid my flip-flops off, plopped down on the couch next to Lyric, and put my feet on the coffee table, crossing my ankles. "What the fuck are we going to do?"

"Kill him."

My gaze drifted from my unmanicured toes to Winnie. "Do you think he's stronger than you guys?"

He crossed his arms, leaning back. "I'm not sure, but my gut is saying yes."

I swallowed the tension building in my throat. "Do you think VRC made him?"

"Shit, I don't know, Sage Stick." He shrugged, his forehead clenched with tension. "Maybe."

Lyric rubbed her hand down my arm. "Everything will be okay."

A hard breath escaped me as I pondered another thought. "What was that word Shayla used? A 'ter' something. What's that?"

"A tercet? It's technically three lines in a poem, but I totally understand the resemblance between that and the three species he is."

"Do you think Ben is the only tercet? Could there be more?"

Winnie's thoughts seemed to wander off for a minute, his face unreadable, before he finally answered me. "Let's hope not."

Winnie and Lyric eventually left while Luka remained asleep, leaving me alone with my thoughts.

With only an hour left before the sunrise, I decided I'd do the dishes before bed, to get my mind off of all the fear I was harboring. I played some music through the Alexa Winnie had gotten me, but kept it low so I didn't disturb Luka.

My kitchen wasn't dirty enough to occupy my brain for long. It only took three songs and I'd finished the dishes, wiped the counters and fridge, and began contemplating reorganizing the almost empty cabinets.

The wood floor was cold against my bare feet and I was about to grab a pair of socks before I moved onto my next task when I heard a creak from behind me.

"How long was I in there?"

I froze, my heart fluttering at the sound of Luka's voice, his question sinking in. My breaths were rapid, and I locked my eyes on the gray laminate counter, staring at the black and white speckles, refusing to meet his eyes.

"Six . . . six months."

He sucked in a hard breath. "Holy shit."

"I'm sorry I didn't come sooner." I bit my lip, the guilt eating at my veins.

"I already told you not to be sorry for anything. I'd happily be locked up forever to keep you safe."

The wood floor creaked again as Luka moved in close, then slid the collar of my shirt over, sending chills down my spine. He placed soft kisses on my shoulder, his hot breath blowing across my skin.

I leaned into him, my eyes drifting close, completely enjoying the moment.

The song shuffled to the next one, changing to "Fade into You" by Mazzy Star, and he gripped my hips, turning me to meet his eyes.

"Kiss me," he commanded in a way that sent shivers rippling through my body—through my damn soul.

I did what he asked and pushed up onto my tippy toes with lips parted. His mouth pressed against mine, warm and inviting, giving me a safe place to be on a cold winter's night.

My heart raced, an aching settling in it. I didn't know if the feeling was fear of losing him again, or if my heart had overfilled with so much love it hurt.

Silent tears rolled down my cheeks as I pulled back, staring into his bright blue eyes. He held my gaze, gently wiping them away with his knuckle.

He leaned down, pressing his forehead against mine, and we silently bonded back together.

The stars had destined our paths to cross because we were two halves of a whole, stronger together than we were apart.

He was the peace to my chaos, the calm to my nervousness.

The universe, that's what he was.

He was life—my life—and I knew I couldn't live without him. Which wasn't something I was used to.

For as far back as I could remember, I kept most men at a distance, and I finally realized why.

As a small child, I was a daddy's girl, following him around, awaiting the day I'd finally get his approval—one that never came. My uncle also made me feel unworthy, constantly reminding me of my inadequacy to hold my proud position as a member of Venom.

As I got older, I was afraid of becoming a victim, making the unconscious vow to never let another man hurt me. It mostly worked. I'd had romantic relationships with both men and women, none of them successful. When things ended, I'd blame them, saying they were too clingy or some other excuse, not acknowledging I was the real problem. With me came a giant suitcase of emotional baggage that I refused to unpack.

There were only a few men who'd made it through the stronghold I had surrounding my heart, and one of them was Marcus. He'd stepped up, slowly teaching me about integrity and showing me the fatherly love I'd never experienced with my real dad.

Another was Erik. Being born in the Venom society just a few years before me, we'd become family before my walls went up. He was a brother to me and a person I trusted with my heart.

Then there was Winnie. Our friendship had experienced significant growth over the past six months, making him my family now.

Finally, there was Luka. Despite all the hate in the beginning, he'd always looked out for me, sacrificing his own needs for the sake of mine. Somehow, he'd slowly inched his way across my thresholds without either of us knowing. And as I stood there, my forehead pressed against his, his scent once again gracing my nose, I knew he'd broken down my barriers and completely moved into my heart.

And I . . . had let him.

He shifted, letting go of me for a split second to gently guide my hands to his shoulders before dropping his own back to the curves of my hips. His body swayed gracefully with the music, mine naturally following . . . and it forever would. I'd follow him off a cliff without hesitation because he was a piece of me now. A piece of my heart and soul.

As the wood beneath our feet creaked, the cabin floor felt less chilly. His warm blue eyes stayed locked with mine while we swayed away the darkness.

CHAPTER 32

LUKA

After being rescued and sleeping for numerous hours, I finally asked the dreaded question. Although I didn't want to, I needed to know how the fuck long I had been in that hell hole. Sage hesitated at first before she finally broke the news, telling me I'd lost six months of my life.

The torture I had endured while strapped to that table was unbearable. The only wave of relief was when my consciousness became consumed by hazy dreams. As I became more awake and aware, the memories of my time in captivity replayed in my mind, each moment etched vividly in my memory.

Doctor Cuntface snaps on a pair of latex gloves, the sound a haunting reminder of the last two times she was near my groin.

"I will be taking samples of your scrotum and testicles again today."

I don't give her the pleasure of answering, instead, I tighten my fists, praying it doesn't hurt as bad as the previous time.

She clutches her hand around my balls and squeezes, sticking in the first of three needles.

A stinging pain radiates through me and I grit my teeth tightly. The overpowering torture yanks a tear from the corner of my eye.

She sets the last needle down, exchanging it for a scalpel. My fists tighten more, causing my nails to dig into the palm of my hand, and I hold my breath as she slices into my sac. A whimper slips through my teeth, and I swallow down a second one, refusing to let her hear the pain she's causing.

Once done, she puts the surgical instrument back and grabs the lubrication. As soon as she begins to lube up a finger, I squeeze my eyes shut, not wanting to watch as she strips me of my virility.

"Are you okay, bro?" Winnie asked, ripping me out of my memories.

A thin layer of sweat coated my entire body while my heart pounded against my chest. As I leaned back in the recliner, the soft fabric gently caressed my skin, offering a much-needed comfort, unlike the cold, spiked metal bed I laid on for six months. I threw an arm over my head, letting out a sigh of relief, grateful to have escaped the torment of hell.

"I'm good, man. Sometimes I get these flashbacks and . . ." I swallowed my words, knowing damn well I'd never reveal what happened to me while I was in VRC. "Don't worry. I'm good."

A motorcycle engine roared, pulling into the parking lot, and Winnie looked toward the door. "Lane's here."

Knowing we needed cold beer for this conversation, I hopped up from the chair and quickly headed to the kitchen, where I snatched three from the fridge.

Making my way back to the living room, I placed a beer in front of Winnie and another on the opposite side of the coffee table before settling back into my spot.

The wood planks on the front porch creaked, the scent of a wolven entering my lungs. "Come on in, Lane."

Annie started barking at the door as it opened, and Lane entered with a huge smile. "My man, I'm so glad you're back."

He headed toward me and I stood, giving him a quick hug. "I got you a beer."

"Awesome." Lane copped a squat on the couch by Winnie, twisting the top off of his bottle. "Settling in good?"

I nodded, picking Annie up and setting him on my lap, not wanting to talk about what happened to me. "Winnie said you had some information."

"Possibly. I was up at the new Save building, fixing a pipe in the kitchen because Evelyn asked me to. No one knew I was there, and I saw Finneas on the cameras talking to a man right at the edge of the property. I didn't know how to download the footage, so I just took a video of it." Lane pulled out his phone, clicked on a few things and then handed it to me. "Do you know the man with him?"

In the slightly blurry and dark video, two men could be seen engaged in conversation before ultimately shaking hands beside a white Cadillac. The shorter, plumper guy was Finneas, one of the leaders of the Supernaturals Against Venom Elitists. The other guy had a muscular build, darker hair, and was completely unfamiliar to me. He entered the Cadillac and proceeded to depart, while Fin made his way toward his black Escalade.

"I've never seen him before." The video started over as I handed the phone to Winnie, then stroked my fingers down Annie's short fur.

The second his eyes locked on the screen they flared in disbelief, his jaw dropping open. "What. The. Fuck. I fucking knew it." He shook his head, holding up the phone, furiously pointing at it. "That burly dude, that's Ben Fucking Argent. Sage's uncle."

Even though I didn't recognize the man, I knew exactly who he was talking about. Just an hour ago, Winnie had filled me in on *all* the details I'd missed, including the revelation that my girlfriend was a witch, and her uncle some kind of triple hybrid.

A low growl left me, veins rippling across my face in a flash, and a weird throbbing radiated in my gums. Annie hopped off my lap, running toward the bedroom.

Winnie cocked a brow. "Chill, bro. We ain't killing anyone today."

Lane's nostrils flared as he inhaled deeply, his confusion evident. He locked eyes with Winnie who nodded, and a sense of suspicion washed over me.

My eyes darted between the two of them. "What?"

Winnie's body language spoke volumes as he leaned forward in his seat, his elbows planted firmly on his knees. "Umm, we weren't going to say anything yet, but you smell weird."

"I literally showered before you got here." I raised my arm and sniffed my pit. "Smells fine to me."

"It's not that." Lane shook his head, his nostrils widening as he sniffed again. "I don't know what it is. It's earthy, like old soil mixed with a pungent rotten fruit smell."

My brows lifted. "Are you sure? I can't smell anything."

"We're sure," Winnie said, yanking his beer up. "Every wolven and vampire in this camp has smelled it, yet none of us can pinpoint what it is."

"And when you growled it became stronger for a minute," Lane added, his nostrils flaring once more. "It's a lot calmer now, but it's still there."

Winnie took a sip of beer, then leaned back into the couch. "Perhaps that doctor loaded you up with steroids or some other unknown substance, bro."

Lane picked his phone back up, his head shaking as he eyed it. "Shit. Based on your description of Ben's scent they might have injected him with something too."

A wave of coldness washed over me, causing my back to immediately tense up and sending a prickling sensation across my entire body, as if warning me of some impending danger.

The three of us locked eyes and the tension in the room became palpable, our expressions silently acknowledging the unspoken truth.

It's possible the Vampire Research Center had altered my nature.

Winnie cleared his throat, finally breaking the silence in the room. "Do you think they turned you into a freak hybrid?"

"No," I quickly replied, my hands trembling with fear of what the truth might reveal. "You said you'd detected the scent of the multiple species on Ben, but mine doesn't smell like that, right?"

Winnie ran a hand through his dark, shaggy hair, the shaved sides contrasting against the longer top. "No, but they definitely did something to you."

"Let's stay on topic. Back to Sage's uncle and the meeting he had with Finneas."

Winnie's intense glare clarified we'd be continuing this conversation in private, whether or not I wanted to. He finally broke eye contact, tipping his head toward Lane. "If they're working together, you're not safe. I think you should pull back from meetings."

"I agree with Winnie."

"Will do." With a nod, Lane reached for his beer, finishing it off in one swift gulp before he rose from his seat. "Well, this has been eye-opening, but I gotta get back. If you guys need anything, let me know."

The cabin door flung open and Sage and Lyric giggled their way through the door. Annie came back out, barking again, before happily wagging his tail.

"Oh, hey, Lane, how is umm," Sage side-eyed me and Winnie, "that thing we were talking about?"

A wide smile spread across Lane's face. "Beyond amazing. Once I get time, we can sit down and I'll tell you the entire story."

"That would be great."

Before Lane even got out the door, Drag poked his head in. "Has anyone seen Laren? I need more torch oil. Oh, hey, Lane."

"She went to the store for Ollie again," Lyric said, her brows tightening. "He needed limes and something else for the bar. I can't remember."

"My dad is a pain in the ass." Drag sighed, his eyes landing on Lane. "Hope all is going well at your place."

"Thanks. I'm settling in nicely."

Drag nodded, his face filled with urgency. "Good. I can't stay and talk because I have to finish this project. See you guys later."

He shut the door and Lane turned back toward us.

"What's wrong with Drag? I've never seen him so energetic."

Winnie snickered. "Ever since he rejected that chick from Ironclad, he's been running around putting up tiki torches, solar lights, and hammering on shit. I think he's nesting or something."

Lane laughed, his hand on the door knob. "Aluna is a sweet girl. He should at least acknowledge her. But it's none of my business."

With a smile, Lane left, and it only took a few seconds for the door to open again.

I threw my hands up. "What the fuck is this, Grand Central Station?"

Lynx stuck her head in. "Someone wants to see you." She pushed the door open and Carmen stepped into the house.

She nervously glanced around, pulling on one of her curls before her eyes landed on me. "I was just seeing if we could talk for a minute before I leave."

According to Winnie, Lynx was taking Carmen home and planned to stay at her house for a while as she figured out her next steps. I was sad to see her go, but was happy she was free from VRC.

"Uh, me and Lyric were about to take off," Sage said, taking my finger in her hand. "We're going to go shoot targets with Peach. We'll be back in a little while." She gave me a quick kiss and smiled at Carmen. "It was nice meeting you." Sage headed toward the door with Lyric in tow.

"Don't be out too late, mama, I have plans to be inside of you tonight."

Lyric froze in the doorway, whipping toward Winnie, her face red. "Winston!" She exhaled sharply, slamming the door shut.

Winnie shrugged nonchalantly. "I was just being honest."

"Stop torturing that girl," Lynx said, heading into the kitchen and opening the fridge. "She's going to dump your ass."

"Doubtful. She knows what daddy Winnie has to offer."

Winnie's outgoing personality left Carmen puzzled, her face contorting with confusion. "Is this a bad time?"

Winnie grinned, showing off his fangs. "Nah, I'm always this arrogant."

I rolled my eyes, then gestured toward the couch. "Have a seat, and be careful, he bites."

Nervous laughter escaped Carmen's lips, but it was short-lived as her face turned somber. "I don't have time to relax. I have to get on the road now if I want to make it home before sunrise. I just wanted to say thank you. Without you and your friends, I'd still be trapped in a never-ending cycle of torment. I owe you all so much."

Her eyes took on a gentle, watery shine as tears began to pool in them.

"I wouldn't have left without you," I said sincerely, before standing and pulling her in for a hug. "You take care of yourself."

"You too, Luka."

My heart was heavy as she bid us farewell and walked out of the cabin with Lynx by her side.

"I'm going to get us another beer so we can talk about the possibility of you being a freak."

As Winnie stood, making his way toward the kitchen, a lump formed in my throat, which I struggled to swallow down.

The front door flung open once more and I was beginning to wonder if anyone knew how to knock as a dude with thick glasses stumbled in, his eyes filled with fear.

"Who the hell are you?"

"I'm Jimmy. We met before and you told me to run instead of killing me."

"I told you about him," Winnie hollered from the kitchen. "He's chill."

Jimmy had sweat beads forming on his head, his heart thundering in my ears. "Why are you panicking so bad?"

"We're all being hunted by Venom. They're offering reward money to anyone who captures us." He hurriedly made his way toward me and slapped down a pile of papers on my lap.

My heart bounced against my rib cage, my breaths becoming choppy when I saw the top page. It had a vivid picture of Sage, accompanied by a thorough description of her appearance, notable markings, and any other relevant details they had gathered. They also had a considerable amount of reward for her capture, and half that amount for her death.

"Holy shit."

Winnie was by my side in a flash, taking it from my hand. "What the fuck! They have a million dollar bounty on Sage."

The next portfolio in the pile was mine. It had the same categories, and went into great detail about every tattoo I had. Just like Sage's, my bounty was a hefty million.

I panicked, thumbing through the rest quickly.

The next three had unknown names and were Ravage, Winnie, and Lynx. Then Carmen's had a name attached. Each of their profiles only had descriptions of them and semi blurry pictures taken from video footage inside and outside of VRC. A half a million in bounties on each, dead or alive.

The profiles with names and pictures attached were all the ex-Venom members. Lyric, Erik, Marcus, Zeke, Jimmy, Nellie, and Randi were less wanted criminals with bounties reaching two-hundred fifty thousand each, dead or alive.

"Why the hell am I worth more than you?" Winnie asked, his brows tightened. "You're a damn ex-member."

Jimmy's shoulders rose and fell. "I'm assuming because you're a vampire. Other than Sage, all the humans have a low bounty."

"Winnie, call Lyric and tell her and Sage to get back here, then call Lynx and tell her and Carmen the same. Jimmy, you go find those two other Venom girls and bring them to the fire pit." I hopped from my seat and headed toward the door. "I'll get Ravage and the others."

"What are we doing?" Jimmy asked, his fear so thick, I could almost smell it.

"Family meeting time."

The bonfire crackled and roared, its flames dancing high into the night sky. All eyes were on me, filled with curiosity and anticipation.

"We received something important tonight that requires serious attention." I held the papers in my hands, fiddling with them. "Now, don't freak out when I tell you this but . . . Venom has bounties on most of our heads."

Gasps and incoherent words echoed from every direction.

"How many of us?" a young woman asked, her tone low.

My brows knitted together. "Who are you?"

"Oh, I'm Randi," she said with a warm smile.

"You're on their list." I approached her, extending the paper with her information and she took it with a large gasp. My gaze flicked to the other woman I didn't know. "And I'm assuming you're Nellie." She nodded and I handed her paper over. "And so are you."

Patiently, I went from person to person, delivering the papers to their rightful recipients, until I reached the last two. Mine and Sage's.

She nodded knowingly. "Just give me it."

With shaky hands, I reluctantly handed it over.

"They have a million dollar bounty on my head!" she screeched, her mouth stretched wide in a horrified expression.

Winnie snickered. "Mine's only half of that."

"All the vamps who went on the mission are half a million. The only ones less than that are the ex-Venom members."

"Mine's only a quarter of a million," Nellie said, shaking her head in disbelief. "I'm not sure if I should be happy or sad."

"How the fuck am I the most wanted? They must really hate me," Sage pondered aloud, her words tinged with a touch of insecurity.

"You can't be everyone's cup of tea, darling, not when you reside in a well-aged barrel of whiskey," Ravage stated, holding up his glass and winking.

A hard sigh left Sage, then her eyes met mine. "Wait, what does yours say?" She yanked it from my hands. "Fuck, they want us both more than anyone."

"That seems to be the case, Princess."

Small sobs left Nellie, bringing my eyes to her. "How can they do this? If they hadn't gotten a bunch of us slaughtered, we wouldn't have left."

Sage laughed, her expression amused. "They couldn't care less about any of us. They wouldn't have led you to a slaughter if they did."

"I just don't understand," Nellie whimpered, wiping tears from her cheeks. "One day we are in a prestigious society, the next we have bounties on our heads. And you're just okay with that?"

Sage shrugged, a small frown playing on her lips. "You get to the point where your animosity overrides your integrity."

"Hear! Hear!" Ravage held his glass high. "That's my girl."

Sage smiled, and when she turned her back toward everyone, it immediately dropped. "We need to get my mom out of there," she whispered, her voice filled with a mixture of fear and determination. "I only want a few of us to know about it."

I took her hand and headed fifteen feet away from the bonfire surrounded by people, and whispered low enough the vampires would hear but no one else. "Hey, Winnie. Be chill and come here."

He got up and messed around with the fire, then slowly made his way toward us, his brows knitted together. "What up, bro?"

"You got a burner and a few minutes to spare?"

He tilted his head. "Always."

I tipped my face toward Sage. "Go with him and call your mom."

She nodded, quietly walking off with Winnie.

Despite the urge to take her to call her mom, the toll of today's repeated conversations weighed heavily on me, a reminder of my long incarceration in mostly silence.

Seeking solitude, I headed into the woods and walked around for a few minutes and took in a few deep breaths, savoring the earthy scent of the trees.

I had been longing all day for a chance to have a private moment with Sage, and then I had a perfect idea.

CHAPTER 33
SAGE

Once me and Winnie arrived back at the bonfire, Ravage had music on and Luka was nowhere to be found. I sat there quietly with my thoughts before he finally plopped down next to me.

"We good?" he asked, with a sly smile that didn't really fit the situation.

"Yeah. Why are you grinning?"

His gaze locked on mine, the bonfire flickering in his beautiful blue eyes. "I just love you."

Emotion overwhelmed me, and my heart swelled with intensity. I was about to respond when the fast-paced music abruptly stopped.

The song changed to "Unchained Melody," the Smith and Myers version.

Zeke stood and took the baby monitor from April, setting it on the ground. "Come on, babe."

He pulled her to her feet and she wrapped her arms around his neck. They swayed to the music, and my chest filled with love while I watched them.

Enjoying the moment, I leaned my head on Luka's shoulder and felt the warmth of his arm as he slid it around me, gently drumming his fingers down my back.

Jimmy got up and approached Nellie. "Would you like to dance with me?" His voice was uncertain, but it filled me with pride knowing he had stepped out of his comfort zone. She graciously accepted his offer and began dancing with him.

"Shit, mama. We can do better than them." Winnie pulled Lyric to her feet as she giggled. I was happy they were back together.

Erik said nothing as he took Kimber's hand.

Marcus stood, peering down at Peach with more love than I'd ever seen in someone's eyes, and held out his hand. "My lady."

Peach graciously accepted and a happy sigh left me. I had found him earlier, and he assured me he was grateful to be alive and knew I forced Winnie to change him out of love.

Lynx and Carmen had returned to camp earlier, not long after leaving, because they were on the wanted list and Ravage said it would be safer here. I didn't know Carmen at all, but she seemed nice to me.

Lynx took her hand, leading her to the dance floor.

"Aw, shite," Demi mumbled under his breath. "I'm not gonna let a woman sit." He rose from his seat and reached his hand down to Stephanie.

She stared wide-eyed, looking around as if confused.

"It's just a dance, darlin', not a proposal. Don't get your knickers in a twist."

She laughed, then happily took his hand.

I glanced at Heston, seeing if he had any thoughts about asking Randi. He crossed his arms, leaning back in his lawn chair, attempting to make himself invisible. It took all my strength not to laugh.

Other than us and Ravage, everyone was dancing.

His eyes locked on Luka. "I know I taught you better than that, son."

Luka pulled his arm from around me and stood, lowering a hand, and I shook my head profusely. "Oh, no. You don't have to."

"I don't have to do anything I don't want to."

My heart sped up with the familiar words. Before I had a chance to resist, Luka had my wrists, dragging me to my feet, pulling me into the middle of the other people on the makeshift dance floor.

His hands slid onto my lower back and he yanked me into him. Even though I hated being controlled, the casual possessiveness had me melting in his arms. I wrapped my hands around his neck, laying my head on his chest, swaying in peaceful bliss until the song ended. When it restarted, I popped my head up and Ravage winked at me, and I realized Luka had planned this.

He brought my attention back by grabbing my chin, forcing me to make eye contact. "Look right here, Princess."

When I locked eyes with him, a sense of calm washed over me, making all my worries and stresses melt away.

Ravage played the song three times while we enjoyed our lives for just a few brief minutes.

Once the song finally changed and everyone began mingling, Luka pulled me away from the bonfire. I didn't ask where we were going because as long as I was with him, I didn't care.

We went to the side of our cabin, my forehead wrinkling when I saw my Jeep because I knew I hadn't left it there. Luka's hands gently rested on my hips as he effortlessly lifted me up onto it, joining me with a graceful hop.

After pulling me to my feet on the roof of my car, he lifted me once again. "Grab the edge."

I did what he said and clung to the roof of the cabin before pulling myself up onto it. Luka jumped up next with ease.

"What are we doing?" I asked, catching my breath.

Luka took my hand and guided me to the peak of the roof where a blanket laid and I finally realized he had planned this too.

He took a seat, pulling me down with him. "Showing you this. Look up."

I tilted my head back and marveled at the vast twinkling stars. "I've been out here for months and I don't think I have stopped worrying long enough to look at the sky at night."

"I think it's healthy to take twenty seconds for yourself and look at something beautiful."

As I glanced over, I noticed that his attention wasn't on the stars but on me with admiration. I laughed. "Then why aren't you looking at the beauty?"

His eyes shimmered with a mixture of emotions as he softly whispered, "I am, Princess."

It may seem cheesy to some, but my heart *completely* melted. Perhaps only figuratively, but it might have if it weren't so cold away from the bonfire.

The way he gazed into my eyes compelled me to confess the passion, the happiness, and the affection which stirred inside of me, but the intensity of my feelings rendered me speechless. Each emotion which engulfed me was indescribable, and *almost* unbearable. It appeared as if there were no words in existence that could help me accurately express my emotions to him.

Well . . . except there actually was.

I diverted my gaze, counting the stars above to gain time. When I got to thirteen, Luka's fingers slid in between mine, and when he locked them around my hand and squeezed, I felt safe. Secure. A feeling I hadn't experienced in a long time.

This man was my world, and as I thought about how much he meant to me, pain filled my chest.

He was a vampire and my brain was stuck on that stupid fact. Not because being with him was wrong. Fear consumed me, knowing that one day he would inevitably lose me.

"Your tears are going to freeze." His voice was deep, sexy, amazing. His free hand raised to my cheek where he ran his thumb across it, wiping away my sadness. "What's wrong, love?"

When my face turned toward him, his beautiful blue eyes were watching me again—wanting me, needing me. I swallowed my vulnerability and turned my head, making his hand fall away. More tears filled my eyes and I closed them tight, forcing them to stop.

"You're going to outlive me since I'm human."

"I can turn you," he stated with ease.

"That's not what I meant." I took a deep breath and exhaled softly. My eyes stayed locked on the sky as I finally said the words we both needed to hear. "I wanted to say I love you. In case that happens."

His hand was warm as it slid under my chin, forcing me to turn my head. "Look right here. Especially when you say something like that." The arrogant grin on his face was almost too much to bear. I had missed it dearly.

I sucked in a couple of deep breaths as I stared into his eyes. "I love you, Luka."

His thumb softly glided over my bottom lip, stopping it from quivering. "It took you long enough."

I let out a breathy laugh, the warm air from my lungs sending small puffs of smoke into the chilly night sky.

"I love you, Sagelynn. With every breath I take, every drop of blood I bleed. I love you with everything I have. And I don't know if you know this but . . . ." His eyes filled with tears—something I had only seen once before. "You're the only thing that kept me alive in there."

"And you're the only thing that kept me alive out here," I confessed, sniffing back sobs.

He leaned in close, his nose brushing delicately across my cheek, breathing me in. "I missed that scent. Lavender and vanilla."

"I love you too," I whispered against his mouth.

His tongue glided over my bottom lip before he tenderly nipped it. When his lips pressed against mine, the warmth of them consumed me, making me forget the world even existed.

His kisses came harder, faster, exploring the depths of my soul before moving away from my lips, leading down my neck. I tilted my head, giving him room to proceed.

He slid his hand up my shirt, gripping my breast, and I found myself leaning into his touch, craving more.

"Fuck," I moaned. "I feel like I haven't been touched in a thousand years."

Luka moved with urgency and intensity, every touch and kiss sending shivers down my spine. His hand glided down my soft leggings and a realization hit me.

Oh god. I'm so hairy.

"Um, this might not be the right time for this."

Luka unlatched from my neck just long enough to say, "Every minute of the day is the right time, Princess."

With his mouth back on me, every ounce of resistance seemed to fade away, leaving only a powerful desire. His hand was between my legs, sending waves of pleasure coursing through my body.

I was stuck between wanting to have my brains fucked out and not wanting to scare him with my winter coat.

I whimpered in a not so sexy way, and Luka pulled back. "Do you want me to stop?"

"God no. It's just," I panted out fast breaths, "I haven't shaved. We've been so busy that—"

I didn't even have a chance to argue when he pressed on my stomach, forcing me to lie back. "I don't give a shit if you grew a beard while I was gone."

"We are literally on a roof," I whispered, feeling a slight breeze against my face. "All the vampires are going to hear. They can probably hear me talking now."

"And all the wolven are going to smell you when I make you come in my mouth." He ripped my shirt and sports bra both up.

"Luk—aaaaah." My pleas of resistance quickly faded into moans of pleasure as he skillfully latched his mouth onto my breast, my nipple ring clinking against his teeth.

My hands dug into his hair, gripping tightly as a dire need flared in my lower abdomen. I pushed him down my body, shoving his head between my legs. He latched his mouth on me, sending a warm breath through the fabric of my thin leggings. My pussy clenched, wetness filling my panties.

"Take them the fuck off," I screeched, and he yanked at the waist band, pulling my leggings down enough for my thighs to fall open.

With skilled fingers, he gently spread my lips apart, his mouth hungrily seeking out my throbbing clit, sucking it with an insatiable appetite.

Intense pleasure washed through my body, causing my back to arch off the roof, a moan escaping my lips. "Oh, fuck. Don't stop."

Gripping his hair tightly, I pushed and pulled, grinding my hips with urgency, desperately using him to fulfill my needs.

"Bite me," I whispered, and he pulled back, my tense body relaxing slightly.

He gazed up at me as his finger dipped into my wetness, capturing my juices, before gliding it along my sensitive clit. He dipped his head back down, and I let mine fall against the roof. With each circular motion of his hand, his lips traced a tantalizing path along my inner thigh.

The sensation of his fangs grazing my skin caused me to inhale sharply and my wetness intensified, trickling down onto my ass cheeks. Clutching the plush blanket, my fingers trembled in anticipation of his impending strike.

My breaths came in short bursts, my muscles began twitching, an urgent need, ready to be released.

In a flash, his fangs sank into my inner thigh, causing a sharp, searing pain that was quickly relieved by the warmth of his venom spreading through my veins.

With each gentle suck of blood from my inner thigh, ripples of euphoria washed over me, ripping a moan from my lips. "Oh, god!"

The orgasm hit me like a powerful rush, causing him to release my vein and eagerly suck on my clit while I rode the wave of euphoria. My moans echoed through the night sky, the stars above us blurring.

My muscles went lax, my fingers gently releasing the death grip I had on his hair as my body quivered, before finally stilling with satisfaction.

Luka crawled up to me, settling between my legs. "They definitely heard that."

My cheeks flushed and I quickly covered my face in response. "Oh, god."

"Yeah. That's the exact words they heard."

A mortifying giggle left me and I dropped my hands above my head. His eyes locked on mine almost as if he still couldn't believe I was real. I blinked a few times, sleepy from the venom in his bite.

I grabbed his cheeks, pulling his face toward me. "I love you."

"Lavender and vanilla," he said with a grin before he pressed his lips against mine.

CHAPTER 34
WINNIE

The events of the next evening revolved around our mission to retrieve Sage's mother. Not being able to trust anyone, we broke our team up into four groups, each one leaving at a different time, telling a random story of where they were going.

Luka, Sage, and myself were in the last group. Our story was we were going to Luka's house to retrieve some things. As the final team to depart, we had more than an hour remaining before we had to leave.

Settled into the comfortable rocking chair at Luka and Sage's cabin, I balanced my laptop on my thighs as I combed through a collection of VRC files, meticulously reviewing each one. Unbeknownst to Luka, I was hoping to find something specific on what that doctor did to him.

Sage was in the shower and Lyric had taken her "morning" run with Erik. They usually left right before the sun went down, and came back not too long after I woke up, so I knew she'd be back in about thirty minutes.

Annie barked, then Chewy hissed at him. "I thought they couldn't live together?" I asked, watching as Chewy swatted Annie in the face.

"Too damn bad. They're going to have to get used to it."

"So, was last night your first time fucking on the roof?' I asked, wiggling my brows.

Luka snickered. "Shut up, Winnie."

"That was fucking loud. Or loud fucking. Same difference."

Luka chuckled lightly, then pushed himself back into the couch, plopping his feet up on the coffee table as his smile faded. "We didn't have sex."

With a subtle tilt of my head, I shot him a disbelieving look. "The moans echoing through the forest says otherwise."

Luka's distant eyes seemed to carry a heavy burden. "I assure you we didn't. I took care of her, but then we stopped."

"You or her?" I subtly asked.

His eyes locked on mine and the torment in his face was evident. "Me."

I straightened my expression, letting sincerity replace my sarcasm. "You were probably tired. You've been through a lot of shit."

"No, I just . . ." He shook his head, crossing his arms in front of him. "I was in VRC for a long time, Winnie. Lying on a cold table, not in the warm embrace of a woman. Shit happened to me. Bad shit." He inhaled sharply, releasing a hard breath. "Her lure was so strong, I knew she wanted it, and I wanted to please her, so I did. But once it was my turn, I backed out. I told her she looked tired from my venom and we should just go to bed, and we'd fuck tonight. She was in such a haze, she didn't even realize something was wrong."

"Fuck, dude. That's some serious adult shit."

He chuckled at my light joke and both our heads whipped toward the door when two scents filled the air.

"Who's that?" Luka asked, sniffing the air.

"Zeke's wife, April and their baby. I'll get it." I hopped up and opened the door. "Come on in."

April moseyed her way into the living room, the baby asleep in her arms, and Annie was sniffing curiously. "Hey, Luka. it's nice to finally meet you."

"Likewise."

"Do you know where any of the girls are? I need someone to watch Scarlet while I shower real quick, and Zeke left with Marcus and Drag to help them at Drifters."

Lie number one.

"Sage is in the shower and she took two razors with her so she'll be there awhile," Luka said and I laughed.

April's gaze went to me.

"Lyric is out running with Erik. They'll be back in like twenty minutes. We can watch her until then if you want," I offered before remembering how much I hated changing diapers.

"Are you sure?" April asked, a guilty expression on her face.

"We're sure," Luka said with confidence. "We've been around Drag's nieces and nephews their whole life."

"Thank you." April slid Scarlet into Luka's arms, then held her bag out. "She just ate, so she should be good until

I get back. If she starts crying, just rock your hips. She loves that. The pink blanket is her favorite, so keep that one on her, but if she spits up on it use the green one. That's her second favorite."

Luka nodded. "We got this. Go have twenty minutes of self care."

April's tense shoulders sagged. "Thanks again."

She left the cabin and Luka rocked the baby in his arms. "It's crazy how tiny she is." Scarlet stretched, a bunch of farts exploding in her diaper, and Luka stopped moving. "That doesn't sound good."

The smell hit me like a ton of bricks. "Geezus. That's worse than Drag's farts were that night he was in the chili eating contest."

"Oh, god, I can't." Luka turned his nose into his shoulder, his eyes watering. "I can feel her poop bouncing off my hand."

I wrinkled my nose. "Eww."

Annie sniffed, then ran off, and I burst out laughing.

Once Scarlet was done handling business, Luka laid her on the couch. "Change her."

My brows arched. "Why do I have to? You're the one who agreed to watch her."

"Actually, that was you." Luka picked up the diaper bag and handed it to me.

"We aren't friends anymore," I said, snatching it from his hands.

Even though I hated changing diapers, I'd mastered the science, and was able to do it in less than a minute.

After getting out a diaper and some wipes, I rubbed my hands together, warming them up. "Time me."

Luka said nothing as I quickly unzipped her onesie and pulled her little legs out, not letting the cuteness of her tiny toes distract me from my mission. I undid her diaper, lifted her legs and wiped, then wiped again, and then again, all while Luka made a gagging sound. For such a small thing, Scarlet could really drop a load.

With one hand, I rolled up the old diaper with the wipes in it, setting it aside and slid on the new one. Then I latched it up, zipped her onesie, and she was smelling fresh again.

"Time?"

"Thirty-seven seconds."

"Hell yes! New record." I pointed to Scarlet, who yawned, but remained sleeping. "Watch her while I wash my hands."

I yanked the diaper up and headed to the kitchen, sealing it in a ziplock bag before dropping it in the trash. That thing was horrendous.

After a quick scrub, I came back and picked the baby up. This time, I took a seat on the couch, laying her across my thighs. I couldn't stop staring at her. Her tiny nose, her pink cheeks, her red hair. She was perfect.

"Babies are so lucky, bro. They have no worries, their soul is still pure, and they have someone to wipe their ass for them."

"Are you wanting someone to wipe your ass?" Luka asked, and I popped my head up.

"I don't think Lyric is the ass wiping type." We both laughed and I turned my attention back to the baby. "I think I love her."

Luka took a seat next to me and brushed his hand over Scarlet's head. "I just met her and I already love her. Well, as long as she doesn't shit again."

"I meant Lyric."

His eyes bulged, his hand falling away. "That's huge for you."

I nodded. "I know. And I didn't want to, but it just happened." I glanced back at Scarlet. "Lyric is going to want kids when she gets older. I can see it in her eyes. She's so loving and nurturing. She was born a mom and doesn't even know it." I shook my head with a sigh. "I don't want to break her heart or take that experience away from her. And I think that's why I tried so hard not to love her. And probably why I haven't told her."

"Sage told me she loved me, man. I knew it already, but it's a whole different vibe when someone actually says it to you."

A hard breath left me. "She's just too innocent. I can't hurt her."

"Are we talking about the same woman here?" Luka asked, tightening my brow.

"What's that supposed to mean?"

"Did you see her at VRC? I only got a glimpse of her, but she was blood-soaked and made it out without a scratch on her. Which means she's tougher than you think. Maybe take her off that pedestal you put her on and give the girl more credit."

My eyes darted to him, mouth agape. "I just want to protect her from getting hurt."

"It's okay to protect her, even worship her. However, thinking she's weak is a mistake. Given her ability to kill a man or even a vampire, I'm sure she can endure the pain of a broken heart if it happens."

A snicker left me. "Where the fuck were you a month ago?"

"Waiting for my friends to rescue my ass."

We both chuckled and I turned my attention back to Scarlet as I thought about Luka's words. They were one hundred percent accurate. Lyric had the most pure soul, and deep down, I wanted to shelter her because of it. Even during our sparring sessions, I held back, refraining from using my full strength. Despite my hesitation, she always pushed forward, throwing out strong kicks and punches.

She was a warrior and I made her a princess.

As my mind reeled with this new revelation, I started to list some of her bad qualities. Though low, I came up with a few.

"You know what, maybe I shouldn't have her on a pedestal. She leaves hair ties everywhere. I found one in the refrigerator once. No clue how it got there. Oh, and water cups. She has at least one in every room. I'm starting to feel like I'm trapped in that movie where water is the aliens' ultimate weakness. It's like Lyric's waiting for an invasion."

Luka laughed, shaking his head. "Sage bites her fingernails and picks her cuticles when she's nervous. The sound drives me nuts. But I love her anyway." He slapped his hand on my shoulder. "Welcome to a real relationship, man."

Just as the scents hit me, Lyric and Erik barged through the door.

"Hey, oh, you have the baby?" The sound of Lyric's squeal echoed through the room, and I couldn't help but share a smug glance with Luka, silently confirming my previous statement. "I gotta wash my hands so I can hold her."

Erik plopped down in the chair, leaned forward and whispered, "You gotta start running with her. I can't keep up. She's like deer, galloping through the woods, never getting tired."

Lyric came into the room, and Erik leaned back in the chair with a heavy sigh. She set a water cup on the table and held her hands out. "My turn."

"Hold up, mama, I need to say something."

Lyric eyed me, seemingly confused, and I let every thought I had burst out my mouth.

"I know you love your braids, but I literally found a hair tie in the fridge and one in my shoes. I also hate that you leave your water cups lying around waiting for the aliens."

Her face turned confused, her eyebrows arching upwards.

"Regardless of that, I plan on being with you forever, unless you stay human, then I'll be with you until you die."

I shook my head. "I can't really tell you what I'll do after that, because my heart hurts even thinking about it."

I glanced back at baby Scarlet and she smiled in her sleep. The cuteness gave me just enough courage to say what I needed to without shying away. With a deep breath, I met Lyric's eyes.

"All I'm saying is, I never want to spend a day without you. And if that means I might have to steal you a baby in the future, then I guess that's what we're doing. Because I love you more than anything, including hacking, and that's actually crazy. So, yeah. I love you, mama."

With her bottom lip caught between her teeth, tears filled Lyric's eyes. "I hate the way you cut your toenails in bed. It's disgusting. And don't get me started on the way you talk to your computer like it's a hot girl." She shook her head. "Regardless of your ease with kidnapping, I plan on being with you forever because I love you."

She leaned down, pushing her lips against mine for a brief moment.

"Also, there's no reason to steal babies when so many need homes. If we decide *we* want one, we'll figure it out."

Her genuine and comforting smile spoke volumes. Although my words weren't poetic, Lyric understood me as a person, confessing her love the same way I did, and he made me love her even more.

The door opened and April rushed in. "Thank you for giving me time to shower." She made her way over and stopped next to me, peering down at the baby. "Was she good for you?"

"She was an angel." I looked down at Scarlet and took her hand in mine, giving her a fist bump. "You can hang out with Uncle Winnie again later." I carefully lifted her and she extended her body, arching her back as I held her out. "Time to go back to your mom."

April sucked in a breath as she took her.

"Is she okay?" I asked, my brows narrowing, concerned I did something wrong. "I'm not good with babies, but I was gentle with her. I did change her diaper earlier. And if you think baby shit smells bad when you're a human, try being a vampire."

I stuck my tongue out, making a gagging sound.

"It's just," April's voice trembled as she choked back tears, "no one has ever called me her mom before."

"Oh." My gaze darted across April's face and I realized how huge of a life-changing event this was for her. "Well, I'm not in charge of anyone or anything, but you knew what blankets she liked, so I'm pretty sure you're her mom."

"I'm her mom," April whispered, eyeing Scarlet. "It sounds so weird to say aloud."

A smile tugged at my cheeks as April began to sway her hips. Lyric peered down at the baby, a radiant smile lighting up her face, and I knew no matter what challenges life presented, we'd make it together.

With a deep sigh, I glanced at my phone, noticing that it was Lyric and Erik's turn to leave. I sent him a text, reminding him.

A minute later, he said, "Hey, Lyric, are you still going to ride with me?"

"Where are you guys going?" April asked curiously. "I need to go to the store to get diapers and a few other things. I'd really like to check out the baby aisle myself to make sure I'm not missing anything."

"We're headed to do a property check on our grandparents farm," Lyric said. "We're concerned that the storm might have caused some damage."

Lie number two.

"That's okay. I can try getting a ride from someone else."

Lyric and Erik left for their mission, April took Scarlet back to her cabin, and Luka went to check on Sage because we were set to leave next. He came back a few minutes later with her in tow.

She let out a hard sigh that echoed through the small cabin. "I'm not ready for this."

"I told Lyric I loved her," I blurted, attempting to take her focus off the nerve-wracking mission.

Sage smirked. "About time, Asshole." She gave me a genuine smile, then sighed, heading outside, Luka trailing behind her.

With a deep breath of my own, I stepped out the door, pulling it shut behind me. Descending the porch, the moon's eerie red glow caught my eye.

Must be a blood moon.

CHAPTER 35
SAGE

The night had a gut wrenching hold on me. We had to go on a mission to get my mother, and although it wasn't as dangerous as infiltrating VRC, there was still a sense of concern. We had gone over the plans a few times, making sure that only the people going knew about it, and no one else in the camp. When I got out of the shower, there was another foreboding sensation growing in my chest, exactly like the one I felt at the hotel. I'm not sure if I was correlating the feeling with the one I had before Marcus's death or if my witch senses were working, but I absolutely knew one thing.

Someone is going to die tonight.

We hopped in my Jeep, heading to our meet up and I refrained from mentioning the nervous alarm to Luka.

He drove the thirty minutes and I absentmindedly picked at my cuticles, feeling a mix of anticipation and anxiety. Eventually, we turned onto a dirt road with tall pine trees forming a natural canopy on either side. I glanced at the GPS and swallowed the lump in my throat, knowing we were only a minute away. And possibly only a few minutes from the death of one of my friends . . . again.

"What's your mom's name?" Luka asked, bringing me from my wretched thoughts.

Tearing my gaze away from the towering trees, I turned my head toward him. "Janene, why?"

"Because I can't call her mom. I haven't even met the woman."

I let out a nervous laugh, trying to hide my unease. "She's sweet. You'll love her."

Luka turned into a large gravel parking area where my mother and Naomi stood illuminated by our headlights. He parked, then killed the engine.

My breaths quickened and I instinctively turned to my breathing techniques to regain control over my racing heart.

Winnie laid a hand on my shoulder. "Remember to push the necklace if you feel uncomfortable."

I nodded, then opened the Jeep door.

Meeting Luka at the hood of the car, he took my hand in his, Winnie walking on my other side.

My mother stood nervously next to Naomi, fidgeting with her hands. Her eyes shifted from me to Luka, her face lighting up with a radiant smile.

With a sudden tug, Luka pulled my hand, forcing me to come to an unexpected halt. "There are others here. I can hear them."

"Sounds like three extra heartbeats," Winnie added.

"Are you alone?" I asked, my eyes scanning the empty parking lot.

My mom's face turned confused. "Of course we are."

While I trusted her, I couldn't help but cast a skeptical glance toward Naomi, unsure of her intentions. "Who's with you?"

She held her hands up in a non-threatening manner. "I swear we came alone."

"That's a lie," Winnie snapped, his voice sharp. "We can hear their heartbeats."

A shadow on the ground caught my attention seconds before my father emerged from the darkness with two armed guards. "I knew the spray the lab made would keep you from smelling us, but I hadn't considered you hearing our heartbeats."

Growls left both Luka and Winnie, and if I could have growled, I would have.

"Fuck, that's not good," Luka muttered in a low tone.

Within moments, the roaring of four vans filled the quiet night air as they zoomed into the parking lot, causing small pebbles to scatter.

Luka locked eyes with me—a silent question.

"I'm not leaving my mom," I said fiercely. "I'll die first."

"This will be fun," Winnie mumbled, cracking his knuckles as tons of people piled out of the vans.

Over twenty Venom members surrounded my dad, one of them pressing a handgun to Naomi's temple, causing her to freeze.

When another guard grabbed my mother from behind, doing the same to her, terror shot through me, stealing the air from my lungs. But the fear that consumed me quickly vanished, leaving behind a seething anger.

I yanked my hand away from Luka's. "I suggest you get your fucking gun away from my mom!"

Luka pulled me back by my arm. "This is what they want. Don't react."

My dad's gaze went to the guard. "Remove your weapon from my wife's head if you want to live." The soldier lowered his gun, and my dad locked his eyes on Luka, tilting his head. "So, you're the one my daughter threw her entire life away for."

My attention immediately shifted to Luka. His jaw flexed before he uttered, "And you're the one who's willing to kill everyone to keep her from being with me."

"Because she was raised to kill vampires, not fuck them," a familiar voice echoed, sending shivers through me.

Every bone I had locked, each muscle quivering as my uncle strolled out of the treeline and into the glowing lights of the parking lot.

Luka squeezed my hand and I forced myself to look in his direction. His eyes briefly flickered to my necklace before averting his gaze. I raised my hand, forcefully pushing the pearl necklace over and over, sending an alert to our friends as fear ran through my body. Hopefully, they had a better plan than our non-existing one.

Ben's hazel eyes raked over me, siphoning every ounce of self-confidence I had, leaving me feeling like a teenager again, vulnerable and helpless.

A small whimper left me, as small as I felt under his malevolent stare before his eyes went from us to my father. "Maybe you should've had a son, instead of a slut."

Knowing how Ben was, I should've expected something horrific to come out of his mouth, but his words utterly shocked me, causing my jaw to unhinge.

Luka snarled, veins adorning his face like strings of lights on a Christmas tree. "Say another word about her and I'll rip your fucking throat out and savor every drop of your blood as I drain you dry."

My head turned toward the oncoming headlights, hoping it was our friends, and more concern filled me when two cars pulled in with a van behind them.

The white Cadillac passed behind us, the windows so tinted I couldn't see inside. Whoever drove parked the car facing the exit, far away from where we all stood. They stayed inside, the engine running.

The black Escalade parked to my right, behind where Naomi had, and when the short, stumpy driver emerged, I had no clue who he was.

The man slammed his car door. "Well, I see everyone showed just as planned."

"What a conniving weasel," Winnie shouted. "I see you like hanging out with the enemy, Finneas."

Finneas.

He was one of the leaders of Save who Winnie and Luka both had suspected was a rat working with Venom. Now their suspicions were confirmed.

"I could say the same about you two." He cocked his head toward Luka. "Back from your *vacation*, already? I knew we should have sent you to another state like your brother."

"Fuck you, Finneas!" Luka snarled, his fists balled to his side.

Another snarl filled the night sky and I shuddered when I realized it came from my uncle. He left his mouth wide open as he panted.

Even though I'd learned about him being a new species that we were unfamiliar with, reality hit when I noticed his fangs. Like all vampires, Ben's two canines had elongated . . . but next to those were two sharp incisors. Four fangs ready to strike at a moment's notice.

With his growl, the van unloaded another five people, each of them marching their way to stand beside Ben.

Winnie sniffed the air. "Those are fucking hybrids." There was a tinge of fear in his voice I'd never heard from him before.

My gaze darted across the hybrids guarding my uncle, before it went to the Venom members with my father. They seemed confused by the situation, and I immediately realized they had no clue what was going on. They were mere pawns being used for a sinister game.

Another black Venom van skidded into the parking lot, slinging rocks. Erik and Lyric jumped out, both carrying AR's. When Lyric noticed my uncle, her gaze darted to me, her eyes wide. She stood next to Winnie and raised her gun, pointing it at Ben.

"Holy fuck," Erik muttered from the other side of Luka before locking his gun in the same direction.

Engines roared and tires screeched as the rest of my friends arrived. Zeke and Marcus exited first and ran toward us, pistols ready, and I had no idea where Drag was.

Ravage and Peach got out of the other van, leisurely strolling toward us. She stopped in front of me, hands on her hips. "Hello, gentlemen," she snickered, "and Finneas. Did you miss me, old friend?"

Finneas' face twisted with fear, revealing just how terrifying Peach could truly be.

His fingers nervously smoothed down the front of his dark suit jacket, his attempt to appear composed, but falling slightly short. "Ah, Heather, when did you start associating with wanted criminals?"

"Since the day you decided to ruin everything I built from the ground up." She shook her head. "Mixing Save with Venom was never in my plan. You went against your own kind and must be punished."

Ravage tsked. "Do you want me to kill him for you, Peach?"

"No," she answered sharply, before raising her finger toward Finneas. "That kill is mine."

"Kill her!" Finneas screamed, and the hybrids all lifted their guns.

Peach didn't even flinch. "At my age, it would take a thousand bullets to take me down."

A door slammed shut and I caught sight of a naked Drag seconds before he shifted into a large wolven. The second his gray paws hit the ground, he howled, the haunting sound making the hairs on the back of my neck stand up.

The forest unleashed a menacing presence as wolven, some with red fur, others with black or gray, along with one white, prowled out. Their snarls and snaps echoed, creating an eerie symphony as they took up roost behind Drag.

Two enormous wolven—one black, the other red—took their places on either side of Drag. It became clear that these three were the alphas of their packs.

My uncle locked gazes with me, attempting to make me shrivel in terror once more. But this was a war, and he had once told me something I would never forget.

There is no room for fear during a battle.

I grinned arrogantly, ready to take on the challenge. "Your move, uncle."

With speed I've only seen from a vampire, he grabbed my father from behind and locked his arm across his throat, pinning him against him. "Do you actually think you can control this situation? The destiny? I've been controlling everything that has happened."

He raised his gun to my dad's head and my heart stopped.

Of course, I was still angry with my father for everything that happened since my induction night, but I didn't want him dead.

"Every play made has been done with my approval," Ben continued, his voice confident and unwavering. "From you killing that arrogant vampire to Sorin waiting to kill Luka. If you wouldn't have been there, he'd be dead, and none of this would be happening! You've repeatedly fucked up my plans."

Luka growled, along with at least half of the wolves.

"Did . . . did you send Mannie to kill me?"

Ben's eyes betrayed him, answering my question when they darted to Finneas.

Pure hatred zoomed through my veins at lightning speed and I clenched my fists. "You're my uncle! My blood! How the hell could you do this to me?"

"To you?" Ben clicked his tongue and sneered. "It's always been about you since you were born. You took everything from me!"

Confusion filled me and I shook my head profusely. "I've taken nothing from you."

"Do you have any idea what it's like being born two years after the person who inherits everything, Sage? I've been second place to him my whole life." Ben tightened his hold on my father's neck, making him groan. "I was promised I would become the president once he retired, but it would only give me a short time to be in power. You can't turn an entire society around in two years. I was going to kill him in his early thirties, giving me enough time to take Venom to the next level. Then you were born only one year before, leaving you as the heir to Venom, ending my plans for any future career." Ben's lips curled into a scowl, his four fangs showing. "I should have suffocated you when you were a baby instead of waiting until you became a bitch!"

Luka growled, stepping forward. I tightened my grip onto his shirt sleeve, as I drew deep breaths, my own anger threatening to consume me. "You'd kill me for Venom?"

Ben cocked his head, his gleaming smile filled with arrogance and malice. "Venom is worth much more than your pathetic life would ever be."

The anger took hold and the trauma of everything I'd been through in my entire life consumed me. "I know how much it's worth," I spat, taking a step forward, my fists clenched. "I've repeatedly paid the price for being born into this society! My childhood was nothing but begging for your and my dad's acceptance. I have lost my family, my home, my life, my friends, and all because I paid the price over and over and over! All because *you* wanted to be the president! You can fucking have it. I don't want a tainted society filled with hate and lies!"

"I don't need to take it because I already have it. I only need to kill all of them," he nodded his head toward the Venom members, then to my dad, "him," then his cold eyes locked on me, "and you."

My dad scowled, pulling on Ben's arm. "The hell you—"

A gunshot rang through the night sky, echoing through the woods, making me wince and my mother scream. I stared wide eyed as my father's limp body tumbled to the ground, blood oozing from his skull.

The howls of the three alpha wolves covered the sounds of my mother's horrific screams as they commanded their packs to attack.

The world in front of me darkened and every feeling that once threatened to consume me unleashed, a primal need to kill taking over my every move.

With my gaze narrowed on my uncle, I yanked the gun from my holster, aimed it toward him, and pulled the trigger twice. Two bullets landed dead in the center of his chest. One of his hands went over the wound and the other lifted his gun at me.

With no time to move, I squeezed my trigger again, aiming for his head, and a force slammed into me, sending my bullet on a wayward trajectory. My side smashed into the rocky parking lot, and one of the hybrids landed on top of me. I lifted my fist and punched him twice and he didn't even flinch.

Luka snarled, forcefully yanking him off me and hurling him ten feet away. In an instant, another hybrid charged at him with incredible strength.

By the time I jumped up from the ground, people were shooting, throwing fists, snapping necks, snarling, scratching, and biting.

Finneas' scream rang through the night as Peach ripped him to shreds.

Suddenly, my attention was diverted as a Venom woman lunged at me from the side. I swung a right hook into her face, then lifted my leg, kicking my boot into her chest, causing her to fly backwards.

"Ahh!" my mother screamed, and when I looked toward her, she was being shoved into the Cadillac by a hybrid . . . and my uncle.

Fast shallow breaths left me, my body now propelled by pure hatred and a need for vengeance. I yanked my gun from the ground and sprinted toward them, shooting the hybrid in the back twice.

He let go of my mom and she fell to her knees crawling away. I plowed into him from the side, slamming him into the car door.

My actions were fast as I pushed off on my feet, hurling myself toward my uncle. My nails caught his face and a deafening noise resonated in my ears, sending vibrations throughout my head . . . and my heart raced.

Thump thump. Thump thump. Thump thump.

CHAPTER 36
LUKA

Fear was more than just an emotion. Fear was a villain, cunning and wicked, always prepared to dominate the unsuspecting, stripping them of their strength and savoring in its victory.

There were only a few times in my life that I'd faced the relentless power fear possessed.

And tonight was one of them . . .

After beating the last guy that touched me to a bloody pulp, I glanced around to find Sage running toward a car, shooting a hybrid in his back before hurling herself at her uncle.

Ben raised his gun at the same exact time I used all my strength to get to her in one second.

The gunshot went off next to my head, and my ears rang as thick wetness splattered, staining my face and neck. The smell of blood filled my nostrils as Sage's body tumbled into mine, my arms wrapping around her.

"No!" Janene screamed louder than the gunshot as she scrambled off the ground. The terror of a mourning parent not only stopped most of the fighting, but it puckered my skin and raised the hairs on the back of my neck, sending panic through my body at lightning speed.

"No. No. Stay with me, Princess. Don't you fucking stop breathing!"

I carefully placed her body on the rough parking lot, the rocks digging into me when I fell to my knees beside her.

My eyes were just as frantic as my mind, searching Sage's chest and stomach, looking for an injury. The scent of her blood was still pungent in my nose but I couldn't find a wound.

I lifted my arm, and just as I was about to sink my fangs into my wrist, I caught sight of her left cheek.

Black hair clung to her face. . . along with blood.

Quakes of panic shook my insides and I reached for the gaping hole in her skull before my body froze, locking my attempts.

Janene kneeled on the other side of Sage and fiercely grabbed my arms, shaking me back to reality. "Save her! Please!"

Despite knowing brain injuries were permanent, I was determined to do anything I could to keep Sage breathing.

Lifting my wrist to my mouth again, I sunk my teeth into it, ripping a chunk away. Blood gushed out, splashing onto Sage's chest, and my heartbeat pulsed in my ears, screaming this wasn't going to work as I pressed it against her mouth.

"Drink, Princess," I begged, my voice quivering with raw vulnerability as my cheeks dampened. "You have to drink for me. Please, baby. You have to."

Sage's soul had bonded to mine, and I knew if she died, a part of me would die with her. It was impossible to live in a world where she didn't exist.

"Don't you fucking give up on me," I whimpered, the air escaping my lungs, refusing to return. "You're not allowed to give up!"

I sharpened my senses, straining to hear the faint sound of her swallowing, instead her heart thundered before it began to slow.

Thump . . . thump . . . . . thump . . . .

As her final heartbeat echoed in my ears, a wave of grief washed over me, making my chest tighten. My own heart beat twice as hard as if it attempted to help keep her alive.

"Is it working, Luka?" Janene saying my name, made my eyes drift to her.

I opened my mouth, but my words dissolved into silence. The tightness in my throat felt like a thousand razor blades had moved in, slicing me to pieces.

Sage's sweetness, her integrity, her fears . . . her entire existence fleeted away with every ounce of blood that oozed from her head.

"No," I finally whispered, closing my eyes tight, attempting to block out my waking hell as tears rolled down my cheeks.

Pain ran through my veins like a forest fire, burning and eating at me. Any control I had over my body diminished when I balled my fists, letting out a tremendous scream, flooding the quiet night with my agony.

"Fucking no! She's fucking dead. She's fucking dead," I screamed over and over.

Janene jumped up from the ground and hurled herself at the closest Venom member, violently swinging her fists at every part of his body. "You bastards!"

The rest of the soldiers pointed their guns at her and my friends pointed their guns at them. Screaming and fighting commenced and the world stopped, no longer moving forward as my life fell apart.

I tumbled onto Sage's body, my hand lying across her stomach, my ear pressing against her chest and a hollow white noise radiated from within her.

A heart that didn't beat.

Blood that didn't rush.

A soul that didn't survive.

My soulmate had departed from this world, leaving me empty, a mere physical manifestation of the person I once was.

My lungs gave up, refusing to take in air which no longer held her fragrance.

My heart pumped faster, begging me to keep breathing. But since hers had stopped, I couldn't. I didn't want to.

Life was empty without her.

Once upon a time, I had lavender and vanilla, and now I have nothing.

The despair ate at me, and my eyes became blurry, unfocusing on the world around me.

In a flash, the pain vanished, giving way to pure un-bridled hatred. A powerful growl conjured within me, rumbling my insides before erupting from my mouth with vehemence.

My canine fangs throbbed, elongating with thirst.

Then my gums tightened, a strange, unfamiliar sensation coursing through me as if something primal and dangerous was awakening within.

Two more fangs emerged, ready to unleash wrath onto the world.

I lept to my feet, my gaze darting from person to person. Another large growl left me and every hybrid and wolven took a few steps back, acknowledging my power.

Fueled by impetuous anger, I charged for the first person in front of me. The Venom member was unable to react before my sharp fangs impaled him, violently tearing away a chunk of his cheek.

The sound of a gunshot reverberated as it struck the back of my arm, prompting my immediate reaction. I swiftly turned around, seized the fucker with the gun, and snapped his neck.

A third member stared wide-eyed and I yanked him toward me, sinking my fangs into his throat. The metallic yet sweet flavor of his warm blood pooled in my mouth before slinking down my throat with delicious satisfaction.

The world brightened with every gulp, fueling my fury, and driving me further over the edge of insanity.

A sensation of power crawled through my insides and each vein on my face throbbed, increasing in size. My four fangs became longer and sharper, ready to attack my next victim.

When my strength started to double—triple—I vaguely knew bloodlust had taken over, but not one ounce of me cared.

My anger allowed me to spare no one, including my friends.

Anyone who moved would be my target.

Twisting my body toward the now faceless people, I lunged for the nearest one, biting into her neck and ripping a chunk away. Strangled cries filled the air as I chewed the flesh, which was as juicy as a rare steak.

With a sense of satisfaction, I savored the delectable meat before finally swallowing and searching for my next meal.

The person closest to me raised his gun, shooting me in the stomach. The stinging pain disappeared as I yanked them toward me, sinking my fangs into his cheek. I'd hardly taken a bite when someone violently collided with me from the side, throwing me off balance.

With my new superpowers, I recovered quickly, hopping to my feet.

The one who knocked me down glared at me, fists up and ready, awaiting my next move. Though she seemed highly trained, her scent told me she was human.

An easy meal.

In an attempt to catch her off guard, I leapt forward, but she deftly dodged me, countering with a forceful kick to my abdomen, causing me to be pushed backwards. I recovered quickly and charged her again. This time I knocked her to the ground with me landing on top of her.

With fangs bared, I leaned into her neck and a pair of arms went around my throat, choking me back.

"Luka, stop. That's Lyric!" someone yelled, the voices as foreign as the faces. "You're in bloodlust."

I stood up with him still on my back and attempted to fling him off. "Let go!"

"It's me, Erik."

With me still in a choke hold, he kicked the back of my leg, pulling me backwards, and I tumbled to the ground with him below me.

"Grab his legs, Lyric!"

She laid her entire body across me, wrapping herself around my legs, and asked, "Can we weaken him with silver?"

"I don't know, but I'm suffocating under him!"

My rage remained uncontrolled and I growled and thrashed.

"We have to do something. Sage needs him!" she screamed, and although I didn't recognize the name, a sense of panic flowed through me.

Sage?

"You guys did this shit. Help before he kills us all!" I had no clue who the Erik guy yelled at, but threatening snarls left me when more hands pulled at my body.

Four, five, six people held me down as I fought for my freedom.

Another person ran up and placed a palm on my chest. "Luka, stop! It's me, Ravage. Remember your oath, son. The darkness shall not command thyself. Thou shall command it."

Who is Ravage and why do his words seem . . . important?

Lyric let go of my legs, freeing them, and Erik screamed, "What are you—"

Erik's question got interrupted when someone slapped the shit out of me.

My face stung for only a second before a pair of soft hands gently rested on my cheeks. "Sage needs you, Luka. Come back to her."

Memories of a woman with black hair, a beautiful smile, and a perfect body flashed through my mind and my movements slowed.

"Keep talking, Lyric," Ravage said through panting breaths. "It's working."

"Sage won't make it without you. She almost died staring into those woods because she loves you. Lavender and vanilla, remember?"

Lavender and vanilla.

My body eased as additional memories of Sage flooded my mind. She was my mate. She loved me. She had saved me.

I couldn't protect her . . . and she died.

No.

Agonizing pain spread throughout my heart, causing it to shatter. I blinked a couple of times and the faces in front of me came into focus, my eyes landing on Ravage. "Where is she?"

"Let him up," he instructed, and everyone released me.

I hopped from the ground, my mind frantic as I glanced around and immediately noticed a handful of people kneeled around Sage.

A large growl rumbled from my chest as I headed toward them.

CHAPTER 37

SAGE

Intense pain licked the inside of my skull as if a million hornets decided I was their enemy, while scorching lava coursed through my brain, spreading to my muscles and traveling through my veins . . . beelining straight for my soul.

Thump. Thump. Thump.

The Angel of Death himself flawlessly controlled each beat my heart took, his delicate hands squeezing, compelling it to finally abandon the only job it ever had.

My brain rapidly fired signals to my body, instructing it to accept the death I'd earned and euphoria spread through me.

The thunderous sound beating in my ears slowed to a few small thuds, *Thump . . . thump . . . . . thump . . . . . . before* my heart finally stopped.

The fire licking my senses turned to ice, shivering through my veins and quieting me. Quieting my soul.

Then came . . . silence. Nothing but silence.

No trumpets blared enchanting melodies, nor did violins serenade me while beautiful angels escorted my soul to the other side.

Only a silent tomb of white noise. A soundless cage with no way out.

With that came darkness. Nothing but darkness.

The bright welcoming rays of light and pearly white gates many speak of were absent, as were the puffy clouds, the bottomless wine cups, and feasts of plenty.

Only a void of nothingness.

A black plague rotting my body by the second.

Until a new sensation buzzed through me, tickling every nerve I had.

Fresh flowers caressed my nose, expanding my once empty lungs, and a voice, more beautiful than a songbird, danced into my ears.

"Open your eyes."

How can I open my eyes when I'm dead?

Soft, gentle fingers brushed against my cheek, the warmth of them comforting me enough to allow my eyelids to drift open, and I now stood upright in a beautiful, plush field.

The sun above casted its rays upon a beautiful woman with golden skin and russet hair as she grinned with pride.

No . . .

She wasn't a woman.

Adorned in a white, almost transparent dress, stood a goddess. A subtle glow of golden light radiated from her, spilling onto the vast field of flowers below her bare feet.

Contemplating the possibility of a heaven, I asked the only question that came to mind. "Are you an angel?"

"No, my sweet child. I am one of the Keepers, the Goddess of Vigor. My job is to remind you of the power you now have. The power you must contain. Never let the bloodlust carry you away."

Before I had a chance to speak, a flood of sweet warmth rippled through me, now licking my body with pleasure. Waves crashed against my soul, filling it with an immeasurable strength.

Images of everyone and everything I had ever loved flashed at rapid speed, a lingering reminder for me to keep my humanity while I harnessed the power of immortality.

Her voice spoke to me once more but this time, her lips didn't move.

Never let the power take hold. If you give it permission, it will own you.

Many have succeeded, others have failed. When in doubt, remember these words.

The darkness shall not command thyself. Thou shall command it.

Do you promise to honor yourself while upholding the oath of humanity?

Something deep inside of my soul compelled me to agree without hesitation. "I promise."

With a flick of two fingers that reminded me of Shayla, my body plummeted back into the darkness, a whirlwind of emotions consuming me.

A divine spark discharged through my existence, lighting my veins on fire and bringing my soul back to the land of the living.

The sound of my heart pounded through my ears.

Thump thump. Thump thump. Thump thump.

The smell of blood stroked my nose, landing on my tongue and sending a yearning pain through my twisting gut.

Hunger. Nothing but hunger.

A tightening sensation similar to the feeling I get when my nipples harden, radiated through my gums, pulling at my canine teeth. They grew longer, stronger, sharper, ready to be plunged into their first victim.

As my eyes opened, the world appeared brighter, more vivid. A part of me wanted to enjoy my newfound senses, but I had no time to gaze at the beauty of a still tainted world.

Someone growled, and with speed I didn't know I had, I leaped to my feet in one swift move.

My hunger being the only thing which mattered now, my eyes darted to the people of all shapes and sizes surrounding me like a buffet of fresh cuts of meat.

Something inside of me drew my body to one of them more than the others, and when I yanked her toward me, she resisted. The woman was much stronger than I was, holding me back like I was nothing more than a small child.

Someone growled again, causing the hairs on the back of my neck to stand, and my body told me *he* was mine.

His soul was mine.

"Move, Peach!" The man yanked me toward him, his intoxicating scent taking over my entire existence. He didn't hesitate to grab my waist, lifting me off the ground.

Craving the feeling of our bodies intertwined, I locked my legs around him. He moved one hand to my ass, holding me up, and the other went to the back of my neck before fingers slid into my hair, gripping it.

When he pulled my face into the crevice of his neck, the swishing of blood rushing through his veins filled my ears. The scent of his skin was familiar and delicious when it met my lips.

My predatory instincts took over, pushing me forward. The flesh beneath my mouth surrendered far too easily when I bit down, allowing me to fulfill my hunger. Blood squirted for a split second, the sweet yet somehow savory flavor hitting my tongue was beyond mesmerizing.

Can you taste beauty?

If so, it was the most beautiful thing I'd ever tasted.

"Suck hard."

I did what the man said and latched on, causing his blood to pool into my mouth. Each gulp I took left me invigorated. Intoxicated.

A breath of life filled me as the energy from his blood spread through my body, satisfying my frantic soul. In a perfect world, I would stay wrapped in this man's arms for eternity, suckling at the life force his blood gave me.

"She's had enough. You need to stop her."

He groaned, the hum of it vibrating against my lips and sending shivers through me. "Just a few more seconds, Peach."

"No, Kid. Help her remember the oath she took."

He released my hair and dropped his hand to my back before rubbing it in soothing circles. "That's enough, Princess. The darkness shall not command thyself. Thou shall command it."

The words he spoke were transpicuous, a gentle reminder of the vow I took to keep my humanity. I unlatched my mouth from his neck and met his beautiful blue eyes.

Luka.

The smell of lavender and vanilla tickled my nose, filling my heart and soul with more love than I'd ever be able to indulge in.

Even though I'd known I loved him for months, in that moment, I truly believed he would be mine for eternity.

He laid his hand on my cheek and looked at me like he'd never really seen the true essence of my beauty until now.

My breaths were fast and hard, my entire body yearning for him to touch every inch of skin. The scent of lavender and vanilla now mixed with citrus caressed my senses and my core tightened, ready to be pleasured.

Luka yanked my face toward him and pressed his warm lips against mine. The kiss was passionate, sweet, and gentle, stroking my soul with each move our lips made.

Wanting to consume every piece of him he would give me, I slid my tongue into his mouth as I fantasized about spending eternity lying naked next to him, running my fingers along his lean muscles, completely worshiping his body.

Someone cleared their throat, causing Luka to pull his mouth away, and I instantly missed the feel of his closeness.

"Are you okay, my love?"

I was more than okay. I was in a state of bliss most people could only dream of. "I can feel it. Feel the bond. It's like a spark flickering inside me." I laid my palm against his heart. "I can feel you. Feel you alive."

He let go of my hair, moving the hand to my cheek before gently running his thumb over my lips. "Our hearts beat as one now."

He grinned and despite the blood covering his face, I couldn't help but smile back. His joyful look faded, a puzzled one replacing it.

"What's wrong?" I asked, and Luka shook his head.

His heart sped up and I was astonished I could hear it.

"I'm not your origin, Princess."

"No, you're not. I am," Peach said, causing my attention to go to her. "She fed from me before she went to rescue you. My powerful blood is the only reason she is alive and she needs to feed."

Luka lowered me to the ground and turned me toward her, and I shook my head. "I don't understand. I just drank his blood."

"You have to do what's called a sire feed from your origin to seal the sentinel bond or you'll die."

I wrinkled my nose at him. "But you said when we're bonded, other people's blood tastes bad."

"Mine'll taste similar to Luka's, but it'll have an earthy background," Peach said before placing a hand on the back of my head and pulling my face into her throat. "You only need to take a few draws, and after that, you'll never have to feed from anyone else."

Wanting this to be over with as soon as possible, I opened my mouth, sank my fangs into her, and took forceful sucks.

Once I swallowed a few times, I felt a new connection in my soul. My love for Peach grew tremendously. I was a part of her and she was a part of me.

She was a protector. A provider. A parent.

She was my origin.

"That's enough," she whispered, pulling me away.

My breaths came out ragged, my mind attempting to catch up on what had happened in a short amount of time.

Erik cleared his throat. "I hate to break up this beautiful moment, but we're surrounded by dead bodies."

Memories of tonight's events flooded through me. I looked around, my eyes bouncing across each dead person. I counted more than a dozen lifeless bodies.

A wave of sadness washed over me when I saw the two wolven, their wolf-like features frozen in death. Three hybrids laid dead, their twisted forms a chilling sight. Finneas was hardly recognizable, his body mangled and torn apart. Among the remaining corpses were the unsuspecting Venom members, all of whom my uncle betrayed.

When I realized none of them were my mom, I took a deep breath of relief that caught in my throat. None of them were my uncle, either, and the white Cadillac was gone.

"Where is my mom? Where's Ben?"

"I'm right here, sweetie." My mother stepped out from behind Erik and I closed the distance between us in a second, yanking her into me.

Her rapid heartbeat thundered in my ears, causing me to pull back, my gaze wandering her face in concern. "Are you okay?"

She nodded, her eyes sparkling with concern. "As good as I can be, considering the evening. Are you a .. ?"

She couldn't finish her sentence and I wasn't sure I could either.

"I am. Is that okay?"

Nervousness etched lines on her face. "Whatever keeps you on this earth."

I glanced at Luka. "Where's Ben?"

"He got away," he said, and my gaze locked on him in disbelief.

The sensation of spiders crawled across my face, anger filling my body, and I let out a low growl.

My mother sucked in a surprising gasp, her hands covering her mouth.

I quickly turned away from her. "How do I get these to go down?"

Luka grabbed my arm, leaning into my neck. "Just breathe, Princess. Calm yourself and they'll go away in a second."

After taking a few deep breaths and thinking about cute little kittens, my anger dissipated. I turned back around and gave my mom an apologetic expression, hoping to ease the tension in her face. She gave me an uneasy smile.

Before I had a chance to blink, Lyric plowed into me with a huge hug. "If you would have stayed dead, I would have slaughtered everyone." She pulled back, her golden brown eyes locked on me. "Blood of the coven."

"Blood of the coven," I repeated.

She released me from her death grip and her eyes darted across the dozen Venom members nearby, one of them talking to Ravage. I immediately recognized the man as Andrew Pace, one of the senior-ranked officers in Venom. Naomi was standing with them.

"Come here, girl," Ravage shouted, his hand waving me over.

I glanced at my mom, not wanting to leave her alone.

"I got her," Winnie said, his blood-soaked body assuring me she was safe with him as I headed toward Ravage.

"What's going on?" I asked him, confused.

"I think it would benefit everyone for you two to chat." Ravage pointed to Andrew, then me.

"Nice seeing you again, Sage." He extended his hand and I shook it, my brows furrowed. "We were at a loss coming to this battle. President Argent appointed me to lead this team with the objective of protecting Mrs. Argent and you. We were completely clueless about the hybrids that Ravage just informed us of, or Ben's involvement."

"Yeah, we knew some things, but not how deep this really went."

Andrew gave me a sympathetic smile. "I figured I should tell you, in article four, section A2 of the Venom employee handbook it states, 'If the current president should succumb to death, their oldest child shall immediately gain all rights to the society and its members, taking command without an induction ritual, a defusion trial, or discrimination from the cabinet or any of the society members without prosecution.'"

We were required to memorize the handbook, so I knew exactly what he was referring to, but I had no idea why. "And?"

"And it doesn't say a damn thing about you having to be human, President Argent."

President Argent? What does he . . . oh god.

My heart raced, my mouth falling agape.

Andrew smiled, seemingly amused by my shock. "All you have to do is accept."

A weird pooling pinged in the pit of my stomach, confusing me. I assumed any of my short-lived witch abilities would have died with me, but they hadn't. Then Shayla's words replayed in my head.

As a born witch, even in fanged death, she is still family.

My instincts told me one of my ancestors attempted to communicate with me, advising me to accept what was being offered to me.

The sound of shuffling filled my ears as each surviving Venom member stood up straighter, turning toward me.

Swallowing down the lump in my throat, I nervously scanned the group, an unwavering loyalty in the eyes of each member.

Having watched my father command the Venom society my entire life, I was well-versed in what the role required. I had also learned what *not to do* to the people who hold nothing but loyalty.

Taking a deep breath, I had no idea what I was going to say as I placed my hands on my hips and walked down the line of the members.

"I accept the role given to me, however, things will be changing. If any of you don't feel like you could adapt to new regulations or work with supernaturals for a greater cause, then leave now. None of you will be harmed." I pointed to one of the black vans left behind. "Get in there and go live a normal human life or possibly die with me making a better one."

My breaths were shallow as I awaited their decision.

One girl ran toward the van, then two guys. The rest stayed put, ready to die for the greater good.

"Thank you, President Argent," Andrew said, bringing my eyes to his brown ones. "If you would like, I can lead the rest of the team back to the compound."

I nodded, still unsure what the hell I was doing. "Let everyone there know they can leave if they want, and anyone who stays is under your command for now. Tell them there will be a meeting. I'll send you info with the details."

"Yes, ma'am."

"I'm going to go with him for now," Naomi said, and I leaned in close.

"Keep me updated if anything seems odd."

Naomi nodded before trailing off behind Andrew and the rest of the Venom members.

I turned around, surveying the rest of the people still lingering. Three packs of wolven, a bunch of vampires, and one Venom society hub ready to follow *me*.

I accidentally started an army.

Ravage began directing everyone toward the vehicles and Peach got on the phone with the mortuary guy preparing plans to dispose of the bodies, and making sure he knew my father needed to be preserved until my mom was ready to deal with the arrangements.

I turned toward Luka, unsure of what to say and he yanked me into him

"President Argent?" He cocked a brow, then wore a proud expression. "The way you took control over those men, you looked like a natural."

On the outside, I may have appeared to be a true leader, but on the inside, I really had no fucking clue what I was doing.

I shrugged. "There is no room for fear during a battle."

Luka gave me a quick kiss, then took my hand, pulling me toward my Jeep, my mother in tow.

The ride back was mostly quiet. Luka drove and I sat in the back seat, holding my mom's hand, her face a mixture of loving, mourning, and confusion.

"I'm sorry about dad," I whispered, squeezing her hand. "I know he never liked me, but I did love him."

"Oh, honey. Your father was hard on you because he had to be. You were set to be the president and he knew you'd never survive Ben if you were soft. He loved you dearly, even if he didn't always show it."

She turned her head out the window, wiping away the tears in private.

Her words hit me like a punch to the gut, causing my heart to twist in pain. Although me and my father never saw eye to eye, I could understand why he was hard on me, especially as I aged.

My mind began to reel, pulling up old memories of him. When I got my bike, he spent hours following me around, making sure I never so much as skinned a knee until I was a pro. We may have had different agendas, but that day he showed me love.

He loved me.

Once at camp, we exited the vehicle, my mom's eyes darting over anything she could see amongst the glow of the new tiki torches.

The lights inside of them flickering with multiple colors, the smell so strong it stuck in the back of my throat.

Then I realized, I was looking at the world through a new set of eyes and I gasped.

The first time I met Shayla she had said, *"Your new eyes will see the beauty this world has to offer."* The third time, when we were discussing Marcus, she said, *"His new eyes will see the beauty this world has to offer. As yours will soon."*

The memories brought on thoughts about destiny. During our conversations, Shayla never once uttered the word maybe when she said those sentences. She knew without a doubt, I would turn when I saw her yesterday, because I had already taken Peach's blood. But the first time, I hadn't yet.

She also said, *"Our choices harbor the capacity to alter the predetermined trajectory of destiny."* How was she sure from the first time meeting me?

Is she hiding more than she's revealing?

Someone dropped a wood log into the fire pit, the crackling getting my attention. Everything was brighter, louder.

"Is there a place I can wash up? And possibly have a minute to myself?" my mom asked, and I whipped toward her, a lot faster than I meant to.

I pointed to my cabin. "You can go to my place. The bathroom is down the hall on the right. If you want to lay in peace, the next door down is the spare bedroom."

"Is Chewy in there?" she asked, and when I nodded, she let out a settling sigh. "Thank you, Sweetie. In case I fall asleep, I love you."

"I love you too."

She gave me a hug, then as she walked toward my cabin, the tiki torches flickered across her clothes. The little things I never noticed when I was a human now had my attention.

"Are you okay?" Luka asked, bringing me from my thoughts.

The scent of fresh rain caressed my nose when the wind whipped past me. "I'm noticing little things. Things I've never paid attention to before. Beautiful things."

"Come here." Luka grabbed my hand, dragging me to the edge of the woods, and when he stopped, I gasped.

Despite it being nighttime, I could see deep into the forest with my new vampire eyes. Like the sun was about to set, but lit the world just enough to see.

The stream that wasn't close enough for my human ears to hear now played a melody for my senses, and the lake nearby had frogs croaking, then one jumped, splashing the water.

"Whoa. This is crazy."

Luka slid his hands around me from behind and pulled me into him. "Amazing, isn't it?"

"I can't even describe how wonderful it is."

"Most of it you will eventually drown out unless you want to notice."

He ran his nose across my ear and I tilted my head, giving him better access to place soft kisses on my neck, sending shivers down my spine. I pressed my butt against him and he moaned softly.

A hint of cedar caressed my senses, reminding me of my grandmother's old cedar chest at first. The scent became stronger, more intoxicating as it blended with sweet bergamot oranges and warm vanilla.

I ripped out of his embrace and faced him. "What's that delicious scent?"

His blue eyes sparkled as he gave me a smug grin that made me want to rip his clothes off. "Me."

"There's no way you smell like that." Grabbing his face, I yanked his head toward me, eliciting a grunt from him, then ran my nose up his neck, inhaling the most arousing scent ever.

The tantalizing fragrance made my mouth fall open and my fangs elongate. The sensitive skin of my areolas puckered, hardening my nipples. The smell was beyond delicious. I wanted it. I wanted to strip naked and bathe in the aroma. Bask in its phenomenal glory. Wanted to drink the scent's blood.

"Did you start wearing cologne?"

He shook his head, and it surprised me to see his sparkling blue eyes in the dead of night. "It's not cologne, it's my essence."

"What's that?" I asked, my body burning with a primal longing.

"It's like a lure. When two supernatural's bond, it's the scent they release to show love or their level of arousal. And the cool thing is, only your bondmate can smell it."

"Holy fuck. That's what that is?"

Luka laughed and the deep timber of it sent my blood pumping.

"The feeling I get is similar to yours, Princess. Your citrus and vanilla scented lure was extremely delicious."

"What do you mean, it *was*?"

"You won't have it now that you're a vampire. Your lure has blended with your amore, which is your love scent. And it makes up your essence. Now you smell like delicious lavender and vanilla when you're showing your love, and add citrus to that when you're horny. It's beyond intoxicating."

I stood on my tippy toes, bringing my face to his. "You're underestimating how amazing yours smells."

Jimmy came running up to us, his face flushed and sweaty, gasping for air. "I need to talk to Luka."

CHAPTER 38
WINNIE

*L*uka is a fucking hybrid!

A thousand thoughts raced through my head, my heart beating against my ribcage as I hopped in the front seat of a van with Drag, and Zeke and Erik got in the back.

"Carmen said the doctor at VRC pushed Luka to his limits, torturing him more than her. Almost like she was looking for something. Do you think she was trying to get him to snap? Is that how they change?" I shook my head, then turned my face toward Drag, not giving him a chance to answer. "You saw those hybrids, man. They smelled like vamps and wolven combined. And now Luka smells like that. Did you see his four fangs? That bitch turned him into a hybrid somehow!"

"I saw his fangs up close when he tried to eat my sister," Erik said from the back. "Way scarier than a normal vampire."

I furrowed my brows, attempting not to be offended by Erik's comment.

"My senses were in overload with the amount of mixed breeds there," Drag said, pulling out of the parking lot.

"It was so strange, my vinculum buzzed just like when a new member is asking to join my pack. When I reached out to see who, it surprised me when it was Luka. The second I accepted it, I could hear some of his random thoughts because he doesn't know how to mindlink properly."

I think my heart stopped beating. "What. The. Fuck. He's a vampire but has four fangs and can use wolven telepathy? How is that possible?"

Drag shook his head. "I don't know. I need to talk to my dad or one of the elders. Maybe they've heard of this before. Or maybe VRC made a new species. And another thing . . . he wasn't *just* a hybrid."

Fixated on Drag, my breath caught in my throat as I braced myself for the news.

He glanced at me, his eyes wide. "He's an alpha."

My heart definitely stopped. "How is that even possible? I thought you couldn't have two alphas in one pack."

Drag shook his head, eyes locked on the road ahead. "We can't, but it happened. He's a part of my pack now."

"Holy fuck." I pushed myself back in my seat, pressing one of my black combat boots against the dashboard, my breaths heavy.

"Get your damn feet down before I make you walk home."

I yanked my foot off the dash. "Sorry. I'm just nervous and can't sit still. This is a lot of shit. Even for us."

"On a positive note," Zeke said from the back, "Luka seemed like himself once he was out of bloodlust."

A small bit of relief swept through me. "Yeah, I noticed that. I also noticed none of the hybrids or Ben shifted." I turned my head back to Drag. "I guess you couldn't hear their thoughts."

He let out a hard sigh. "No, but my inner wolf sensed they were wolven before I even shifted, not that their smell wouldn't have given it away. I don't think they have the same capabilities a true born shifter has because they seemed surprised when the packs started coming out of the woods, which means they didn't sense them hiding."

I let out a hard breath, directing my gaze out the window.

The rest of the ride was quiet, all of us deep in our thoughts. My mind reeled with the hybrid situation. Between them and what Sage was calling a tercet, we had two whole new species to deal with.

Ravage had always been the science guy and I was grateful he was already back at camp when we pulled in because I had a million questions for him.

Sage's Jeep was also sitting there, so I knew she and Luka were also back.

"This is going to be an awkward conversation," I said, pulling the door handle and exiting.

As soon as I got out of the van, the back door opened, Zeke and Erik getting out. They'd been so quiet the rest of the ride, I almost forgot they were there.

Zeke squatted, stretching out his long legs. "I'd never seen anything like that before." He stood, shaking his head. "I'm going to check on April and my daughter."

A small smile pulled at my cheeks as he headed toward his cabin.

Erik stood there, his eyes distant.

"You good, bro?"

"A man murdered his own brother in front of his wife and kid. The woman I consider my sister died, then turned into a vampire, and is now running a Venom hub. There are hybrids and tercets and witches and all kinds of shit." He took a deep breath through his nose, blowing it out through his mouth. "I'm as good as I can be."

I clasped my hand on his shoulder. "But did you die?"

Erik laughed, and it was nice to know he was getting used to my sarcasm. "No, because I was with a damn good team." He held his fist out and I bumped mine into it. "I'm going to find Kimber. Maybe she can massage these knots in my shoulder."

"Take her on the roof. I heard it's a nice place for a date."

Erik smirked. "Goodnight, Winnie."

"It's Winston!" I hollered, my smile fading when my eyes met Drag's.

"Are you ready?"

Of course, I wasn't ready to confront my friend and reveal that he was a hybrid freak, but I nodded.

We headed toward Luka's place and Nellie's laughter caught my attention, the joyful sound contrasting with the fear and anger coursing through me. The fire residing in my chest flared higher with each step I took before

I finally flung around, the veins on my face pumping, a large hiss leaving me.

"Winnie!" Drag screamed, and I ignored him as I took off.

In a flash, I was next to the bonfire, standing right in front of Nellie. Before I had a chance to rip her throat out, a powerful force tugged me backwards, causing me to crash onto the ground, the impact vibrating through my spine.

More anger filled me as I hopped to my feet and Ravage was immediately in my face. "Don't you fucking move, boy!" he spat, his voice filled with authority.

"She's a fucking rat! Her and that whole fucking society are the reason we're all in this fucking mess."

Peach instinctively pushed Nellie behind her, shielding her from me. "And we can talk about that, but if you lay one hand on her . . ." Peach shook her head. "Don't make me hurt you, Winston."

"You want to talk, fine! Let's fucking talk about how she made sure to tell my girlfriend and Sage when we went on a mission to the Venom compound. Or when she said 'we' when mentioning Venom. Or when she was in the woods making a phone call. Let's talk about that!"

"Wait, a damn minute!" Nellie screeched, coming out from behind Peach. "I don't know what you're talking about with the 'we' thing, but Randi is the one who said I should tell Sage what happened. I didn't know I wasn't supposed to. She also told me to ask Peach if I could call my mom because I missed her." Nellie's mouth dropped open simultaneously with mine as we both had the same thought. "Oh my god, is *she* a rat?"

"Fuck," I whispered, my eyes darting around, looking for Randi. "How did we miss this?"

"You were too busy blaming me," Nellie retorted, pointing at herself. "I didn't betray you. I have no plans of going back to Venom or doing anything to put this group in jeopardy."

"Lower your voices," Ravage said in a hushed tone, fearing Randi might overhear us. He glanced at Lynx, he had left her and Laren in charge. "Where's Laren?"

"She went to the store for Ollie."

"Are you fucking kidding me?" Ravage's face contorted with anger, and my heart went out to Lynx. He shouldn't be mad at her or Laren, considering no one we left at the camp knew about tonight's mission. We had done that for a reason, and it could have possibly backfired on us.

Zeke came running up, a concerned look. "Has anyone seen April and Scarlet?"

Lynx shook her head. "She went to the cabin earlier to feed the baby. She never came back out. I assumed she fell asleep."

"Ravage, Sage, somebody!" Jimmy hollered from a distance, and I wondered what the fuck else could be going on.

Ravage let out a hard sigh. "Peach, you find Laren and April and I'll deal with whatever he wants."

Ravage took off and Peach turned toward Drag. "Can we get some of your men to check out the area for April and Scarlet's scents? I'm going to find Randi and bring her here. This needs to be handled tonight."

Drag leaned forward and grabbed his chest, an aching scream coming from him. "Ahh, shit! Someone in my pack is injured." He straightened his spine, his fear-filled eyes meeting mine. "It's my dad."

Drag took off toward his truck with me, Heston, and Demi right on his tail. Nervousness ate at me as we hopped in the vehicle, headed toward Drifter's.

CHAPTER 39

LUKA

Jimmy had come running up to me and Sage asking to speak to me and I had no clue what he wanted.

"I'm going to check on my mom real quick," Sage said, before kissing me. She headed toward the cabin and Jimmy started rambling.

"The witches visited us while you were still locked up. Shayla took my hand and told me something. At the time, I had no clue what it meant, but I finally figured it out."

My brows pinched as I wondered what this had to do with me. "Go on."

"There are nine figures for the house, which means it's nine numbers long. Seven will lead the race with nine on its tail, so seven and nine are the first two. The snake eyes come in last so the number sequence ends with two ones back to back. The two shall not pass the other three, and that's the part that confused me, until I realized there were two different threes and the number two had to be between them. Then she said, the five shall follow it, which meant the five had to follow the two, along with six. So the answer would be 793256311."

I glared at Jimmy, wondering where this conversation was going. "Okay. I don't know what any of that means."

"Well, at first I thought the numbers were a security code but something deep down told me that was wrong."

"Is there a point to this story?" I asked, baffled by the dude. He seemed cool, but I barely knew him.

"Did you know you had a code attached to you at VRC?"

Winnie screaming about Nellie being a rat, brought my attention in his direction. Seeing that Peach and Ravage had the situation under control, I turned back to Jimmy. "I actually didn't."

"They call it a patient identification number. While I was going over files, I saw your ID and even though the numbers started in a different sequence, they were still nine digits, like the one Shayla told me, so I figured it wouldn't hurt to pop the numbers into the patient registry. When I did, I found a vampire who they captured a year and a half ago. There's no name attached, but they caught him in the same zip code as yours. His description closely resembles yours, leading me to suspect it may be Strike."

Worried Jimmy was about to say my brother died while being experimented on, my mouth fell agape and my heart thundered in my chest.

"At first, I thought it could have been a coincidence until I saw this." Jimmy held out a piece of paper and pointed to a section which said *known markings*. "The tattoo described on his sternum is exactly like the one you have."

I placed my hand over the goat skull tattoo in the center of my chest, barely sticking out through the top of my T-shirt.

Not long after Ravage figured out how to tattoo vampires, me and my brothers decided to get matching ones. Andrei drew a goat skull with etchings inside of it that looked cool, so Strike and I both agreed to get it tattooed with him. At the time, I just wanted a tattoo and didn't care what it was. But as I reflected on it years later, I realized the three of us having matching ones was a part of who we were. A bond that nobody could ever break.

Shoving my memories aside, I let my hand fall and took a shaky breath. "Is . . is he dead?"

Jimmy pushed his glasses back onto his nose. "No. He's being held in a VRC location in Nevada and I have the address."

Knowing my brother was alive, everything stopped—time, emotions, my breaths. The only thing that continued were the memories that flashed through my brain, reminding me of the months of torture I'd suffered at the hands of VRC.

Glass shards seemed to fill my throat as my heart pounded loudly in my ears. I'd barely survived what they'd done to me, and my brother had been there much longer. I needed to get him out of there—if there was anything left of him.

I yanked the paper from Jimmy's hand. "Is this the address?"

"Yeah, but . . ."

"When Winnie's done trying to kill Nellie, tell him to meet me in the parking lot in ten minutes."

I turned away from Jimmy and headed toward my cabin to grab some supplies before I hit the road.

"Ravage, Sage, somebody!" Jimmy hollered before running up and blocking my path. "You can't go yet, Luka. We need to get a team together like we did for you."

"You know I can kill you before you even blink," I growled.

"If that's what you feel like you need to do, then do it because I'm not moving!"

Even though I hadn't known Jimmy long, he'd helped rescue me, so I wouldn't kill him, but I had no problem scaring the shit out of him.

A hiss left me as I opened my mouth and bared my fangs. Jimmy's eyes widened, then his chin stiffened, and I had to give him props because it was the bravest I'd ever seen him.

Before I had a chance to shove him aside—because seriously, he weighed about a buck fifty and I could remove him with my pinky—Ravage slid in between us.

"What's going on, son?"

"I have to find Strike," I said, holding up the paper. "I have the address to the VRC location he's at and we need to get him out of there today."

"We'll have to get a team together and come up with a plan."

Shaking my head, I stepped around him.

"Luka, wait."

I ignored Ravage, continuing toward my cabin, but I knew damn well he wasn't going to let me get far.

"I swear to you, boy, this is my only warning. If you take one more step, I'm going to hand you your ass!"

Even though I didn't have time to fight with my origin, I stopped dead in my tracks and turned around. With fists tightened, I moved in close, going almost nose to nose. "You have no clue what they did to me in there! How they starved me, cut me, fucking tortured me. They stuck fingers in every goddamn hole of my body and needles into my balls to extract semen and they did it all in the name of fucking science!"

A gasp came from behind us and when I looked, Sage had both her hands clasped firmly over her mouth. It was mortifying to realize she'd overheard the one thing I wanted to keep secret.

The dampness on my cheeks made me quickly rub my face against my shoulder, using my shirt as a tissue before I turned back to Ravage. "Like I was saying, we need to get my brother out of there now."

Ravage gently laid his hand on my shoulder, his eyes softening. "Okay, son. Let's find Winnie and Drag."

I bit down my feelings, forcing my gaze back to Sage. She didn't look at me with pity or like I wasn't a man anymore due to what happened to me. There was a fire in her eyes, the same kind I had brewing inside of me. A fire that said we would not only save Strike, but we'd take down every VRC and Venom location we'd find.

"We'll get him out of there as soon as we can," she said, picking up my hand, gently holding it between hers. "However, it's important to avoid risking our lives or the lives of our friends by rushing in without a plan. If anyone knows how hard it is to wait out that time, it's me, but we have to be strategic, Luka. For the sake of everyone."

Just as I was about to reluctantly agree with her, Peach ran up. "Something is going down at Drifter's and it's not good."

CHAPTER 40
DRAG

When I found my fated mate, my mind became overwhelmed with a flurry of emotions. Though I had convinced myself that I was ready, reality proved me wrong.

Before I brought her home, I wanted everything to be perfect. For the last two nights, I'd done anything I could to make sure the camp looked good for her. I'd installed tiki torches and solar lights to brighten the pathways, cleaned my entire house, threw away a bunch of old junk, and I even fixed the leaky sink in my bathroom.

But that all changed in an instant.

A vinculum is the bond we wolven have with our pack—on this plane and beyond. The vinculum I had with my pack was strong, unbreakable. It let me know who was under my care at any moment. Most of the wolven were born into my pack, some of them mated in.

The golden magical strands looked similar to veins and could only be seen in wolf form . . . but I could feel them at all times.

The invisible tether connecting me to my pack vibrated, then sent pain coursing through me, indicating that someone had suffered an injury. The bond told me it was my father.

When I slung the door to Drifter's open, my heart took a few seconds to catch up with the chaos my eyes were seeing.

Blood filled my nostrils, my gaze darting around the room, bouncing off each dead body, most of them Venom members.

Laren was the first person I recognized. She had her hands clasped over a wound on her stomach, writhing in pain.

As I ran toward her, I immediately wondered how long it had been since she'd last fed because she hadn't healed yet.

She lifted a blood-soaked hand and pointed toward the bar. "Ollie!"

My thoughts scattered like a thousand arrows raining down on a war, each of them waiting to strike me down. I swiftly rose to my feet and proceeded to dash across the room, skillfully leaping over any obstacles such as broken chairs, glass, and dead bodies that obstructed my path to the bartop.

My feet slid to a halt on the slippery, beer-coated floor as I rounded the corner, my eyes landing on my father who was lying on the ground, covered in blood.

Forcing myself to move, my heart raced with each step I took forward, before I tumbled to my knees next to him, taking his hand in mine.

"Feed room," he whispered, gasping for air.

Tears dampened my face, a sense of unworthiness filling me. "You can't leave me, pops. You haven't taught me everything I need to know. I can't even fix the fucking jukebox without you . . ."

His eyes were still open, staring directly at me when he gasped, taking his last breath . . .

The vinculum released a signal, suddenly jolting my body when his soul left our world.

I found myself wide-eyed, unable to process the events unfolding.

The jukebox began randomly playing "Bittersweet Symphony," by the Verve, enticing bar patrons to part with their money.

While listening to the lyrics of the song, I realized with my father's death came my own.

My soul felt tainted—stained. Any thoughts of fated mates or bonding wilted away from my reality, being replaced by a dire need to seek vengeance.

The agonizing scream I released was a warning that retribution was imminent.

Death himself was coming for all who had scorned us.

My dad's hollow gaze peered up at me, piercing my soul as if they were saying revenge wasn't the answer. His voice echoed in my thoughts, warning me to avoid any actions that could lead to my demise.

I ignored it and ran my fingers down his eyelids, forcing them closed, then laid my hand on his chest.

Tears tickled my cheeks as I whispered the words of honor to a wolven who had passed. "Although your soul may be at peace, our vinculum with you will never cease."

"Eternal bond," Heston said from across the room, sadness lining his voice.

"Eternal bond," Demi added, sniffing back tears.

The song continued, the words fucking with my head, as a fire fueled inside of me. I let go of his hand, gently laying it upon his chest, and stood, heading toward the Jukebox.

I exerted all my strength, fiercely striking it with my fist and the glass shattered easily, shards biting into my knuckles, chunks flying in all directions.

But that had failed to pacify my anger.

Madness took over, driving me to kick, and punch, and growl, obliterating the machine until it stopped playing music and all lights went out.

My breaths were choppy, my jaw tightening as my teeth clenched.

Winnie gently placed a hand on my shoulder. "I'm sorry, bro."

I took a few shaky breaths, attempting to make myself look like the alpha I was born to be. Straightening my shoulders, I went back into my role. "My dad whispered something about the feed room. Did you check it?"

Winnie shook his head, then went toward the closet. I took a second to pull glass from my bloody fingers.

"Drag!" he screamed, just as the scent of humans filled my lungs.

April and Scarlet.

I sprinted toward the closet connected to the feed room and Winnie shook his head. "She won't let me near her."

Peeking into the small six-by-six room, my heart fluttered. April was curled into the back corner, her entire body shaking, baby Scarlet in her arms.

I knelt down beside her, keeping my voice calm even though my insides were screaming. "April. It's Drag."

"Don't touch me! Where's Zeke? I need my husband. I can't trust anyone after Randi betrayed us."

"She's dead," Winnie said, sending surprise through me. "Looked like Laren got her ass."

"I need Zeke," April cried, shivers rippling through her.

The front door burst open, and the scent of Sage and Luka instantly filled the air. Footsteps pounded against the floor as they headed toward us.

"Oh, my god!" Sage yelled, and April sucked in a gasp.

"Sage," she whispered, tears rolling down her cheeks.

Sage squeezed her way into the closet and Winnie and I moved out of the way. She knelt beside April, calming her down.

"Winnie, call Zeke and tell him we found April," I commanded, before turning toward Luka. "You're in charge of my pack until I get back."

Luka's forehead creased. "Where are you going?"

I headed toward the front door.

"Drag!" Luka called out and I ignored him.

Once outside, I shifted into my wolf form and ran as fast as I could.

Lost and uncertain, I clung to one motivation: vengeance had become my closest ally.

Hunted by Venom
Sage

en have been starting war for countless generations due to competition over land, religious dif-
ferences, racism, slavery, imperialism, and other notable
issues.

The war I started was to save the man I love, but as I reflected on the situation, gaining a broader understanding
of what's important, my plans took a sudden detour.

Regardless of the number of people I killed for my
loved ones, both Venom and the Vampire Research Center
would continue their heinous acts with hybrids actively
protecting them.

In order to ensure the safety of both the vampire and
wolven species, we needed to eliminate those in control
and bring the entire system down. Even if that meant
outing Venom, VRC, and the United States government
to the entire country.

Our primary targets were Viktor, an exceedingly an-
cient vampire, whose brother we killed . . . and my uncle,
Ben Argent.

My eyes darted across the one hundred twelve Venom
members who had sworn their loyalty to me, then glanced

at the paper in my hand showing the locations of seven different research centers in the country, and one Venom organization in every single state.

Fuck, this is going to be a long fight.

AN ARGENTIUM VAMPIRE NOVEL

HUNTED
BY
VENOM

P.S. Nail

Unclaimed

Kaysa

Sobs rumbled up from Summer's chest and Aluna rubbed her hand up and down her back, soothing her.

"I just . . . I just want to run away," Summer whispered, a thought I had had many times before.

During my initial year with Galen, I carefully strategized my escape from the moment I left until my ideal happily ever after. In my made-up scenarios, I'd flee this place and go into hiding on the east coast far from the reach of Galen. With my newfound freedom, I would start a homestead, dedicate my time to volunteering at shelters for victims of domestic violence, express myself through any hairstyle I chose, and fulfill my lifelong dreams of finally owning a dog.

But I never attempted leaving because I knew exactly how the scenario would play out.

Galen would exhaust all the pack's resources to find me, subject me to the harshest punishment possible, and then mercilessly slit my throat in the middle of camp while forcing my loved ones to watch.

It wasn't the fear of dying that kept me here because I'm sure it would be more peaceful than being beaten and raped. But since Galen lacked the dedication to do the work I'd been doing for my pack's prosperity, without me to lead, the members would suffer. He'd let the children starve, the women go without tampons, and refuse to support the pack with anything he'd deem unnecessary.

If I stayed, they'd always have someone fighting to make sure they had anything they needed to survive.

And that . . . that was worth the years of pain.

Galen thrived on making people suffer, feeding off their screams and basking in their torment. The pack being scared of the alpha gave him power, and realizing that quickly after I came here, I refused to do that.

That's why I faked it to survive.

I faked it by lying, smiling, and sometimes even flirting, no matter how pathetic it made me feel.

It was difficult hiding my misery every time he was near.

Hiding how disgusted I was at night when his skin touched mine.

How sore my body was the day after he abused me—violated me.

To hide how I'd given up on him . . . how I utterly despised him.

The happy mask on my face acted as a spartan shield, protecting me from any further damage.

My lies were my shelter, my smiles were my blades, and if those failed, my flirting was my last minute tactical gear.

But the worst thing I had to do was pretend I still loved him.

My whole life I waited to become a luna of a pack only to end up unclaimed, all while having my heart broken, my body assaulted, and my soul damaged by a psychopathic dickwad.

Tears streamed down Summer's face, staining her cheeks with black mascara and unfathomable shame—a feeling I was far too familiar with.

Her piercing blue eyes met mine, begging for comfort, sympathy, or possibly a hug.

That was the moment I realized everything I'd ever thought about her was incorrect. She wasn't the woman that was going to free us from the alpha's grip. She wasn't a blonde blessing in disguise, our saving grace, nor our ticket to freedom.

Summer was a broken soul, tortured and unvalued, slowly losing her will to live. A chained woman, being used and abused for the sake of the alpha's pleasure, imprisoned in a place that would make most people long for death.

Summer wasn't our enemy.

She was one of us.

Aluna and I had endured abuse for so long, and even though we pined for the day we'd be free, we were good at bearing Galen's sadism.

But I was unsure Summer would survive.

The radiance in her eyes had already faded and in such little time. The abuse would be too much for her tender heart to endure much longer.

AWAKENED SHIFTERS BOOK ONE

UNCLAIMED
P.S. Nail

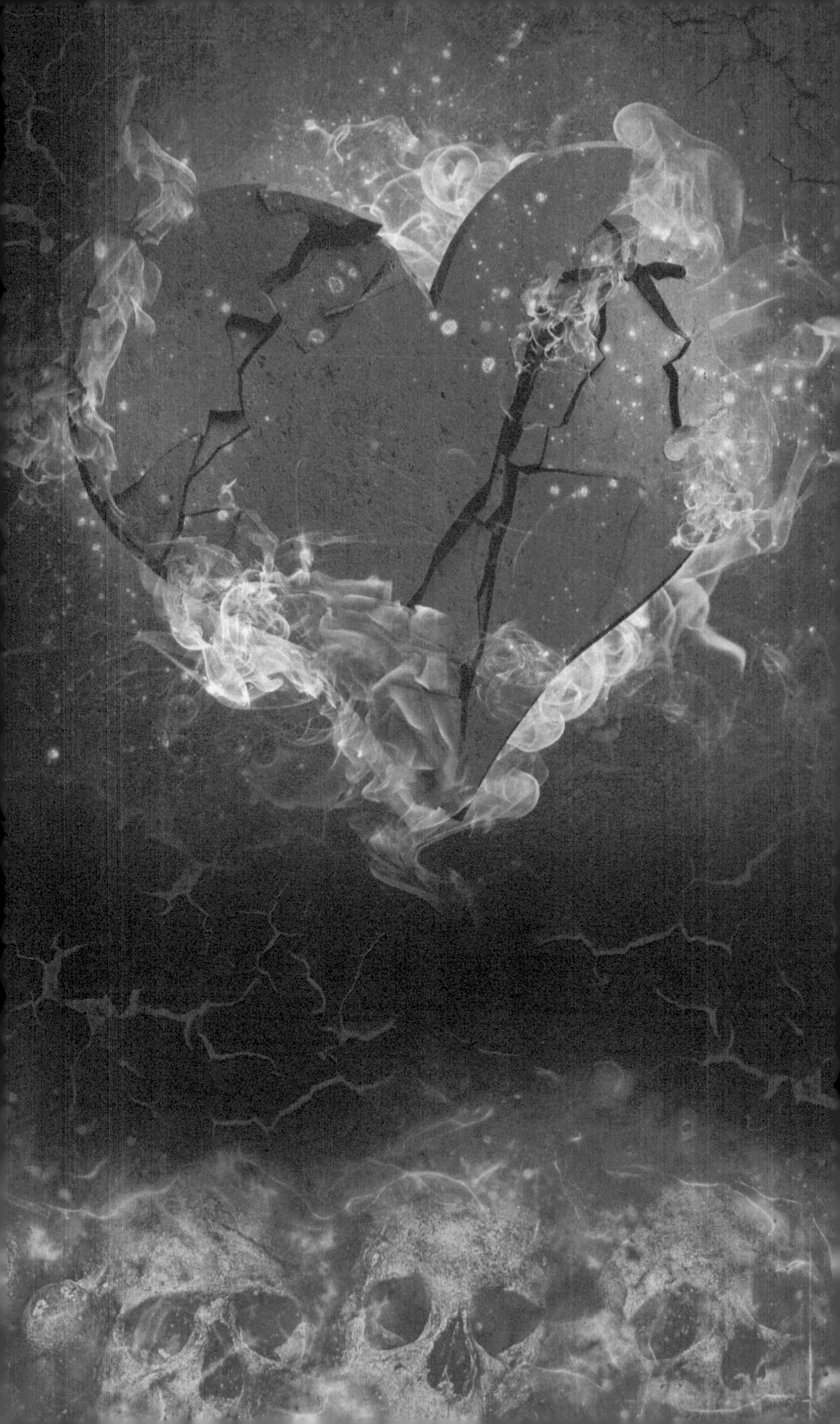

GLOSSARY

Alpha: A male dominant leader of a pack.

Amore: The scent a person emits when in love with someone. Humans can't smell it, but vampires and wolven can.

Ardent: When a *sentinel* bonded pair of vampires forms a lenxus. *See also, Sentinel.*

Bonded: The supernatural version of being married, but on a higher mystical level. Two souls entwined as one.

Essence: The scent a bonded vampire or wolven emits when horny or expressing love that only their bondmate can smell.

Fangsters/Fangasizers: A human who fantasizes or wants to be fed on by a vampire.

Fated Mates: When two people, supernatural or human, are biologically and/or spiritually destined to be together.

Fangdom: A group of humans who obsess over vampires.

Hybrid: A vampire and wolven combined to make one species.

Intimate: The person which a wolven has a *nexus* with is considered their intimate. *See also, Nexus.*

Lenxus: A bond which a vampire has formed with their mate.

Luna: A female dominant leader of a pack.

Lure: The scent a person emits when sexually attracted to someone. Humans can't smell it, but vampires and wolven can.

Mark: Vampires can mark a person with their scent, showing other vampires they're taken. It also protects them from enemies.

Mindlink: Wolven have the capability to talk using telepathy, while shifted into wolf form, and only to members of their pack.

Nexus: The bond which a wolven has with their mate. Time spent together can create certain bonds while fate determines others. *See also, Fated Mates.*

Nosh Pit: A group of dancing Humans.

Origin: A vampire who *turns* another human into a vampire becomes their origin.

Pulling: An internal feeling a vampire or human gets when their bonded mate needs them.

Promised Luna: A woman who's obligated to marry an alpha male due to hierarchy and family ranking.

Sentinel: A bond which a vampire has with their origin. *See also, Origin.*

Shifter: A person who shifts from one form to another. *See also, Wolven.*

Sire Feed: A newly turned vampire must drink blood from their origin to complete the bond. If not achieved in a specific amount of time, the vampire transition will not be complete, and the human will die.

Supernaturals Against Venom Elitists or Save: An organization who is protecting vampires and wolven from being used for research.

Tercet: A witch, vampire, and wolven combined to make one species.

Vampire Eradicating National Organization of Malice or Venom: A government-funded society who trains its members to hunt vampires for research.

Vinculum: A non-sexual bond a wolven has to their pack. The invisible thread starts at the alpha and weaves through the pack, connecting them as a whole.

Vampire Research Center or VRC: A government-funded facility and/or laboratory that does investigations, collection, analysis, and experimentations on vampires so they can use the information to make a multitude of products.

Wolven: A person born with the power to shift from human to wolf form.

None of Us Are Perfect

All vampires are reborn with different powers and unfortunately predicting grammatical errors is not one of mine. If I made a mistake in any of my books, feel free to send me a screenshot to peggysue@primordialtree.com and if you are the first to report it, I'll send you a free bookmark and sticker! This also includes any trigger/content warnings I may have missed.

Love, hugs, and vampire blood,

PS Nail

About the Author

Dreaming of becoming a vampire, I mean author, since she was a youngling, PS Nail finally fulfilled her prophecy by self-publishing her first paranormal fantasy romance novel, with many more to come.

She enjoys playing guitar to soothe the draw of the moon, video games to help pacify her blood lust, reading romance and smut books, since she never sleeps, and having a fangtastic time with paranormal friends. Once a month, when the full moon calls, she and her coven dance naked around a magical blazing fire . . . but don't tell her we told you.

We think she currently lives in the United States, or possibly Romania, with her shifter husband, three hybrid sons, and their pet demons. She lovingly calls them her immortal family.

She will continue to quench her thirst for writing until death, dismissal, or dishonor.

FYI: She hates the sun, but loves garlic.

Websites: primordialtree.com and psnail.org

All social media: https://linktr.ee/authorp-snail

Free Book with Newsletter Sign-Up: https://dl.bookfunnel.com/x395y7zcm9

Acknowledgements

Holy fucking shit, what a ride this book took me on! The emotional grip it had on me was like no other.

First, I want to thank my readers for patiently, and not so patiently, holding on for a year and a half after I left them on a massive cliffhanger! Your patience and kindness has kept me going through the unexpected losses I had. Thank you for truly being amazing.

To my big-bearded, wolf shifter husband. Just so you know, I've never screamed 'Oh god' from a rooftop and I seriously feel like I'm missing out. I found your ladder and will be waiting with bated breath.

To my three full-grown, adult sons, don't ever read any of my books!

If anyone has a mother-in-law and an aunt as amazing as mine, congratulations! Terri and Vicky, without both of you constantly reassuring me I can, I would have stopped. Thank you for being not only understanding but also harassing me for the next book. I love you both.

April D. Berry, my sister, my friend. The last time I referred to you as my scrunchie, this time, I only have four words for you:

Blood of the coven.

Heather 'Peach' Shields, thank you for all the amazing, hard work you did editing as you alpha read. I love you Peaches and Cream!

To my editor, Vanda, thanks for putting up with me and my constant need to change things, and reassuring me I could do this. You did a wonderful job on my manuscript!

My alphas, Katie, Ashley, Janene, Anna, and Kelli, every single comment you made, every angry face you sent me, and every laugh we had was worth the tears we shed together along the way. I appreciate every one of you. I can't wait to do it all again in book three.

To my entire team of Bloodsuckers, thanks for alpha, beta, or ARC reading, sharing things on social media, constantly hyping me, and supporting me along this journey. You are all amazing and I couldn't survive without your kind words, your love, and even the pictures you send me of you flipping me off. I love you all!

9 798218 369040